PENGUIN BOOKS

THE INNOCENCE OF AGE

Neil Bissoondath was born in Trinidad in 1955. He has lived in Canada since 1973 when he came to study French at York University.

Neil Bissoondath burst onto the literary scene in 1985 with the publication of his first book of short stories, *Digging up the Mountains*. This success was followed by his first novel, *A Casual Brutality*, which won international acclaim (*The Sunday Times* of London said "The assurance and maturity of *A Casual Brutality* make it hard to believe that it is a first novel", and *The New York Times* described it as "rich in sensibility").

Neil Bissoondath recently wrote and hosted a documentary on fathers and sons broadcast on *The Journal*. He lives in Montreal with his wife and daughter.

The
Innocence
of Age

Neil
Bissoondath

Penguin Books

PENGUIN BOOKS
Published by the Penguin Group
Penguin Books Canada Ltd, 10 Alcorn Avenue, Toronto, Ontario,
Canada M4V 3B2
Penguin Books Ltd, 27 Wrights Lane, London W8 5TZ, England
Penguin Books USA Inc., 375 Hudson Street, New York, New York 10014,
U.S.A.
Penguin Books Australia Ltd, Ringwood, Victoria, Australia
Penguin Books (NZ) Ltd, 182-190 Wairau Road, Auckland 10,
New Zealand

Penguin Books Ltd, Registered Offices:
Harmondsworth, Middlesex, England

First published by Alfred A. Knopf Canada, 1992

Published in Penguin Books, 1993

1 3 5 7 9 10 8 6 4 2

*Publisher's note: This book is a work of fiction. Names, characters, places and inci-
dents either are the product of the author's imagination or are used fictitiously, and any
resemblance to actual persons living or dead, events, or locales is entirely coincidental.*

Manufactured in Canada

Canadian Cataloguing in Publication Data
Bissoondath, Neil, 1955 -
The innocence of age

ISBN 0-14-017307-2
I. Title

PS8553.I77I66 1993   C813'.54   C93-093944-1
PR9199.3.B68I66 1993

For Élyssa

who makes the world new again

"A horror is not an idea, as a shudder is not a conviction."

— Donald Hall
"Purpose, Blame and Fire"
Harper's, May 1991

Chapter One

THE MOMENT the door swung shut behind him, Pasco undid his coat. The Starting Gate was always too warm, the air stale and singed by tobacco smoke.

In summer, Lanny opened the large windows to the street, but that served only to flood the room with more humid air mixed with the noises and exhaust fumes of the traffic on Dundas. The moment the weather turned cool, though, Lanny would fire up the furnace—he couldn't abide the cold himself—and the heat of the radiators would be such that fingers could not rest long on them without pain and a quick redness.

The food, as Montgomery had rightly said, tasted like horse dung liberally sprinkled with black pepper; and the beer, even the well-known brands, like slightly cooled piss. Montgomery blamed the food on the cook; the man, he said, could make butter rancid by just spreading it on toast. The flavour of the beer he attributed to the mugs, some of which had grown opaque from years of washing, all of which displayed distinctive chips.

Sometimes one of the street people would wander in and Lanny would hurry over from behind the bar. He was a small, wiry man who, after failing to make a living as a professional jockey, had spent twenty years in the army, rising only to the rank of corporal. The first thing he did when he left the forces was to let his moustache have its way with his face. The second thing he did was to use his savings to open the Starting Gate. Lanny didn't allow begging in his establishment. Customers came here for a drink or two or three and a bit of R and R, as he put it, and he wasn't about to let anyone pour hard-luck stories all over them. If the street people cooperated, which meant they made no protest, Lanny would take them to a table way at the back and serve them a beer and a meal on the house. If they resisted, he would pick them up, man or woman, big or small, and toss them back out onto the street, a feat he always managed with a minimum of fuss. Some thought Lanny hard, but Pasco knew that the Gate hadn't exactly made Lanny rich. The room was large, but it didn't feel so much spacious as empty. Its high ceilings, webby lighting and dusty racing paraphernalia displayed on the walls—a couple of English saddles, several riding crops, jockey caps, a set of faded silks, a pair of riding boots—were just about all that stood between Lanny and the street. So while Pasco agreed that Lanny was hard, he insisted that he wasn't hard-hearted.

Pushpull, Marcus and Cruise were already there at the usual table beneath one of the saddles. Montgomery would probably be along before too long, worn out from his mail route and badly in need of a beer.

Pushpull, still wearing his electric-orange crossing-guard's vest, looked up and winked as Pasco slipped off his coat, folded it over the back of his chair and sat down.

Marcus, forearms on the table, one hand resting lightly on the other, was leaning with his usual intensity towards Cruise. "—talkin' twenty, thirty percent, man—"

"No shit." Cruise was not impressed. As befitted an ageing hippie, he never was. He leaned back in his chair, hand rubbing thoughtfully at his unshaved cheeks. Today his shoulder-length hair, black shot through with grey, was tied back in a pony-tail.

"Not only that," Marcus continued, "but a lot of these guys take Canadian at par."

Pushpull nudged Pasco with his elbow. "Marcus here," he said, raising his half-empty mug at Marcus, "is tryin' to sell our friend Cruise"—he swung the mug towards Cruise—"on the glories and wonders of shopping in Buffalo. Seems our money goes elastic when it crosses the border."

Cruise took a gulp of his beer. "Same thing used to happen to our dicks a couple dozen years ago. Remember that, guys?" He smacked his lips. "The good old days in T.O., eh? When a hot night on the town used to mean a trip down to Buffalo, Noo Yawk, for Chris'sake!"

Marcus turned his spare, intelligent face towards Pasco. "How 'bout you, Pasco? Interested in a little shopping down in Buffalo? Twenty, thirty percent—"

"Right now, all I want is a beer, Marcus."

"Aw, c'mon, Pasco—"

"Yeah, Pasco," Pushpull whined in mockery. "Give the poor guy a break. His old lady's bugging him to go down and he's lookin' for company. All that time alone with his old lady'll drive him crazy."

Marcus grimaced at Pushpull. "You're so full of shit, man."

Lanny put a beer in front of Pasco. "Hey there, Pasco, served lots of lunches today?"

"A few, my friend, a few."

"Enough to pay the bills?"

"And a bit more."

"That's what counts, eh?" Lanny flicked his dish towel over his shoulder and headed back to the bar. It was as lengthy a conversation as Lanny ever had with anyone.

"Well, Pasco?" Marcus said impatiently.

"Well, what?"

"Twenty, thirty percent...."

"Marcus, I saw my dad working his tail off to make his living here, and I see a lot of people doing it everyday. So why should I drive for hours just to help foreigners—"

"They're not foreigners, man, they're Americans. Besides, the prices—"

"The prices, ahh, yes!" Pasco's eyes widened, his head nodding. "What's yours, Marcus?"

Marcus slouched down on his seat, intensity diminishing throughout his lanky body.

Cruise slapped the table. "Atta boy, Pasco. Remember the—"

"Ohoh," Pushpull moaned. "Here it comes, the fuckin' oil-tanker."

Although he was the only one to remember it, Cruise—who held that Canadian historical memory reached no further into the past than yesterday's dinner—swore the story was true. Long, long ago, he claimed, back in the mid-seventies when the Arab oil embargo had Americans lining up at the gas pumps, a tanker of oil on its way from Venezuela to Canada was diverted to the U.S. on orders from the American oil monolith that controlled the Canadian oil monolith. Fuel for Canadian industry was being hijacked—Cruise tended to turn up the rhetoric when telling his tale—by "our friends down south". Somehow the story had leaked out, the media creating enough bad publicity that the order was cancelled. Cruise recounted the story frequently, and with a passion that always managed to be slightly more comical than embarrassing. This evening, though, he fell silent.

"What?" Pushpull said, smoke streaming from his mouth and nostrils. "No bedtime story?"

"I'm trying to reform," Cruise said.

"Hallelujah!"

"But on the other hand—"

"Here it comes, guys."

"—where would you all be without me? I mean, when's the last time you read a newspaper, Pushpull?"

"Read a what?"

"Marcus?"

"I was lookin' through one on the subway just yesterday."

"I said *read*, not drooled over the Sunshine Girl." He winked at Pasco. "As for Montgomery, well, we can guess. See what I mean? How would you guys know what's goin' on in the world if I didn't—"

"Editorialize," Pasco said.

Cruise shrugged. "I don't know. Around you guys, I feel like a fuckin' philosopher sometimes."

Cruise owned a used-book store on Queen Street. It earned him his living. He had been a Rochdale College radical in the sixties: grass for the taking, sex for the asking, philosophy and politics lurking around every corner. He claimed to have particularly enjoyed arguing Kierkegaard while "banging away during group gropes". Everybody was a poet or a folksinger, everybody was "into freedom". And then one day a girl claimed the ultimate freedom by launching herself off the roof without a parachute. Cruise had known her only slightly—they'd slept together just once or twice—but her death proved to be a turning point in his life. There was nothing sadder, he'd once told Pasco, than a handful of hippies standing around watching the broken body of one of their friends. "That kind o' brought the swingin' sexties crashin' down for me," he'd added wistfully.

So he'd moved out, back to his parents' house in High Park. He eventually completed his degree in English literature at the University of Toronto and, by the early seventies, was a lecturer at the university. By the mid-seventies he was bored. Correcting his students' essays, he insisted, had just made him an expert in waste management. The chance came along to buy the used-book store. He managed the down payment with a loan from his parents, changed the name to "The Booksore", and moved into the flat upstairs with his books and his typewriter. He claimed to be working on "projects", but the only one he'd revealed, a literary magazine for prison inmates, hadn't progressed beyond the title of "Prose and Cons".

"S'not good for the eyes," Pushpull said. "All that readin' you like to do, I mean."

Pasco swallowed a mouthful of beer. "So who is it this week?" he said to Cruise. Last week it had been Euripides.

"Plato. *The Republic.*"

"What's it about?" Pushpull asked.

"It's about a Greek philosopher named Socrates."

"What's with these Greek guys anyways? They don't have first names?"

Pasco glanced sceptically at Pushpull. At times it was difficult to tell whether he was joking.

Cruise nodded sagely. "It was in the paper just the other day. Seems there's a shortage of names in Greece. They're rationing them, one per person."

"Any sex?"

"Plato was gay."

"Oh Christ."

Marcus ran his hand through his thinning hair, shook himself from his brooding. "So, Cruise," he said, "with all this reading you do, you must know just about everything. So can you tell me where he"—he stuck a thumb in Pushpull's direction—"got a stupid name like that? What kind of a name is Pushpull, anyways? Yugoslavian or something?"

Cruise doubled over in silent laughter, beer spraying from his mouth.

Pasco strove to suppress a grin. Pushpull was his oldest friend. They'd gone to school together and it was there, so many decades before, that he'd acquired the name. Somehow, for reasons Pasco never got clear, he'd become known as a "wanker", a "pocket-billiard player", a "jerk-off artist". And so the name Pushpull was given to him because, as Pasco remembered someone saying, "He's always pushin' and pullin' on it." Pasco had nothing against all the pushing and pulling—in fact, he was doing quite a bit of it himself at the time—but it had seemed ridiculous to call his friend Manfred when everyone else was calling him Pushpull. The nickname had stuck to him throughout the years.

"Yeah, Marcus," Pushpull said, doing his best to look offended. "It's Yugoslavian or something like th—"

"Hey there, fellas." Montgomery threw himself into the chair beside Pasco's. "What's the joke?" He was, as usual, chewing on a toothpick. Cruise had once said that toothpicks were Montgomery's health food: they had no calories and they provided roughage.

Cruise jabbed his thumb towards Marcus. "Ol' Markie here wants to know where Pushpull got his name." He choked on his laughter, coughed. "And not only that. He wants someone to go shopping in Buffalo with him too."

Montgomery removed his mailman's cap. "All that, Marcus? And the fellas givin' you a hard time to boot?"

Marcus shrugged. "Fuck 'em."

Montgomery unzipped his parka, acknowledged Lanny with a nod when he placed a full mug on the table in front of him. "Well, my friend, I ain't able to help you with either problem." He took the toothpick from his lips, sipped his beer, put the toothpick back. "So, Pushpull, tell the man where you get the name, nuh. And Cruise or Pasco, go with him, okay?" He shook his head in mock chagrin. "But all-you like chil'ren, eh."

Pushpull mumbled a low obscenity and headed off to the washroom.

"S'no use, Montgomery," Marcus said. "Cruise doesn't believe in saving money, Pushpull doesn't have any money, and Pasco's too good to go shopping in the States. Won't give his money to the goddam Americans."

Montgomery took a pocketknife and an orange from his bag, began peeling the rind off in one continuous, curling string, orange on the outside, white on the inside. "But what you have so against the Americans, man, Pasco?"

Cruise said, "The oil tanker."

Pasco rolled his eyes.

"I ain't know, man." Montgomery sliced the orange in two, sucked at one of the halves. "I ain't have nothing against nobody, but especially not against the Americans. American boys dead freein' my country, they help my people out. How I going to hate them?"

Pasco nodded. "I know, I know."

"Before the Americans hit the beaches, man, nobody ever hear 'bout Grenada. Even when the one-time P.M. went off to New York and lecture the UN 'bout UFOs, who pay attention? And when the folks who overthrow him cozy up to the Cubans so much that people was 'fraid to talk too loud in their own house, in their *own house*, I tell you, who pay attention? Nobody, is who. Well, Reagan send in the boys, a few people get kill, but he free up the place, thank God, send the Cubans back to Fidel. Life still hard, but my people learnin' to laugh again, life easier for my family down there now."

Cruise said, "You still got folks down there, Montgomery?"

"A brother and two sisters, nieces and nephews, cousins." He leaned back in the chair, picked up his beer. "So how I could hate America?"

"And this country?" Pasco asked.

"I ain't have nothing against Canada. Is a good country, life okay here."

"Nothing more than that? So why didn't you emigrate to the States instead?"

Montgomery sighed, belched into his cupped palm. "Pasco, my friend, I respec' the way you feel, believe me, but you have to understand that the day I pick up and leave home, the country I was goin' to wasn't important, only the job was. That's what I come here for, the work and the money, not the place."

"Funny, eh?" Pasco said. "Marcus was born here, and he thinks the same way."

Cruise said, "Friend of mine went to the Big Apple once, and when he came back he couldn't stop talkin' about the variety of things on store shelves. If we have a choice between, I dunno, say, five kinds of mustard here, they have fifteen to choose from down there. You should have heard him, it was unbelievable. He was dazzled. But who the fuck needs fifteen kinds of mustard?"

"Who's talkin' about mustard, eh?" Marcus said irritably. "I'm talkin' about clothes and liquor and VCRs, important stuff." Then he leaned across the table, intensity returning. "So, Montgomery, you interested in going shopping in Buffalo?"

But before Montgomery could reply, Cruise's voice sang out lowly: "Do-do, do-do, do-do, do-do. Twilight Zone time."

Everyone turned towards him.

"Take a look," he said, nodding towards the door. "Pasco's younger double just walked in."

———————

The Starting Gate turned out to be the kind of place Danny had always imagined, or feared, it would be. Hot, stuffy, with the glutinous ambience of a beer trough. Formica tables, chairs of old chrome with leatherette seats, fluorescent lighting fairly swirling with smoke. The little attempts at decoration—all that dusty horse-racing equipment—served simply to heighten the bareness of the walls. All it lacked, he thought, were a couple of pool tables with attendant sharks.

He had gone by the house, but his father was not at home; had driven to his dad's greasy spoon, but that too was closed. There was only one other place he was likely to be at this time of the evening. His father had been meeting his friends at the Gate for years, once, sometimes twice a week. Danny had never been there. It had been, for so long, the slightly disreputable place where his father went. He himself preferred the glitzier spots where the social intercourse wasn't so starkly stripped to beer and idle chatter.

Even though he was tired, as he frequently was, Danny's business eye was dependable. By the time he spotted his father at a table in the far corner, he was already seeing the possibilities of the place, one part of his mind speculating idly—in a kind of mental exercise—on what could be done with it. A paint job in pastel shades, he thought, indirect lighting, two or three slow ceiling fans, a few pictures tasteful enough to embellish but not so appealing as to distract, a few deftly placed potted palms, rattan chairs all around....

The exercise was pointless, though, and by the time he was at his father's table he'd already dismissed the notion. The location, downtown east of Yonge, was all wrong, the place could never attract the right clientele.

His father remained seated, his the only head at the table not turned in Danny's direction.

"Hi, Dad."

"Danny."

One of his father's friends half-stood, extended his hand. "Hi, I'm Manfred." He was a short man with dark, tired eyes, his hair unevenly greyed. The flaps of a crossing-guard's vest hung loosely on his beer belly.

"Daniel," Danny said, shaking his hand. "Glad to know you, Manfred."

"Most people call me Pushpull."

"And most people call me Cruise," said another, raising his beer mug at Danny. "And this here's Montgomery, your friendly mailman." He indicated the black man sitting beside him. "I'm afraid that the fifth member of our distinguished little group, Marcus over there, is taking a mental leak right at this moment."

Danny nodded, constructed his professional smile. So these were his father's friends, a bunch of middle-aged men sitting around as their bellies got too big for their shirts and their balls too big for their underpants.

Pushpull said, "You want a beer, Daniel?"

"Thanks, Manfred, don't have the time. I just stopped by for a quick word with my dad."

"Catch you next time then, eh?"

"For sure."

Pasco got to his feet, his chair scraping back. He let Danny follow him away from the table.

"Hi, Dad," Danny said.

"What's up? Somebody died?" Pasco's tone was not friendly.

"I've been trying to reach you."

"Been busy."

"We have to talk about the bedrooms."

"You're kidding." Pasco swallowed the absurdity. "What's the grand hurry?"

"Just the old equation, Dad. Time, money. I've been thinking we should do the bedrooms next instead of the kitchen, they—"

"I still don't understand what you're doing here."

"I—"

"Look, Danny, I come here to relax. I don't come into your fancy Yorkville hangouts chasing after you."

"We have to talk about the renovations sometime, Dad."

"Sure, fine. But there's a place and a time. And you've got them both wrong."

"So when—"

"You know where the restaurant is. I'm there all day, six days a week. That's where I conduct my business, all my business."

Danny stuffed his hands into his coat pockets, glanced around. "Mom always hated this place."

"She was never here."

"Fine, Dad, have it your way." It was an old battle and Danny, fatigued, had no desire to prolong the skirmish. "I'll give you a call."

"You do that."

Danny turned, walked to the door without a further word.

Back at the table, Pushpull said, "He's your kid, Pasco, no question there. It's like lookin' at you, say, fifteen, twenty years ago."

"Yeah, well." Pasco drew his chair closer to the table.

Cruise chuckled. "Nice-lookin' young fella anyway, though."

Pasco, frowning, said, "Don't forget looks can be deceiving."

"You not jokin', man," Montgomery said unhappily. He banged his empty mug on the scarred tabletop, his gaze swivelling around the room, searching out Lanny. His fingers signalled with impatient grace for another beer.

"Easy," Pasco said. "Easy, friend." But he knew it could never be. For any of them.

———————

Marcus left after a couple of draughts, heading home for a nap before taking his cab out for a twelve-hour shift. Cruise and Pushpull, hungry, decided to hop a streetcar across to Chinatown for dinner.

Pasco and Montgomery signalled Lanny for another round. The smell of frying chicken wings drifted oily and unappetizing around the room.

Pasco had known Pushpull the longest, but he knew—or felt

he knew—Montgomery the best. They had met several years before when the regular mailman fell ill and Montgomery temporarily replaced him. The route took him by Pasco's restaurant. One cold day during his rounds, he stopped in for a coffee. Sitting at the counter, he introduced himself to Pasco with a becoming dignity: "Muntgumery Bird de t'ird," he'd said, extending his hand. Then he removed his cap, revealing the most hideous haircut Pasco had ever seen: short almost to baldness in spots, long and tufty in others. Pasco burst out laughing. Montgomery, looking hurt, said, "You jealous, eh?" And in that moment, as Montgomery explained that he'd made the mistake of going to a barber who'd never cut a black man's hair before, they became friends.

For a time, Pasco had thought that Montgomery bore a passing resemblance to Harry Belafonte, only darker. "And poorer, too," Montgomery had said in his characteristic rasp to Pasco's observation, "but the voice just as sweet." But Montgomery also had knobbier features, a less glaring grin, a stockier build. In fact, when you came right down to it, Montgomery didn't look a bit like Harry Belafonte, and Pasco had to admit to himself, with some shame, that he hadn't been able to look past the colour of the forest to see the individuality of the tree.

Montgomery's rounds usually wore him out, especially in winter, but this evening he looked more tired than usual. His face was puffy, his eyes yellowed and traced with red veins, the skin under them darkened as if by ink-stains. Clearly he hadn't slept much the night before.

"You look like you could use a holiday," Pasco said.

"Things not so good in Paradise, man." *Paradise*: it was how Montgomery usually referred to his home.

"Nothing serious, I hope."

"A little family problem, nuh. No big t'ing."

"Your son?"

"No-no, he doin' okay. He was first in his class at Ryerson last year, I tell you that?"

"Only a couple dozen times."

"No, the boy goin' to be okay. He goin' to be a 'lectrical engineer if it kill him." He sipped at the beer, took a fresh toothpick from his coat pocket and put it between his lips. "I ever tell you I wanted to name him Doctor?"

"Name him what?"

"You hearin' me right. I figure that way he was goin' to be Doctor Bird all his life, and there ain't nothin' like a title to bring respec'." The toothpick danced along between his lips, from one corner of his mouth to the other. "His mammy put her foot down though. Tell you, Pasco, is a hard-head woman that I marry there."

Pasco smiled. "Well, at least now I know who's got the brains in the family."

"Well, it ain't the girl I'll tell you."

"Ahhh." Pasco had known that Montgomery would get around to it sooner or later.

The daughter had come as a welcome surprise to Montgomery and his wife. Mrs. Bird—Pasco had never met her—had emigrated first, to a job as a domestic servant, twelve months to the day after their marriage. Montgomery had followed three years later with the infant son to whom she'd given birth two months before leaving. Once Montgomery had found a job as a loader for a moving company, they decided to have another child. They were a year without success and had just about given up hope when the daughter announced herself with morning nausea and evening cramps.

"How old's she now?" Pasco said. "Sixteen, seventeen?"

"Sixteen goin' on twenty-eight."

"Bad years."

"The boy was easier, I tell you. Quieter. A shy little fella. But Nutmeg...." His voice fell off into a contemplative silence.

Nutmeg: they had named her Charlene, but Montgomery had taken to calling her Nutmeg from the first time he'd held her. "She was the sweetes' smellin' baby," he'd explained to Pasco. "Just like the nutmeg spice back home."

Montgomery contemplated his beer, his head twisting slightly as if in regret or in puzzlement, Pasco couldn't tell which. He appeared more than simply tired now; looked old, as if his vigour weren't just momentarily drained but permanently impaired. In the dusky fluorescent lighting his short hair, carrying still the impression of his cap, seemed thickly sprinkled with silver. Age was marking itself on him, marking itself on all of them.

"A baby's a frightening thing," Pasco said. "You just can't tell how they're going to turn out." Images of Danny—the baby, the boy, the young man on the make—flashed through his mind.

"You not jokin', man." Montgomery sucked his teeth in a juicy screech of frustration. Then he closed his eyes, massaged them gently with the tips of his fingers. After a moment, he said, "It all goin' to work out in the end, God willin'. She still our daughter, she can't be so different from her family. The heart good, the soul good, the spirit strong." He smiled uncertainly at Pasco. "Right?"

"Right."

Montgomery took a big gulp of his beer. "Talkin' 'bout chil'ren, your boy lookin' good. How he goin'?"

"Fine, as far as I know."

"They finish the livin' room yet?"

"You kidding?"

"But he have ambition. Is a good thing to see in your chil'ren, Pasco."

"Yeah, I suppose. But sometimes it's difficult to tell greed from ambition."

"But is natural to want, man. As I say, is the work I come to Canada for. And I'm only a mailman, but"—his eyes rapidly blinked away moisture—"is a kind of success, not so, Pasco?"

Pasco, embarrassed at the unexpected emotion, stared into his beer mug. After a moment, he said, "You provide for your family. I'd say that's success."

Montgomery sniffled, spat the half-chewed toothpick to the floor, took another gulp of beer.

"But I don't know what Danny means by success," Pasco continued. "Maybe it's not greed, maybe it's just a kind of possessiveness." He paused, deep in thought. "It's funny, eh, seeing a whole life, seeing a person take shape. You start connecting things up."

"I hearin' you, man. When she was still small-small, Nutmeg cry two whole days till we let her put on nail polish. Now miss dressin' up like a Chris'mas tree. She even take to wearin' a ring on every finger excep' the t'umb."

"Danny hasn't changed much either. I remember one day, he must've been three or four, I guess, I was sitting in the living room looking through the paper or something when all of a sudden Danny dashes past me heading for the stairs. Both hands between his legs, holding on tight."

"Don't tell me…."

"You guessed it. Suddenly, boom!, the dam gives way. And the kid just stands there. Dumbstruck. Looking down at the pee soaking his pants and legs. A little puddle starts spreading around his shoes and he's— Like, he can't figure out what's going on. Then his eyes grow as big as saucers, his face goes all red, and he starts screaming *Put it back! Put it back! Put it back in my penith.*"

Montgomery, shaking with laughter, slapped the table.

"And you know, Montgomery, the kid hasn't changed, he's still asking for the impossible."

Montgomery shook his head. "*Put it back, put it back,*" he repeated quietly. "Oh Lord, what you goin' to do, eh?" He drained his beer. "Well, call it what you want, is just chil'ren bein' chil'ren. Sometimes I does think that the trick to being a parent is jus' learnin' how to survive."

There was a great deal of truth in what Montgomery had said, Pasco thought. There were few rules, few guidelines: you simply made it up as you went along. His palm wiped at his forehead: he was sweating. "Christ, it's hot in here," he said, tugging at his collar.

"Is why I like it, man." Montgomery glanced reluctantly at his watch. He took a long, slow breath. "I guess is time to set off for Paradise."

Pasco had never before heard regret in his voice at the prospect of heading home.

They called good-night to Lanny, Montgomery zipping up his coat and then helping Pasco on with his.

Outside the temperature had dipped. A light, cold rain was coming down. Cars slowly followed each other on the slick road, their lights sharp and bright but without merriment.

Before they headed off in opposite directions, Montgomery said, "You know, Pasco, recently I been thinkin' that another winter in this country goin' to kill me. It gettin' me in the bones, man."

"You and me both, my friend." Pasco's arm reached up, his hand briefly grasped Montgomery's shoulder. "You and me both."

Chapter Two

P ASCO sat up in the bed, blankets falling away from his shoulders and chest. He was perspiring, his undershirt, white and growing ratty at the seams, cool where it clung damp to his skin. He studied the round face of the alarm clock. It was six A.M., early still. The dull glow on the windowpanes came from the streetlamp.

As so often, he'd been awoken by a familiar mumbling. Only after several seconds of searching the darkness did he realize, with irritation and a deep hurt, that the sounds had come from inside his head, his mind making real the undecipherable prattle that had often surfaced from Edna's dreams. At such moments he felt as if he had briefly reclaimed her from afar, but he resented, in his growing awareness, having nothing substantial to hold on to.

When Edna died five years ago, Pasco thought that the weight of memories would kill him too. The day after her funeral, in his first moments alone, he went around the house collecting the photographs of her. They were many, all in black-and-white, none recent, most dating back to Danny's high-school interest in photography. He wrapped them in newsprint, placed them carefully in a box and put the box on a shelf in a corner of the basement.

But as time went by, he discovered her absences to be more virulent than he would have guessed. They came at him from unexpected angles, at unexpected moments. In the mornings he missed the rasp of her lighter and the bite of her first cigarette, missed the heavy aroma of her brewing coffee. The days at the restaurant were made easier by activity, but evenings imposed a deep silence on the house, a silence that nothing—not the radio, not the television—could adequately fill; it was a silence in which the broadcast sounds of the world, the music and the newscasts and the joyous lilt of advertising jingles, were thinned and hollowed, revealed a chilling emptiness. And nights brought their own absences: her warmth beside him in bed, the press of her slight body against his back, the caress of her cold feet on his.

He could hide her images, but he could not escape the sense of her that continued to hover insubstantial and rigorous.

He had, after some time, got to the point of wishing to sell the house. He would move into a flat, preferably in the neighbourhood—for he had grown accustomed, after twenty-five years, to walking to and from the restaurant and could not imagine changing his routine.

It was Lorraine Neumann who pointed out that to change homes would be simply to move the pain to a different location. "Give it time," she'd said. "Get over Edna first, at least as much as you can. Then if you still want to, I'll help you look for a new place myself." Her words gave him pause, not because she was a crisis centre counsellor and not because she had been Edna's best friend, but because she too had lost a spouse and survived well. Experience: it was an authority Pasco had always respected.

So he'd given it time, inhabiting only parts of the house: the kitchen, the bedroom, Danny's old room which he turned into a workroom for his hobby of making old furniture new again. He was still giving it time five years later.

He turned onto his side, the old bed creaking under him. He was too warm under the blankets but a deeper chill shuddered along his bones. The heating system, like the house, was old and inefficient. Water gurgled noisily through the pipes, the bathroom and kitchen taps were frequently incontinent. The cold damp of autumn had taken hold of the walls and there were days when it was warmer outside than in.

He reached down and massaged his thighs, fingers pressing hard into the kneecaps where the cold seemed to gouge most deeply. By December they would be waking him well after midnight so he could massage heat into them with a medicated rub.

He sighed. "What to do, Pasco?"

Sometimes his ankles hurt too, but he accepted with a certain equanimity the signs of age: the aches, the wrinkles, the greying of the hair, the bleaching of the skin, the growing stringiness of the muscles.

"Nothing much to do, that's what."

Middle age: he wondered why they called it that. He wasn't likely to live to a hundred and ten, and he wouldn't want to see the state he'd be in if he did.

He switched on the bedside lamp, tossed the blankets aside and eased himself out of the bed. His slippers were there on the floor, as neatly composed as cat's paws. They were almost shapeless with use, the leather cracked, wisps of whitish stuffing peeping out in places. But they were comfortable, for Pasco a vital quality.

Rolling his neck at the morning stiffness, he pulled on his bathrobe and shuffled to the bathroom, the urgency bringing back Montgomery's gravelly voice teasing him about his growing inability to "tighten the tap". Pasco had simply shrugged and grinned away the uneasy laughter, for he knew he wasn't the only one of the group to find himself visiting the Gate's washroom—condoms for a dollar, combs for fifty cents—before he'd seen the bottom of his second mug of draught. When, some months before, the washroom at the restaurant backed up, Pasco had been embarrassed by the number of times he'd had to pop next door to the cubbyhole at the back of Fong's Fruit and Vegetables. But

Fong, who sold fruit, vegetables and just about everything else, was understanding, shrugging in sympathy each time Pasco hurried past him.

The toilet hissed and gurgled. He switched on the radio. The news had already given way to last night's sports scores. The Leafs had lost again: so what? Pasco paid scant attention. Hockey, like all professional sport, held no particular fascination for him.

He faced himself squarely in the mirror. This was one of those mornings when it was hard to believe that once so many years ago he'd fancied himself, with scant proof, a bit of a ladies' man. The hair was still intact—he had it regularly trimmed and it had retained its fullness—but the grey of his pupils had liquefied, and prominent half-moons had etched themselves below his eyes. His skin had acquired a chafed quality, as if thinning through to the underlying flesh. He worked up a lather with the soap, spread it on his stubbled cheeks and opened up the razor.

From the radio came a familiar voice. "Ten years. Maybe less. We have to, we *must*, turn it around."

The Doctor: didn't the man ever sleep? Pasco's jaws tightened, and he had to lift the razor from his skin for a second or two.

"And the answer is right here, in each and every one of us. If we don't, we will go the way of the dinosaurs, we will—"

Pasco turned on the hot-water tap hard, the hiss and splatter breaking up the Doctor's words. The Doctor was a man driven and insistent in his concern for the future of the planet. He had a following. Pasco at times lent an ear to his fervour—like the tele-vangelists, he was a diversion, offering a wrinkle on their message of eternal damnation—but this early in the morning he wasn't in the mood. He took his time rinsing the blade of the razor.

"We are consuming our mother, not just suckling from her breast but actually cutting out her flesh—and eating—"

"Thank you, Doc—" The interview was cut off by an advertisement for a tropical resort.

Pasco rinsed his face, gargled, spat. Then he brushed his teeth vigorously and took a quick shower.

As he dried himself off—his belly was soft, but not so soft that he wasn't trim in pants—the radio host introduced the next guest, a man who ran the city's largest food bank. Pasco knew what the man would say—shortages occurred every year around this time—and he made a mental note to himself to put a bag of groceries together. It wouldn't be hard, not with all the cans and boxes—high fibre, low cholesterol (excessive packaging as the Doctor never tired of pointing out)—that Lorraine was always stuffing into his cupboards.

He snapped off the light and the radio, dressed and trod carefully down the stairs. These days, leaving his bedroom was a bit of an unwelcome adventure, like stepping from the ordered and the familiar and descending directly into a construction zone.

The living-room walls had been torn down to their guts: wooden beams, electrical wires, lead piping. Bare bulbs dangled on plain cords from the ceiling. The wall dividing the living and dining rooms had been removed altogether, opening up "the space", as Danny referred to it, his impersonal language effectively effacing all memory. The floor, dusted white and littered with stray bits of wood and wire, showed the tracks of work boots. The fireplace, not used in years, had been partially stripped of the white paint Edna had layered on so many years before; the revealed brick showed red and surprisingly fresh.

The front window, changed at Danny's insistence from small frosted panes to a large sheet of plate glass, disclosed an unpromising day. Grey, wet, the light filtered by heavy cloud: the worst kind of day for the bones. The house across the street, renovated the year before by new owners, sat unlit and inanimate, its walls sandblasted raw. At night, chandeliers and brass glittered through its windows. The branches of the young tree out front— it had been inserted into a small circle of soil left when the front yard was redbricked—trembled in a light breeze.

That house on the other side of the street was the incarnation of his son's dream. Pasco wasn't quite sure what to make of it: he could not deny there was a certain beauty to the house not unlike the beauty he gave to battered pieces of furniture in his workroom upstairs; but while he sought, with his stripping and sanding and polishing, to retrieve a concealed beauty, the house across the street had been completely remade, had become new and unrecognizable. Intimidating.

Danny had logic on his side though. The boy was quick with figures, could make them dance, could conjure magical images with them the way the people at an Amway meeting he once attended had done. Sitting in Pushpull's friend's living room with a dozen other people, Pasco had quickly recognized the manipulative construction of dreams, the making of nothing from nothing, heightened fantasy used as motivation for the selling of household cleaners. The technique reminded him of the trick of the lottery corporation: the romance of burgeoning wealth for minimum effort.

It had begun one hot evening the summer before. Pasco had just come in and was in the kitchen wolfing down, straight from the fridge, a small shepherd's pie Lorraine had brought him when Danny dropped by. He hadn't called first and Pasco remembered not being thrilled to see his son—so often, their encounters ended in disagreement. He wondered what Danny was doing there. At that time of the evening he would usually be still running around doing Simmons's bidding or, free, popping into the Yorkville nightspots, picking up women, becoming part of the glitter.

Danny had brought a six-pack of imported beer, a large bucket of fried chicken—and a bottle of Glenlivet with a red ribbon on it. "What's that for?" Pasco had asked, suspiciously eyeing the Scotch. "Christmas isn't for months yet."

"So merry whatever," Danny had replied with uncharacteristic levity. Then he'd opened two of the beers, helped himself to a chicken leg and placed a folder on the table between them, the folder that contained the plans and estimates that were the raw material of his visions.

Although he'd recognized Danny's approach, and although he'd argued—feebly—against the disruption to his life, he couldn't in the end bring himself to deny his son. He was not the kind of man to say the words out loud, but he loved his son; and he recognized that he had never been the perfect father, or even much of one. To say he'd done his best was inadequate, not to mention humiliating. So in some remote and unexamined part of himself, he felt he owed Danny.

Pasco hadn't, in truth, realized that his son's plans were more ambitious than sandblasting on the outside and a paint job on the inside. Danny, in making his pitch, had somehow managed to paint pictures of enhanced beauty and value without mentioning specifics: like the enterprising enthusiasts who never mentioned the humiliation of trying to sell to friends and family, or the lottery pushers whose exhortations ignored the odds.

Danny had left the house that night pleased with his father's tentative agreement.

Pasco had heard nothing more about Danny's plans for several weeks. He put it out of his mind, supposing that some detail hadn't worked out. Maybe one of Danny's calculations had been off, maybe Simmons was keeping him busy.

Then one Saturday morning when Pasco was already at the restaurant, a crew arrived at the house and, under Danny's direction, set about gutting the living room. They removed the wall. They knocked out the front windows and prepared the space for the new glass, covering it up temporarily with a sheet of plywood. They pounded and hammered and scraped and sawed. And only then, as this work was proceeding, had Danny, in jeans and a hard-hat, come down to the restaurant to inform his father that the renovations were underway.

Pasco, busy preparing ten Breakfast Special Number Ones (two eggs, bacon, hash browns, toast and coffee) for a group of hung-over conventioneers, had paid little attention. "Call me when you get home," Danny had said over the sizzle of bacon. "Leave a message if I'm not in."

So Pasco wasn't prepared for what he found when he let himself into his home around seven that evening. His living room had been thoroughly wrecked, as if by a pack of blindfolded delinquents let loose with power tools. As he stood in the midst of the carnage, the same feeling came to him as on the night when he and Edna had returned home from a late movie to find they'd been burglarized: a palpitating sense of violation.

He'd immediately telephoned Danny, but of course—*Hello, Daniel here,...you know what to do after the beep*—he was never in. Pasco left as coherent a message as he could.

It was the following Monday evening before Danny called back. His apologies were brief: just what, he wanted to know, had his father expected—a couple coats of paint and some aluminum siding?

Well, yes....

Pasco, his back turned to what had once been his living room, smiled with grim satisfaction at the silence his response had elicited.

Finally Danny had said, "It's just the beginning, Dad. You won't recognize the place—"

"I don't already."

"—when I'm through with it."

"Danny, just what are you planning?"

"Sorry, Dad, can't discuss this now, gotta go, I'm late." And he'd hung up, the dismissive click giving way to the mockery of the dial tone.

Probably dashing off to answer Simmons's call, Pasco thought bitterly. With employees like Danny, the old fart wouldn't even need toilet paper.

Danny and his work crew hadn't achieved much in the two weeks since. They'd managed to replace some electrical wiring, reinforce beams, patch cracks in the remaining walls. And they'd installed the plate-glass window. The problem was that they couldn't come every day, another detail Danny had neglected to mention. The men were hired on the side from The Simmons Construction Company; they worked only when they were free— and when Danny could afford to pay them. Danny had evaded the question when Pasco asked whether old man Simmons himself knew about it.

Why, Pasco wondered, did children so often assume that their parents were prepared to put up with anything just for them? Maybe, he thought, it was because parents often did. And in his mind he heard Edna's voice, or the approximation of her voice that stayed with him: Boys will be boys. She had used the cliché to excuse horrors. Boys will be boys: even when they were caught cheating in exams or sneaking dollar bills from the food money, even when joints were found in their school lockers. Boys will be boys: Pasco had never figured out whether the phrase revealed Edna to be a loving mother or a resigned cynic. Whichever it was, he'd never admitted, not even to her, that he himself had merely put up with it all as best he could—as he was now, years later, still putting up with it all as best he could.

The lights came on in the living room of the house across the street, a chandelier sparkling warm in the wet morning. Pasco glanced at his watch. It was getting late. He picked his way through to the kitchen, flicked the light on. After the living room, even its dinginess seemed welcoming.

The kitchen had been next on Danny's hit list, if his crews ever managed to get the living room done.

The wall between the dining room and the kitchen would go too—"Open concept, Dad, the latest thing"—to be replaced by a work counter, "all wood, the real stuff".

What precisely, Pasco had wanted to know, was "all wood, the fake stuff"?

But Danny was intent on pursuing his vision. "You see, you can be in the kitchen cooking—I've put lots of thought into this, Dad—and your guests can be at the dining table, and you can still chat, see? No more Excuse-me-while-I-stir-the-pot."

"Pot?" Pasco had said. "What pot? What guests?" Then—and he didn't know why it happened just at that moment—he noticed the thinning patch on the crown of his son's head.

"New cupboards, something colourful. New fridge, new stove, microwave."

"Danny—"

"Don't worry, Dad, I'll get you a two-burner for the living room till it's done."

"Danny, you're losing your hair, just like your grandad."

"Dad—"

"Bald as an eagle before forty."

"Dad!"

"Blamed the mustard gas." Approaching thirty years of age, Danny was acquiring a striking resemblance to his grandfather: the same high forehead, the same suspicious eyes, the mouth set in such a way as to say, Here is not a man easily amused.

"It's being taken care of, okay? Can we drop it now?"

"You buying yourself a rug?"

"Drop it, Dad."

"A little flying carpet?" His hand swept upwards. "Whoooosh!"

"Fuck!"

Pasco had laughed alone. Danny had never known his grandfather, and Pasco was at a loss to explain how the boy had grown into a similar humourlessness.

Pasco filled the kettle and turned on the stove, the gas hissing for a moment before popping into flame.

The bottle of instant coffee and his mug stood on the table beside the kitchen window. He picked up the telephone and hydro bills and put them into his shirt pocket.

Danny referred to the table as his father's office. It was small, unsteady on its chrome legs, the top hidden by untidy piles of old bills and ripped envelopes, dog-eared magazines and unread newspapers, pens, pencils, notepads, store receipts, the white and yellow pages, reams of junkmail offering clever gadgets at discount prices. In one corner, balanced on a stack of ancient department-store catalogues, was a small black-and-white television which worked only when the weather was good.

He spooned some coffee into his mug, one of a pair that was a gift from Lorraine "just because". One, which he kept in its package in a cupboard, had a lascivious barber twirling one end of his moustache with the declaration that BARBERS LIKE IT SHAVED. The one he used showed a chef salivating beneath the words COOKS LIKE IT HOT. It was a large mug, solid, glazed white, the interior brown with coffee residue built up over time. The residue was layered smooth, silken to the touch. Pasco fancied that this lent extra flavour to each cup of coffee and would let it go as long as he could, until it began flaking off and dissolving gritty between his teeth. Then he would take a steel-wool pad to it, scrubbing until it gleamed white once more.

Bachelor habits: Edna would never have let him get away with it, would have declared the mug *filthy dirty* with her look of disgust.

Edna: She had taken so much away with her. The familiar sadness came to him, a dull ache expanding in his chest. It rarely came in the mornings—he thought it must be the weather—but was usually prompted by early evening, in that quiet time when the daylight had faded to a suggestion of itself, shadows multiplied and the world seemed to hold its breath: a kind of paralysis, an emotional dread.

Pasco, by nature not a disconsolate man, did not enjoy the looming despondency. He struggled against it, as he always did.

The kettle whistled. He filled the mug with boiling water, stirred it and sipped carefully at the scalding bitterness. Then he sat on a chair and took a deep breath.

He thought: You see, Edna....

A rapping at the kitchen door pulled him away from his thoughts.

Lorraine was standing at the top of the stairs, clutching her sweater shut. She smiled at him. "Morning, Pasco. Saw your light."

"Morning."

In her unlaced work boots Lorraine was as tall as Pasco in his socks. She was a year or two younger than he, and in better shape. Not careless of her looks, but not fussy either, she used no make-up except a light glaze of lipstick. Her hair, brown with some grey, was usually tied into a careless bun. She wore her age well, which was more than Pasco could say for himself.

"Here," she said, proferring a basket swathed in a kitchen towel. "Muffins. Fresh baked."

He took the basket; it was warm to the touch. Supposed he should ask her in for a coffee.

"I'll take a raincheque," she said. "There's another batch in the oven, don't want 'em to burn."

He asked why she was baking at this time of the morning, and she explained that the crisis centre's baked-goods supplier had been forced into bankruptcy. The staff had decided to make their own supplies until a new donor could be found. "Gotta do what you can," she said with a resigned twist of her head.

He thanked her again, and offered to ask the restaurant's suppliers if they would consider donating to the centre.

"That'd be great. Thanks, Pasco." She shivered in the early morning chill. "Enjoy," she said, turning to go. "They were Rick's favourites."

"Old family recipe?"

"Right off the box-top," she laughed, descending the stairs.

Pasco remained at the door watching her walk back to her house through his excuse for a backyard, the ground soggy and uneven, the grass patchy and not so much cut as hacked short. She didn't bother to latch the gate in the waist-high fence that separated their properties before hurrying through her own backyard, in summer a marvel of shrubbery and flowers but now well prepared for winter, the lawn tightly mowed, the flowerbeds cleaned, the shrubs battened down under constructions of wood frames and burlap. A plastic bird-feeder sat full of seed atop a wooden pole.

Lorraine's endless labour out there from early spring to early fall had earned Danny's derision—"What a waste of time. Same thing over and over again, year after year." But he accepted with gratitude the giant lettuces, tomatoes and zucchini she grew in one corner. Pasco had bristled with anger the day Danny remarked in passing that Simmons really appreciated the vegetables.

Pasco himself admired the results she coaxed from the soil, but he'd never felt the urge to do the same himself. The backyard was just extra space that had to be trimmed back from time to time. On blazing summer days, Lorraine would position her sprinkler so that the spray arched over the fence, dampening his own parched grass. To Pasco, this was neither here nor there; if it made her happy to do so, that was fine by him. He had refused her offer a couple of summers back, however, to put in wild roses along the fence. He feared that the rose bushes would lead to further labour, to a request to put the lawn in order, maybe, with all the requisite rolling and planting and fertilizing and watering and pruning and mowing that would require.

Thanks but no thanks, he had said to her, and he wished he had found the strength to deal with Danny's plans in the same way. He thought it revealing, though, that Danny had everything to gain, and Lorraine nothing.

Lorraine turned at her kitchen door and waved before going in, as if she knew, or hoped, that he'd still be there watching her. He raised a hand in hesitant acknowledgement before closing the door.

At the table, he threw back the folds of the kitchen towel and took one of the muffins. He didn't often have breakfast; his stomach felt tight in the mornings, contracted somehow, and he was usually content with a slice of toast at the restaurant later on. But the muffins were warm, fragrant with cinnamon. They awoke an unusual hunger. He broke the muffin open, put a chunk into his mouth. Cinnamon, yes, and bran. Walnuts and raisins. Honey, too, with strands of desiccated coconut.

He finished his coffee, lukewarm now, while watching the seven o'clock news on television. There was nothing new. Native unrest, immigration policy, the Soviet economy, African starvation, Ottawa corruption, lake-water pollution: each topic got its thirty or forty seconds, not enough to inform but quite sufficient to ensure that the world was, as ever, lurching from one crisis to another.

Afterwards, taking his time, he shrugged into his coat, slapped at his pockets—wallet, keys, handkerchief—and slipped on his shoes. He was already on the porch about to pull the door in when it occurred to him that he should give Lorraine a call. He hurried back to the kitchen, dialled her number. He felt awkward at such moments and when she answered he spoke quickly, his voice, he thought, lacking sincerity, his compliments on the muffins sounding hollow. But she was more pleased than he'd expected, and when he hung up his face was hot.

He let himself out, testing the door to make sure it was locked. The air was heavy with the sense of the city stripping down and tucking itself in for winter. He set off for the restaurant at his usual easy pace.

———————

Aldo turned up minutes after the first pot of coffee had been brewed. Pasco poured him a cup, balanced two creams and two sugars on the saucer and watched Aldo's manicured fingers carefully peel open the tubs of cream, slowly tear open the packets of sugar, watched him empty them with a kind of grace into the coffee. Aldo had the hands and the motions, Pasco decided, of a man accustomed to reaching into an open chest and probing at a living heart.

Aldo was a cardiologist, middle-aged and good-looking in a world-weary way. He favoured turtlenecks and sportsjackets, and for several weeks now he'd been stopping in at Pascal's for a morning coffee. A fairly talkative man, he seemed unusually pre-occupied this morning.

"Torronto is a *won*derful city, Pas-co," Aldo suddenly said in a tone that was clearly leading elsewhere.

Pasco nodded, wiped his hands on his apron.

"*Beau*tiful. The hospital, first class. The doctors, first class." He was spending some time in Toronto, perfecting his English and acquainting Canadian heart specialists with an innovative recovery programme he'd developed back home in *Pahdwa*. "But one thing I don' un'erstan'—"

"And what's that, Aldo?" Pasco swirled a damp cloth on the countertop.

"It's delicate, Pas-co...."

"What's delicate, Al-do?"

"Bidets."

"Bidets?"

"Yes. In Canahdian houses, where do they keep it, the bidet?"

"Ahh, well...." Pasco could not help smiling at the picture of Aldo, eminent cardiologist, a man of a certain elegance, squatting on a bidet, pants around his ankles. "The usual place, I guess. If they have one."

"*If.* That, you see, Pas-co, is my problem. I am staying with a coll-eague not far from here. An authority. World respected. And, believe it or not, there is no bidet in the house."

"No bidet, eh?" Pasco crumpled the washcloth into his hand.

"That's right. No bidet. I don' un'erstan'."

"Aldo, my friend, you know most Canadian houses don't have bidets."

"Ah no! But this is horrible! Then how—forgive me, Pas-co, there is no delicate way—how do Canahdians wash their bottom after they go to the toilet?"

"Generally speaking, they don't. *We* don't, I mean."

"You don't!" Aldo's eyes widened in disbelief. "But,... you are such a cle'n people. All the deodorant they sell on television—"

"Hey, we use toilet paper."

"Yes. But, Pas-co, this is not enough, one must wash, too."

Pasco threw his hands up. "Hey, what can I tell you, Aldo? Ask your friend to lend you the garden hose."

But Aldo was beyond humour. He slid off the stool. He paid, was obviously still troubled.

Pasco could see that the esteem in which Aldo held all that he had so far encountered in the city was taking a battering. He wished he could somehow reassure him, but Pasco knew that certain things—especially in matters of habit and custom—simply *were*; they couldn't be explained, couldn't be changed.

Pasco helped him on with his coat. "Aldo, some things you can't do anything about, you know?"

Aldo smiled thinly, eased his hat onto his head. "Pas-co, you believe me, in my business it is the one thing I know for sure." He raised the collar of his coat up around his ears, briefly shook Pasco's hand as he always did on arriving and departing, and stepped through the front door into the rainy morning.

Pasco watched him hurry across the glittery street. After clearing away the cup and saucer, he fetched the mop and began washing the floor. The radio played quietly in the background. Jose Feliciano was *weash*ing everyone a *Merry Creasmas*. It was the first song of the season Pasco had heard.

Chapter Three

"CHRIST!" Danny turned in the bed, tugged the duvet higher and tucked its edge under his chin. His body felt leaden in the trapped warmth of the bed. His eyelids would not rise, lips would not part. His mind was fogged with a deep fatigue.

The clock radio had awoken him from where it sat on a dresser on the other side of the room, deliberately out of reach. Gritty music and the morning man's comfortable babble filled the room.

Random bits of thought and image flitted unordered through his drowsiness: his desk cluttered with half-finished reports and stacks of pink requisition slips. Mr. Simmons smiling: *Dano*. His fist pounding at an unpainted door. The sounds from the radio— weak jokes, commonplace philosophy—nudged at him, prickling at his consciousness. He felt faintly hung over. A wall in his father's house being ripped away. Sal's hooked index finger punching at his calculator. A hand—fingers startlingly white, nails startlingly red—unzipping his trousers in the dark. Mr. Simmons grimacing: *SkyDome? They should've called the damned thing the ConDome. You see the prices they're charging, Dano? They're giving it to the public, putting it right up there where the sun don't shine!*

His recollection of Mr. Simmons's fury brought a thin smile to Danny's lips. *Right up there where the sun don't shine*. Of course, that was precisely what thousands of Mr. Simmons's tenants said he was doing to *them*. But whether it was the prices the SkyDome charged for baseball tickets, beer and hotdogs, or the rents that Simmons Construction demanded, Danny understood—as did Mr. Simmons—that business was business. The law of supply and demand. There was no right or wrong, good or bad, it was merely economic fact. *Right up there where the sun don't shine.* It was all part of the game governed by the tensions of the marketplace, except that Mr. Simmons—whom Danny would never have guessed to be a sports fan—didn't enjoy being the recipient.

Gradually he became aware of the disinfectant that hung about the room. It wasn't sharp, was more like an unsubtle suggestion of cleanliness, a reminder that Estelle had been here the day before doing her weekly wiping and dusting and scrubbing and vacuuming. The industrial smells of her profession usually remained behind for a day or two, a grander version of the trail left in the wake of a heavily perfumed woman. When, every Tuesday morning, he slipped fifty dollars into an envelope and left it for her on the breakfast counter in the kitchen, his nose anticipated the scents he would come home to. They were part of Estelle, helped define her, just as whenever he pictured Mr. Simmons the sweet smell of fresh banknote ink came to him; or when he pictured his father the smells of his little greasy spoon—an oily mixture of old grease, fresh coffee, burnt toast, singed bacon—seemed to materialize around him. He wondered what smell suggested itself when people thought of him. None, probably. He felt he hadn't yet sufficiently defined himself in life. Besides, did M.B.A.s give off a distinctive smell? He thought not. At least, not before they hit the boardroom.

Then he remembered.

Red-haired, pale-skinned, small-breasted. Lipstick that tasted vaguely of strawberries.

His hand burrowed under the duvet searching for her. She wasn't there, the mattress wasn't even warm.

An artist of some kind. Sandy. Advertising? Clothes design? She'd had a large black portfolio with her. Clothes for her soul, advertising for her food. Favoured—she'd told him this—black outfits, red scarves. Her colours. Lived up on Balliol, Ball*oil*, she'd said. Not one of the Simmons buildings.

She wasn't there. She was gone, and that was good. He disliked the early morning dance, the intimacies of the night before become the inadequacies of the morning after. Lips that offered nocturnal passion seemed, in the spent aftermath, the bruised relics of abuse. He always felt like shaking their hands.

He relaxed, thinking himself alone, and so he wasn't prepared when she called out to him.

"Morning, Dan."

"You're still here." He sat up, the duvet falling from his chest.

"Breakfast's ready." She was standing in the kitchen doorway wearing one of his shirts. "Would you like it in bed?"

"No, no, I—" He stood up, wrapping the duvet around himself: morning brought a modesty that had been absent in the urgencies of the night before. He felt himself absurdly small, shrivelled even, while last night he had revealed himself with pride.

She laughed, an easy, open chuckle. "Covering up, eh?" Shook her head. "Some guys."

He ignored her and hurried to the bathroom, shutting the door firmly behind him.

He scrubbed himself hard in the shower. Her familiarity of tone bothered him more than her presence, more even than her presumption in preparing breakfast. For familiarity indicated an assumption of rights and, as far as Danny was concerned, rights to his privacy were not there for the claiming—it was why he rarely answered the telephone at home, letting his answering machine take a message instead—but had to be earned by more give and take than was possible from one night of vigorous tumbling between the sheets.

He took his time shaving, slapping on after-shave lotion, brushing his teeth. He decided against his usual cologne: Sandy had commented favourably on it the night before. He slowly massaged in the hair tonic that promised to arrest the premature thinning on the crown of his head. Haunted by photographs of his grandfather's clean and shining scalp, he'd already inquired about hair replacement, but it was too soon for that.

His grandfather's hair: his father was probably right about that. But different qualities of light brought out different features. Sunlight seemed to highlight certain aspects of his mother, a resemblance not displeasing to Danny. Electric light, though, heightened the features he had inherited from his father: when people mentioned the resemblance, Danny usually felt like stepping into another light, offering another angle, bothered not so much by the observed presence of his father as by the unremarked presence of his mother. Yet in his bathroom mirror he'd begun seeing more and more of his father: the eyes, the nose, the shape of the chin.

There was a light rap at the door. "Don't take forever, Dan. Food's getting cold."

Danny reached for his clothes. He felt hunted by her voice.

She was still wearing his shirt when, knotting his tie, he entered the small kitchen. She had set plates and cutlery on the breakfast counter and was sitting there with a cup of coffee, gazing through the window at the lake stretched out down below like a field of pewter. A light mist hid the horizon. "Looks cold, eh?" she said.

Danny grunted, straightened the tie.

She pushed her chair back, reached into the oven. "I've been keeping it warm," she said.

Bacon, scrambled eggs, toast. From the fridge, slices of fresh tomato decorated with a sprig of parsley.

"Where'd you get all this stuff?"

"I popped downstairs to the convenience store."

"You shouldn't—"

"Why d'you bother having a fridge anyway? Decoration?"

"I don't spend much time at home. Stuff just goes bad."

"So you going to eat, or what?"

"Haven't got the time."

"It's all ready, you might as well—"

"I never have breakfast." He spoke firmly, resentful of her insistence.

"Fine, suit yourself." She jumped to her feet and pushed past him to the living room.

He poured himself a coffee, lingered at the window for a moment. Grey sky, a few lonely gulls, a Cessna, fragile against the immensity, touching down at the Toronto Island Airport. He wondered, and not for the first time, what a man like Mr. Simmons might be up to at this time of the morning. But no images presented themselves; it was impossible to construct for the boss any semblance of a life away from the office.

When he took his coffee into the living room, Sandy—black blouse, black slacks—was knotting her scarf around her neck. She said, "I'm sorry, one-night stands shouldn't—" He didn't miss the bitterness in her voice.

"Forget it." She wasn't bad-looking, though not as attractive as he'd thought the night before.

She pulled a hairbrush through her hair, fluffed and patted it. "I'm—" She tugged at a knot, brushed it out. "I don't know the etiquette."

"Don't worry about it." He thought it best to ignore the crack in her voice.

She sighed, tossed the hairbrush into her handbag. "How come you live in a bachelor?" she asked suddenly. "I thought a Simmons employee would have his pick—"

"I don't need more," he said, on his guard. He didn't remember discussing his job.

"You get a break on your rent at least?"

"Mr. Simmons believes in treating everyone the same, tenants or employees. Business is business, you know."

"Yeah, right." Struggling with an earring, she began wandering slowly around the room. Tapped her foot on the pot of the stunted orange tree. "Needs water." Examined, unimpressed, his framed posters for various art and archeological exhibitions. Glanced briefly at his university degrees. Paused before the one photograph mounted on the walls. "Who's that?"

"My mom."

"Looks like a nice woman."

"Think so?"

"Isn't she?"

"She's dead."

"Recently?"

"About five years ago." Danny drained the coffee, tapped the empty cup against his palm. Examinations of his life made him uneasy, but he sensed this to be a moment when he could indulge curiosity without attracting consequence. "What do you see?"

She planted herself firmly before the picture, her eyes narrowed.

Danny was reminded of a city housing inspector challenged by some aspect of his assessment.

"Not a happy woman," she said after a moment. "Not unhappy either, though. Maybe kind of content. Tired, for sure."

"For sure." But he knew that his mother had been angry at the time, that there had been tension between his parents. For weeks the house had pulsed with silences and whispered fights, averted eyes and refused caresses. He had heard his mother sobbing in her room, liquid sounds that had caused his heart to pound; and one afternoon, in an attempt to cheer her up, he'd cajoled her into posing for him out back. It hadn't worked.

"Is that your parents' house behind her?"

"No, a neighbour's. Widow *Noymann's.*"

"Widow Noymann?"

"Yeah. N-e-u-m-a-n-n. *Not Newman, Danny, Noymann. It's German, you know. Cherman.* That's how her old man used to say it."

"And your dad?"

"What about him?"

"How come you don't have a picture of him?"

"But— he's still alive."

Sandy turned wordless towards him. Raised her eyebrows. "Well," she said, "it's time I got out of your hair." She retrieved her purse and portfolio, stepped briskly towards the door.

Danny hesitated. "Look, I've got some calls to make. Business. You can wait, or—" He reached into his pant pocket, took out a ten-dollar bill. "Or you can take a cab."

Her eyes glittered disbelieving at him. "No thanks, I'll take the bus."

Danny realized his message had been too awkwardly sent, too bluntly received. He hadn't intended to wound her pride. Now it was too late. "Suit yourself," he said.

She put her hand on the doorknob. "You know, technically you're pretty good in bed."

"Thanks." But he was wary.

"Must've read all the books, eh?"

Wariness gave way to venom. "Hey, you're not such a bad lay yourself."

"But you don't know the first thing about making love."

Love? No, she didn't know the etiquette. "Hey, you came, didn't you? Two, three times?" He too could be brutal.

"See what I mean?"

Danny forced a chuckle. His own pride demanded it. "Have a nice day, Sandy."

"Yeah, you too." She closed the door quietly behind her.

He was some time in regaining his equanimity, his agitation, as always, demanding movement. He made up the bed, folded it back into its sofa; tossed the breakfast and used condoms into the garbage can, poured himself another coffee. Then he settled back on the sofa to work out perspective. He considered, briefly, what Sandy had cost him. A couple of drinks. Bloody Marys. What— ten bucks? Better than, what was her name? Evelyn. A professional virgin, that one. He'd spent nearly five hundred dollars on her— dinners, movies, the ballet for Christ's sake—and she hadn't even agreed to sleep with him.

He knew what the problem had been with Evelyn: he'd found out too much about her. Her life was her favourite topic of conversation; she had spent hours telling him about herself. And he eventually came to realize that her sharing this knowledge with him implied, for her, a handing over of a certain responsibility. It was as if, in revealing the unhappiness of her childhood, she was demanding action of him, looking to him to create the conditions that would ensure happiness in her adulthood. Her needs and expectations he felt to be alien; they were simply her way of staking a claim on him. He'd made himself busy, too busy to visit, too busy to go out, too busy to call. And he had, in this way, let the relationship taper off.

All things considered, then, a parting insult from Sandy didn't upset the balance sheet much.

When, sometime later, he pulled out into the traffic, Sandy was still waiting at the bus stop. It was a blustery morning and her coat was thin. But he decided not to complicate matters. He drove on past her, seeing as he did so that she had seen him; and seeing, too, that each was pretending not to see the other.

———————

Viv, the superintendent, was kneeling in the lobby securing the Christmas tree to its base when Danny let himself in.

"Marnin', Danny."

"Marnin', Viv."

Viv straightened up, but remained on his knees. His belly, pendulous and solid, hung over his belt. His shirt, untucked, wasn't fully buttoned. "So how you doin' this marnin', mahn?"

"Just fine, Viv. You?" It was obvious to Danny—and not without a certain satisfaction—that Viv would never get used to calling him by his first name. At first he had called him *Mister* Danny, but that had come to an abrupt end the morning Mr. Simmons overheard him. Without missing a beat, the boss had said, "There's only *one* mister here, Viv."

"As usual, mahn, as usual."

Viv was a black man in his fifties from Guyana. He was rarely without a smile, but one that seemed to emanate less from good humour than from that part of him, unmistakable in the eyes, that was sly and assessing. He was neither the fastest nor the most enthusiastic of workers, but the work usually all got done anyway, thanks mostly to his wife, Deanna, a woman unfailingly pleasant despite her constant and obvious fatigue. It seemed to Danny that, whenever he ran into her, she was always on the way to, in the middle of, or on the way from one physical task or another. Deanna was the one to scrub the laundry room, mop the floors, vacuum the corridors, wash the windows and sweep the stairwells; the one to clean vacant apartments, chase down late rent cheques and supervise the parking lot out back. Viv mowed the lawn, shovelled the snow, spread the salt, took charge of the garbage and super-vised the underground garage. And he drank, his eyes usually burning red from the alcohol often dense on his breath.

Danny supposed that Deanna suffered countless indignities behind the locked door of their apartment. Something in Viv's manner suggested a brutal side, and while he was not obviously a bad man, while he was a friendly man in his way, Danny sensed that there were parts of him that were better left undiscovered.

Danny nodded at the Christmas tree. "Isn't it a little early for that, Viv?" The tree, of wire and plastic, had been used for years. The decorations were never removed, the tree stored whole, lights, bulbs and tinsel permanently in place. It spent the year in the basement enclosed in a coat of garbage bags taped together, and simply had to be unwrapped before Christmas, rewrapped afterwards. This was a time-saving innovation by Mr. Simmons, who had been unhappy over the monumental waste of time involved in lifting the tinsel, strip by strip, from the branches and laying it carefully in a box, only to have to replace it at the same painful pace the following Christmas.

Viv shrugged, grimaced at the tree, his fingers reaching out to straighten a twisted branch. "I don't make no decisions aroun' here, mahn. The boss tell me put it up, I put it up. I ain't think he have a special time, sometimes is November, sometimes is Decem-ber. Whenever he remember, nuh. And orders is orders, eh?"

"Right. Good rule to live by, eh?"

"Yeah, mahn." Those sly, assessing eyes took him in. "Yeah, sure." He picked up a can of Pine Forest air freshener, directed a long burst of spray at the tree. This was another of Mr. Simmons's innovations, a "refinement", he called it.

"Mr. Simmons appreciates loyalty."

"Yeah." Viv scratched at his belly, then he smiled broadly. "Right, mahn."

Could Viv be laughing at him? Danny had often wondered, but

proceeding past the elevators to the cramped office he shared with Sal the accountant, he dismissed the thought as too absurd to entertain.

Sal, a fleshy, balding man given to toothy grins, was already at his desk. He nodded in greeting. As Danny hung his coat on a wall hook and settled in behind his own desk, Sal said, "What d'you think he really does every morning, Daniel?"

"Who cares, Sal?" Danny glanced up from the stack of pink requisition slips brought in by the maintenance manager from building superintendents across the city. "Who gives a damn?"

"It's not that I care, Daniel." Sal's long fingers caressed the pages of his open ledger. "I just wonder, that's all. I mean the man hardly ever comes in before midday."

"And he's here till all hours of the evening. So what? He's the boss, he can set his own hours."

"It's kind o' funny, don't you think?" He rubbed at his right eye with a knuckle, his left blinking rapidly across the cramped office at Danny.

"So ask him then." Danny shuffled through the requisitions. Bathurst needed paint and equipment; a pipe had burst, water seeping through and staining the walls of several apartments. Mount Pleasant needed major repairs on its elevators, and one of the St. Clair blocks, following a visit by a city building inspector, needed signs and new lighting for its underground garage.

"You saying you're not curious, Daniel? You probably know him better than anyone else."

"No better than you, Sal." The police had called about one of the Sherbourne Street buildings. The garage door had been broken for months and the public access had led to a steady stream of drug and prostitution problems. Sal had taken the call and, in his memo to Danny, had added "public access leading to pubic excess, so to speak." Danny scratched out the comment.

"Does he have a wife at least?"

"You've been here longer, Sal. You tell me."

"Kids?" Sal was on a rhetorical roll.

"Your guess is as good as mine, Sal."

"Not likely. Our Mr. Simmons isn't—"

"For Christ's sake, Sal, I'm trying to concentrate, d'you mind?"

"Maybe he's a late sleeper?"

"Sal, I really don't think the boss's private life is any of our business."

"Or maybe he catches up on his paperwork?"

Danny's lips were already forming around an expletive when a sharp rap at the door interrupted him. Deanna bustled in, several cheques clutched in her hand. She laid them on Sal's desk. "Seven-o-six not there an' twelve-o-nine promise the cheque for this evenin'."

"What's twelve-o-nine's excuse?"

"He run out o' cheques, he say he goin' to the bank today."

"Tell him we accept cash."

"I jus' tellin' you what he say, Sal."

"Okay, Deanna, I'm not blaming you."

"Better not be." She was coolly serious.

Danny smiled at her. He admired her directness, the sense of sturdy resolution with which she conducted herself. "How's it goin', Deanna?"

"As usual."

"Too bad."

She smiled wearily in response. "By the way," she said, "it have somebody peein' in the elevators again."

Danny sighed, leaned back in his chair. He tossed his pencil onto the desk in exasperation.

"It does really make you wonder 'bout people, eh?" Deanna said.

Danny shook his head, gestured helplessly. "What can I say, Deanna? Keep your eyes peeled."

Anonymous protest was not unknown. Occasional graffiti showed up on the walls questioning Mr. Simmons's parentage, and not a notice was posted—advising tenants about fire-alarm tests or balcony repairs—without various hands commenting, questioning, threatening. All this was part of the game, part of the natural give-and-take between strict landlord and demanding tenants; but using the elevators as urinals was something else again, as were the swastikas in black marker and spray paint that had been popping up in the last few months. Mr. Simmons was clearly growing more unpopular with his tenants, but he refused to be fazed by it. "They must think I'm a Yid," was all he said the morning they found a huge swastika painted on his office door.

Danny turned back to the requisition slips. One of the High Park town houses needed electrical work, and a couple of the downtown rooming houses were requesting new locks because of a rash of thefts. And then there was the apartment on Lawrence that had been damaged by fire, careless smoking as usual.

It would be a busy day. Even though he already knew that the town houses would be dealt with sooner rather than later while the rooming houses would have to bide their time, Danny faced a day of running around to evaluate the urgency of each request. This done, he would then have to write a report on each—concise, no more than half a handwritten page—for Mr. Simmons's consideration.

He had begun sorting the slips into stacks of ascending priority when his telephone rang. Mr. Simmons, with no pleasantries, said, "Meet me out front in five minutes, Dano. I have a house to show you." Then he hung up before Danny had a chance to reply. Danny tossed the sheaf of slips onto the desk—they would have to wait for another day—and reached for his coat.

Sal looked up from his calculator. "Going out already?"

"That was the boss."

"This early?" He glanced at his watch.

"He's got a new house."

"News to me."

"Guess there's a lot you don't know, eh, Sal?"

Sal sat back in his chair, eyes narrowed in contemplation, a pen ticking against his lower teeth. "Maybe he spends his time—"

"I don't want to hear it." Danny shut the door on the accountant's disappointed shrug.

———————

Danny said, "I grew up in this neighbourhood."

"Is that right, Dano?" Mr. Simmons drove hunched over the steering wheel, gloved hands clutching tightly at it.

A light snow had ended, leaving no trace of itself, and the sky had begun to clear. In the distance, out over where the lake lay unseen, snatches of blue showed cold and brittle.

"My dad still owns a greasy spoon not far from here, on Carlton Street."

"Maybe we should stop in for a coffee?"

"My dad isn't one of your admirers."

Mr. Simmons chuckled, thumped his horn at a passing car. "On Carlton, eh? We wouldn't be talking about Pascal's, would we?"

"You know it?"

"Haven't been there in, well, ages. But old man Pascal couldn't be your father. He'd be well into his nineties by now. Or cemetery fertilizer."

"He retired back to the Soo when my dad bought the place off him."

Danny had never driven with Mr. Simmons before. His old Ford LTD was in good condition, but Danny couldn't help noticing as he'd got into the passenger seat that the interior smelled just like Mr. Simmons himself, the lavender scent of a powder he associated with the elderly. As he fumbled with the seatbelt, his eye had fallen on a small plastic lion glued onto the dashboard. As they drove along, Danny could have sworn several times that his eye caught the lion stepping stealthily forward.

"The Soo? My memory must be shorting out, I swear he said he was from France."

"I only met him once, when he came to the house to turn over the keys. He and my dad got piss-drunk celebrating—"

"You must have been young at the time."

"Five or six. But some things you remember."

Mr. Simmons grunted, punched the horn at a drunk lurching across the road. Sherbourne Street slid steadily by. After the busyness around the hospitals farther north, the street had settled down into a genteel desertion, an empty ribbon between shabby lowrises.

"I was really surprised how thin he was," Danny said. "I remember my dad joking that all Pascal needed for pants was a couple strands of boiled macaroni."

"That's right. A skinny cook. Funny, eh? Like a bald barber." Mr. Simmons changed lanes. Tires screeched behind him, a horn blared in protest. "What's he going on about?" Mr. Simmons said in an aggrieved voice. "Driving's getting worse in this city every day." As the car roared by, he raised a middle finger at the driver. "You were saying, Dano?"

"Anyway, Pascal got all weepy—"

"It happens in old age."

"—and blurted out that he'd always pretended to be from France, he'd never even been there. But it was the only way for a French Canadian to get respect in this city. That and money."

Mr. Simmons raced through yellow traffic lights at Carlton Street.

Danny couldn't resist a quick glance backwards at the plate-glass window of his father's greasy spoon. In the park, he glimpsed the woman his father called the pigeon lady desultorily tossing crumbs at the birds. He used to play in the park when he was young, chasing pigeons—there were fewer back then—and panicking seagulls in cowboy pursuit of Injun friends. In their games, only the Injuns died; the rules had specified that cowboys could only be shot in the arm.

"You see, Dano," Mr. Simmons said with a glance into the rearview mirror, "what you're saying is that Pascal didn't understand that the best businessmen, like the best currency, really have no nationality."

Danny nodded, his gaze drawn once more to the dashboard: the plastic lion had taken a graceful step forward.

———————

Danny wondered about the house Mr. Simmons was taking him to see. It was not unusual for his boss to make sudden purchases—he struck quickly when he saw opportunity—but it was unusual for him to show off a new acquisition himself. Normally he would hand Danny the plans, go over the renovations with him and send him off to arrange the details. He kept a close eye on the work in progress, sometimes making unannounced visits to the sites, taking notes and passing along criticism and, rarely, compliments the following day.

At Dundas Mr. Simmons turned left, the street flattening out and spreading the farther east they drove. Closer to Yonge, it was dense and seedy, but now, approaching the Don River, the downtown bank towers retreating into the distance, there was a greater sense of space between redbrick lowrises, industrial depots, milk stores with bars on the windows. The people Danny saw seemed to be all from elsewhere: blacks, East Indians, many Chinese.

Just past Broadview Avenue, Mr. Simmons began slowing

down and pulling to the side of the road. He braked briefly beside a schoolyard teeming with sprightly children, their coats bright and colourful in the thin light. He checked his mirrors, swung around in a squealing U-turn and pulled up immediately on the other side of the road, the walls of the tires scraping against the curb.

Mr. Simmons was fastidious in turning off the car, putting the gear into park, setting the emergency brake—more fastidious, in fact, than he had been in the actual driving. "Here we are, Dano," he said, opening his door and causing a passing cyclist to swerve and swear.

They had parked in front of a stretch of row houses, each tall, narrow, decrepit in its own way. Each had been painted, and not recently, in a different colour: red, green, cream, blue and shades thereof. Some of the tiny front porches, reached by wooden stairs that rose directly from the sidewalk, had been boarded up, one or two had been encased in plastic and the rest left open to the street.

Mr. Simmons led Danny to the unit at the end of the block. It was the grimmest of the houses. Much of its white paint had peeled away to rashes of old red brick. Its porch was exposed, the wood rotting in spots. The first-floor windows had been sealed with warped sheets of plywood, while a broken pane on the second had been patched with cardboard and masking tape. Its abandonment, heightened by the shouts and cries from the schoolyard across the street, seemed almost to detach it from its neighbours.

Danny thought of dank rooms and bat droppings.

Mr. Simmons stood at the bottom of the stairs, one foot perched on the first step: a hunter posing with his fallen prey.

Danny said, "You bought this thing, Mr. Simmons?" His professional eye told him that this house, in this neighbourhood, was grist for, at best, another rooming house.

"I inherited it, Dano. This is where I grew up."

Danny nodded. "I see." Mr. Simmons as a child: an impossible image.

Mr. Simmons looked hard at him. "You see? What do you *see*, Dano?"

"I—" In the growing brightness of the day, Danny saw as if for the first time Mr. Simmons's age: the sparseness of his hair, the loosening of his flesh, the wrinkles that ran riot around his eyes and his lips and down his neck, the skin folding into his shirt collar. The outdoors aged Mr. Simmons, dwarfed him. To Danny he looked a tired and unwell man.

"You see nothing." Mr. Simmons spoke sharply. "So don't pretend."

"Yes, sir."

Mr. Simmons went quiet. He clasped his hands behind his back, swept his gaze up and down the street. "Forgive me, Dano," he said after a long moment. "I'm a little edgy today. This house is a special project."

"There's nothing to forgive, Mr. Simmons."

Mr. Simmons took a deep breath, smiled. "Did I ever tell you why I hired you, Dano?" His eyes wandered around the busy schoolyard.

"No, sir. I never really—"

"I know what you're thinking, but you're wrong. Not for your B.Sc. or your M.B.A. or any other letters you have on your résumé. I'm sure those degrees are nice pieces of paper to have, but they had absolutely nothing to do with my hiring you. No, Dano, I hired you"—light laughter rippled his words—"so I'd have someone to call Dano, just like that guy on Hawaii Five-O."

Danny snickered with scepticism.

"Shocked?"

Danny shrugged. Surely the boss was joking—but the possibility that he was not made him uneasy.

"Don't be," Mr. Simmons said. "That's how the world really

works. It's capricious and sentimental—that's what old boy networks are all about—and people spend a lot of time catching up to reality and claiming they've wilfully created it." He rubbed at his nose with his gloved hand. "I'm sure you studied hard to earn your letters, Dano, but sometimes I think that wearing the same school tie, or being named Daniel, is more important in the end." Mr. Simmons gave him a sly look, openly assessing the effect of his words. "You know the show, Dano? 'Hawaii Five-O'?"

"I've seen it a few times." Getting in late from work, Danny had sometimes wound down by watching midnight reruns of the series, the intrigue incidental to its little escape into televised sun and sand.

"Best series they ever made. I must've seen just about every one, got lots of them on tape."

"So if I'm Dano," Danny said, "you must be—"

"Steve McGarrett, of course. And Sal's the Chinese fella—what's his name?"

"Chin? Chan?" Sal wasn't Chinese, he wasn't anything decipherable, but Danny left the thought unspoken.

"Something like that. Or is he the bad guy? My memory really must be going." Mr. Simmons laughed, his hands fumbling through his pockets.

It seemed curious to Danny that Mr. Simmons would see—or want to see—himself as Steve McGarrett, a cold, calculating and, for the most part, sexless television character. He remembered Steve McGarrett as a man who strutted around his office and the island encircling criminals the way a carnivore stalked dinner. Suspicious of romantic involvement, Steve McGarrett was in many ways an automaton, his affections sublimated, his sexuality submerged. Work seemed his only pleasure, his power an obvious source of satisfaction. Steve McGarrett of all people! What a curious fantasy life the boss must have, Danny thought.

Mr. Simmons found his keys and led Danny up the stairs.

On the wall beside the door, someone had painted in large black letters:

DOWNTOWN TOMMY
GO HOME TO MOMMY

The words might have been a simple plea, a taunt, might even have been the lyrics of a rock song. But whatever their source, whatever their intent, Danny found them unsettling in their plaintiveness.

Mr. Simmons opened the door and ushered him in.

Into darkness. Into a sudden claustrophobia.

Then a webby light splattered on and Danny saw that he was standing in a long and narrow corridor. It ran the entire depth of the house, to a staircase at the very end. The wooden walls to either side were pierced every few feet by a closed door.

Mr. Simmons, close behind him, said, "This is how I got started in the business, Dano. I converted the family home into a rooming house."

As Danny's eyes grew accustomed to the light, he saw that the walls were heavily scrawled with drawings and scribbles, some hasty and desperate, others more considered. One door read JESUS SHAVES. Another displayed two hearts, one broken, one pierced. Here were spitting male genitalia, there sweating female genitalia grotesque below ballooning breasts.

"The living room used to be on the left," Mr. Simmons said. "The dining room on the right."

Some scribbles offered sex while others demanded it. Many promised violence.

"Farther down on the left was the bathroom, on the right the kitchen and pantry."

One lengthy note described in detail a fantasy of enforced fellatio. Around it, as if to fence in the words, a careful hand had penned several biblical quotations complete with references.

"There aren't any tenants left, the last one took off about six months ago. I've kept it that way."

Running his eyes over the walls, reading, Danny was reminded of the stalls in public washrooms, where the darkness of the public mind bared itself most explicitly.

"Makes interesting reading, wouldn't you say, Dano?" Mr. Simmons, strangely expressionless, glanced at him. "Their little squeals of squalor. The Hansard of the poor. You see, Dano, the people who lived here, this is all most of them will leave behind when they die." In the narrow space, Mr. Simmons's words echoed lightly, then faded into the dingy light. "I've left it all, this legacy of theirs, as a kind of reminder. A kind of inspiration, if you know what I mean."

Danny felt numbed. The stale air, mingled with Mr. Simmons's smell of lavender, became oppressive. He turned away from the frenzy on the walls, his chest tight.

Mr. Simmons pushed at the nearest door. It swung slowly open, squealing through its arc. Danny peered into the tiny cubicle gloomily lit by the light from the corridor. A wooden mattress frame took up much of the space, a broken chair standing beside it, a bulbless socket hanging above it.

"We could rent them all in a minute," Mr. Simmons said. "Imagine, I used to rent them out for fifteen bucks a week. That was money in those days. What d'you think we could get these days, Dano?"

"Two hundred a month?"

"Easily."

"More, if we gussied them up a bit."

"That's the other reason I hired you, Dano. I like the way you think. You have the mind of a businessman."

"I guess all those courses were good for something then."

"No, no, Dano, this isn't something a course can teach you. It's instinct, pure and simple. You have it or you don't." Mr. Simmons walked slowly down the corridor, pushing the doors open one by one. Each squeaked agonizingly. "You remember the orange I gave you when you came in for your interview, Dano?"

"Who can forget something like that?"

"When I handed it to you, you probably thought, what is it with this doddering old fool? He must be going senile, blathering on about fruit and vitamins, no wonder he's looking for an assistant."

"Not for a second." But Danny couldn't suppress a smile.

Mr. Simmons considered him slyly. "No, I suppose not. Not you. The other applicants, they sure did. I could see it on their faces. And they all treated me as if I *was* a doddering old fool, they told me what they thought I wanted to hear." He worked his mouth as if diluting a bitter taste. "You remember the interview, Dano?"

"I remember the orange."

"We covered the usual stuff. Your qualifications, your working experience, all the usual crap that doesn't mean a damn when you get right down to it." He chuckled. "I like giving job applicants what *they* expect too." He pulled his gloves off, crumpled them into his coat pocket. "And then after ten or fifteen minutes I stand up, we shake hands, I show you to the door, promise to call. But before I let you go, I ask what you're planning to do with the orange. One bright young fella actually peeled it right there in front of me and ate it. Another one said he was going to save it for breakfast. And yet another one thought he'd impress me with his frugality by saying he'd save it for a rainy day. You remember what you said, Dano?"

"Sure, I do."

"You said, 'Mr. Simmons, I'm going to take this orange home and I'm going to squeeze it dry tomorrow morning. Then I'm going to drink the juice, because I like fresh orange juice. But I'm going to save the seeds. I'll plant them and grow some trees. And when they bear fruit, I'll pick them and sell them right back to you. Small overhead, big profit.' Now that, Dano, was the answer of a businessman. That's when you clinched the job." Mr. Simmons slapped the back of his right hand into the palm of his left, a sharp, dry clap. "Profit, profit, and more profit. That's what counts, right?"

"That's what business is all about, Mr. Simmons. What's the point otherwise?"

Mr. Simmons pursed his lips, nodded slowly. A stillness seemed to settle on him. "At least at your age, Dano. But when you get older, when you've had a bit of success, you start considering other things too. I know lots of executives, rich, successful men at the top of their fields, who dream of opening up country stores or retiring to farms. It's just a fantasy, of course, most of them can't do a thing about it. But I...." He looked around the corridor, eyes rising to the ceiling. "This old house, for instance." He went silent for a moment. "If I were your age, I'd rent these rooms out, make a bundle. Hell, that's what I did when I *was* your age. I know that's what everybody would expect me to do. After all, I'm old man Simmons, the money-making machine, right?"

Danny, uneasy, said nothing.

"It's all right, Dano, I don't mind. I've been called worse. But you know, I just wish they'd call me a job-making machine too. Just think of the number of people Simmons Construction employs, Dano, and more and more every year. Do they think of that? Course not. They only see what I take, they don't want to see what I give. Don't get me wrong, I'm not trying to make myself out as some kind of philanthropist."

"I've got a little orange tree growing in my apartment right now, Mr. Simmons."

Mr. Simmons's face brightened in delight. "I wasn't wrong about you, eh, Dano?"

Danny constructed what he hoped to be a smile of transparent

modesty. Mr. Simmons was the kind of man who would appreciate the confidence that lay behind it.

"The reality's that every company's got to seed future profits
by pandering to the public," Mr. Simmons continued. "Some
sponsor sports or cultural stuff, some spend millions on useless
publicity. We're spared that at Simmons Construction, at least our
rental division is, thanks to the tight housing market. People
grovel to us, not vice versa. But if people are going to pay rent,
they have to work—and one of the things Simmons Construction
does is create jobs. I employ hundreds of people directly or indi-
rectly. Nobody remembers that."

Danny had never suspected that Mr. Simmons cared about his
public image. The boss was full of surprises today.

"But this house, Dano," Mr. Simmons said with summoned
energy. "It gave me my start, it was the beginning of everything I
have achieved." He pressed a hand delicately to the wooden wall.
"But I had to destroy it in the process. That was unavoidable. Now
it's time to pay it back. With full restoration, *not* renovation, mind
you." The boss's eyes latched onto his. "And I'm putting you in
charge because it's too much work for me, I'm not up to it. I've
seen how you work, Dano, I've come to trust you as much as I can
trust any man. You must promise me your best efforts."

Danny held his gaze, nodded with deliberation.

"Good. Now let's go upstairs."

"What's upstairs?"

"I have a little place up on the third floor, a little hideaway, if
you like. I do a lot of my thinking there. There are some photos
you'll find useful."

Danny, reflecting on Sal's speculation about what the boss did
every morning, followed Mr. Simmons up the stairs.

———————

Mr. Simmons's hideaway on the third floor consisted of a sizeable living room, a tiny bedroom and a white-tiled bathroom. Dusty windowpanes allowed in little light. The lamps Mr. Simmons switched on—of slender brass with crocheted shades—cast dusky circles on the wooden floor.

"It's not grand," Mr. Simmons said. "But it's comfortable." He motioned Danny to a seat and disappeared into the bedroom.

The furnishings—armchair, sofa, coffee table—were old and mismatched but cared for. The glassed doors of an ornate wooden bookcase enclosed statuettes of lions in various sizes and attitudes: resting, feeding, stalking, pouncing, wrestling, mating. On the walls framed photographs showed lions in the wild, many of them peaceful, even bored. One, in close-up, seemed to be yawning. In the corner beside the two small windows, an animal crouched unmoving on a pedestal. It turned out, on closer inspection, to be a large grey tomcat with marble eyes; it was stuffed in an attack posture, teeth bared, claws extended.

"I see you've met Simba." Mr. Simmons emerged from the bedroom with a stack of photo albums.

Danny looked around. "Cute little fellow."

Mr. Simmons chuckled and Danny realized with some surprise that he felt at ease here. He understood why Mr. Simmons would spend time in these rooms. There was something reassuring in the settled atmosphere. The rooms had, in an unselfconscious way, the feel that Mr. Simmons had tried without success to re-create in his office.

"Like the pose?" Mr. Simmons asked. "He was a good companion for sixteen years. The claws aren't real, by the way, I had him declawed when he was a kitten." He perched on the edge of the sofa, spread the albums out on the coffee table. "As for the ferocity, that's a little joke. I always suspected Simba had a fantasy life. He'd run to the door and spit and growl whenever he heard a tenant moving around. So I had a taxidermist bring it out after he died."

Danny lowered himself into the armchair. "You live here, Mr. Simmons?"

"No, but as I said, I spend a lot of time here. Dreaming, planning."

Danny noticed that the boss had answered his question without revealing where he lived.

Mr. Simmons opened up the first album to two black-and-white photographs hinged onto the black page. He shifted the album towards Danny. "This," he said, pointing to the first photograph, "is what the living room used to look like. And this is the dining room," he added, as he moved his finger, the nail flesh-coloured, to the lower photograph. He pushed the album closer to Danny. "There are pictures of almost every room in here, Dano. They're your starting point."

Danny took out his notebook and pen.

Mr. Simmons turned the pages, pointing out details in a quiet voice, going so far as to specify the design, colour and shade of drapes and upholstery, of doilies on the sidetables.

Danny, mind boggling at the scope of the project, scribbled quick notes. Some of the photographs included people grave and self-conscious before the camera. But Mr. Simmons didn't explain who they were, never even acknowledged their stoic presence. And Danny, though recognizing Mr. Simmons's traits in several of them, didn't dare ask.

———————

The siren of a firetruck wailed in the distance.

Mr. Simmons looked haggard as he stacked the albums on the coffee table. They had been at it for hours, viewing photo after photo, Mr. Simmons's fatigue first showing itself in the trembling of his hands as he pointed out details, then in the little sigh he took before beginning each sentence.

Danny's neck went stiff. His stomach growled. He hadn't noticed the hardening of the light outside into afternoon. His writing had grown progressively worse as his hand tried to keep up with the flow of words. For the last hour, he hadn't really seized what the boss had said; he'd just jotted it all down in the hope of making sense of it later, when he needed to.

Mr. Simmons got slowly to his feet, his hand massaging at his lower back. "There's just one more thing you should know, Dano. There aren't any tenants left, but there's still a—"

From deep within the house came the sound of a door being shut.

Mr. Simmons looked up expectantly, cocked an ear. "There she is now," he said. "Come."

Danny followed him out to the landing, waited as he paused to lock the door to his hideaway. "If you need to consult the photographs again, Dano, just let me know." They descended the stairs slowly, Mr. Simmons feeling his way, less vigorous going down than he had been coming up.

A young woman was standing at the bottom of the stairs, following them down with her eyes. She was thin, brown-skinned, with long black hair. Danny guessed that she was in her late teens, maybe early twenties. "This," Mr. Simmons said, "is Sita. Sita, this is Daniel."

She didn't offer her hand, just gazed at him with large, uneasy eyes.

"Sita is, shall we say, the last resident of the house. My special friend. She isn't quite legal in this country, you see, Dano, but I like her, I let her stay here. I even let her have some money from time to time. And in return she helps me." Mr. Simmons smiled gently at Sita. "Don't you, dear?" He gathered her long hair in his hand, stroked it. "She cuts my hair, dyes it for me—you know I dye my hair, Dano, don't pretend. She even gives me a perm when I need it." His smile grew tentative, eyes uncertain. "Don't you, dear?"

Sita didn't respond, but Danny didn't miss the sudden rapid blinking of her eyes, the light tremble in her lower lip. He thought: Sal would give his right arm to see this. The secret life of passion.

"Anyway," Mr. Simmons continued, "we'll work something else out for her when you're ready to start work, Dano. Maybe one of the Parkdale rooms, we'll see." He took her chin in his hand, nudged her face towards his. "This young man will be around once in a while just looking around, Sita. There's no reason to be afraid. He's a good boy, he'll leave you alone." He patted her cheek, turned and headed down the corridor to the front door.

Danny followed him, brushing past Sita. She pulled back sharply, as if startled by his touch.

Mr. Simmons grasped the doorknob, hesitated, then turned around to face Sita.

She was standing as if frozen at the end of the long corridor, looking back at them, her hand resting on the railing of the stairs.

"Remember," Mr. Simmons called out. "His name is Daniel. You know, just like the guy in the lion's den."

His laughter, echoing down the corridor, caused Danny's stomach to tighten.

Chapter Four

THE lunch-time rush had come and gone. There was only one client left, a young man dawdling over his coffee and the employment pages of *The Toronto Sun*.

Pasco, weary, poured himself a glass of orange juice and, elbows on the counter, hunched over his lettuce-and-tomato sandwich. His appetite was not great, but after the constant exertion of cooking and serving, his energy was low.

As he ate, his gaze wandered through the window to the park across the street. The trees, stripped bare, were clustered against the sky, each branch twisted into a form as unique as a fingerprint. The park itself looked a lonely place, a larger, less friendly version of Lorraine's garden. The path that dissected its length was dark with absorbed moisture, the greenhouse stolid and lifeless in the dull light. One corner off to the right was taken up by a church, an empty lot separating its heavy stone walls from an abandoned apartment building, the boarded-up windows thick with posters advertising plays, concerts, protests of one kind or another.

It was difficult, on such a day and in such weather, to remember that this very park was a place which, in the warm months, resounded with the distant screams of toddlers and the barking of dogs, a place where the aged could soak up sunshine and admire

the flowers. Now, in the gloom, the park seemed to reflect the reputation it had acquired in recent years as the hub of a neighbourhood whose night-time dangers left its grid of streets and
alleyways littered with bloodied needles, used condoms and pools
of vomit.

There were moments, on grey days, when Pasco felt that he
was being shoved aside by the growing contradictions of the city.

The radio emitted a time tone and the news came on. Pasco
lent half an ear to it. The announcer told of an airplane that had
lost one of its jet engines in flight but yet managed to land safely.
When he explained that the plane could, of course, fly without all
its engines, Pasco put down his sandwich and changed stations.

"Hey," the young man protested mildly from his table, "I was
listening to the news."

Pasco spun the dial rapidly past the rock stations. "What good
is news that tells you a plane can fly without its engines?"

"Come on, you know what he meant."

"Sure I do, but isn't he supposed to be a journalist? He should
say what he means, eh? Or get into politics." He twirled the dial
some more, finally settling for the sounds of swelling strings. The
music, inoffensive, seeking to do no more than cushion the day,
provided background sound to fill the empty spaces of the restaurant. Although he was susceptible to music, Pasco's ear made no
great demands on it. He cared little whether a tune was being
played by a great orchestra, a second-rate bar band or a group of
drugged musicians. He was impervious to the dexterity of the
playing or the inventiveness of the arrangement. All that counted
was the pleasure the sounds gave him, his reaction elemental and
unencumbered.

"Christ," the young man said. "I might as well be in an elevator."

"Why not close your eyes and pretend then."

The young man turned back to his newspaper.

Afternoons were usually slow at Pascal's. A few people would stop in for a coffee or a piece of pie, usually the street whores—cornered women, as Pasco thought of them—coming in to rest their feet after the lunch-time shift or killing a few hours until it was time to head back out to the street. Pasco didn't mind so long as they behaved themselves, which they did for the most part. Once in a while, one of the younger ones would offer to trade a blow job for a meal, but he was never tempted to accept. He had learnt to differentiate between the playful and the desperate. The playful met with a curt refusal; the desperate received a free meal. This was why they gave him no trouble, the regulars keeping the newcomers in line: the rules were clear, and so long as they were followed Pascal's would be a haven.

After twenty-five years, Pasco had grown accustomed to the rhythms of his business. The glow of ownership—the sheer recollected audacity of it—had long since faded, as had the bigger dreams of the time. As had the restaurant itself. Danny had, from the beginning, referred to the place as a "greasy spoon", a characterization Pasco disliked. But time, he recognized, had somehow fit the reality to the term.

Pascal's was longer than it was wide, the clarity of the fluorescent lighting dimmed by the old cream-coloured wallpaper. Ten booths—Formica tables between seats of red leatherette—ran down the right side, each with its aluminum coat-rack. Once miniature jukeboxes had hung on the wall above each table—a song for a quarter—but they'd been more trouble than they were worth and he'd had them removed. The other side of the restaurant was taken up with a counter, lined with stools, that directly overlooked Pasco's stainless-steel work station. At the back, a more formal dining area, never used now, contained bare tables and a cigarette machine. The rubber-tiled floor, swept and mopped every working day, had lost much of its colour, its gold crown pattern fading into the blue field.

The newest object in the restaurant was the price-list—he had no menus—mounted on the wall beside the work station. He had changed it the year before after years of stability, a coffee going from fifty to sixty cents, an order of fries from eighty-five cents to a dollar, a club sandwich from three-fifty to four. The old list had included several dishes that were rarely ordered—his clientele preferred cole slaw to Caesar salads, mashed potatoes to scalloped—and Pasco, not one for doing something just for the form of it, had simply left them off the new one.

Pascal's could have been something much grander had Edna taken a greater interest, but she hadn't been enthusiastic about buying it in the first place. Through the years she had shown scant concern for its operation except so far as it affected the family finances. And for the most part, Pasco had provided well for his family. If they had never managed Edna's dream holiday down south, they at least had wanted for nothing.

Edna had insisted on working at her job selling women's clothing in a store downtown. She didn't earn much, but what she brought home was hers. She spent it on herself, bought birthday and Christmas gifts with it. This independence—Pasco had always liked strong, intelligent women—was what had attracted him to her in the first place, so he'd swallowed his pride. They lived a quiet life while the sixties happened around them, Pasco and Edna too old to be part of the turmoil, Danny too young.

And then the seventies had brought a recession, at least to him. As the city grew visibly richer, the restaurant grew progressively poorer, his debt at the bank straining his ability to pay. He kept the news from Edna, hoping for better times. They were slow in coming. Finally, on the verge of bankruptcy, he could hide it no more.

Edna reacted quietly, more quietly than he'd feared she would.

She was angry, as he'd expected, but not because of the state of the restaurant's finances. She was angry because he had kept the situation to himself until almost too late. Why hadn't he told her? This keeping of secrets: it was one of his failings. Had he forgotten it had once almost broken them up? Hadn't he learnt his lesson?

Pasco had felt helpless before the sadness that tempered her anger.

Then, gathering her energy, Edna had studied the books and come up with a plan. First, to ease the pressures of the bank loan, they would sell the cottage. It was, in truth, hardly more than a cabin. They had paid little for it but had never had the money to winterize it and so had never bothered with the expense of running water or electricity; but it was well located, with its own little stretch of lakefront. Rising real-estate values in cottage country would ensure a sale price sufficiently generous to keep the bank happy until they could revitalize the restaurant.

Pasco wasn't thrilled at the thought of selling the cottage, but there was little choice. Besides, as Edna pointed out, they hadn't been going often since Danny grew up. Yet, Pasco was a while letting go of the dream—the fantasy, Edna said—of fixing up the place and retiring there.

The second part of Edna's plan took Pasco by surprise. She announced that she would become the new supplier of baked goods to the restaurant. Pasco would save money by having to pay only for the cost of materials, and he could advertise home baking to attract new customers.

He was hesitant, unsure that this would work the necessary magic, and Edna, in her usual way, had slammed her pencil down on the table and said, "Fine, so let's hear your plan." Then, as she'd always done when angry, she'd folded her arms and wrapped herself in silence.

But of course, he'd had no plan.

She sat there, giving him time.

He felt himself drowning in the inevitability of it all.

Edna was as good as her word. On Saturdays, she rose at dawn to buy fresh fruit at the St. Lawrence Market before heading off to work. Saturday evenings she stayed up late kneading dough and crusting pie plates. Sundays she spent in the kitchen—she refused to use the restaurant facilities, insisting that only her own oven would do—cutting and kneading and stirring and baking. She made bread, buns, strawberry and raspberry turnovers, vanilla and chocolate doughnuts, apple pies and coconut cream pies for which she grated the coconut herself.

The first Sunday night, once her labour was over, she sat at the kitchen table with coloured markers and construction paper making up signs for him to hang in the window: HOME BAKING, FRESH BREAD, HOMEMADE PIES.

Pasco was not allowed to help beyond sprinkling sugar on the hot turnovers, coloured dots on the iced doughnuts. Protesting that he was a cook, for God's sake, was useless. He wasn't a cook, Edna retorted, he just heated up disguised chemicals and singed defrosted meat.

And it had worked. The signs and the food attracted enough new customers to stabilize the business. The financial pressures eased. Edna, spurred on by her success, convinced him to replace the paper placemats with paper tablecloths—pink, she insisted—and to lay the napkins on the tables with the cutlery instead of loading them into their metal dispensers.

A new kind of clientele began drifting in, people who were better dressed, more discriminating. "Not exactly upscale," Edna said, "but at least we're *on* the scale now."

All the extra work, however, wasn't long in taking its toll. Pasco suggested Edna give up her job. She wouldn't hear of it, and he knew better than to insist. He then suggested that she spread out the kitchen work: couldn't she do a little each evening instead of everything on the weekend? She decided this made sense, but rebuffed his renewed offer to lend a hand.

Edna's involvement, and the success it brought, revived Pasco's interest in the restaurant. An incipient boredom had been heightened by the flagging cash flow—or maybe his boredom had contributed to the slowdown in the first place, he wasn't sure which. But with Edna—he toyed with the idea of renaming the restaurant The Golden Touch, in her honour—he found himself beginning to dream again: maybe they could take that trip down south, get another cottage, retire early. One evening he shared his dreams with her and she, in her practical way, told him he was way ahead of himself. But she had softened, grown tender, opened her arms to him.

Her death had changed everything. Emptied Pasco, imposed an unnatural silence on the house.

At the restaurant, the signs she had made were eventually taken down, Pasco unable to bear the sheer weight of their untruth. The pies came once more in boxes, the powdered eggs and potatoes in cans. The cream was not whipped and spooned but shaken and sprayed. Hamburger patties, perfectly formed by machines, were delivered in frozen stacks. Steaks were bought pre-striped in imitation of charcoal grilling, coffee grounds measured and packaged. Even the butter for toast came in liquid form, convenient for painting on with a brush.

A mustiness built quickly in the restaurant, corroding the brightness Edna had brought. The atmosphere turned murky. Business wasn't long in falling off, but stabilized at a level comfortable enough to pay the bills. Keeping going: Pasco had lost all desire for anything more.

The young man rolled up his newspaper, stuck it under his arm and stepped over to the counter. He paid his bill with coins. "See ya," he said on his way out.

"Later," Pasco said. He tossed the remains of his sandwich into the garbage can and got to work washing the dishes from the lunch-time rush.

———————

The light was fading outside, a blurry greyness settling on the city.

Pasco lightly grasped the spoon by its stem and held it up to the ceiling light, turned it slowly so that its oval bowl sparkled in his eye. There was not a blemish but he passed the chamois cloth over it once more for good measure.

It was a large serving spoon, ornate and gold-plated, with an inscription on the convex side of the bowl: *To Pasco, Happy 20th, The Guys at the Starting Gate.* At least once every month, when he had an idle moment, Pasco would take it from its plastic display case and polish it up. While he wouldn't have described himself as a sentimental man, the gift was special to him. Two months after Edna's death, his friends had held a little party to celebrate the twentieth anniversary of his buying the restaurant. They had presented the spoon to him with mock solemnity and spent the rest of the evening joking and laughing. Returning home late that night to the dark and silent house had been difficult, but the evening—the sense that life continued beyond the personal tragedy—had gone a long way in helping him emerge from the greater numbness.

He was drawing the cloth along the stem when the door opened and a familiar voice called out, "If I've told you once, I've told you a thousand times, don't leave that fucking thing here, Pasco, somebody's going to make off with it one day."

Pasco didn't have to look up. He would have recognized Sean's voice anywhere. "And if I've told you once, I've told you a thousand times, this is where it belongs." He laid the spoon in its case and pressed the cover down until it clicked. "The usual?"

"Plus an orange juice for my young friend here." Sean, closing the door on the leaden dusk, indicated the younger man with him. "Kurt, Pasco." They shook hands, Sean and Kurt sliding onto stools and resting their elbows on the counter in front of them.

Sean had, over the last few months, become a regular. They had met the February before, the day Pasco found the body of a young runaway in the park. Sean had been passing by in his cruiser when Pasco, hurrying back to the restaurant to dial 911, flagged him down. He was a middle-aged man, tall and impressive in his uniform, but on the heavy side with a bit of a paunch. It was difficult for Pasco to imagine him chasing a criminal along the streets and through alleyways.

He had been efficient that freezing winter morning, calling an ambulance, taking notes, supervising the removal of the body. Then he accompanied Pasco back to the restaurant. As he sat at the counter, hat pushed back on his head, his face sagged, lost a professional tension. While Pasco poured him a coffee he silently ran through his notes, pen in hand. "Name," he said. "Pascal…?"

"Actually, no."

"You're not the owner?"

"No, no, I am."

"So who's this Pascal, then, your pet?" He spoke wearily, as if too tired for jokes. But a thin smile tightened his lips.

Pasco laughed a touch more heartily than he'd meant to. Uniforms in general made him nervous, they were shields to the human being. That, at least, was how it had been with his father. Busying his hands by swirling a washcloth on the counter, he explained that his name was really Taggart. Gilbert Taggart. Once upon a time Gil to some, Bert to others. He now used the name so infrequently, usually only to sign cheques, that it felt strange on his tongue, sounded foreign to his ears. Even Edna had eventually accepted that the Gil she'd married had turned into Pasco.

"So who's this Pascal character?"

"He's the guy I bought this place from years and years ago. Folks just kind of took to calling me Pasco, and I didn't see any reason to object."

Sean nodded and scribbled, snapped his notebook shut and rose to go. He moved slowly, heavily, gazing through the window. The ambulance was gone, the park as it had always been, an expanse of trampled snow. "They're getting younger and younger," he said, pulling the visor of his hat low on his forehead. "And it ain't getting any easier." He zipped up his parka, tipped his hat at Pasco. "Maybe I'll stop by for lunch sometime," he said.

And he had, once a month, sometimes twice. He ate little, usually half a hamburger or a club sandwich washed down with a can of diet cola, the food almost incidental before his desire to chat. Pasco assumed it had something to do with the way he'd once described himself, as "a bachelor—well, divorced". There were no children. He lived by himself in a one-bedroom apartment up on Bathurst, a Simmons building, Pasco had ascertained. His wife had remarried and moved to Florida with her new husband. "He's not a cop," he'd said. "So now she can sleep nights."

Sean had mentioned Kurt before, with some unhappiness. As Pasco put their drinks in front of them, as he waited for them to count out their change, he took the opportunity to examine the young man. Long eyebrows that met in the middle, straight nose above thin lips, regulation haircut that brought out his youth, sparse moustache that emphasized his baby face. If Sean in street clothes called to mind a slightly seedy insurance agent or a used-car salesman, Kurt looked more like a slick bouncer, or perhaps a professional hockey enforcer too rich too young.

Pasco scooped the change off the counter into his cupped palm. "They're getting younger and younger," Sean had said of Kurt, strangely echoing his words of the winter before. "The Metropolitan Toronto Police Force and Daycare. Shit! Oh, don't get me wrong, Kurt's a nice kid. Good name for him, by the way. Young and kind of high-strung, y'know? Granpa was in the force, dad was in the force, older brother's with the RCMP up north. And now here's junior lookin' real nice in his uniform and packin' a pistol. Likes to keep his hand on the butt whenever there's a situation. Trying to break him of that habit but it ain't easy, I'll tell ya, Pasco."

Was he real police material? Pasco had asked.

"Well, he's one of us now for better or for worse," Sean sighed. "They usually manage to weed out the misfits. Oh, he'll be all right, I guess." But he hadn't seemed thrilled at the prospect of, as he put it, "showing the kid the real world for the next few months".

Sean sipped at his cola, wrinkles gathering on his face. "So how's it going, Pasco?"

"As usual. You guys hungry?"

Sean refused with a shake of his head.

Kurt said, "I could use something." His eyes looked up at the menu on the wall.

"The kid's always hungry," Sean said. "Vacuums it in."

"Got any prunes for the old man, Pasco?" Kurt said sardonically.

"Ain't he cute? *Old man.* Cracks me up, this kid. We should book him in at Yuk Yuk's. Make a fortune, eh?"

"You want something from me, old man?"

"Yeah. You still upset about last night?"

Pasco glanced at Kurt. There was no reaction, but his eyes were frozen on the menu board. The soft sounds coming from the radio grew intrusive, drifting in the tension of the moment from background to foreground. Kurt swung around on his stool. "Mind changing the radio station?" he said.

Pasco nodded towards the radio. "Help yourself." His eyes met Sean's.

"Accident last night on the 401," Sean said. "A tractor-trailer ended up on top of a Toyota. What a fuckin' mess. Like an elephant sitting on a cardboard box. There was a couple inside, and a kid in the back seat. Not a pretty sight, I'll tell you."

Kurt stood at the radio twirling the knob past snatches of static, conversations, advertisements, music. "It was on the radio this morning," he said. "You don't listen to the news?"

"The local stuff, almost never," Pasco said. "What do I get from knowing about fires and accidents and robberies?"

"You get nervous, that's what," Sean said.

"It's all over the paper too," Kurt said. "Front page, full colour. Or don't you read the papers either?"

"Sure I do, but never right away. I give it two or three days. You don't bother with the filler and the gore then, you just read the important stuff."

"The important stuff, eh?" Kurt snickered. "Yeah, right. Three people turned to pulp. Just the important stuff." He snapped off the radio.

Sean turned towards him. "So, you're still upset."

"What d'you think?"

"Look, kid—"

"No, you look. I can't do whatever it is you do, I can't just shrug off things like that."

"That's what you think, eh? I shrug things off, just like that. Have a hot chocolate, go to bed and sleep like a fuckin' baby. You listen to me, sonny, my stomach's still churnin', okay? Happens every fuckin' time. Still. Only I don't usually throw up any more. Don't worry, it'll happen the next five, ten times, then you'll learn. Don't get me wrong, you never get used to stuff like that—and if you do, get the fuck out of the force 'cause that means you're really screwed up. You just learn not to stew in it, you learn not to let it ruin more than one day."

Kurt threw himself into one of the booths, his eyes turning away from Pasco and Sean.

Sean said, "Sorry, Pasco. Just wanted the kid to meet you. Maybe we should've come another day."

Pasco's hands gestured away Sean's concern.

"Pasco," Kurt called. "I'll have an order of fries."

"Fries are no good for you," Sean said. "Have a BLT instead."

"I said I'll have an order of fries."

"Large or small?" Pasco said.

"Large."

When Pasco served the fries a few minutes later, Kurt salted them and, with deliberation, hid them under a thick layer of ketchup.

Sean left before he was done.

Chapter Five

IT WAS dark out. Sal, counselling moderation, had left about an hour before. Viv had gone off duty, the sign on the apartment door warning that he responded to EMERGENCIES ONLY. Deanna, though, was still washing the stairwells, the clatter and bang of her pail as she moved it from landing to landing echoing down the cavernous shaft and into the lobby.

Driving around the city had drained Danny. Rain, light but constant throughout the day, had turned the roads greasy. Other cars had developed minds of their own, their drivers, all sixteen years old again, distracted and impatient. But he had managed to verify many of the repair requisitions, those he had had to put aside to visit Mr. Simmons's house as well as the ones that had come in since. He arranged his reports into a neat pile and slipped them into a folder for handing over to Mr. Simmons.

The boss would run through each report, questioning Danny on details, his manner prosecutorial, probing for justification to avoid any expense he considered unnecessary or frivolous. Danny already knew what he would say about the rooming houses: Theft? But what do those people have that's worth stealing?

Danny disliked these inquisitions. He was never quite sure whose point of view he was supposed to represent—Mr. Simmons's, the city inspectors', the superintendents' or the tenants'—

and he often felt squeezed between legitimate demands on the one hand and suspicious intransigence on the other.

His reports on the rental applications, though, were easier to deal with. Every applicant was told as a matter of course that there was a two-year waiting list. There was in reality no such list. Vacant apartments were rented out at Mr. Simmons's fancy, and only after the rent had been suitably, and secretly, raised beyond legal limits, the boss doing his best to prevent old and new tenants from meeting so that new tenants would not get their hands on the old lease.

Danny's role was to go through the application forms, verify credit ratings and references and write up reports of the usual brevity for Mr. Simmons. Should Mr. Simmons, for whatever reason, take a liking to the portrait presented in the report—"tenant profiles", he called them—Danny would contact the applicant and invite him or her in for an interview with the owner. At his own request, he regularly observed these sessions. There would be a few minutes of inconsequential chat—the weather, the chances of whichever sports team happened to be playing—before Mr. Simmons got around to a gentle probe of the applicant's background. Eventually the boss would find or create an opening to work in a little speech about the difficulties of being a landlord while the applicant, sitting as if for a job interview, nodded and hummed in noncommittal sympathy. Mr. Simmons would move on to the distress caused "out there" by a housing market so tight that—believe it or not!—some people regularly offered him a "finder's fee" or "key money" of a thousand dollars, two thousand, five thousand.

At the mention of "fees", the applicant would inevitably stiffen, wondering if he was being asked for a bribe. Mr. Simmons would chuckle, deny that he was interested in illegal money. All he sought was responsible tenants. At his age he didn't want any trouble, just wanted to help people live comfortably. Then would come the tentative offer: "I like you, I'd like to help you. Unfortunately I have nothing at the moment but I'll call you as soon as something's available, all right?" Naturally, Mr. Simmons usually knew two or three months in advance what vacancies would be coming up, but he preferred to make applicants wait a bit, sweat a bit. They were all the more grateful that way, more pliable.

It was Danny's job to prepare the ground for Mr. Simmons's manoeuvrings, sifting out the undesirables, the troublemakers, the welfare cases. The boss didn't care what colour they were, what language they spoke, where they came from. What he mostly wanted to know was whether they could afford to pay and how desperate they were to find a place. The rest he could handle—indeed, insisted on handling—by himself.

The Simmons Construction Company hadn't been Danny's first choice as a place of employment. He had, like every other M.B.A-to-be, simply applied everywhere, broadcasting professionally produced résumés to the grand firms and to the lesser ones. He had been called in for a few interviews, but only Mr. Simmons—nobody's idea of a wealthy executive—had called back with a job offer. Danny, at the time, had been unable to separate his relief from his disappointment.

Simmons Construction was no multinational with expense accounts, plush offices and corporate jets. It didn't own billions in real estate, wield irresistible influence in bank boardrooms or pull the strings of foreign governments. Neither the company nor the owner would have made anyone's list for stylishness and daring. Still, Danny comforted himself with the thought that it was no corner-store operation either. Even if the Toronto real-estate market weren't so wondrously inflated, the value of the company assets would easily run to the tens of million of dollars.

And yet it was typical of Mr. Simmons's style—if that was the word for it—that he had never even considered putting up a building to house the various departments of his company. He had, instead, scattered them around to different offices in the various buildings he owned across the city.

Soon after he began working for the company, Danny had suggested that consolidation—having everyone under the same roof—would result in a sharpening of efficiency and financial savings for the company. He had even presented the boss with a sheet of preliminary figures.

But Mr. Simmons, while pronouncing the idea "clever", was not impressed. He made clear his belief that familiarity between employees was to be actively discouraged; it was bad for efficiency, he said, "impacted negatively on productivity". This was the reason the company tolerated no office parties, the reason he had turned down even the idea of a company softball team. He couldn't stop anybody from doing what they wanted on their own time, of course, but he was damned if he was going to pay for their beer or team T-shirts—or, for that matter, bring them all together so they could huddle around the coffee machine or water cooler.

Danny never again mentioned his idea. Among the valuable lessons he had learnt in his M.B.A course—not in so many words, and despite all the paeans to it—was that corporate culture feared nothing so much as innovation, that it valued nothing so much as loyalty. New ideas, he'd come to understand, were intimidating, deference to authority benign. The profit margin was intractable, and everything could be shrugged off before its demands. The most important truth for any employee to accept was that all decisions, but especially those regarding staffing and destaffing—terms such as "firings" and "lay-offs" were anathema to modern business—were made against the background of accountants' reports.

Danny wasn't long in realizing why Mr. Simmons had rejected consolidation. Like so many men of overweening confidence, the boss feared, above all, whispers of dissent. He brooked no challenge to his authority. The Simmons Construction Company was, after all, his and his alone. He had built it from scratch. He insisted that every decision be channelled through him, every purchase, whether of appliances, carpeting, bulbs or screws, made only on his signature.

One winter when he was out of town—the story, actively encouraged by Mr. Simmons, had grown into a company fable— several bags of road salt were acquired without his authorization. It was February, the snow and ice unusually heavy. Salt supplies had run low. The maintenance manager, a man of a certain initiative, had simply paid out of his own pocket, never doubting that reimbursement would follow. Salt, after all, was a regular winter purchase and Mr. Simmons had more than once instructed him to ensure that the superintendents didn't stint on it: he was terrified of the legal implications of a broken leg or dislocated shoulder because of ice build-up on his properties. On Mr. Simmons's return—so the story went—the maintenance manager had presented him with the bill, was duly paid—and promptly fired for disobeying the standing order about approval of purchases.

Danny didn't know whether the story was true or not—Sal, who had told it to him, swore that it was—but he knew enough not to ask. Its importance lay not in its fact, but in its effect. Truthfulness, as Mr. Simmons had once remarked to him, was vital, but only if it was of some use. And lying? Danny had said. "Ditto," the boss had replied with a shrug. "Everything's a tool, Dano."

Mr. Simmons was the kind of man who inspired passion, of one kind or another. He was too definite about who he was, made too clear what he believed in: he left little room for ambivalence. If he thought someone deserved the finger, he gave him the finger, no matter how influential, or inconsequential, the person. Mr. Simmons, Danny knew, had more detractors than admirers.

His office, and Danny's, was in one of the Spadina Road buildings. It wasn't the most attractive in his "pride"—the word Mr.

Simmons habitually used when referring to his properties—and Mr. Simmons explained his choice of location as a purely tactical one. He didn't need to surround himself with glitter, he'd said, the bank books being satisfaction enough. "Besides," he'd added, "just try arguing over money with a supplier or a tenant in a fancy office. Some people think they can overwhelm the opposition with opulence, they think they're going to dazzle them with their wealth. I've always found the opposite to be true. Nothing gets people's backs up more than someone else's money. Toss it in their faces and they'll toss it right back by deciding there's no way they're going to help make you richer. So I take the opposite tack. I plead poverty. No guarantees, of course, but it makes the battles a little easier. Remember this, Dano, there's satisfaction in shouting at a rich man, but only guilt in insulting a poor one."

The red-brick nerve centre of the Simmons Construction Company overlooked Spadina approximately halfway between Bloor and Dupont streets. The parking lot at the northern end offered an obstructed view of Casa Loma, the ersatz castle that formed the nucleus of one of Danny's fondest fantasies, a whole new concept in shopping malls: Henry VIII hamburger stands, Mary Queen of Scots headgear stores, Elizabeth I unisex-clothing boutiques. As business ideas went, it was one of his more spectacular, on a par with the fantasy he sometimes entertained of cornering the artificial turf market and convincing the city to replace the grass in the park systems with it. These, he knew, were just games, they could never be translated into reality, but it was one of the ways in which he kept himself going: by aiming at the sun when the moon would do. He'd never forgotten the joke told by one of his professors at the university: What was the difference between American and Canadian businessmen? While the American aimed to make his first million by the time he was thirty, the Canadian would settle for a couple of thousand.

The apartment block, ten dimly lit floors, hadn't changed with the neighbourhood. Other buildings in the area had been spruced up in an attempt to keep pace with the rocketing property values of their Annex surroundings, to reflect, as much as any apartment building could, the neat, sprightly and moneyed air of their renovated neighbours. Mr. Simmons, however, frequently ridiculed the owners of the other buildings—the "non-Simmons" buildings—for their wasteful self-indulgence. "They're just like old whores," Danny recalled him saying one day. "Prettying themselves up with powder and lipstick. But who do they think they're fooling?"

So not a cent was put into maintaining the older Simmons properties with an eye to the neighbourhood. Exteriors were left as weathered, interiors kept to minimum safety standards. While in summer the balconies of non-Simmons buildings displayed flowerpots or colourful anti-pigeon windmills, those of Simmons Construction tended to be crowded with brooms, mops, cardboard boxes and drying clothes. People with tattoos and lanky hair would lounge on them late into the night, drinking beer to the screeching and teeth-gnashing of heavy-metal music crunching through their open doors.

Danny, without noticing, had taken to entering the building with his head lowered.

Mr. Simmons's office was on the ground floor, to the left of the main door. Danny's, shared with Sal, was straight ahead past the elevators and just beside the rear exit. From his window, he could see the parking lot and the garbage containers awaiting pick-up.

To the right of the main door was the lobby. A few plastic-covered chairs, used by only the older residents of the buildings exhausted after their treks to the supermarket, lined the walls. In the middle crouched the statue of a nude female figure, lips and nipples painted red by some prankster. Viv had pointed out to Danny that the dais on which the statue stood—large and round, the sides tiled, the plywood surface swathed in green carpeting—

had once been a fountain. Sal, prattling on one day, told him that Mr. Simmons had intended it to be a wishing well, figuring that over time the value of the coins tossed in would not only pay for the work and materials but provide a continuing profit, too. However, the pennies had clogged the pipes so frequently, and the plumber's bills had grown so astronomical, that Mr. Simmons had ordered it sealed up. "There are few things sadder," Sal had said, "than a dried-up fountain."

Danny had once tried to convince Mr. Simmons to convert the wasted space of the lobby into a private office for him. The room he shared with Sal was not large enough for them both; it was crowded with their two desks and their filing cabinets. Nor did Danny enjoy Sal's company. He thought his obsession with Mr. Simmons's private life objectionable, and was particularly irritated by Sal's arrogance over a Japanese board-game called Go which he spent much of his free time playing but which he couldn't explain to Danny because, as he had once said, "You'd never be able to wrap your mind around it." Most bothersome of all, though, were Sal's bouts of unsubtle flatulence. Sal seemed, in Danny's word, "unembarrassable". He was the kind of man who could jabber on at length while revealing little about his private life, probably because there was little or nothing to reveal.

Danny's request was rejected without a moment's pause. It wasn't that Mr. Simmons was attached to the lobby; it was that he couldn't justify the expense. "So Sal farts once in a while," he'd said. "So sue him."

But he'd come in the next day with a gift for Danny, a gas mask he'd bought at an army surplus store. He insisted that Danny try it on at that very moment, and without explanation, in front of Sal. Mr. Simmons, poker-faced, had considered Danny's masked visage for a full minute, pointedly ignoring Sal's puzzled expression. Then, spinning around on his heel and stalking out of the office, he'd intoned, "And they say I have no sense of humour."

Sal, leafing through a stack of documents on his desk, wasn't long in asking whether it was Danny's birthday.

"No," Danny said, tossing the mask aside. "Private joke."

After a minute, Sal said he could think of several creative uses for the gas mask, aside from wearing it in a crowded subway car. Had Danny seen, he wanted to know, the movie *Blue Velvet*? No? Well, it wasn't so much *use* as *context*, he said, offering to demonstrate what he meant any evening Danny had the time. Danny declined humourlessly—there were some things he would rather not know about—but agreed to lend him the mask anyway.

Sal developed a curious attachment to the mask and took to wearing it at his desk for extended periods. Sitting across the room from him—enjoying the irony of seeing the mask on Sal, who remained ignorant of the reason for its appearance in the first place—Danny was reminded of another film, *The Fly*.

This continued for a week before Mr. Simmons ordered the mask off. The joke, after all, was no longer his.

As he knocked at Mr. Simmons's office, Danny thought he could see the weariness in the ghostly image of himself reflected in the recently painted door—three coats of Eggshell White had been required to fully efface the large, black swastika. Beyond his watery figure, the lights of the Christmas tree twinkled and blinked like distant underwater traffic lights.

The knock was just a courtesy. When the boss wanted to be left alone, he would hang on the doorknob a DO NOT DISTURB sign he'd lifted from a Holiday Inn and snap shut the safety-latch on the lock. Danny quietly let himself in.

Mr. Simmons was standing with his back to the door, one hand pressing the phone to his ear, the other flicking a handkerchief at his ceramic lion, an ugly beast reared onto its hind legs, its head whipped around in a snarl. He had bought it many years before at a flea market out in Goderich or Stouffville or some such small town and had grown fond enough of it that he'd incorporated its image into the company logo.

Mr. Simmons glanced around briefly, nodded and flicked Danny towards a chair with a snap of his handkerchief. "Yes," he said into the telephone. "This is Simmons of Simmons Construction. I'm calling about your application for an apartment."

Danny made himself as comfortable as possible on the armchair in front of Mr. Simmons's desk. It was an ancient piece of furniture inadequately repaired by Viv when one of its legs had snapped off. He had replaced the broken leg with another; but his calculations had been off and the new leg was an inch shorter than required. Mr. Simmons, amused by its unsteadiness, had refused his offer to take an inch off the other legs.

"Yes, yes, I know. These things take time, you understand, the market's bad, it's hard for everyone, and not only tenants, believe me. But listen, I have a one-bedroom coming up in three months' time. The rent's seven-fifty...."

Mr. Simmons's office hardly befitted the man who had built the company and who still owned every condominium, every apartment, every office, every room, brick, nail and screw of it. The office was no larger than the one Danny shared with Sal—maybe even a little smaller because of the washroom that had been installed at one end—and had been furnished mostly with the discards of former tenants. The lamp with the polka-dot shade that hung above his desk, the bookcases with shelves that weren't quite level, the cowboy prints on the walls, the faded orange rug on the floor, even the kettle in which the boss boiled water for the herbal teas he drank most afternoons. It was waste-not-want-not put into action.

"I know three months is a long time.... Well, all right, look, I have another one. Available immediately. I promised it to someone else, but for you…. The rent? It's eight-fifty…. Steep? Look, I'm trying to do you a favour…."

Mr. Simmons himself was hardly the picture of the successful businessman. His shoes were rarely polished. His suits, while of fine cloth and cut, were not new. There was to him none of the understated flash that Danny associated with the executive look. His watch even had hands.

"Tomorrow? No, I need a decision now. I have to call this other person back…."

But it wasn't just his clothing. It had something to do too with the way Mr. Simmons was built, with the way he stood, walked, carried himself. He was a small man in his late fifties or early sixties, about five eight in two-inch heels. He still had all his hair, but it was not thick, and sat unnaturally curly and golden on his head. The skin on his face and hands was pinkish, but in an unhealthy way. He had no wrinkles, was marked only by age spots. His shoulders were narrow, somewhat rounded, and although he was not overweight, he gave an impression of physical softness, as if he had never lost his baby fat. Yet, sitting or standing, his back remained uncompromisingly straight. Even at the end of the day, there was never any suggestion of a slouch, his vigour testifying to greater health than was apparent. Danny had never known him to take a vacation—Viv had told him that the boss often came in to work even on public holidays—and that was just as well, for he could not picture Mr. Simmons shirtless in swim trunks on a beach.

"You can manage the eight-fifty? Good, I'm so happy I could help. Now, let's see, you have a car? No? Well I'm afraid the apartment comes with a parking space, didn't I mention that? That's fifty dollars more per month, for a total of nine hundred…."

Mr. Simmons turned away from the lion, eased himself into the chair behind his desk and motioned for Danny to pass him the requisition reports. He continued the conversation as he scanned the sheets, the index finger of the hand that still clutched the handkerchief directing his eyes through the texts.

"No, that makes no difference. Whether you need it or not, the space comes with the apartment. It's your choice: take it or leave it."

Some people, ignorant of whom they were dealing with, thought they could outsmart Mr. Simmons. They would accept the parking space and then, more often than not, pin a sign on the laundry-room notice-board offering to rent it out to someone else, usually for a little profit of their own. There was nothing illegal in this, but Mr. Simmons would assume the righteous anger of an Old Testament prophet when confronting the offender: You're not the landlord here, he would growl, I am. I own every goddam inch of this property. What makes you think you can rent out *my* property? There was hardly a tenant who did not fall guiltily silent before Mr. Simmons's apparent rage. Would they be so meek, Danny wondered, if they knew that, when a tenant did not own a car, the parking space usually existed only in the lease, "a parking space *in theory*, so to speak", as Sal had once put it?

"Why should I lose fifty bucks a month just because you don't have a car? Anyway, look, I'm a reasonable man. Tell you what I'll do. Just for you, now, so don't go spreading it around—let's split the difference. I'll let you have the apartment for eight seventy-five, no parking. I'm out twenty-five bucks, but what the hell, so long as my tenants are happy, right?"

Danny began paying closer attention: this was the point at which the applicant would either clinch the apartment or lose it for good. Persistence would cost. The boss didn't like to lose, and an applicant's tenacity over so small a sum as twenty-five dollars a month led inevitably to a call a day or two later from Sal or Danny informing him that there'd been an unfortunate mix-up and that the apartment was no longer available.

"You'll take it? Good for you. No-no, no thanks necessary, I'm just glad I could help. Listen, why don't you come by tomorrow afternoon and we'll take care of the paperwork, okay? After work will be fine. See you then." Mr. Simmons hung up, patted at his forehead with the handkerchief.

Danny could see in the listless gesture, in the slight shrug of his narrow shoulders, that he was disappointed.

"This is getting too easy, Dano," he said. "It's not as much fun as it used to be."

"It's Monopoly," Danny said. "And you have most of the houses and hotels."

"Let me give you some advice, Dano." He smiled for no apparent reason, his teeth wholly bared so that, emerging from the glistening gums, they were like the large yellowed teeth of a canine suddenly, and discomfortingly, revealed. "And I'm telling you this just because I like you."

"Yes, sir."

"You'll get comfortable working for me, my boy, but you'll never get rich. Use that advice any way you want. Or can."

Danny nodded, once more a gesture of mere acknowledgement.

"Risk big, win big, Dano. But of course, risk bad, lose bad. How you play the game doesn't matter. All that matters is that you win, and how you do it makes no difference to anybody, except to those who lose." His eyes glittered across the desk at Danny, lips compressed into a smile somehow more calculated than the one before.

Danny read the smile as playful in a knowing way, and he wondered whether he should tell Mr. Simmons about the renovations to his father's house. He decided quickly it was not a good idea. He would probably not take kindly to the use of Simmons Construction workers. Besides, Danny knew that in business, as in politics, knowledge was power.

Mr. Simmons crumpled up the first sheet. "Paint for Bathurst denied," he said. "If the tenants want it, let them do it themselves. What d'you say, Dano?"

"Fine with me." He made a note on his pad.

From the stairwell came the dull, metallic sounds of Deanna's wash bucket. Danny figured she was about halfway done.

It was after ten when Danny got home. After leaving Mr. Simmons he'd thought briefly about going to Yorkville. But he was too tired, didn't have the energy to invest in the empty banter of pursuit.

A middle-aged couple rode up in the elevator with him. He had seen them two or three times before, knew they were sufficiently well off to afford a penthouse and a Mercedes convertible. They were not so much pointed as absorbed in ignoring his silent greeting. Maybe they were tired, maybe they'd had a fight. Or maybe this was simply their way. They didn't know him; they had never met. His Toronto was the kind of city where simple politeness was sometimes viewed as an invasion of privacy. Danny shrugged it off.

The moment he shut the apartment door, the darkness and the silence surged up around him. For several seconds his nerves were electrified and he felt himself being overwhelmed by a sense that the apartment—*his* apartment—was a place that could never sustain life. His hand trembled as it reached up through the darkness for the light switch.

Relief, and a strange sense of disappointment. The apartment was as he had left it that morning, as he left it every morning, everything in its place. But, as so often when he was tired and alone, it felt abandoned, as if unknown hands had stripped the interior to a spare anonymity during his absence, leaving it with the personality of a furnished room, depersonalized and functional, temporary.

He needed to fill the air with his presence, animate i
sounds and his movements, in order to claim the space
as his own.

He sat on the sofa and clicked th   pper
remote control. On the televis   Reduce
bloated bellies played
chalky. An   rraine?"
Dan

                          uch?"

                        ched him slice the butter in
                      p it into the bowl of potatoes. "A
lit   e, Pasco."

"Ab   of what you've got there. And you call yourself a
cook?"

"Hey, look, at the restaurant it's powder and water, what d'you
want?"

"You've never mashed potatoes before? It doesn't take much
skill."

"That was Edna's job."

"What wasn't Edna's job? She spoiled you silly, Pasco."

"So what's the main course?" he said, removing the butter and
slicing off a third of it. "My head on a platter?"

Lorraine picked up the milk carton, poured a little over the
potatoes. "Sorry, Pasco, rough day at the centre. I don't mean to
dump all over you."

"Don't worry about it." He pressed the masher into the potatoes and the melting butter. "Just keep in mind I'm not a wife-
beater or a rapist or anything like that."

"A fifteen-year-old kid came in today." She salted the potatoes,
peppered them. "Pregnant. She'd been to her doctor. Took all the
courage she had. Only he won't do abortions and won't refer her
to a doctor who will. He lectured her about how conception

makes two patients and gave her a handful of anti-choice propaganda. The bastard can't see that he's just doubling the victims."

"Tough," Pasco said, pumping the masher. "But, you know, Lorraine, you play with fire—"

"Pasco, her dad's the father. He's been abusing her since she was seven."

Pasco grunted. Potato squished through the grid of the masher. "Did the doctor know that?"

"Yeah, and carrying the fetus to term is supposed to make dear old dad face up to his crime."

"I see."

"You do?"

"No, not really." He thought for a moment. "Do you?"

"You kidding?"

"So how is this supposed to help?"

"God alone knows. By giving dear old dad another kid to abuse, I suppose." She opened a drawer, removed knives, forks. "Sometimes I get the feeling we're part of the phantom city, Pasco. Nobody hardly knows we exist, you know?" She took two plates from a cupboard. "Compassion's dwindling fast out there." She reached for a leaflet that was lying on the table. "Somebody dumped a bunch of these at the door of the centre last night." She handed it to him, said, "Sometimes you don't know whether to laugh or cry."

As Lorraine set the table in the dining room, Pasco read through the leaflet.

WHO PROTECTS THE PRECONCEIVED?

Nobody, that's who!!! Let us not mince words: Male masturbation is a *moral outrage*!!! None of the so-called sex experts are willing to confront the bare truth. They will have you believe that self-abuse is normal and natural. But think about it!!! The gratuitous spilling of sperm is nothing less than the *mindless abortion of a preconceived child*!!! Let us call a spade a spade: Onanism by males is mass murder and must be named for the crime it is!!! Help stop this genocide. Write to your MP (no postage required) and demand that male masturbation be put into the Criminal Code of Canada. Write NOW!!!

Pasco said, "This has gotta be a joke."

"Don't you wish," Lorraine called.

"Come on, Lorraine, where's your sense of humour?"

She planted herself in the doorway. "I guess some things just don't seem funny to me any more, Pasco. I've seen too many loonies move to the forefront of one social issue or another." She gestured at the leaflet in his hand. "Today's joker can become tomorrow's adversary. You've got to take everything seriously these days. What kind of propaganda is that girl's doctor going to be handing out next? That?" She moved to the counter, grunted as she uncorked the bottle of red wine he'd brought.

"Where's the girl now?" he asked, sipping the beer she'd opened for him when he arrived.

"Back home. She insisted." She reached into the cupboard for a wine glass.

"With dear old dad?"

"It's dear old mom she's worried about. But I'll give you ten to one mom's known all along what's been going on." She filled the glass, took a gulp of the wine.

"Can you do anything for her?"

"We're providing counselling, we'll arrange for the abortion. And beyond that, we're looking into what we can do about dad. But that really depends on her, and she's only fifteen years old and scared out of her wits." She was silent for a moment. "Son of a bitch!"

Pasco wondered how she put up with it day after day. But he knew better than to ask; that would be like an insult.

She slipped on oven mitts, removed the roast from the oven and transferred it along with the onions and carrots to an oval serving dish. "Grab the potatoes and another beer," she said, carrying the roast into the dining room. "I'll carve."

"What's the matter, Lorraine? You don't trust me with a knife?" For the first time that evening, she laughed.

———————

Lorraine Neumann was a strong, solid woman direct in her ways, frank with her beliefs and attitudes. There was nothing delicate about her. Her hands were large, her fingers plump, but they were not without grace. She had always been a handsome woman but even when younger she had not possessed the kind of beauty that would cause men to turn in the street. Hers was a beauty that came clear only with time; there was nothing superficial about it. Her eyes in certain light did not appear to be a matched set, the right a deeper brown than the left, and their candid gaze suggested at times a puzzlement, a worry, a wariness. When she was engaged in thought, two thick vertical lines furrowed her forehead.

Lorraine gave the impression of great self-sufficiency, a quality Pasco admired, yet one that he also found intimidating. She was the kind of woman on whom others depended, as had Rick, her late husband, as had Edna, her closest friend.

Although he had never grown as close to her as Edna had, Pasco supposed that he and Lorraine were friends. After Edna's death, she continued having him over to dinner from time to time. Occasionally she would stop by the restaurant for a coffee or a glass of water—because she enjoyed wine, frequently in great quantity, she would not touch the homegrown brands he stocked; they gave her headaches. She was always ready to chat, directing conversation with her pointed questions and her insistence on considered answers. But her frankness demanded frankness in return, and her intensity could be draining. An evening with her every couple of months or so was more than enough to satisfy him.

———————

"How're you and Danny getting along, Pasco?"

The wine bottle was almost empty. Pasco was nearing the end of his third beer.

"'Bout the same."

"That bad, eh? You two should talk more."

During dinner, they'd reminisced, about Edna, about Rick, about Danny and her daughter Magda, both aware that they were somehow stuck in the past, both also aware that there was no place more comfortable, no place more secure. But then they'd run out of stories, were left with only the ones they were unwilling to share.

"That's some advice, coming from you." Talk more: it was the kind of remark people made when they didn't know what else to say, the kind of advice that was devalued by its generic quality.

"At least Magda and I try. She comes over once in a while, you know."

"Alone?"

"Sometimes. Not always."

"How do you get along with, you know, her friend?"

"Her name's Linda. A pretty name. I guess you could say we're learning." Lorraine's fingers rapped nervously on the table. "Lord, I wish I had a cigarette. Wine does it to me, you know. Never miss the damned things till I relax with a glass." She picked up the wine glass with agitated hands. "But the really hard part, you see, is that I always hoped Magda would have a baby one day. A boy we could name after Rick. You probably don't know this, but Rick really wanted grandchildren. We always kind o' thought that your Danny would, you know, he and Magda." Her fingers wrapped tight around the stem of the glass. "Not much chance of that now, I'm afraid."

"And the rest of it doesn't bother you?"

She twirled the glass in her hand, its edge sparkling in the light. "Objectively, no."

"And subjectively?"

"She's happy. I guess that's all that really counts."

"Is it?"

"What else really matters? Besides, you learn to live with things. You know that, Pasco."

Did he know that? Well, yes, but it didn't come without a struggle, and he wondered whether deep down she really knew it too.

"What we have to remember, Pasco, is that our kids are okay. We see ourselves as being basically decent people, and we want to see our kids the same way. But they're not us. I know this is nothing new, but it's real easy to forget. We have to see them for who they are. That's all Magda's asking from me, and I suspect that's true for Danny too. The good news is, they're basically decent people only in different ways."

Pasco hoped that what Lorraine said was true, but he felt that with Danny the jury was still out. There were moments when his son seemed such a stranger that paternal instinct gave way and he found himself incapable of offering the benefit of the doubt.

Lorraine, eyeing him slyly, said, "You're thinking about Simmons, aren't you."

"It's that obvious, eh?" Pasco made no secret of his unhappiness over Danny's working for Simmons Construction. Leon Simmons, a real-estate magnate with a high sleaze factor, the city's closest approximation to a slum landlord, was not a man he trusted. He was known for the opulence of his office and condominium developments, and for the dilapidation of his apartment buildings and rooming houses.

"You have to work it out with Danny, Pasco."

"My son," he said after a moment, "doesn't accept notions of clean money, dirty money."

"Is he wrong? Money has a way of buying respectability, no matter how you get it."

"You're a cynic, Lorraine."

"And you're a dreamer, Pasco."

"Danny's the dreamer in the family. Takes after his mother."

"Maybe you're both dreamers then."

Pasco, moving to help her clear the table, found himself taken with the idea.

"Wasn't this Edna's job too?" Lorraine said, a tease to her voice, as he picked up the serving dish.

"No, that was mine. She washed up."

"Who dried?"

"Nobody. We let them dry overnight. Why waste time and energy?"

"Rick couldn't stand that. Clutter."

They both recognized the retreat, away from the discomforts of the present to the safe certainties of the past. It seemed the neatest way to end the evening.

"Do you want me to help you, you know, wash the dishes?"

"I don't want you to help me do anything, Pasco. Besides, I think I've had a little too much to drink. Leave 'em. I'll just do them in the morning."

She fetched his coat from the coat-rack in the living room, stood at the kitchen door as he slipped into his shoes. Through the darkness of their two gardens, the light shone in his own kitchen. Lorraine switched on the spotlight Rick had mounted high on the back of their house after the night they'd been awoken by someone trying to break in. The probing, bluish light lit Pasco's way past her bare flowerbeds to the gate in the fence.

He thanked her for dinner. She thanked him for taking her mind off work.

When he was already halfway across her lawn, she called out, "Hey, Pasco."

He looked back, wondering what he'd forgotten.

"You heard about the guy who couldn't stand wearing condoms? He said they just hurt too much when he pulled them over his balls."

Pasco laughed despite the touch of uneasiness that came to him. *Balls*: he thought he would never grow accustomed to hearing certain words spoken by a woman. Not even Lorraine.

"That's what we call humour down at the centre," she said as she closed the door.

———————

From his kitchen Pasco looked back at Lorraine's house. The spotlight blinked off, filling his vision with spectral butterflies fluttering in the dark. Then the kitchen light went out and he felt keenly the heaviness of his own house.

This heaviness, it wasn't just the clutter in the kitchen, it had always been that way. Edna, like Lorraine, had been a conscientious housekeeper, not an obsessed one.

And it wasn't just the debris in the living room either: the disarray seemed merely physical evidence of a deeper malaise, as if something essential had been ripped from the house. He recognized it was more than the renovations themselves that made the house feel cold and lifeless. They didn't help; but they served to heighten an existing sense of desolation.

He tried, as he had so often, to put a name to the feeling. But he could not. How could you name absences? he wondered. How could you seize the ungraspable? All he knew was that he felt he didn't belong here, felt himself a stranger in his own house.

He turned off the living-room lights and, turning his back on the darkness, fled up the stairs to his bedroom.

Chapter Seven

Danny sat on a stool and opened up his coat. Pasco said, "You took your time." It had been two weeks since Danny's visit to the Gate.

"Been busy." He clasped his hands on the counter.

"Yeah, well...." Pasco nervously wiped his hands on the sides of his apron. "Coffee?"

"Sure."

Pasco filled a cup for each of them. "Listen, Danny," he said hesitantly. "About the Gate, I didn't mean to—"

"Forget it, Dad. You've got your turf, I've got mine." He looked around the empty restaurant. "And this is neutral territory."

And the house, Pasco thought, has become the battleground. "So what d'you want to talk about, Danny?"

"The next step."

"Shouldn't you get the living room done first?"

"We're getting there."

"I've had enough of living in a construction site, Danny."

"A little patience, Dad. It takes time, money—"

"Will you listen to me for a second? What you're doing with the house—it's not right for me."

"What are you talking about, Dad? I'm increasing the value of the house."

"It's not a question of real-estate value, Danny."

"It's the best thing for you, only you don't know it yet. You never did know what was good for you."

"And you do, I suppose." Pasco bit the insides of his cheeks. Talk to him, Lorraine had said, talk to him. He wondered if she often counselled the near impossible.

Danny's fingers caressed the coffee cup. "Why do you think I'm doing all this, Dad?"

"Do you know how many times I've asked myself that, Danny?"

"And?"

"And all I've come up with is, this isn't really for me. It has nothing to do with me. It has to do with—"

"You really don't understand, eh?"

"So explain it to me."

"Let me put it like this, Dad. Here you are, working your fingers to the bone day after day—"

"It's in the feet and legs that it gets me."

"—and everything you own that's worth anything is in the house, you have nothing else to show."

"Exactly, Danny, everything's in the house. And you're stripping it away, wall by wall."

"Can I finish please? Somebody's got to do something. Let me ask you a question, Dad. That bunch you spend your time with—"

"That bunch, as you call them, happen to be my closest friends."

"Fine. Do your closest friends ever eat or drink here?"

"Once in a while, not too often."

"And you charge your regular prices, right?"

"You know me better than that."

"Do you charge them at all?"

"For Chris' sake, Danny, they're my friends."

"C'mon, Dad, friendship's just another word for networking."

"I don't believe in making money off my friends."

"When they're in here eating and drinking they're your customers. Everybody's a client, Dad. That's what leads to profits, and profits are what business is all about."

The years had made his son ravenous. "People come in here because they're hungry. That's what *my* business is all about. I give my customers what they want. Do you? Does Simmons?"

"That has nothing to do with anything, Dad. This is a world of victims and victors, you win or you lose. There's no middle ground."

"I think I'm hearing Simmons talking here." Anger crept into Pasco's voice. "There's a middle ground packed with people, millions of them. Maybe they can't afford penthouses or fancy cars but they don't do so bad. A couple weeks down south every year, some government savings bonds, a movie from time to time, a baseball game, hockey game."

"What power do they have, Dad? They vote every four or five years and they think they have power. But who has the ear of the politicians between elections? It ain't those guys lying on the beach in Cancun or making waves at the SkyDome."

"You think it's all worth it, Danny, all this stuff that you're doing? You think it'll make you happy?"

"I want a gilt-edged life, Dad."

"Is that g-u-i-l-t?"

"Let me put it like this, Dad. Being poor is no turn-on."

"I'm not poor."

"You're not rich either. And it sure hasn't turned you into Mr. Happiness. If I've got to be unhappy in this life, I'd rather be comfortable doing it."

"How'd you ever get so cynical, Danny?"

"Cynical, Dad? Look, you know the old joke about a conservative being a liberal who was mugged last night? Well, I was born mugged. It's just a question of recognizing reality, that's all, only nobody had to punch me in the face."

"There's only one thing wrong with that joke, Danny. Doesn't take much to see it isn't really about liberals. It's about conservatives. Liberals believe in certain things, they have ideas. The joke says that conservatives don't believe in anything, they're just scared shitless." Pasco glanced sidelong at his son. "Is that you, Danny?"

"I know what I want out of life, Dad. You gotta push, and fear's pretty good motivation."

"I don't get it, Danny. Why are you so afraid? Where do you get that from?"

Danny was silent for a long time, twisting the coffee cup in its saucer. "Look around, Dad," he said quietly.

Pasco said nothing. He wondered just what Danny was talking about: the restaurant? the city? the world?

Then Danny said, "Look in the mirror."

Look in the mirror? From a stranger, maybe. "Who the hell do you think you are, Danny?"

Danny pushed the coffee cup away, got to his feet. "I'm not gonna sit here and listen to this." He strode to the door, jerked it open. Then he paused, as if having second thoughts. "What about the bedrooms, Dad?" he said with restraint.

"The bedrooms? I don't believe you."

"I need an answer, Dad."

Hardheaded. The boy had always been hardheaded. "Finish the living room first. Then we can talk about the rest."

"Christ." Danny's colour rose in his face. "You can't make anything easy, can you, Dad? Not a goddam thing." He stepped into the night and slammed the door shut.

Pasco splashed the undrunk coffee from their cups into the sink. One of the cups slipped from his hand, landed on the floor with a crack. "Fuck," he said. "Talk to him? Takes two, Lorraine, takes two."

Yet when the telephone rang a few minutes later he briefly hoped it might be Danny. "Hello?"

"Pasco? Cruise. How ya doin'?"

"Fine. What's up?" The interference on the line, like sheets of wind, told Pasco Cruise was using his new cordless phone, the latest MSD—Money Saving Device—he'd proudly announced at the Starting Gate the week before. He kept the cradle in his flat upstairs and brought the receiver down to the Booksore with him every morning, so that he now needed only one phone line.

"Wanna hear something funny?"

"From you? That'll be the day."

"Your kid, Daniel, was in here yesterday."

"In the Booksore?"

"The one and only."

"What was he doing there? Was he lost or something?"

"Naw, he wanted books."

"Danny wanted books?"

"Yeah. Books." Cruise's lighter rasped three times. "Fifty pounds of 'em."

"Cruise, I don't think I heard you right."

"You heard me. Fifty pounds of books. Hardcovers. All the same height, the thicker the better."

Pasco cleared his throat. "So what'd you do?"

"Hey, I run a bookstore. I gave the man what he wanted. An old set of Britannica that's been gathering dust forever. A Churchill war set, Trotsky's collected works."

"Danny bought Trotsky?"

"He was pleased as punch. It's a great-lookin' set."

"Did he say what he wanted them for?"

"Something to do with work. And I remembered you saying he works for Leon Simmons, so I figured the old bastard could afford it."

"Can't argue with that. By the way, how'd you charge?"

"Do I look like a fool? Twelve-fifty a pound, take it or leave it."

"And he *took* it?"

"Oh, he griped a bit. But I told him, hey, look, books this size are in short supply, there's been a run on 'em lately. And, you know, the law of supply and demand, price goes up. Then I took fifty cents off. He shrugged and, yeah, he took it."

"Fifty pounds at twelve bucks a pound. That's—"

"Six hundred bucks."

"Six hundred! My friend, you are a thief!"

"Plus tax."

"You're kidding. I'm going to have to warn my son about you. I'll send him to Coles next time. I hear the going rate there is ten-fifty a pound."

"Listen, Pasco, seriously, I hope you don't mind, eh? I didn't want you to hear about it from him. I just couldn't turn down a deal like that, you know?"

"You know me, Cruise. As you said, Simmons can afford it."

"And you have my word, if your kid ever comes in here again and really wants a book—"

"Don't worry about it. Not much danger of that."

"Thanks, Pasco. Be seein' ya."

"Right, you take care. And, Cruise?"

"Yeah?"

"Next time at the Gate, you're buying."

"Gotcha."

———————

Anger floored the accelerator. Anger squealed the tires as Danny turned left onto Sherbourne.

He should have put his foot down long ago. At that squalid bar, for instance. He should have tossed a twenty at the bartender, bought them all a round of drinks. Some kind of grand gesture.

Two could play the game of humiliation.

Red lights at Bloor Street. The digital signboard at the bank across the intersection flashed 7:03. Minus one degree Celsius. Traffic, as usual, heavy on Bloor. Only his father could upset him like this. Only his father could inflate the balloon in his belly, the tough spiky balloon that was the repository of all his pains and resentments, all his frustrations and his fears. They seemed so often to be speaking different languages at each other. It was as if they were from vastly different worlds with few references in common, and these only from a hazy past. Their present and future lives diverged as surely as a forked river.

The lights turned green. He swung the car left, joining the line of traffic crawling west on Bloor Street: towards the glitter. But how could he expect his father to understand him? He was a man stuck in time, a man whose vision was formed when Toronto was still a town that considered four o'clock tea and British accents the height of grandeur, a town in which the moneyed of Rosedale, old, secure and comfortable, were God-anointed and anyone who aspired to more than his station a grubber and an upstart. But the city was no longer simply that. It had broken wide open. New money, Chinese money, Italian money, had barrelled in, enlarging the envelope, ripping at its sides, changing forever the shape and dynamic of the city. It intruded everywhere, buying up, building up, merging, forcing the society of gentleman bankers and businessmen to give way before its hunger, practically melting in its hunger the old world of imported traditions and private-school connections. Long gone were the comfortable flab and gentle tug of collegiality. Everywhere now the voracious eye and the glare of the hungry lion. And Danny understood that the city—*the whole fucking city*—was up for grabs. Observe its workings, learn its ebb and flow, and plunge in, hungry and driven, asking no quarter and giving none: do this, and the rewards would come, the millions multiplying like amoeba.

The traffic slowed to a halt. Up ahead, a police cruiser with flashing lights slowly approached the Jarvis Street intersection from the other direction. The bottleneck had all the signs of a fender-bender. Danny swore. He wasn't going anywhere in partic-ular, but even going nowhere he liked getting there fast.

His father's city was a staid and musty place, rundown and fraying at the edges, a place of the aged and the marginal where a future was nothing more than the faint traces of yesterday's fantasy. But his city—the new city—was a bright and shining arena. It sparkled with glass and chrome and spinning, multi-coloured lights. It surged forward to a symphony of cars and trucks and heavy machinery. Danny had once shared his vision with his father. In his father's city, he had pointed out, problems were obstacles. But in his city, problems were opportunities. And his father, with the anger that seemed to come so easily to him, had denounced his arrogance.

His arrogance! His finger tapped impatiently on the steering wheel. He thought he would go crazy just sitting there waiting for the police to clear things up. Peering into his rearview mirror, he eased the car back, peeled out into the eastbound lane and swung left down Huntley. He'd go down to Isabella, work his way across to Yonge, then up to Yorkville for a quick drink.

Huntley was a quiet, nondescript street, an uneasy blend of high-rise, private homes and frazzled apartment blocks. It bisected a no man's land between his city to the west, with its insurance companies and department stores gleaming their wealth, and his father's city to the east, its low-rent behemoths impounding rumours of cockroaches, violence and drug-dealing, while north of Bloor, secure beyond the moat of its heavily wooded valley, sat the camouflaged splendours of lower Rosedale.

He drove past the hulking television studio where people nightly related miracles and bartered prayer for cash, past the deserted sidewalks and dimly lit houses, braking at Isabella to allow another car by. As he was about to turn, something farther down the street caught his eye, a movement of shadows at the end of the next block. His foot hesitated on the gas. Then, without really making a decision, he let the wheels straighten themselves out and he drove slowly ahead.

———

One was tall, one was short, and they seemed to come to life only in the beams of his headlights. They both stepped to the edge of the sidewalk, hands fumbling at coat buttons. The coats opened up. Advertising: tight glittery clothes spilled high breasts and swatches of white flesh. Sequinned legs reached out from the darkness.

"Hi, guy, how you doin'?" It was the short one who came to his window, brought her head close to his.

"Just fine. And you?"

"Fine 'n' dandy, bub." She was chewing gum, its sweetness thick on her breath.

"Cold evening, eh?"

"You can say that again. Looks warm in the car though." She shifted the gum to the other side of her mouth. "You hot?"

"You could say so."

"Want some company to cool off?"

"Depends."

"On what?"

"What d'you think?"

"Fifty bucks'll take care of everything." She stuck her tongue out, wagged it at him before curling it slowly back into her mouth. "Cool you right down, bub. Soften up all those stiff muscles."

Danny ran her words through his mind. He'd been tempted before by the ease of such transactions. No small talk, no social games. No self-revelations or explanations. No morning coffees and awkward goodbyes. This was simple and direct, desires understood, expectations declared. It could be easily tabulated, the account brought to a neat and mutual conclusion, no one hurt, everyone satisfied.

"So what's it gonna be, honey?"

"How much does your friend there charge?" Danny believed in comparison shopping.

"Only thirty," she answered easily. "But then, under all that make-up, his name's John."

"You're kidding."

"So you up for this or not, bub?"

He nodded, reached over and opened the passenger door for her.

She trotted around, got in. In the brief flash of light before she closed the door again he saw that she was pretty.

"So what's your name, honey?" she said.

He paused only briefly before saying, "You can call me Nathaniel."

"Sure, it's as a good a name as any, eh?" She did up her seatbelt. "We wouldn't want the cops pulling us over for a seatbelt violation now, would we?" She laughed.

Danny said, "When do I...? You know."

"My little gift, you mean? Now would be a good time."

Danny took two twenties from his wallet.

"It's fifty," she said.

"Take it or leave it."

"Son of a bitch." But she made no move to leave the car.

Finally she said, "Business is kind o' slow these days." She slipped the bills into her bra, settled back in the seat. "Drive on, Nathaniel."

———————

Danny drove slowly, following her terse directions—hang a right here, left at the next corner, right again—without paying much attention to where they were heading. He was nervous, his eyes roving around. With a spurt of panic, it occurred to him that she might be a police decoy, might even be reaching into her coat pocket at this very moment to flash her badge at him. But she had mentioned money first, he was in the clear: wasn't that how the law worked?

"Take it easy," she said at one point when he braked a touch too harshly. "There's no sign on your car saying Hooker on Board."

"It's my first time."

"Well," she said dryly, "there's always a first time, eh, Nathaniel?"

Nathaniel. Nathaniel Price. Strange how the name had surfaced on the spur of the moment after so many years. His anger with his father had probably dredged it up, as his anger had created it the summer his father almost drowned.

They had been at the cottage, in truth little more than a shack, on Georgian Bay. A strip of lawn out front, and an abrupt falling off of the land to the bottle-green water. His father was a fair way out, dog-paddling; his mother was in a lounge chair, dozing. Danny, tinkering with his camera in front of the cottage, suddenly saw his father's arms flailing, saw his mouth yawning at the sky, his plastered hair appearing and disappearing in silent desperation. And Danny, gazing as if from a long distance at the helplessness of his father, watched a neighbour pull him to safety. Watched as the neighbour pumped his lungs while his mother, straining at calm, caressed his father's head. Later that evening Danny sat on the small porch slapping at mosquitoes and looked at his parents standing arm in arm at the edge of the land, their silhouettes stark against the sunset. The light was thick, blazing fire at the horizon, molten gold on the water. A bright quarter-moon shone in the violet sky above.

Yet it was soon after this that his mother turned red-eyed and retreated from his father.

From all of this—his father's helplessness, his parents' closeness, his mother's tears—came the fantasy of Nathaniel Price. He no longer remembered where the name itself came from, but he sensed still the strength of its sound that had attracted him. It seemed a solid, secure name, not the name of a man who flailed around, made his wife unhappy and wore an apron at work. He had practised saying the name, signing it, had even convinced one or two of his friends to call him Nathaniel, for a short time at least. And he decided that should it ever become necessary or desirable, he would one day make himself over into Nathaniel Price: a man with no past, a man with a future only as he saw fit.

"Pull in there," she said, and he was dismayed to find she was directing him into the Simmons building with the broken garage door. He didn't turn, kept on driving without telling her why. To explain that he knew the police were keeping an eye on the garage until it was fixed would have been to reveal too much. He said simply that he suffered from claustrophobia, preferred the outdoors. He circled around instead, pulling up at the loading bay behind the building. Large garbage containers sat in the dim light.

"Romantic," she said.

"Will it do?"

She shrugged, reached a hand out to the radio. "You mind?"

"Suit yourself." He slid his seat back several notches.

She pressed the buttons one after the other, filling the car with snatches of music, phone-in rage, hockey commentary, urbane conversation. Then a flat voice said: "No, no, in our wasteful modern world fridges and stoves are necessary evils, more or less—"

"Hey," she exclaimed. "The Doctor! Doesn't he just drive you wild?" she said. "I think he's so sexy." She unzipped him, wormed her hand into his trousers.

"...Imagine—gas ranges in the Amazon, TVs in Chinese villages. The waste is enormous. Our consumer mentality is polluting the world—"

"So you're into the whole ecology thing, eh?" Danny said. His breath was growing shorter. Already.

"You know it, bud." Her free hand dug into her coat pocket.

"...As for the Brazilians, they have a thing or two to learn from their indigenous peoples, let me tell you—"

She ripped open a condom package with her teeth.

"...met a Brazilian rubber tapper. Lives in the middle of the jungle and couldn't be happier. Has everything he needs—"

She held up the circle of rolled rubber for him to see. It was green.

"...And he's never been sick in his life. He makes his own medicines from tree bark—"

"I'm not only user friendly," she said, slipping it on him. "I'm environmentally friendly too." Her face sank into his lap.

"...But at least he isn't destroying the environment—"

Danny felt her teeth.

"...He lives in harmony with nature, is at one with it—"

Danny didn't hear the rest of the good Doctor's words. In his belly, the balloon was slowly, deliciously withdrawing its spikes.

———

Danny drove her back to her corner. Her companion John was not there.

"You know, Nathaniel," she said opening the car door, "you're my favourite kind of trick."

"Oh yeah?"

"Yeah, you cheapskate." She stepped out. "You see, I just hate it when they're good-looking." She slammed the door shut and stepped defiantly back.

Bitch, Danny thought. He hit the gas and abandoned her to the night.

———————

He parked in the municipal garage and walked over to RDW, his favourite Yorkville nightclub, so named because, as one of the owners once explained to him, it was what came before s-e-x in the alphabet.

RDW was packed as usual, and loud. He ordered a Screwdriver and leaned on the bar. In the end, it had been an unsatisfactory account. His forty dollars could have been better spent. She had helped distance him from his anger, from his father. But she hadn't banished them. Danny still felt stifled by his father's psychic smallness, a quality he shared with the Gate's collection of aimless people caressing the ruins of small dreams.

It was here, in the midst of pounding music and flickering lights and well-dressed people shaking and shimmying to notions of glitter and life at a higher pitch, that Danny felt his most secure. It was a society of brittle connections and pliable convictions, where interest in others rarely lasted beyond a night. Here, surrounded by people whose visions and desires he understood and shared, was life as it should be. Why disappear into the greyness when you could so easily sparkle in the lights?

He nodded at acquaintances, smiled, winked. Andreas came up, slapped him hard on the shoulder in greeting. He was an ageing but still handsome interior designer who worked from time to time for Simmons Construction, designing opulent fantasies for the lobbies of the condominium and office buildings. Eyes flitting constantly among the crowd, searching, assessing, flirting, he told Danny of his plans for a new nightspot. It would be intimate, he said, with quiet music and mirrors eveywhere: on the walls, on the ceiling, on the floor.

On the floor? Danny said, only half-interested.

Of course on the floor. Especially on the floor. With indirect lighting glowing up from under the glass. That was the heart of the concept: guys'd just have to glance down to see what was up a skirt. And the gals could wear whatever they wanted, depending on how daring they were or "you know, what they're lookin' for".

Then Andreas was gone, pursuing someone into the crowd. That was the way it was here: fast and to the point.

Danny ordered another drink, made useless eyes at unknown women. Two pretty women were dancing together. Sheathed in black, they were alone in their own world, eyes closed, bodies close, hands a-flutter.

He envied them their absorption.

Chapter Eight

THE DAY was not particularly cold. The temperature, two degrees below freezing when Pasco left the house that morning, had risen a little. By mid-morning, when the first snow of the season began drifting down, the flakes wet and heavy, it hovered around zero. The middle of December was early still for snow, but after a lifetime in the city Pasco knew better than to be surprised.

The winters of his youth had been, at least in memory, more predictable. He recalled as many blue days as grey, temperatures sinking until the air fairly crackled, snow coming early and hard, burying the city in a whiteness that would be days turning ugly, and then only on the busiest streets. Blizzards would leave behind crisp, bracing days, the city swept clean and brilliant in the sun.

But this had all changed in recent years. Winter had come to mean a bitter dampness well into January, heavy cloud cover trapping the humidity of the lake, the temperature flirting with snow but always pulling back, unable to commit itself. Some days the city awoke to a roiling fog, and Christmas more often than not now came and went under a sky spitting and dripping and opening up for the occasional downpour. It wasn't until late January or early February that snow came in abundance, but by then it had lost its romance. And it wasn't long in becoming

unsightly, the whiteness quickly trampled and spun into a bronzish slush on most streets.

Marcus had cobbled together an elaborate theory linking the change in the weather with astronauts, the moon, the tides, microwaves, nuclear plants and what he claimed to be the growing structural instability of the planet from excess mining.

Pasco, unconvinced, believed rather that the change in the weather had something to do with the city itself, with its growth in his lifetime from a contained and self-satisfied conventionality to an immense and hungry metropolitan grandeur. Farmland had turned into suburbs, suburbs into cities. Cars roamed where, in his childhood, horses had grazed. Barns and stables gave way to industrial parks as the downtown core grew denser, higher, brighter, even eliminating the seasons by tunnelling out a vast underground city of shopping malls linked by subway lines. The streets, insufficient before the growing demands of commuters and transport trucks, clogged with traffic.

This was all it took, Pasco thought, the bustle and fuss of the city raising the temperature in the sky above. At times heavy snow would be blanketing the suburban fringes while the downtown core was being drenched in a freezing rain. Weather forecasters, confident of their computers and satellite pictures, frequently saw their projections turned to nonsense by the ceaseless fervour of the streets.

So you never knew what the weather would do in this city strangely defiant of expectations in a country bent on fulfilling them. All you could do was put up with whatever was tossed at you, moaning and grumbling and massaging the joints, and trying to remember that summer would be sweet.

Pasco paused as he was clearing the booth closest to the front window—a half-drunk cup of coffee, a half-eaten strawberry Danish, the tin ashtray warm with half-smoked cigarettes—and gazed through the glass past the red mirror-image letters that, from the

street, read PASCAL'S Restaurant & Grill. The snowflakes were
constant and hurried in their descent, touching down and melting
away on the sidewalk, on the benches, on the stripped trees and
dank grass of the park across the way.

Through the flakes he saw that the old woman—the pigeon
lady—was at her usual bench. With her tight hood, shapeless
black coat and plastic boots, she was like a three-dimensional
shadow broken only by the white oval of her face and the steady
fluttering of her large hands. She brought with her a plastic
grocery bag bulky with four loaves of white bread, sat on the same
bench on which Pasco had found the body of the runaway, and
almost apathetically fed the birds. The pigeons and a few seagulls
swooped in from the sky, hopping and skipping and jumping
around her, nipping and pecking furiously at the crumbs she
tossed onto the grass. Squirrels scrambled around seeking their
share.

He couldn't fathom what drove the old woman to come each
day to the park to feed the birds. Her pleasure was not evident.
She neither smiled nor laughed. Her gestures—the shredding of
the bread, the flicking of the wrist—revealed nothing beyond the
monotony of assembly-line labour. Loneliness seemed an insufficient explanation: the pigeons, intent on feeding, hardly made
genial companions. And as philanthropy, her actions seemed mis-
guided in a city with haemorrhaging food banks: on summer
nights, the park was home to countless people who, he supposed,
would appreciate four loaves of bread.

One morning last spring, he'd hung the back-in-five-minutes
sign on the door and crossed the street to the park. He wasn't sure
what he intended to do. Maybe just get a closer look at her, maybe
establish some sort of contact. Hands in his pockets, he'd strolled
lazily towards a bench not far from hers. He would not be particularly conspicuous: it was the kind of morning made for wandering
around in a park. The last patches of snow and ice had all melted.

The grass was bruised, but a thin sunlight softened the air. The soil of the bare flowerbeds showed a rich, deep brown and the shrubbery fairly shimmered with the delicate greenery of new buds. The kind of morning, then, that when he was younger would have made him glad to be alive.

He was circumspect as he sat on the bench and crossed his legs—he didn't want to scare her—but she paid no attention to him, seemed oblivious of his presence. Her face, thick-fleshed, was impassive, her eyes simply following the path of the crumbs from her fingers to the grass. Nor did she focus on the pigeons and their scrambling, and it occurred to Pasco that she would be doing this even if they were not there. She appeared to be offering the bread to the earth itself.

As she began working through the final loaf of the morning, Pasco got to his feet and ambled over towards her. He came to a stop just outside the ragged circle of birds—from close up he saw that several sparrows were hopping and darting among the pigeons—and stood gazing at their frenzied activity for several seconds. Finally, with a smile, he said, "Hungry little buggers, eh?"

The old woman's round eyes blinked slowly up at him. He saw that she was blind in one, almost so in the other. Then she mumbled in a language he didn't know. Czech? Russian? Ukrainian? Something eastern European.

He repeated his words, more loudly and with greater emphasis. "I said, they're hungry, little buggers, eh?"

She mumbled again, shrugged her substantial shoulders and returned her gaze to the ground.

He remained where he was for a few seconds more, then turned and began a slow walk back to the restaurant. He didn't look back until he had reached the road. He saw that she had remained as he'd left her, staring at the ground, a slice of bread in her left hand, a crumb in her right.

He regretted his intrusion.

Many minutes later, well after he'd closed the door behind him, he saw her toss the piece of bread. Saw her enveloped in a surge of pigeons.

The snow continued coming down. Pasco watched the flakes disappearing into the wet pavement. Watched the pigeon lady, her black coat twinkling as the flakes alighted briefly on her and winked out. Watched a couple of drunks waltzing through the park, and a group of skinheads striding by on the sidewalk, the males brash and theatrical, the females huddled in their studded leather jackets.

His dissatisfaction with the failed attempt at contact was still fresh even after so many months. The pigeon lady would always be a mystery, as was her right. His discomfort came from knowing that her anonymity was a sign of the changes that had come to the neighbourhood over the years. There had been a time when no strangers wandered the streets, for newcomers were quickly absorbed, became familiar. Now people came and went with casual regularity, identities tightly guarded. The neighbourhood, once settled, had gone fluid. People now walked here only on the way to somewhere else, rarely for simple pleasure. The community had dwindled, his stable of regulars shrunk. He was saddened that the best-dressed people who now came to the park were the police, and they came not to visit the greenhouse, not to admire the flowers, but to bundle up corpses or to bust drug deals, or merely to sit in their cruisers observing the darkness.

———————

During a lull in the lunch-time rush—everyone had been served, no one new had come in—Pasco made himself some toast and leaned tiredly on the counter. The radio was on, its sounds melding with and only occasionally rising above the buzz of conversation in the restaurant.

As he nibbled at the toast, the memory he had been holding off all morning—there had been no time to entertain it—came to him once more. A childhood memory—he was no more than seven or eight—impressionistic and incomplete and, like so many of his early remembrances, divorced from all context except the personal.

A fall day, bright and cool. Lunch-time. He was on his way home from school: blue socks, brown shoes—patterned leather buckled on the side—scuffed and dusty on the pitted sidewalk. Suddenly car tires squealed. He looked up. Something went thump. Looked around. And half a block away, a little girl was soaring above the windshield of a car. The girl was wearing a pink dress, the car was painted grey. She landed on the roof, bounced, hit the pavement in a splatter of scarlet. He turned and fled.

At home he said nothing about what he'd seen: witnessing, he understood many years later, had somehow implied involvement, and helplessness implied guilt. Lunch that day turned out to be a red-bean soup, with buttered bread. He found himself unable to eat.

He was well into his twenties before he could once more eat red-bean soup, the sight of it never failing to trigger flashes of the accident. He had no idea who the girl was, whether she'd lived or died. He recalled no announcement of her fate at school, no talk of the accident. He had only a vague memory of a policeman talking to the class about road-safety. What he remembered most sharply was the policeman's advice: "Look left, look right, look left again before you cross." Like the squealing of the car tires, like the sight of the airborne girl, the policeman's words had impressed themselves on Pasco. His words, and his eyes. For they were watery and unsure eyes, eyes that undercut, even for a young boy, the confidence with which he spoke.

As Pasco tossed the uneaten crusts into the garbage can, he knew why the images of the accident were forcing themselves on him this morning. The quality he had seen in that policeman's eyes—the uncertainty, the denial of his apparent confidence—he had noticed, too, in the eyes of Sean's young partner. It probably meant nothing, he told himself, acknowledging with a nod a client's mimed request for his bill. Kurt was most likely just suffering the excess of arrogance peculiar to the inexperienced young, and wasn't that the most natural thing in the world?

Pasco double-checked the man's bill, took it over to him. While pudgy fingers dug into a fat wallet, Pasco watched through the window as the pigeon lady gathered herself up and lumbered out of the park. A few birds strutted stiffly around her bench pecking at the last of the breadcrumbs. The sky was clearing, the clouds pulling back to the fragile light that, during fall and winter, seemed to drain the city of substance, turning glass to ice, thinning the air and kindling everywhere a frigid sparkle.

On the other side of the street directly across from the restaurant stood Sklewy, a tall, middle-aged man who'd begun wandering the streets of the neighbourhood three or four months before. For the first few weeks he'd carried around a briefcase, but that had recently been replaced by a plastic grocery bag bulky with mysterious possessions. His face was radiant with a quiet smile; his eyes stared off into an insubstantial distance. He hadn't shaved in several days and his old grey suit had grown baggy around his increasing gauntness.

Pasco had, with disbelief and a quiet horror, watched his decline through the months, a man with the demeanour of a business executive going steadily to seed. His neighbour Fong, with an uncertain command of English but a great appetite for gossip, had heard that he'd been fired from his job with either a large insurance company or a bank. He'd been either a topnotch sales representative or a senior vice-president, had either screwed up a lucrative deal or misappropriated funds. Whatever the story, his decline had been sure, swift and unforgiving. Someone claimed to have seen a cellular phone in the briefcase, while someone else said it contained a movable bar. There were apparently a broken marriage and alcohol problems.

And here he was wandering the downtown streets, not begging but not refusing handouts either. "He sklewy," Fong had said, crossing his eyes and screwing an index finger against his temple. The word had stuck and, in the absence of any other, become his name.

Sklewy, mumbling to himself, began searching through his pockets. He often did this, looking for something never found, searching, Pasco thought, for something irretrievably lost. He shuddered, as he always did when he caught sight of Sklewy, and he wondered where, in all of Fong's ands and ors, lay the true story.

The client held a twenty out to Pasco, thumb and forefinger testing the bill to ensure there was only one. "'Sokay," Pasco said. "Only new bills stick together. This one looks like it's been around the world a couple of times. On foot."

Across the street, Sklewy held his hand curled in his jacket pocket, stiffened his back into a febrile dignity and continued on his way.

Pasco locked the door of the restaurant behind him and crossed the street to the concrete path that bisected the park. The lamps were on, their dull light showing the way to the other side. An ambulance hurtled down Sherbourne, its lights slashing brilliant through the early evening darkness. Clouds had moved back in, and a brief drizzle had once more dampened the ground. The air was heavy with moisture.

The damp cold seeped through his clothing to his joints, sank into his ankles and knees tired from standing all day. The fatigue was familiar and, in a way, not unpleasant. He accepted that it was, like paperwork, a price for the independence of proprietorship. Pasco had always valued his independence; it was the reason he had bought the restaurant from Mr. Pascal in the first place. And he worried that Danny, in working for Simmons, was surrendering his own. How far, he wondered, was Danny prepared to go in pursuit of his dreams?

———————

"Where's Marcus?" Pasco said, tugging off his coat. He took the chair beside Montgomery.

Cruise's eyes widened, his mouth fell open and his palms fluttered beside his ears in imitation of a dancehall minstrel. "In Buffalo, Noo Yawk," he sang, "spendin' his little heart out."

"As God is my witness." Montgomery, pausing briefly in his story, clapped Pasco on the arm in welcome. "I swear is the trut'. For the longest while I thought the CN Tower was the Seein' Tower. Because from up there you seein' the whole damn city." He laughed, his eyes red and watery. Two empty beer mugs sat on the table in front of him, and a third was half-empty.

Cruise screwed up his face in scepticism. "But they've got CN written all over the fuckin' place, how could you miss it?"

"Oh, I see the letters awright, but the idea was a'ready in my head. The Seein' Tower. Everything was so new, man, I jus' didn't connec' the two. When you adjustin' to a new country, it have a lot of things you doesn't connec'. That never happen to you, man, Cruise? One idea fix like cement in your head—"

"Like cement?"

Pasco said, "Sounds like my son. Cement in the head."

Pushpull wiped his lips with the back of his hand. "Besides, Cruise never had an idea in his life."

Montgomery winked at him. "Hey, man, sometimes is not a

too-bad thing, eh? Is ideas that does cause all the problems in the world. Take that daughter o' mine—"

"And it's only ideas," Pasco said quickly, "that can solve them."

"Sixteen years old and skippin' school. All she interested in is money and good times."

"Ain't nothing wrong with that," Cruise said. "This education thing ain't all it's cracked up to be, y'know. Look at doctors, for example."

"What the hell you talkin' 'bout?"

"Well, they're supposed to be healers, right?"

"Yeah?"

"So how come most of 'em end up as heels? They forget to study the *er* part or what?"

"Good point," Pushpull said.

"Right." Pasco winked at Lanny as he placed a beer in front of him. "The kid could always end up as a crossing-guard. Don't need any training for that, right, Pushpull?"

Cruise raised a thumb at him. "Fuckin'-A, man."

"You think is why the wife and me move here? For Charlene to help chil'ren and old people cross the street?"

Pasco wondered what had happened to Nutmeg.

"Hey," Pushpull said in mock anger. "It's a vital public service."

"So's pickin' up the fockin' garbage, but—"

"*Daddy, Daddy,*" Cruise said in falsetto. "*I wanna be a garbage-man when I grow up.* All right, son," he continued in baritone. "But you gotta start at the bottom of the barrel like everybody else."

Montgomery said, "You know, my granny use to say you shouldn't praise the day before the evenin'. Everything look so rosy when we first come here...."

"Don't go getting yourself all worked up over it, man," Cruise said. "She'll settle down. Shit, I was a hellraiser when I was her age."

Pushpull said, "And this is supposed to make him feel better? Cruise, man, I wish you wouldn't use yourself as an example, it's so goddam depressing."

"Is no joke, fellas." Montgomery went serious. "The girl stayin' out till all hours. Goin' out when she want, comin' in when she want, no explanation thank you. Say a word to her and she lettin' fly 'bout her liberty. Her fockin' liberty! Her brother take to callin' her Liberty Bell, because he say she all crack up. The wife and me, we try everything. We try reasonin', but the girl like she have no reason. We try crackin' down, but she slip out when we wasn't lookin' and din't come back till next mornin'. The wife even get to the point of layin' a hand on her. And the child—" Montgomery paused, swallowed hard. "The child lay a hand right back." He shook his head at the memory. "Well, I never see nothing like that, a child raisin' a hand to her own mammy."

After a moment of silence during which the entire bar seemed to hold its breath, Cruise said, "Teenagers. Rough times, man. But don't forget, in the end the seed always comes down near the tree."

"Unless," Pasco said, "the wind happens to blow real hard at the wrong time."

Montgomery said, "You know, if we was back home, the girl would o' know she was taking her life in her hand when she hit her mammy. Is only my son who stop me from beatin' the livin' day-lights out o' Nut—" He looked away, sucked his teeth in a loud display of disgust. "—Charlene."

Pasco thought he had never heard a name said with such despair.

Chapter Nine

THE HOUSE had a dry, musty smell, but no echo. Sounds travelled only short distances before being absorbed flat and dull into the wood. The silence imposed itself, made him circumspect during his visits over the next few weeks. Apart from the occasional inquiry as to how things were going, the boss was leaving him alone, and this trust, heavy with calculation, made Danny unusually nervous about the restoration project.

He spent hours studying the layout, planning the deconstruction, figuring out where the original walls had been. He wanted to know how the rooms had fit together, wanted to capture whatever feeling of the place remained. There wasn't much.

Most of the tiny rooms—cells, as he'd come to think of them—resembled one another in their bareness. Few of the walls had been scribbled on, as if the tenants had seen the corridor as the place for their resentments and their fantasies, their rooms as places not to be defiled. In one room on the second floor, though, the wall beside the bedframe was covered in a neat handwriting.

If right now is already a second ago and if today is fast becuming yesterday is tomorow realy today?

What the fuck did that mean? There was more, in the same

hand but a different voice, as if the writer was arguing with two distinct parts of himself.

No you dimwit it just means that one second past midnite tonite tomorows already beginning to be yesterday

And today?

Easy crapface today doesnt exist. Today is just tomorow becuming yesterday

In that case I am dead for yesterday and alive for tomorow. And today I do not exist

Have it your way asshole

There were more arguments, one voice disquieted and questioning, the other impatient, peppering every reply with expletives. The voices went on at length about the existence of the number zero: if zero meant no thing, *the absence of thing*, then how could it exist? And if it didn't exist, wasn't everything—*mathematicks, physicks, electronicks*—based on a lie? And if the world, ancient and modern, was based on a lie, wouldn't it all come crashing down one day? Existence, truth, lies: The words and their meanings obsessed the writer.

Danny briefly felt sorry for the mind that could produce such relentless ravings; the thoughts, feverish and abusive, seemed to have spilled from a brain molten with uncertainty and anger. Danny had never understood why some people chose to make the world a more complex place than it was. Evelyn, for example, on whom he'd spent so much money with no reward. Having convinced herself she had had an unhappy childhood—all the pop psychology books she read told her it must have been so—she then took it as her divine mission to convince others of her ill-treatment at the hands of her parents: the father who would not hug her, the mother who would not let her be. Evelyn spent much time burnishing her store of psychic pain; it was her way of making herself special. Why couldn't people like Evelyn, having understood the past, simply shrug at it and get on with their lives? What was the self-indulgence that drove them?

The wall-scribbler was just a variant of Evelyn: what was more self-indulgent, after all, than questioning the very reality of existence? As far as Danny was concerned, he was here, the world was here: it was all he needed. He knew his father would call him shallow. But that was one of the basic differences between them. The father's shallowness was the son's practicality. As for truth and lies, they were just variations of reality; what was true and what was not true simply depended on where you stood. Which was the truth, which the lie? Danny thought it obvious: money and success changed everything in a man's life; they redefined all the terms. People who didn't know this, people who spent their time wrestling with questions that had no application in the real world, were doomed to be losers. The world went on spinning, rewarding some, punishing others, while they wrapped themselves in useless speculation.

His father was one of those who, limited by their ideas of right and wrong, good and bad, failed to take advantage of the potential life offered them. If his father let him, Danny knew he could turn Pascal's into a worthwhile business. Translate the menu into French, add an espresso machine, put up a few prints—the Eiffel Tower, the Arc de Triomphe—and there was no telling where it would go. They could keep it exclusive and skyrocket the prices, or they could franchise out and go for the shopping-mall clientele. Either way, they were looking at a million-dollar enterprise. But his father would never go for it and Danny, denied the fast track, had to settle for the slower one of renovating the house with an eye to increasing its value for future sale.

He was still surprised, even somewhat grateful, that his father had agreed to his plans: it showed the power of a well-prepared scheme backed up by a little bribery. The old man had never learnt that money was amoral; he indulged all kinds of strange ideas and attitudes that, in the end, served only to limit him, narrowing his possibilities, hedging his successes. Danny himself had no such illusions, for he knew where all that airy speculation got you: in places like this, scribbling craziness on the walls.

Sita, to his relief, was rarely there, and the two times she had been she'd quietly slipped into her coat and left. Danny wondered idly what she spent her days doing. He figured that, like the illegals he'd read or heard about, she washed dishes here, scrubbed floors there, collecting, if she was lucky, the minimum wage.

That, though, was the easy part. The more difficult question that came to him was what she spent her nights doing. To this he had no answer save the haunting vision of her rattling round in the big, dark, empty house. He had peeked into her room one afternoon to a darkness so total that he had had to switch on the light. The windows had been sealed with plywood so that no brightness from the uncovered bulb could be seen from outside. The walls were bare, the bed neatly made up, a suitcase on a chair beside it. A room of an almost religious sparseness. There was no radio, no television, nothing to offer relief from the weighty silence of the house.

In the end, Mr. Simmons's harbouring an illegal didn't strike Danny as extraordinary. At least, Sita's presence was no more curious than anything else about his boss. His furtiveness, the den on the third floor, his desire to reconstruct a past he himself had razed: elements of a secret life. Sita was undoubtedly one of its more bizarre aspects, but Danny knew enough—was ambitious enough—not to pursue the path curiosity opened up. Part of him was dazzled by the trust Mr. Simmons was showing in entrusting him with a project clearly vital enough to him that he would reveal corners of his personal life so long and so carefully hidden.

He had, on Mr. Simmons's order, said nothing to Sal about the project. Sal had no reason to know. The bills would be routed through the construction and not the rental accounting office, and with Sal's penchant for gossip the less he knew, the better it would be. Still, Danny didn't understand the need for secrecy—the reconstruction of the house was, in the end, just another Simmons Construction project—but he didn't question it. The boss, he had realized, was one of those people who kept their lives neatly divided between the personal and the professional, and then subdivided those divisions. It was a quality Danny admired, for the control it afforded.

Yet he wished he could tell someone—croon a little, boast a little. But he owed Mr. Simmons, and discretion was after all one of the most vital attributes of an executive assistant. An acquaintance of his, another graduate of his M.B.A. class, had in a moment of drunken imprudence told him of the hotel-room entertainments he had to arrange from time to time for the business executives his boss wanted to seduce into signing on the dotted line. It had backfired only once, embarrassingly so, for the recipient, one of the flamboyant successes of Wall Street, turned out to be "not into girls". Danny's friend had had to scramble a bit—the Yellow Pages offered only female companionship—but, as his friend put it, "In this town, you want it, you got it. Everything's just a phone call away." The man signed the next day, a smile on his face.

The house, interior untouched by the sunlight, sat sterile and silent. As he always did on instinct, he stood in the corridor just inside the front door and listened. Nothing, not even a suggestion of the hum every dwelling had, even one long uninhabited. This stillness, this profound absence of life: he'd felt it—for it was felt, not seen—only from his mother's corpse.

He went up the stairs, drawn without knowing why to the room of the argument.

But if I don't exist for today then you don't exist for today either

As far as he had figured out, this cell and the next two had constituted what Mr. Simmons called the sewing room, his mother's, Danny deduced, although the boss hadn't said so.

So what fuckface isn't it enough you and me exist for tomorrow Yesterday doesn't matter so why don't you shut the fuck up

He stood at the window, palm circling dust away from the panes, struggling with the unfamiliarity of the role he had been asked to play. He was a man accustomed to newness, to the banishing of ghosts rather than to the retention of them. But now, Mr. Simmons's wishes required imagination of a different sort: new ways of looking, new ways of proceeding. And as he tentatively sought the way, it occurred to him that this approach—not of remaking the past but of renewing it—might have been more acceptable, less threatening, to his father. This clinging to ghosts: perhaps an effect of age, he thought.

"Mr. Daniel?"

He spun around. "Sita. How did you know I was here?"

"I always know when somebody here."

"I didn't hear you. Were you in your room?"

"No, sir, I just come in. I went out for a walk." She stood in the doorway tightly wrapped in her beige coat. It was big for her, made her head appear shrunken. She was wearing running shoes.

"Nice day for a walk."

"Yes, sir. Nice day."

"I'm, uh—" Danny grew more uneasy. "I'm just having a look around. For the restoration. You know about that, eh?"

"Yes, sir. Mr. Leon tell me everything." She had a thin, piping voice, and spoke with a lilting tone that struck a note of despondency.

Danny smiled, turned back to the window in dismissal.

But she didn't leave. She said, "This was Mr. Bell room, sir."

"Mr. Bell?"

"Yes, sir. He was the las' tenant."

But the boss had said the last tenant had moved out months ago. "How long have you been living here, Sita?"

"About a year, sir."

"And you knew this Mr. Bell?"

"Yes, sir. He din't stay long. A few weeks."

"Did you ever talk to him?"

"No, sir, he frighten me."

"Why?"

"He din't belong here, sir. He not like the other tenants. He was always dressin' up in a suit."

Danny gestured at the wall. "Looks like he had a lot on his mind."

"Yes, sir. He was always thinkin'-thinkin'. Mr. Leon tell me he use to be a big-shot somewhere and he get fired."

"You know what happened to him?"

"I does still see him sometimes, sir. Jus' walkin' around in his suit thinkin'-thinkin'. Before I come here, I din't know it had people like that in this country. Back home people always sayin' Canada rich-rich, it ain't have no poor people up there."

"There are poor people everywhere. It's a fact of life."

"So I findin' out, sir."

Danny took a step towards the door. "Well—" He needed to get away. Although he knew it to be illogical, he felt himself a trespasser here. Still she didn't move, not deliberately blocking his way but as if unaware she was in his path. "It's time for me to—"

"Mr. Daniel, sir?"

"Yes?"

"I—" She became fidgety, fists clenching and unclenching in her coat pockets. Her eyes darted around, tongue flicked briefly from her mouth to moisten her lips.

Danny noticed how small her lips were, dark and finely shaped. He waited for her to go on.

"Nothing, sir."

"What is it?" He suspected she was worried about where she would live once the work had begun. He would tell her what Mr. Simmons had said: We'll work something out.

"You have the key for Mr. Leon room upstairs, sir?"

Danny hadn't expected that. "What for?"

"Is jus' that…." She stared at the floor.

Danny could see she was trying to make up her mind as to whether she could trust him or not. "Go on." He'd meant to reassure her, but the words came out too severely.

"Is jus' that Mr. Leon have my passport, sir, and I was hopin'—"

"Why does he have your passport?"

"For safe-keepin', sir."

"So why don't you ask him for it then?"

"Mr. Leon—" Her right hand jerked from the coat pocket to her mouth. Small white teeth gnawed at the thumb. "You here now, sir."

"I don't have the key. You should ask Mr. Simmons."

Her eyes, already so dark, grew darker. They blinked rapidly. "Yes, sir. I'll ask him, sir."

Danny, fearing she was about to cry, said, "Why do you need your passport?" This time the words came out more quietly.

She offered no answer.

"You thinking of leaving?"

"Is *my* passport, sir."

"Look, if you're planning on going back to wherever it is you came from, I'm sure Mr. Simmons—"

"Is jus' my passport I want, sir. I ain't have the money for a plane ticket, and my old one done expire."

This was getting complicated—was she asking him for money?—and Danny didn't like complications. "Look, I can ask him if you like, I'll be seeing him at the office tomorrow—"

"No, sir! Is awright. Don't say nothing to Mr. Leon. I—" She swallowed hard. "He here every evenin', sir, I'll ask him."

Danny shrugged. "Whatever." This was between Mr. Simmons and Sita, and he had no wish to involve himself in an affair that was no business of his.

She moved aside to let him pass. He left her standing at the door to Mr. Bell's room.

Outside, the light was already beginning to fail.

Chapter Ten

A MOVEMENT deep in the park caught his eye, shadows among the trees. Skinheads, six or seven of them, sauntering with silver-studded arrogance towards the pigeon lady.

Pasco, wary, stepped closer to the window, his vision blurring at the edges as he focused on them forming a semi-circle before her, blocking her from view. He wondered whether it might be prudent to dial 911—but he really had nothing to report. The skins hadn't actually done anything. They were just wandering about the park, as was their right. And it might be, Pasco thought with faint hope, that their curiosity over the pigeon lady was as benign as his own. It might be that they were examining her the way some people examined flowers: with an interest that implied menace only in its frankness.

But when the skins closed in on the pigeon lady, when their circle grew tighter around her—a closer look? examining the petals?—Pasco reached for his broom, quickly unscrewing the head and tossing it aside. He hefted the wooden shaft—it had never felt so light—and with hardly a second's hesitation, having barely paused to consider his options, he found himself dodging traffic to cross the street, striding with diminishing purpose across the firm turf.

He came to a halt several yards behind them. Their leather-jacketed backs walled in the pigeon lady.

"Stupid old bitch. What'sa matter with you? You don't understand English?"

Pasco tried to get a look at their boot laces. Saw that they were red. That wasn't good. He'd read in the newspaper that red laces, unlike black or white, were certain skinhead packs' proud badges of racial intolerance. And they used violence, the article had made clear, the way he used a spatula: as a tool of the trade.

"Fuckin' foreigners."

"Takin' away our jobs."

The voices were male and female, but from where Pasco stood he couldn't separate the sexes.

"Hey old lady, you're a Jew, ain't ya?"

"Yeah, look-it that face."

"A Jew-face if I ever saw one."

"What's the matter, Jew-lady? Cat got your tongue?"

"Lose the scarf, lady—" One of the females, sex revealed only by her voice, stepped towards the pigeon lady. "Let's see your horns."

Pasco's hands tightened around the broom handle. He swallowed, searched for his voice. When the words came—"Tha... that's enough"—they faltered, emerging with less decisiveness than he'd hoped for.

The skinheads turned as a group to face him, their faces young and abused, menacing in their uniformity.

"Lea...." His voice failed him again. "Leave her alone." Pasco's breath went shallow. His voice sounded thin to his ear, every word he said further diminishing his authority.

Their leader—the eldest, Pasco guessed, in his early twenties—stared hard back at him. Veins strained prominent down his forehead and he seemed, in the reddening of his face, to be working himself up into a fury. "Fuck off, old man." He spoke quietly, cracking his knuckles—one hand followed by the other—in theatrical emphasis.

"Yeah, old man," drawled another. He was a boy with damaged teeth. "You ain't got no business here."

"Go stick your head in an oven, man," laughed a third.

"He's a real cutie pie in that apron, ain't he?" said a fourth.

And as their attention turned steadily from the pigeon lady to him, it occurred to Pasco what a ridiculous figure he must cut: a middle-aged man, wrapped in an apron, armed with a broomstick, facing down an urban wolf-pack.

Recognizing the tenuousness of his situation, feeling himself grow frail, he only vaguely heard the distant screech of car tires, but the skinheads reacted instantaneously, their gaze shifting beyond him to the street. The tension left their bodies, their stances grew casual. Arms folded, hands slid into pockets. The leader reached into his coat for a pack of cigarettes.

Pasco glanced quickly over his shoulder. Sean and Kurt, nightsticks in hand, were striding towards them.

"Trouble, Pasco?" Sean said.

Pasco couldn't find his voice, gestured at the skins and the pigeon lady.

Sean waved his club at the leader. "Beat it, Emile."

Emile coolly sucked at his cigarette. "It's a public park, man."

"Don't give me any trouble, Emile."

"We're just hangin' around, man. Mindin' our own business."

"Go hang around somewhere else," Kurt said. He was slowly circling to the right of the group.

"You gonna make us go?" another skinhead said. "You and your little stick?" He grabbed his crotch, laughed mockingly. "I'll bet my stick's bigger'n yours."

Kurt hesitated only a moment. Then he lashed out, tumbling the boy and pinning him to the ground.

His companions yelled in protest, but they didn't move.

Emile, eyes narrowing, said, "Temper temper."

"Let him up, Kurt," Sean said with easy authority.

Kurt released him, pulled back. The boy sprang to his feet, dusted off his leather.

Sean said, "Move it, Emile. I'm not askin' a second time."

Emile tossed his cigarette to the grass, ground it under his boot. His pack grouped around him. As they moved off, he said to Sean, "You better watch your friend there, man. Nasty little temper he's got." Then he winked at Pasco. "As for you, old man, we know where to find you, right?" He snickered. "Maybe we'll stop by for lunch sometime."

Sean seized Kurt by the arm, pulled him several paces off. A squirrel scampered away from them. They exchanged furious words in hushed voices.

The pigeon lady still sat immobile on the bench. She hadn't moved.

Pasco took a step towards her.

Her good eye panicked. She seized up her half-empty bag and, without a further glance at him, shuffled off in the direction from which she'd come.

When he got back to the restaurant, Pasco found Sklewy sitting at a table, his plastic bag bulky on his lap.

"Help you?" Pasco said. According to Fong, Sklewy was not a beggar. He occasionally stopped in at the vegetable and fruit store to buy an apple or a banana, a handful of grapes.

Sklewy responded with a childlike smile.

"You hungry? You want lunch?"

He nodded once, a slow and graceful movement of his head.

"Hamburger? Fries?"

The smile again, and a slow blinking of the eyes.

"Costs five bucks. You got five bucks?"

Sklewy's face went inert.

"So, how much you got then?"

He held up two fingers, the nails long and blackened.

"Well you're in luck. Today's special is burger, fries and a coffee, all for one dollar."

Sklewy, his face serious, gave a brief nod.

Pasco prepared the meal, served it.

While Sklewy ate, Pasco leaned on the counter and reviewed the tensions of the past few minutes. He ignored his own performance: that was incidental. Concentrated instead on the greater anxiety, the one that had remained with him: not the skinheads—their only surprise was their postured submission to authority—but Kurt and the flash of violence that Sean had had to dominate.

Sklewy, finished, patted his lips with a napkin and motioned for the bill. Pasco brought it to his table. Sklewy fished two dollar coins from his pocket, put them into Pasco's hand.

Pasco shook his head. "It's only a buck," he said, giving back one of the coins. Then he collected the dishes and took them around to the sink.

When he went back to wipe the table down, Sklewy was already halfway out the door. And lying squarely in the centre of the tabletop was the dollar coin he had returned.

Pasco, staring at his tip, marvelled.

———————

The wind picked up gradually and by the time he got home that night, buffeted by its gusts, his cheeks numb from the cold, he knew he would not be sleeping well. For windy nights, the provocations of their clamorous darkness, made Pasco restless. The silken whispers, the breathless silences, the moaning and whistling and subtle creaking of the house were like voices nagging themselves with ragged insistence into his head.

In his bedroom he pulled on his dressing gown, a terrycloth robe so ancient that when Danny was eleven or twelve he'd worn it to play Joseph in a school nativity play, with one of his mother's headbands holding a dishtowel around his head. Holes gaped under the arms and the collar hung detached on one side. Danny had given him a new one a couple of Christmases back but he'd never bothered to remove it from the box. He liked his old robe, was attached to it and saw no reason to change simply because it had seen better days.

He had always been that way, most comfortable in clothes only when all traces of newness had been ground from them. One of his clearest childhood memories was of a particular pair of pants—navy blue, with an elastic waistband and heavy stitching along the seams—that had practically become part of him. He'd gone everywhere, done everything, in them. They had come, in time, to fit him like no other. As tough as leather on the outside, they were on the inside, against his skin, as tender as the calfskin gloves his client Aldo wore. Putting them on in the mornings, he felt prepared for the challenges of his rough-and-tumble world. Even when their colour had faded, their knees worn through and their hems shredded, he insisted on wearing them.

He looked, his mother said with a deepening frown, like a hobo. And one day when he was in the shower, she tossed the pants into the garbage.

When she told him what she had done, he was horrified and, with a towel preserving modesty, dashed to the rescue.

She would not be swayed, though, and promptly threw them out again. Once more defiant, he fished them from among eggshells and rotting vegetables.

She tried tempting him with a brand-new pair.

He objected to the colour. Sky blue, he said, was for girls.

But they weren't *sky* blue, she pointed out, they were *baby* blue. He almost choked.

But she remained unsympathetic, wrested the old pair from his grasp and sent him to his room.

The moment he was allowed out, he went digging through the garbage. Old envelopes, mouldering bread crusts, chunks of meat turning interesting colours, chicken bones, blackened potato remains: his bare hands dealt with them all. But his pants weren't to be found. And there was no point in looking further, his mother told him, they were gone, he'd never see them again: she had buried them in the garden. "Say a prayer for them," she suggested to the temper tantrum reddening his face.

When the first hole appeared under the arm of his bathrobe, Edna offered to buy him a new one. To Pasco this sounded like a threat. He became wholly unreasonable. Edna mended it as best she could and never brought the subject up again. The clasp of the old bathrobe, she came to accept, told him he was home. Its very rattiness—the word she used—was a kind of security to him.

Pasco poured himself a beer and, tugging the bathrobe more closely around him, prepared to spend the rest of the evening at the kitchen table going through the newspapers. He sifted through them, tossing out the advertisements and the sports and business sections.

They had stacked up. Every morning he bought copies of both the *Globe* and the *Star* at Fong's, but he rarely read either on the day it was published. He'd once been a voracious newspaper reader, especially back in the sixties when the world seemed to be tailspinning towards oblivion. Nuclear tensions, military confrontations, political assassinations, drugs that could be smoked, swallowed or injected. Cities down south dissolving in gunfire and Molotov cocktails. Racial anger, ideological anger, sexual anger. The times had been such that a man, if he was to survive, had to know what was going on.

Years later, Pasco would view as obscene the longing and nostalgia with which people looked back on the decade, as though all there had been was the music.

At the time he had thought it a return to barbarism, the world rocking and rolling around a dissolving centre. He found himself living with a continuous tension, rising every morning and turning on the radio expecting—fearing—to hear news of U.S. and Soviet troop movements, of nuclear bombers and missiles on alert to reduce the world to cinders.

Once in a while anger would flare. Tough words would be exchanged, sabres rattled, governments overthrown. Maybe a few thousand people would be killed in some distant country ruled by men with unpronounceable names—although no country was ever distant enough to prevent politicians from glimpsing tottering dominoes. And their visions of apocalypse, breathlessly shared, would present Pasco with his own personal vision: the front windows of the house shattering before a hot white blast, Danny and Edna and him crouched at the base of the far wall melting to their skeletons before they could feel any pain.

Yet somehow the world trundled on. He went about his daily business, dealing as always with the bills and the little crises, all the minutiae of domestic life—his stomach never quite settled, his tensions never quite stilled.

And gradually the waiting wore him down. He grew weary of the suspense, longed for the Armageddon anxiety to be over and done with. Some people protested. They marched, or they wrote letters. Pasco was inclined to neither. He instead reduced his intake of news by waiting several days before opening a newspaper.

He soon came to the conclusion that the incomplete immediacy of daily journalism served only to encourage heartburn. Today's murder was replaced by tomorrow's fire and the following day's robbery—all destined to be forgotten by the following week save for a residue of unease.

The frozen runaway he'd found in the park had been page one news the day after he discovered her. The *Toronto Sun* tabloid even covered its front page with a colour photograph of the body being wheeled away, comforting its readers two pages later with a swimsuit-clad beauty who had found happiness cheerleading for the Toronto Argonauts football team. The day after, the story was on page five, receding within days to page eleven and then oblivion. What, Pasco wondered, had been the bloody point? Nothing had been learnt, no conclusions drawn, no steps taken. A teenaged runaway had died, and her death had sold a few newspapers.

Pasco pulled the folds of the bathrobe more tightly around his exposed legs as he continued scanning the papers for something worth reading. Bouncer shot outside tavern. Woman raped. Cab driver's throat slashed. Bus driver stabbed eight times. Police accused of racism. Crack house raided. Fire kills two, arson suspected.

He no longer read these stories, had come to see them as a kind of journalistic gossip. It wasn't so much that the events themselves were unimportant—the runaway's face, a greyed mask of defeated youth, had haunted him for months—as that their presentation diminished them, the people involved, like the runaway, lost in the drama.

Newspapers, aiming simply to titillate with tragedy, told Pasco little about life. He concentrated instead on the longer feature articles, usually written with an eye to the larger picture and not burning with the heat of the moment. The radio kept him up to date on what was going on in the city, the country, the world. Informed, then, but not battered. He owed the world no more than that.

A dull ache pulsed in his eyes. He had run through articles on the federal debt, apartheid, the Amazon rainforest, nuclear disarmament. Yet the reality of it all eluded him.

The wind still howled outside. He yawned. He knew he would not sleep, not for a while yet, but he needed at least to close his eyes. Pushing the newspapers aside, he turned off the light and went up the stairs. He took two aspirins for the pressure that was building in his forehead and as he got under the covers he thought:

You see, Edna....

———————————

The wind whistled through his mind, the images liquid, the thoughts wayward: strangers and friends, smiles and grimaces. Snatches of song and pieces of conversation. Lorraine in the garden, the guys in the Gate. Danny slapping the back of one hand into the palm of the other, for emphasis.

Nothing complete, everything senseless: the world swirled disordered within his head.

He twisted around, the old bed rocking gently under him, its springs squeaky with rust. Some nights, merely shifting in the bed would be sufficient to soothe him, to cap the runaway flow in his brain.

Not tonight, though.

Already his knees were chafing, the dampness probing into the caps.

It was too late to muffle the wind. Once rooted in his mind, it took on a life all its own, raging unhindered as it pulled the havoc of yesterday into the havoc of today.

Wind, and noises unsettling in their namelessness: it had been like this the night his father died.

A storm had sprung up in the darkness, the wind almost smothering the rumble of heavy rain. He had got out of bed, stood at the window watching nature on the rampage: the trees swaying and pitching and spitting leaves into the night; lightning diffusing into the clouds; the crackle of muffled thunder. As he watched, he dimly heard the sound of splintering wood seconds before the window sprang open, rain spattering cold onto his face, wind pushing and swiping at him.

At that moment somewhere in northern Ontario, on a narrow unlit road between two one-motel towns, his father lost control of the car.

Chilled flesh, watery eyes.

The casket was sealed. His father had gone through the windshield, the glass shredding his face and bald head like a grater. The disfigurement, the funeral director insisted, was beyond the skills of the most talented cosmetician, was no sight for a bereaved widow or a nineteen-year-old boy. Watching the pallbearers from the local Legion Hall struggle with his father's casket, Pasco—still Gil to everyone—remembered the wind, felt anew the lash of it in the still afternoon. And he knew that he would never forget the way it had surged into his room, sudden and inescapable.

His first responsibility had been to keep from his mother the news that a woman had been found in the car with his father, a woman "with a certain reputation", as the sympathetic policeman had whispered. Her neck was broken, there was no known family, it could all be hushed up, "out of respect". Respect for whom? Pasco had wanted to ask the policeman, but thought better of it.

His second responsibility as he saw it was to set aside his plans for an education. His father, it was immediately clear, had left only debts. There was little money in the bank and he'd allowed the insurance payments to lapse. Until his mother found her equilibrium, and she never really would, he had to find a way to earn money. A full-time job was the only answer. The day after the funeral, he withdrew from the university. In the circumstances, his dreams of a professional career—unformed, flirting with the practicality of law but attracted to the more fluid notions of philosophy—seemed fanciful.

The footwear company his father had worked for offered him the one vacancy it had—his father's job. He declined, and was given with obvious relief a cheque for his father's final earnings, minus the cost of replacing the company materials lost in the crash.

He wasn't long in finding a sales job in a gentlemen's apparel shop on Yonge Street. He wasn't, like his father, a natural salesman. He had to work hard at the tricks of the job to ensure that a customer left not just with a suit but with various accoutrements as well: a shirt to go with the jacket, a tie to go with the shirt, a pin to go with the tie, a belt to go with the trousers. It was difficult working through his initial distaste at having to convince a man who wanted only a suit that he needed the accessories as well, but his boss hovered, a constant reminder that his continued employment depended on his powers of persuasion. And he surprised himself by doing well enough that his father's creditors stopped sending intimidating letters.

Every morning on his way to work, and every evening on his way home, he would stop in at Pascal's restaurant for a coffee. It was here that he met and got to know Edna, another breakfast regular. She was a small, feisty woman who had moved to Toronto from a tiny town in Saskatchewan—no big dreams, just a hankering after a life more promising than any possible in a small farming community. She lived in a rooming house in the area and had a job, just a few doors down from the gentlemen's apparel shop, as an inventory clerk in a family-owned hardware company. The first time they met at the restaurant counter he surreptitiously checked her hand for a wedding band; he had never done that before with any woman. He saw that her hands were well cared for and, to his relief, that the ring finger was bare.

He took to her quickly. Her directness attracted him—she had the steadiest gaze he had ever encountered, her light brown eyes never wavering from his—and he admired the strength that was evident in the way she moved, the way she held herself: Edna appeared at times a taller woman than she was.

Yet she had felt her size keenly, claimed that people—not only men but women too, which made her angrier—missed her in a crowd. Not seeing her, they made her the unwitting victim of their wayward elbows, careless shoes, their pushing and shoving. Her response had been to wear bright colours and, even though they hurt her feet, high-heeled shoes. She reasoned that even if people couldn't see her, they couldn't miss the clothes, a sensible enough theory, Pasco had thought.

The days before Christmas were the worst of times for her. She swore every year that she'd get her shopping done weeks ahead of the crowds, but she'd never succeeded. Once, as she stood on an escalator in Simpson's, a hurrying man jostled her hard enough to leave a bruise on her ribs. Her high heels gave way. By the time she got back to the rooming house her right ankle had swollen to twice its size. X-rays showed only a severe sprain—she was able to hobble into Pascal's the next day, limp in the day after that—but she brooded for weeks afterwards, consoling herself with boxes of Black Magic and bags of her favourite chocolate-covered almonds. "You see, Edna," Pasco had remarked, "theory is always battered by reality." She didn't thank him for pointing out the little philosophical truth.

They began meeting for lunch. Lunch led to dinner, dinner to movies and dances.

After six months he accepted that he was in love. Walking her home one snowy evening after a movie, he casually asked her to marry him. And she refused. They were too young, she said, it would be impractical. He agreed to wait.

He continued at his job, doing so well that he was even able to put aside a few dollars every month after the household expenses had been paid. Yet this very success, his proven ability, engendered in him a desire to claim his independence. His father had always complained bitterly about his boss, and Pasco, silently chafing under the gaze of his own boss, began thinking what a fine thing it would be to do what his father had always threatened to do but had never come close to achieving: to go into business for himself, spurred on by fantasies not so much of wealth as of freedom.

Edna, listening to him dream out loud, agreed that, yes, it would be a fine thing, but risky. Her caution, which he interpreted as concern for his welfare, touched him.

One year later—he had noted the date—he again asked her to marry him and, to his surprise, she accepted. When he asked what had changed her mind, she said, "You're still working at that job you hate. I like that. You have your dreams but you're not reckless. I like that, too. You have character. I think you'll make a fine husband." He blushed at her words. Noticing this, she promptly added: "You're not terribly imaginative, though. But then again maybe that's not such a bad thing. Too much imagination can lead to trouble."

But did she love him?

"Of course I do," she replied, clearly surprised that he had felt compelled to ask.

After a quiet wedding at City Hall witnessed by Pushpull, a few friends of Edna's from the rooming house and his mother, Edna moved into the house.

They lived a quiet life, Edna and his mother establishing a polite but distant accommodation between themselves. By the time Danny was born a year and a day later, Pasco had moved to a better-paying job selling insurance. From selling men accessories they didn't need to selling them policies they didn't want: despite his growing unease, there was no choice. His mother was practically bedridden, the baby had to be fed and clothed. Edna had, with great reluctance, been forced to quit her job.

His mother died only a few months later, praising the memory of her husband with her diminishing breath. His name was the final word she said. At least, Pasco comforted himself, she had breathed her last unhappy over his absence but not bitter over his memory. It wasn't much, but it was something. Only after her funeral did he tell Edna about the woman who had died in the car with his father. She assured him he had done the right thing.

Pasco was too good at selling insurance for his own comfort. He accepted praise and bonuses with a reticence his bosses put down to modesty but which he knew sprang from a darker, less praiseworthy source. For despite himself he told his clients the standard tales with a conviction that haunted him afterwards.

A shake of the head, a look of sadness: *Just lost a client, you see. Didn't have much life insurance. Tried to tell him he should raise the level of coverage. The price of living today, you know, think of the wife and child trying to make it without him. But he wouldn't go for it. The wife wanted to use the money for a new dishwasher instead. It was delivered two days ago. Just heard this morning the guy had a heart attack on the way to work. Dead before he hit the ground. Now his wife has a new dishwasher but she'll probably have to sell the house, find a job.* A shake of the head, a sigh of regret. *Tried to tell him: You can never have too much life insurance.*

The story worked almost every time. The unfortunate client had died so often, Pasco had almost begun believing in the reality of him: late thirties, unruly hair, dishevelled, overweight, harried—and the wife and child, each perfectly put together in a house that fairly glowed. He even dreamed from time to time of the man's demise: a hot, crowded streetcar, a pallor on a sweaty face; then puzzlement, shock; a hand clutching at a chest, knees buckling and the man falling among a forest of skittish legs.

So Pasco was more than prepared to act when, not long after Danny's fifth birthday, he noticed the FOR SALE sign in the window of Pascal's. He inquired. Mr. Pascal was friendly but sceptical. What did he know about running a restaurant? And then there was the question of the down payment.

He left the restaurant with his excitement tempered, but his mind made up. Certainly cooking couldn't be that difficult; Edna, or even Mr. Pascal himself, could teach him what he needed to know. The house, long paid for, would serve as collateral for a loan. The only difficulty would be that down payment. His savings fell fifteen hundred dollars short of Mr. Pascal's minimum, and the thought of emptying the kitty, leaving nothing to fall back on, frightened him.

That night after dinner, he and Edna discussed buying Pascal's. She was not enthusiastic. Neither of them knew anything about the restaurant business, and she wasn't terribly thrilled at the thought of his being a short-order cook. While she was no snob, her notions of respectability hovered well above the picture of her husband wrapped in an apron serving up hamburgers and fries.

He was stung. The apron was of no consequence; it was just a uniform, like the jacket and tie he wore to sell fear. What mattered was the freedom Pascal's represented. As the words poured from him, the persuasiveness with which he sold insurance crept into his voice. He knew it was there, could sense it. He spoke with passion of the years he'd spent at jobs he detested; with pain about the people he'd fooled. He told of the man who died again and again in his nightmares; complained about his bosses, men who cared nothing for the individuals behind the sales figures, hearing to his dismay his father's voice in his.

And eventually, though with reservations, Edna gave in. "If you really want to do this…." she said, and fetched from the bedroom a bank passbook he hadn't known she had. She handed it to him. "There's almost two thousand dollars here. Now you have enough for the down payment." These were her savings, she explained, the nest egg that was her way out if the marriage collapsed, that was to have been Danny's university fund if it didn't. "This money represents *my* freedom, Gil. Don't waste it." He swore that he wouldn't, even promised to pay it back with interest as soon as he was able, but he could see that she was not reassured.

A few weeks later, Mr. Pascal came by to turn over the keys. They celebrated, but Edna would not join them. She was not generally a superstitious woman but as she left them to their bottle she made clear her feeling that at least one of them should maintain a sober head at the beginning of this new venture. Pasco respected her anxieties.

When he rolled into bed that night, his head spinning, she told him she had decided to return to work. He was too drunk to argue.

Pasco tossed the blankets aside, pulled the bathrobe around his shoulders and got the rub from the bathroom. His knees and ankles were all, as he thought of it, acting up. He massaged them, feeling the warmth working its way down into his tissues, soothing them.

He flexed his knees, stretched his ankles to the edge of a cramp. The wind was moaning outside, gusts of it hissing and whistling through the myriad gaps in the roof. He stood up, wandered over to the window. Through the dusty glass, shadows wobbled in the swaying light of the streetlamps. A plastic garbage can rolled and bounced down the street. The lights still blazed in the renovated house. Several brightly dressed people were seated around a dining table, their dinner party dragging into the small hours of the morning.

Wind and its noises: it had been this way, too, the night before Edna died.

They had both slept badly. Edna had been having headaches for about a week. Aspirins and the massages he gave her had little effect. She'd gone to the doctor for a check-up and he'd pronounced her as fit as a horse, to which she'd replied, "A pony, maybe. I'm not *that* big." He'd scheduled further tests for the following week and sent her off with a prescription for stronger pills. But the new pills were also ineffective and she had spent much of that night tossing and turning. Pasco could do little for her, dozing off for short periods only when she did.

They gave up on sleep when dawn brightened the windows. Edna sat up in bed and tried to distract herself from the pain by working on her nails while Pasco went downstairs to make coffee. When he came back, she was cleaning her nails with a cotton wad and nail-polish remover, the polish on the cotton looking like blood swabbed from a wound.

He put her coffee on her night table and sat on the other side of the bed. Her eyes were red, dark circles forming beneath them. He asked her how her headache was.

"Getting worse," she said in the even voice she used when putting up with distress.

He offered more pills, but she just shook her head in refusal. Their only effect was to upset her stomach, so what was the point?

She closed her eyes for a moment, then shook herself and reached for her nail file. As she drew it along the curve of a nail, she began speaking about Danny. He was always so busy, he rarely called, hardly ever came by, and whenever she called he seemed to resent the intrusion. There were times, she confessed, when she wondered whether he loved her, although deep down she knew that he did, he must, she was his mother after all.

Pasco nodded, murmured reassurance, but he had his own questions about Danny.

"I just wish," she said, "that we could have helped him more. I always wanted to."

Pasco thought about the two thousand dollars he had never managed to pay back, and which she had never mentioned.

"Help put him through university or something," she continued. "It's so expensive these days. He has dreams, Pasco. Just like—" Suddenly her words broke off and she gasped.

Pasco, sipping his coffee, looked up.

Her eyes were shut tight, her mouth falling open. Her fingers flared, the nail file tumbling to her lap.

Pasco said, "Edna?"

Her hands clamped onto her head, as if trying to contain an explosion within.

His coffee mug fell from his hands, and he scrambled across the bed to her. The moment he touched her elbow she went slack, her head collapsing backwards, her arms falling to her sides.

"Edna?"

At the hospital, the doctors explained the meaning of the word "aneurysm".

Days passed before her heart ceased beating.

He remembered standing dazed beside the satin-lined coffin in which she lay, Danny to his right, Lorraine to his left, each with a hand lightly grasping his arm. He was grateful that someone had painted her nails. And as he watched her face grown younger in death, his mind picked up their interrupted conversation. He thought: You see, Edna....

And he hadn't stopped since.

Chapter Eleven

ANDREAS, smartly dressed as usual, was in the barren lobby of the new condominium building poring over a sketchpad. He was preoccupied, eyes darting from his drawings to the bare concrete walls, pencil darting here and there on the paper, erasing, sketching, scribbling. He barely looked up when Danny and Pasco came in, their footsteps echoing in the emptiness he was planning to fill.

"Working on Sunday, Andreas?" Danny said.

"Art knows no holidays, Danny."

Danny didn't bother to introduce his father. Andreas at work was all business. He would acknowledge the presence of others and grudgingly exchange small talk, but his eyes and hands remained engrossed. He specialized in themes, viewing an empty space, he'd once said to Danny, the way a sculptor did a chunk of raw marble or—in typical Andreas style—the way a lover approached a fresh virgin: as material for spinning fantasies. In one lobby he'd constructed a tropical jungle, full-sized trees reaching up behind glass to simulated suns. In another, he'd re-created a corner of the Alhambra, the Hall of the Kings captured in a *trompe-l'oeil* of seductive perfection. For this lobby he had in mind a desert oasis. Sand, date palms, the illusion of dunes, maybe a Bedouin tent. A spring would gurgle from a crystal-studded rock formation, although it would offer only plain water and not the chilled Perrier Andreas had hoped for.

Pasco followed Danny across the rough concrete floor to an elevator. The gloom of the unfinished lobby effectively banished the day, the cold brightness surviving only in reflection in the smudged brass of the elevator door.

Lorraine had been at the house earlier that morning—she'd brought a hot apple pie—when Danny had called to ask if he could come over. Not up to arguing with his son on a Sunday morning, Pasco's instinct had been to refuse—there's a time and a place, as he'd said to Danny at the Starting Gate—but Danny was insistent. He wasn't far away, he said, could be there in minutes. Lorraine, eavesdropping with her usual candour, had planted her face inches from Pasco's and mouthed the words *Talk more.* Under her prodding, Pasco compromised: he suggested a drive.

Danny, in apparent good humour, readily agreed. "Like the old days," he said.

"Sort of," Pasco replied, his eyes rolling at Lorraine's wink of approval. The old days: Edna had enjoyed spending the occasional Sunday afternoon in the car "tooling around", as she called it, going here and there with no purpose other than movement. As he drove, she would roll down the window to feel the wind and, if Danny was with them, she would put on the radio so the two of them could hum to the music. The old days: they felt like the very old days now. After her death, Pasco sold the car for a pittance; it was, after all, of no further use to him.

Danny pressed the button for the fifteenth floor. The elevator, of brass and mirrors, reminded Pasco of a fancy washroom, and he found himself patting his hair dishevelled by the wind into place.

Danny, amused, said, "Exactly. A little touch for the ladies."

"The gentlemen, too. But if you don't watch out,"—Pasco patted the crown of his own head—"you won't be needing a mirror 'cept for shaving."

Danny grunted in displeasure. As far back as he could remember, his father's attentions had carried an edge equivocal in its intention: the humour meant to tickle rankled instead. He self-consciously smoothed his thinning spot.

———————

Talk more, Lorraine said. But talk had come no more easily in the car than elsewhere. They had commented like polite strangers on the weather, going on at embarrassing length about the crispness of the air, the blue of the sky, had informed each other about the forecast for tomorrow and lamented the inaccuracy of weathermen armed with satellite pictures and computer projections.

Danny had headed north on the Don Valley Parkway. An autumn drive through the valley was one of the most spectacular in the city, the thickly wooded hills on either side seething with colours bewildering to the senses. But it was much too late in the season. The leaves had long fallen. The hills, moist and greyish brown, were shabby with pockets of snow and crusted ice.

Pasco said it was too bad.

Danny agreed: Yes, it was too bad.

Danny hadn't said where they were going—his driving, Pasco could see, was not aimless—and they'd ended up in a part of the city unfamiliar to Pasco, one of those sections which had, not that long ago, been all open field and horse pasture. Now, claimed by the city, divided and subdivided, it had been turned into real estate, developers putting in sewers and roads and stamping out houses identical except in colour. Pasco didn't mind—progress always exacted a certain price and this seemed a reasonable one— but there was something startling in the realization that whole sections of the city in which he'd grown up had become strange to him.

Danny slowed as they approached an unfinished building of

monolithic proportions. At the entrance to the driveway a signboard announced:

THE HEIGHTS OF AVALLON

Luxury Condominiums From $250,000
"An Exclusive Lifestyle For Discriminating Adults"
A Simmons Construction Company Development

The company logo—a lion standing upright against a stylized
S—was embedded in the front wall of the building. Pasco suppressed a chuckle when, on seeing it, he remembered the term
with which disgruntled tenants referred to Simmons's properties.
Yet he couldn't help saying, "You're not taking me to see an S-hole,
are you, Danny?"

Danny ignored the question. Without a word, pulled up into
the unfinished driveway.

"You've got to be kidding." Pasco shook his head. He felt as if
they had driven up to a *House & Garden* advertisement. "What are
we doing here?"

"I thought that since we were in the area—"

"By accident, I suppose."

"I thought I'd show you our latest project."

"You trying to impress me?"

But Danny had already stepped out of the car.

———

The elevator opened to a narrow corridor, long and dimly lit, the
carpet springy underfoot. As they walked past the naked walls,
Pasco thought of something Sean had once said. He had been
talking about tight situations policemen faced, had mentioned, as
an example, corridors just like this one and the nightmare of
being confronted by a gunman bursting from one of the apart-

ments. "With all those doors," Sean had said, "there's no place to go, nothing to do except crouch and fire."

"Crouch and fire," Pasco muttered as Danny opened one of the doors.

"Pardon, Dad?"

"Nothing."

"This," Danny said motioning him inside, "is our presentation suite."

It was like stepping from a construction zone into the ordered and the unfamiliar. Chrome and plastic, steel and glass. Furniture that looked less like furniture than like equipment for a spaceship. The only wood in evidence—and it was obviously fake—was a bookcase that devoted more space to a television, VCR and stereo than to books. Danny noticed his interest in "the home entertainment centre", but pointed out that it was just for display, it didn't come with the condo.

"Two bedrooms and a den leading to a sunroom," Danny said, his palm indicating a corridor. "Kitchen with breakfast nook, separate dining area, totally private sundeck with a kitchen garden off to one side. Jacuzzi in the bathroom with a view of the city. Recreation and workout facilities in the basement, pool and tennis courts out back. The works."

Pasco stood in the middle of the living room, not certain what to make of it all.

"Maximum comfort for minimum effort," Danny said.

Pasco nodded. He knew he was supposed to be impressed, but—

"Well?" Danny said, his voice expectant.

"Well…."

"What d'you think?"

"Give me a minute."

"Sure. Take your time. Look around."

"I'm not in the market, Danny."

"Good thing too, Pops—"

Pops? Danny'd never called him that before.

"—this place'd set you back a cool half-million. And if you need underground parking, that's another thirty."

"Dollars?"

"Thousand."

"All this for that, eh?" Where did his son get his ease with, even enthusiasm for, such difficult sums? Not from him, certainly, and not from his mother—*Moms*?—either. What would Edna have thought of all this? Pasco wondered. "And what d'you get for a quarter-million like the sign says?"

"One bedroom, no sunroom, no breakfast nook, no kitchen garden."

"Jacuzzi?"

"Of course. It's aimed at the singles market."

Pasco approached the bookcase: hardcovers of uniform height. There were the Britannicas and, to his delight, Trotsky. "The books," he said. "Nice touch."

"Got them from your friend on Queen Street." Danny slid open the door to the sundeck. "He gave me a nice deal on them."

"The man's a thief."

"What's that?"

"Just talking to myself. That Cruise, one hell of a nice guy." He followed Danny out to the sundeck. At this height, the wind was constant, with a greater bite than on the ground. Pasco's eyes immediately burned and watered. His ears and cheeks prickled hot. But the view, which Danny enthusiastically pointed out, was impressive: to the north, a few recent buildings widely scattered among evergreens, rolling hills burnt by the cold; to the south, the downtown core hard and immutable yet almost translucent, like a formation of rock crystal at this distance.

The kitchen garden was a disappointment: a trough of soil, three feet long by three wide, maybe a foot and a half deep. It wasn't intended for growing vegetables, Danny explained, but for raising herbs. Pasco thought it would be put to better use as a fish pond or, at a pinch, a children's wading pool. Danny, deaf to the sarcasm, pronounced it an interesting idea.

Back inside, Pasco said, "Do people really buy places like this, Danny? Where do they get the money?"

"Let me put it like this, Pops. Most of these suites are already spoken for. And most of the buyers are in their thirties. Up and comers. Stockbrokers, financial consultants, lawyers, several CAs, entrepreneurs of one kind or another."

Pasco rubbed at his cheeks, warming them. "Danny, have I ever told you about a man named Sklewy?"

"I know, I know. Pops, gimme a break." They had been through this argument before, had traded all the old familiar disagreements. It was a subject particularly unsettling to Danny, for the homeless and the panhandlers, the *street people* as he preferred to think of them, terrified him. He would not dwell on the dismal details of their lives, hardly dared even acknowledge their existence any more. They—the lion's food, in Mr. Simmons's phrase—were in many ways a mystery to him. While he understood the reasons for their descent to be many and varied—ill luck, laziness, lack of initiative—what he could not fathom was why they continued to live as they did. They struck him as people more than resigned to their fate, as people who had resigned from life itself. With their ragged clothes and oily skin and eyes darkened by neglect, they were what he feared he would turn into were he not focused and ruthless in pursuit of his goals. He couldn't contemplate holding out his hand and asking for loose change: he would rather die.

"Listen, Pops, I'm in business. And business can't afford to be sentimental." Danny banged the sliding door shut, bolted it, as if, Pasco thought, fearing a break-in fifteen floors up. "Sure we could build low-cost housing, but that's just a way of buying off your conscience. We can't afford to think that way. If we don't make a profit we sink. You've got to move forward, do better this year than last year. That's the bottom line. Black ink." Danny, confidence showing in his stride, moved farther into the living room. "That's what makes the country tick, Pops."

"I'm comfortable just floating along."

"Can't float forever."

"So gurgle-gurgle."

"You're impossible sometimes." But there was no anger in his voice. Pasco thought he even heard a note of affection, as if Danny recognized it as a quality they shared.

"You know what your problem is, Danny?"

"No, but I'm sure you're going to tell me."

"You don't know the difference between your country and your company. Only a fool would say money's not important— God knows I know better—but, you know, I'd be willing to put my life on the line for my country like your grandad did, but d'you seriously think I'd do the same thing for a company?"

"I have commitment, Dad. I believe in the pursuit of happiness."

"You're sounding like an American. It's just another way to say the pursuit of money."

"What's wrong with Americans?"

"You're not hearing me, Danny." What Pasco wanted to say but dared not was, Danny, you're my son and I love you but you reek of Simmons, and for all your grandeur and your talk of millions, you and that company you work for carry around the stench of rooming houses. His energy left him. "I don't know, Danny. Maybe you're right. Maybe...." Was he just constructing excuses for his own lack of success? "God knows, your mother always wished we had more money, she wished we could have taken it a little easier, helped you out a bit more...."

Danny's lips tightened against one another and slowly twisted into a small smile. "Mom would've loved all this, eh, Pops?"

"Danny, do me a favour, stop calling me Pops."

Danny nodded. "You got it." He removed his hands from his pockets, gestured around the room. "So tell me." He cleared his throat. "D'you think Mom would've, you know—"

"Loved all this?" Pasco immediately regretted his tone of condescension: there was something intense, needful, in Danny's gaze. "It's really important to you, eh?" he said, with some surprise. Danny looked away through the window to the sundeck.

Would Edna have loved all this? Pasco didn't think so. It was too glittery, too precious, too shrill in its demand for adulation. Despite her clothes, there had been no real ostentation to Edna. Maybe she would have admired it, though, in some distant way. And maybe—who could tell?—she would have been impressed with her son and his achievements. "I think she would have been very proud, Danny," Pasco finally said. "Very proud, despite everything."

Danny smiled, his teeth nipping at his lower lip. And for those few seconds, he was a boy again.

"By the way," Pasco said as Danny ushered him from the condominium and locked the door behind them. "Why the Heights of Avallon?"

"Marketing."

"Aren't we in Scarborough?"

"Dad, who wants to shell out for a luxury condo in the Heights of Scarberia, for God's sake?"

———

Danny drove them to a restaurant he knew at Yonge and Eglinton. The area, though vastly changed in the years he had not come north, brought memories back to Pasco. They now called here "midtown", Danny informed him, but back when he and Edna

used to take their occasional Saturday evening walk in the neighbourhood the city had not yet begun to think of itself in sections.

Edna had liked the residential side streets. She was attracted to
their air of settled calm: to the leafy trees that overhung the sidewalks, to the houses fronted by well-tended gardens that suggested ease and a kind of gentrified comfort: stone fireplaces,
plush rugs, heavy furniture. The kinds of houses in which people
would serve sherry to company and play bridge to pass the time.

Younger, Pasco had been prey to momentary impatience with
the familiar and he had, more than once, suggested a walk
through High Park instead, not so much because he enjoyed its
vast expanse and the natural solitude it offered in the midst of the
city, but for a simple change of scenery. Edna had rarely accepted.
She didn't seek retreat from the city, or the illusion of it. A woman
firm in her convictions, she didn't believe in half-measures.
Selling the cottage had meant resolutely putting the rural behind
them. Yet she occasionally needed a taste of unruffled solidity, and
took delight in the thoughtful urban blend of the quiet side
streets.

He had once asked her if she wanted to move into the area and
she replied, with no hesitation, that she didn't, she was happy
where she was. Pasco remained grateful for that answer; it showed
that even if Edna had had her dissatisfactions with their life—for
what were these walks if not sniffing around the edges of a
fantasy?—she had not been unhappy with what they had been
able to build together.

Danny said, "What's up, Pops—I mean, Dad? It's like you're in
a different world."

Pasco shook himself. "Well, I am, aren't I." He looked around
at the packed restaurant. "It's kind of like being in a black-and-
white TV, if you get my drift." The walls of the restaurant were a
check of black and white tiles; the tables were black, the chairs
white, the servers in black and white outfits; even the majority of

the customers were dressed in black with white or silver high-
lights. The only colour was a red rose in a white vase on each table.

"Like it?" Danny said. "Andreas had a hand in it. It's his chess-
board concept."

"It's all right." The decor was attractive, with a pleasing lack of
frill and neatness of line, the qualities Pasco most admired and
sought to bring out in the old furniture he restored. Yet there was
something unsettling about it too—not just in the decor but in
the fact that this was Sunday, in Toronto, and restaurants were
legally open and bustling. Once upon a time you would find such
a Sunday crowd only in church, or in jail. Now people thronged
everywhere eating and drinking, browsing and buying. To Pasco
there was still something audacious in that. It had been such a
tight-ass city—Cruise's term was crude but apt—and still was in
some respects, despite the ripping of the corset.

The food—*frites* and *hambourgeois à la Newyorkaise* with a
salade du chef on the side—was edible if a bit on the bland side.
The waiter hesitated only a little when Pasco asked for ketchup
instead of the homemade mayonnaise.

"You eat here often, Danny?"

"Once in a while."

"So how come you don't come by Pascal's? I serve the same
food, only better and cheaper and without the fancy names."

"For Christ's sake, Dad—"

"Okay, never mind."

He and Edna had always ended their walks at Fran's on Yonge
Street with a hot chocolate and a Danish, strawberry for her, apple
for him. She had had a ferocious sweet-tooth which she indulged
as often as she wished and yet remained wiry throughout her life.
Even pregnant with Danny, she had seemed merely to be carrying
a football around in her dress.

"You go for sweet stuff, Danny?"

"Never have, you know that."

Yes, he did know that. Danny had been the only boy on his baseball team who had reached for water instead of pop after a game, probably the only child in history who requested an apple instead of ice cream for dessert—and who threw a tantrum when told there was no fruit and he had a choice of chocolate cake or apple pie. The inexplicability of genes again, Pasco thought, wondering about the betrayals they so casually produced.

"You know, Danny," he said putting a *frite* into his mouth. "I guess it's that change worries me sometimes."

"Change is what it's all about, Dad. Nothing stays the same."

"I know that. It's just that...." He wasn't sure of what he wanted to say: something unformed about change and continuity, about retaining the essential while embracing the new. "A few years back a young guy came into Pascal's. A film student or something. He had this remarkable story. He'd borrowed his dad's film equipment for the day and somehow forgot it in the subway. Camera, lenses, everything, you name it. Got home and called TTC Lost and Found. Nothing. Sweated bullets that night. Next day he calls again and guess what?"

"And he lived happily ever after."

"Something like that."

"Dad, that's just another fairy tale out of Toronto's past. So the city's joining the real world." Danny shrugged. "Gotta take the good with the bad."

"That doesn't bother you?"

"I'm a realist, Dad, not a dreamer. I take what life hands me and I work with it."

"I'm not a dreamer either, if that's what you're thinking. I just believe that what you do today affects tomorrow."

"For every action there's a reaction, so what else is new? You can't always control the consequences, but you can't let that paralyse you either, you'd never get out of bed in the morning. You've got to be more practical-minded, Dad, like me."

"Like you." How strange that was: the son telling the father he should be more like him. Pasco said, "You're going to be rich one day, Danny, no doubt."

Danny flushed with pleasure. "Thanks, Dad, you can count on it."

Pasco wondered that Danny hadn't heard the sadness in his voice.

Chapter Twelve

A LAWYER?" Danny heard a frown in Mr. Simmons's voice but his face, so practised, retained a look of passing interest. "Which firm are you with?"

"I'm not a litigation lawyer. I do research." She was a pretty young woman with an expensive briefcase and a becoming self-confidence, the kind of woman Danny found both attractive and intimidating.

"What's your field?"

"Medical law."

Mr. Simmons broke into a wide smile. "Malpractice and all that stuff, eh?"

"Well—"

"You should move to the States. A couple of lawsuits and you'd be set for life."

"Actually, my research is aimed at preventing that situation from developing here. I don't believe that suing people solves any-thing, in fact it—"

"I see." Mr. Simmons went sombre again, his hands shuffling through the application forms on his desk. "Credit references. Good. Professional references, personal references...."

She was just about the perfect candidate for an apartment, Danny thought. A young lawyer who didn't believe in lawsuits:

what more could a landlord want?

Mr. Simmons said, "A two-bedroom, eh? Are you planning on getting a room-mate?"

"I need an extra room as a study. I do a lot of work at home."

"I see. Well, I'm afraid I haven't got anything right now but tell you what I'll do. I'll keep your application on my desk and the moment something comes up I'll give you a call."

She gathered her coat about her, picked up her briefcase. "Thank you, Mr. Simmons, I appreciate that. Any idea how long it might be? I'm in kind of a hurry."

"You can never tell with these things. Three months at the most, hopefully before that."

"That'd be great."

The boss smiled. The moment she left the office he crumpled up her application and tossed it into the wastebasket.

Danny did not hide his surprise.

"Dano, Dano," Mr. Simmons said indulgently. "There's an important lesson here for you. If there's one thing you trust less than a lawyer, it's a lawyer who's more interested in principle than money. You can't read people like that, and if you can't read them you can't understand them. If you can't understand them, you can't find out their price. And without knowing their price, well…. Get my drift?"

Danny shifted in his seat, the uneven chair rocking under him.

Mr. Simmons said, "If you don't become a lion—"

"—you'll become his food." The evening was getting on. Through the sheers hanging in the window behind Mr. Simmons, Danny could see the glow of the lamps that lined the driveway.

"And every dollar lost—"

"—is a little freedom lost."

"Precisely, Dano. Viv and Deanna understand that. That's why they can afford to quit on us like this. They've made themselves into lions."

Snow was predicted for this evening but it hadn't started yet. There was no movement against the light.

"They knew what they were doing, those two. Rent-free apartment, salary, Wednesday afternoons and every weekend off. And they knew how to take full advantage of the situation."

"I still can't believe they managed to buy themselves two houses. Superintendents here, landlords there—"

"Not to mention the cabinet-making business. That was Viv's contribution, believe it or not. Deanna managed their finances. She kept Viv on a tight rein, too. Did you ever notice he was at his worst on Monday mornings after his weekend binge? By mid-week the booze was usually all gone and she made him wait till Saturday for his—what would you call it?—his allowance, I guess." Mr. Simmons smiled in admiration. "Smart woman, that Deanna."

"Did you know about any of this, Mr. Simmons?"

"Not a thing. As I said, Deanna's a smart woman. She knows how to keep her mouth shut."

"And if you'd known?"

"They'd have been out of here like this." Mr. Simmons snapped his fingers. "I pay good wages, I expect one hundred percent in return. But what's done is done, there's no point in stewing over it."

"When are they leaving?"

"Couple of weeks. They want to be all settled into their new place by the new year. They're moving fast. They're even getting rid of their stuff instead of shipping it. Going to buy everything new, move back in style."

Two weeks: that was sufficient time to interview and hire a new couple. Danny scribbled a note to himself to place the newspaper advertisement first thing in the morning.

"That's why, you see—" Mr. Simmons sighed. "You know I'm a cautious man, Dano. And frankly, two weeks, well, it doesn't leave us much time. As you know, I don't believe in rushing these things. The right people can be everything, the wrong people can be a disaster. So if need be, in the interim, I'd like you to handle the superintendent's duties yourself."

Danny felt his brain swirl just a little. "But Mr. Simmons, with everything else I have to do—"

"You'll manage."

Danny didn't miss the finality of the *you'll*: he wasn't being asked, he was being told.

"I'll get Sita to help you. You remember Sita, don't you?"

"Still, Mr. Simmons—" Danny was struggling to keep his tone reasonable.

"Dano." Mr. Simmons swung his chair around, got to his feet. He took a handkerchief from his pocket and brushed it lightly over the ceramic lion, as if to burnish it. "Don't think of this as a burden, Dano. Take it as a lesson. Viv and Deanna are a great success story. They've worked their butts off. Well, at least she has. And now they're going back to wherever it is they came from with half a million dollars in their pockets. Deanna tells me that with the exchange rate they'll be millionaires several times over. They'll live like kings."

"But, Mr. Simmons, I've never been a superintendent, I wouldn't know what to do." Distress made his words tremble as if in barely suppressed laughter. There was even a smile on his lips, but it wasn't really a smile. "I'd be a disaster."

"You're a smart young man, Dano. You'll learn. Besides, it'll only be for a few weeks, no more."

But even for a day, Danny thought. The humiliation was overwhelming.

"We're all part of the same team, Dano. You know what that means."

"How about Sal?"

"Sal? Don't make me laugh. All he knows is numbers. Now, *he* would be a disaster, whereas you, I have confidence in you." Mr. Simmons picked up the lion, cradled it against his belly. "You look so stricken, Dano. Don't be so sensitive. Don't make a tragedy out of this. Would I have entrusted my house to Sal?" The fingers of his right hand caressed the lion's head, probed into the snarling mouth at the fangs.

"But Sal's always here. I have to run around the city—"

"Sal's out of the question. It's a matter of efficiency, Dano, using your resources in the best possible way. Efficiency means profits, and where profits are concerned pride has no place—and pride's your problem here, isn't it, Dano?" Mr. Simmons smiled knowingly. "It's your weak spot, get rid of it. Did you know that most businessmen out there, yours truly included, belong to two political parties? I'm a card-carrying member of both the Liberals and the Conservatives, and I'd buy in to the socialists too the day they form the government. You see, it's all smoke and mirrors, Dano, no matter what they say. Money has no loyalties except to itself." Mr. Simmons's gaze rested hard on him. "You understand that, eh, Dano?"

Danny found himself nodding against his will. He understood that only too well, had even applied it once in a small way. He had put himself through the M.B.A. programme by working at a bank, first as a teller then as a foreign-exchange clerk. He had detested both positions. Despite the jacket and the tie, despite his dexterity with the low-tech equipment impressive only to elderly customers, he had had no illusion that in each job he was little more than a glorified cashier. He'd felt demeaned by the simple manipulation of other people's money, even the grand sums, and he saw no point in labouring for an organization in which the path to the top was too slow and too painstaking for his impatient ambitions.

His father had been unhappy about his accepting the job at Simmons Construction, but Danny had refused to budge, had seen as pointless his father's talk of dirty money. *Money has no loyalties*: he had used practically the same words to justify himself in the argument they'd had.

"You've got to get every cent, every asset, working for you as soon and as efficiently as possible, Dano. Not tonight, not tomorrow, *now*! Why do you think I nickel-and-dime every tenant? Not for the fun of it, that's for sure. It's because an extra buck here and an extra two there make one hell of a difference in the long run."

Didn't he know that? Hadn't he lectured his father about this? But Mr. Simmons wasn't talking to him any more, he was really talking to himself. Danny realized that he had upset the boss.

"You've got to be brutal, Dano. Hold nothing back. Tenants, my boy, are shitholes. They'll try to get away with anything and everything. They'll gripe, they'll complain to rent review, they'll even take you to court. Fight them all the way, don't give an inch and they'll back off faster than you can say 'rent hike.'"

So the discussion was over. Mr. Simmons had decided that he would be the interim superintendent and now he was telling him how to handle the job.

Through the window he saw dark specks falling fast and furious past the glow of the driveway lights.

Mr. Simmons put the lion down in the middle of his desk. It shone in the glare of the desklamp, points of light shimmering on its mane and snout.

"And by the way, Dano, you don't have to move into the super's apartment if you don't want to, but emergencies do happen and it might prove more convenient than having to hustle up here in the middle of the night." He stuffed the handkerchief into his pocket, smiled. "Okay?"

Danny nodded. His hand, moving by itself, drew circles on his notebook.

"Now," Mr. Simmons said, resuming his seat. "How's it going with the house?"

Danny, in a desultory voice, brought him up to date, spoke as frankly as he could about the problems he was having "wrapping his mind around" the second floor.

Mr. Simmons suggested that they meet at the house the following evening to look at more photographs.

Danny said that might help and then, dispirited, took his leave. Outside, a light coating of snow covered the ground. The flakes, glistening in the headlights, had already shrouded every car in the parking lot.

———————

Mr. Simmons said, "The second floor. Yes, that's more complicated. There aren't many pictures of the bedrooms." His hand shuffled around in the cardboard box. "Privacy, you know, Dano. In those days it was more highly valued." He examined a sheet of paper, let it fall back into the box. "We live in such an exhibitionistic age now, don't you agree, Dano?"

Danny leaned forward in his chair, discreetly trying to see into the box. On the pedestal in the corner behind him, Simba crouched in snarling lifelessness. When they first entered the room the movement of heavy, wet snowflakes through the window had created a brief illusion: Danny thought he saw Simba stir. And now, sitting in his marbled gaze, Danny felt the presence of the cat like a chill on his back.

Mr. Simmons's hand emerged from the box clutching a messy pile of papers: letters, photographs, a little booklet hardcovered in green which he quickly tossed back into the box. "Here." He held out a sheaf of photographs. "They're not terribly clear most of them, but maybe they'll help."

Danny shuffled quickly through them. They were overlit, whitish, impressions of images rather than images themselves: heavy beds, chests of drawers, wardrobes. One photograph included an oval mirror. In the glass was the reflection of half of a woman's face startled, perhaps, by the flash. Apart from her, there were no people.

Mr. Simmons put a protective arm around the box and launched reflectively into a description of the master bedroom.

As Danny scribbled on his notepad—the dimensions of the room, the colour of the drapes, the pattern of the wallpaper—it occurred to him that he was being asked to construct a museum. Or, maybe more accurately, a mausoleum. The shape of the lamps, the size of the bed, the placement of the furniture. His writing grew almost illegible. The chill, he realized, had worked its way from his back into his hand.

"I have lots o' family back home, Mr. Daniel. T'ree breddas and two sisters."

Mr. Simmons, to Danny's relief, had grown tired after about an hour. Leaving the photographs strewn on the coffee table, the boss had unceremoniously ushered him from the den, locked the door behind them and tested it. He left Danny unreeling his measuring tape on the second floor.

Not long after, Sita had appeared, treading soundlessly in her running shoes. She had her coat on, and Danny wondered whether she constantly wore it indoors in order to ward off the stubborn chill of the house.

"I does write them all the time but they not able to write back, I can't give them my address, Mr. Leon say it too dangerous."

Lonely people: they became either taciturn or loquacious. Sita belonged to the second group. With no encouragement, the words poured from her, her accent thick and disconcertingly melodious. Her mother, she said, had always called her a chatterbox, and she couldn't count how many times she'd been whipped at school for talking in class.

"You know what it like, Mr. Daniel? Is like talkin' to a wall."

What an appropriate choice of words, Danny thought as he unspooled the tape along a baseboard.

"You writin' and you writin' and you never gettin' a answer, you ain't even know if your letters reachin' them."

I could tell you a thing or two about that, he wanted to say; he felt he had explained so much about himself and his dreams to his father yet so little of his meaning seemed to have got through to him. But he said nothing, instead busied himself noting down the measurement.

"It so strange. They livin', you livin'. They know what you doin', at leas' they know what you want to tell them. I doesn't tell them everyt'ing, you know, I can't bring meself to tell them everyt'ing. So they have a kind o' picture, but the only picture I have is of all o' them at the airport jus' the way I leave them, as if they never go back home, as if they still waitin' there for me to come back."

Danny consulted the sketches he'd made from the photographs, identified the window. Mr. Simmons's parents would have seen this view—the sidewalk, the street, the house on the other side not dissimilar to this one—thousands of times. But it would probably have been different back then, newer, less dilapidated.

"My little sister, Poola, she was carryin' child when I get on that plane, she had about a mont' to go. And I still ain't know if I have a nephew or a niece—"

Danny stepped back from the window, turned to face her. "How old are you, Sita?"

"Nineteen, sir."

"You were—what?—seventeen, eighteen when you came here?"

"Seventeen an' a half."

"So how old was your sister? The pregnant one—"

"Sixteen at the time, sir." Being questioned, Sita assumed an air of formality, like that of a disciplined schoolgirl.

"Sixteen's young—"

"My mother was fourteen when she bring my oldes' brother in this world, sir." There was pride in her voice.

"And your father?'

"He was about sixteen, sir."

"What does he do?" The question came easily to Danny, even though one part of his mind urged caution while another part wondered what harm, in this instance, satisfying his curiosity could do.

"He dead, sir. About two years ago he catch some fellas thiefin' in our vegetable garden. He try to stop them but they chop him up. Where I come from, Mr. Daniel, food wort' more than money, people does kill for some tomatoes or some dasheen. American dollars, Canadian dollars—that mean something. But our money only good for buyin' a plane ticket out o' that place. Can't buy nothin' else with it. Is why I come up here. We use all that wo'thless money to buy one plane ticket. And everybody back home dependin' on me. I tell them I workin' hard, I tell them I happy, I tell them how pretty the snow is. I tell them everyt'ing goin' to be awright. What else I goin' to say? But they mus' be wonderin' why I not sendin' more money, only a few dollars here and there. Ain't no way they could understan' what my life really like up here, Mr. Daniel."

She was silent for a while, her eyes following him as he went from wall to wall, corner to corner, taking and checking his measurements. He became self-conscious under her gaze; he made useless notations, mumbled to himself. He wished she would leave.

"Mr. Daniel?"

"Yes, Sita?"

"What you think of Mr. Leon?"

"What do I think of him?" It seemed an impertinent question. "I think he's a great man."

"You like him?"

He motioned her towards him, showed her where to hold the end of the tape measure while he stretched it the length of the wall. If she was going to hang around, she might as well make herself useful. "It's not a question of like or dislike—" No one had ever before asked him his opinion of Mr. Simmons in such simple terms. Usually people already had a view of the boss which they held in waiting like a hidden club. His father was typical; he bristled at the mere mention of Mr. Simmons's name, launching an attack that grew virulent as Danny grew defensive. "Mr. Simmons is a complex man," he said, kneeling in the far corner and pressing the tape against the baseboard.

"But you like him or you ain't like him?"

Loyalty told him he should simply say, yes, he did like Mr. Simmons. That would have ended it. But Mr. Simmons wasn't the kind of man you could simply like or dislike. "Now for the other wall," he said after a moment, motioning Sita into the other corner.

"So you ain't like him?"

"I didn't say that." He was growing irritable. The question was simple enough. The answer, too, should have been.

She held the tape as he directed, flush into the corner.

"Just like that. Don't move."

"Yes, Mr. Daniel." Her tone was submissive, but for the first time there was a glimpse of the anger that underlay her submission.

Danny made a note on his pad, noticed the measurements weren't fitting together. He knew his sharpness had hurt her. "How'd you meet Mr. Simmons anyway?" he said more gently, seeking to nudge the conversation—if there had to be one—in another, safer direction.

"Mr. Sanford bring me here."

"Mr. Sanford?"

"Mr. KelvinSanford, Immigration Consultant. He put a advertisin' in the papers back home. He promise to get papers, job, everything. Twelve hundred dollars. He meet me at the airport, bring me here—and I never see him again. Mr. Leon say he don't know him, he jus' come by one evenin' and rent the room for a week, cash."

Danny let the tape reel back into its spool. Its swift metallic sucking startled Sita. Her nerves, Danny thought, must be raw.

"Did you look for him?"

"Yes, sir. I did have his address from the advertisin'. A old buildin' down on Adelaide Street. But the office on the fourt' floor was empty, it only had a number on the door and a hole for letters. And a old Chinese man next door tell me he never hear 'bout no Mr. KelvinSanford, Immigration Consultant. Far as he know the office empty for months and months."

"Had you paid him?"

"Is the first t'ing he ask for."

"Cash, I suppose."

"Mr. KelvinSanford don't believe in cheques, sir."

"You should have gone to the police."

Her gaze held him, unwavering.

Danny understood from her silence what absurd advice that was. They lived in the same city, but their worlds—their references, their reactions—were, like salt and sugar, similar only on the surface.

"After the week," she continued, "Mr. Leon tell me I have to pay rent or leave. Where I was goin' to go? Then he start askin' me questions and I end up tellin' him the whole story, I was so frighten. He say maybe he could help, and he ask me for my passport and my return ticket for safekeepin'. Is the last time I see them. He didn't ask me for no rent after that, though."

"And you—" Danny wasn't sure he wanted to ask the question—its imprudence made him hesitate—but Sita had already revealed so much. "You help him?"

"He does give me a little job from time to time, sir. Sweepin' out, cleanin' up. And"—she swallowed hard—"yes, sir, I does help him."

Danny remembered Mr. Simmons's remark about Sita's giving him a perm when he needed it, and the picture came to him of Sita wrapping Mr. Simmons's hair—was that how it was done?— in big pink curlers like the ones his mother used to have. The scene struck him as pathetic.

"By the way, did you ask him for your passport?" He slipped the notebook and tape measure into his pocket.

Her face hardened. "Yes, I ask him." And before Danny could say anything, she spun around and fled the room. He heard her thudding down the stairs. A minute later the front door slammed.

Before turning off the lights and heading out, Danny quickly ran through his notes, comparing what Mr. Simmons had said with what the tape measure had revealed. And he saw that Mr. Simmons's dimensions, culled from memory, were wholly inaccurate. They represented a much larger, much grander house, the facts of feet and inches offering a vision a great deal humbler than that in his boss's mind.

Chapter Thirteen

WHEN the policemen left, Pasco picked up the larger pieces of broken glass and carefully placed them in the box Fong had brought over. Then he swept up the smaller shards both inside and on the sidewalk, wrapped them in newspaper and deposited them in the box with the rest.

A dusting of snow spun and eddied prettily along the street, lithe and alive in the slight breeze.

As he cleaned up, he wondered what had taken them so long. They couldn't have been busy; their type never was. Patience, it seemed to him, would indicate a certain playfulness, and he'd never thought them particularly playful. Calculating then, which would make them dangerous. They had waited, letting time diminish his little play at heroism, letting it distance their vague threat—finally making good on it with a volley of stones through the window. Their vengeance, he reasoned, could have been worse. Surely arson had figured at some point in their calculations.

Fong soon returned with several boxes stacked inside one another. Pasco had arrived at the restaurant some time before to find him standing on the sidewalk, a sweater over his soiled apron, staring disconsolately at the smashed glass. He was eager to help, but equally anxious to assure that he'd heard nothing, seen no one. Pasco understood his fear. Everything he owned was in that fruit and vegetable shop; its loss would kill him.

Together they sliced the boxes open, flattened them out and taped them together. After they had affixed the cardboard to the window frame, Fong took a black marker from his apron pocket and wrote PASCALS OPEN on it. The lettering was shaky and the Ss were the wrong way around, but Pasco was touched anyway.

———————

The restaurant had warmed up a little by the time Lorraine stopped by later in the morning. "New concept in windows?" she said, stuffing her mittens into her coat pockets and leaning forward on the counter. "Windows you can't see through, food you can't eat. What's next for Pascal's? Doors you can't open?"

"It's not funny, Lorraine." Pasco smoothed the shirt sleeves rolled up to his elbows.

"What happened? Food critic?"

"Skins." He motioned her over to the front door, pointed to the pigeon lady in the park. "They were bugging her. I sort of got involved."

"My, my…." There was no missing the gentle mockery in her voice.

"This was their way of thanking me." He shook his head in puzzlement at the pigeon lady. "Look at her, day after day. I just don't get it."

"But it's simple." Lorraine shrugged. "It's her responsibility."

"How so?"

"You see anybody else feeding the pigeons?"

"No, not usually."

"So she's taken on the job. A little one, sure, but it helps, y'know? Something to do. Keeps us aliiive." She drew out the final word in languid emphasis. "There's a saying: Nurture nature and it'll nurture you."

"Christ! You sound like the Doctor."

"Who?"

"You know. Doctor Environment or whatever his name is."

"Oh him." They returned to the counter, Lorraine perching on a stool and rubbing warmth into her hands. "He's all right."

"I suppose he must know what he's talking about. I just don't enjoy being called monstrous for living in the modern world, you know?" He set out two cups on the counter, poured them each a coffee. "He bugs me sometimes."

"That's his job." She warmed her hands on the cup. "To reform sinners like you and me. He means well."

He gestured at her coffee. "Something to eat with that?"

"Why not?" She peered suspiciously at the steaming coffee. "Might as well add some cardboard to the dishwater. How about,…" She eyed the menu board. "A piece of apple pie, no mode."

"Coming right up." He reached down to the fridge, removed a new pie from its box. "But it's not just him, Lorraine. Just seems that wherever you turn these days you've got somebody trying to save you. And it's not just your soul, now it's your body too. Don't smoke, don't drink, buckle up, exercise."

"It's the Janefondarizing of life, Pasco. Slim down your hips, firm up your tits!"

"It all just gets to me sometimes." Pasco deftly sliced the pie into eight equal pieces. "It's like the Jehovah's Witnesses or whoever. Insurance people. They mean it when they say the world's going to end tomorrow. But still all they really want to do is sell you some fear."

Lorraine grinned. "Lecture number one ninety-five."

The words froze on Pasco's tongue. *Lecture number....* Lorraine's teasing took him back years. There had been a time that, whenever Pasco's frustrations overwhelmed his reticence, Lorraine would assign a number to the resulting tirade, as if he had a mental library of speeches and needed only to have a button pressed to engage the appropriate one. She and Rick and Edna would then roar with laughter while he, stifling irritation, lapsed into a foolish silence.

She picked up her fork, smothered her grin with her other hand. "Sorry, Pasco. Couldn't help it. Go on."

"No, never mind." He hid his irritation by turning away and busying himself with the pie box.

"Don't pout. It doesn't suit you."

"Who's pouting?"

"So what do you call that look on your face? Radiance? Go on."

The sincerity in her voice mollified him. He leaned back against the work station and folded his arms. "It's just that sometimes the Doctor reminds me of Danny and Simmons. People who know what's best for everybody else and God help anyone who gets in their way...."

"Simmons, Danny and the Doctor? You're pushing it, aren't you?"

Pasco took a deep breath. Pushing it? Well, after all, maybe he was. Maybe age was making him into the kind of man he frequently saw at the Starting Gate, the kind of man who, living alone in an emotional idleness, began developing theories about the way the world worked. "Sorry, Lorraine. Guess I had to let off some steam. Everyday I see more and more people with no place to live, I see these punks roaming around and bothering old people, creating all kinds of trouble"—he gestured at the cardboarded window—"and nobody seems to be doing anything about them. Know what I mean?"

Lorraine's eyes met his. She nodded in silence: who knew better than she?

Sudden Pasco felt sheepish. "Steam still coming out my ears?"

"Just a little bit. Looks good on you." She forked a piece of the pie into her mouth, chewed, grimaced. "Changed my mind," she said. "Load on the mode."

Pasco took a tub of vanilla ice cream from the freezer.

She said, "I like your passion, Pasco. I've always liked it."

He dug the scoop deep into the hard ice cream, thinking as he did so that if it had been years since Lorraine had teased him, it had been years since he'd given her reason to.

"Where's it been all these years?"

After a moment, he said, "Mourning."

———

Before she left, Lorraine insisted on helping him put up the Christmas decorations. It was about time, she said, and with the new decorator windowpane he and Fong had installed, the place needed jazzing up more than ever. There wasn't much to work with, just the usual battered decorations he'd used for years. Some plastic mistletoe, a glowing Santa, a cardboard Rudolph with a bit of his nose ripped off.

Lorraine bought some cheap balloons from Fong and while Pasco huffed and puffed at them, she went around the restaurant stringing up flattened paper garlands. Then she fastened the balloons to an old plastic wreath and had Pasco climb onto a stepladder to hang it from the ceiling.

All in all, the decorations made the restaurant look just a little less dismal, not a little unlike a party room after the party's over.

"Well, it's better than nothing." Lorraine, dispirited, zipped up her coat and pulled on her mittens.

He walked her to the door and she hugged him lightly just as Sean walked in. He held the door open for her, removing his hat and sticking it under his arm. "Who was that?" he asked, jerking his head towards the door.

"A friend."

"Nice-looking friend."

"She's all right." Pasco found himself just a touch uneasy thinking of Lorraine in those terms.

"You and she, ah, you know?"

"No, nothing like that. We're neighbours. She was Edna's best friend." And as he pronounced his wife's name, he knew that he'd said it out loud as an act of self-defence: *Edna.*

Sean grunted, took a long look at the cardboarded window. "Sorry I couldn't get here earlier, Pasco."

"It's all right, some other guys came and took the report."

"Anything missing? The spoon?"

"Just the glass. I don't think they came in. I've called the repairmen."

Sean laid his hat on the counter. He looked tired. "Guess who's the number one suspect."

"I'm just grateful they didn't torch the place."

"Any witnesses? How about Fong next door? He see anything?" Pasco shook his head.

Sean sighed, perched on a stool. "I think I'll invite Emile for a private chat," he said. "Not much else I can do." He nodded at Pasco's offer of a coffee.

"Where's the kid?" Pasco asked.

"The kid." Sean scratched his head. "Home, resting up. He had a rough time last night."

"What happened?"

"We took a call about a situation outside the Starting Gate. A couple o' guys got rowdy, Lanny had to toss 'em out. They didn't exactly greet us with open arms, if you know what I mean. I had one pinned against the cruiser in no time and Kurt took on the other one. I was 'cuffing my guy so I don't know exactly what happened, but next thing I know the kid's bashing away at his guy like there's no tomorrow. Like he went crazy or something, I dunno. I had to pull him off the guy." He paused, rubbed at his face with his large hand.

"Was the guy hurt?"

"No harm done. A few bruises, nothing broken. But if this gets into the papers the usual shit'll hit the fan, and we can kiss Kurt's career goodbye. Remember how he reacted with Emile and his bunch? He's got this fuckin'—"

"Temper?"

"That's the damned thing, eh? I'm not sure it's his temper that's the problem. If you ask me he's more scared than anything else. His dad got beat up real bad once and the kid remembers it like it was yesterday."

"So he lays into 'em before they can lay into him. So what are you going to do about it?"

Sean sipped his coffee. "Don't know yet. He's basically a decent kid, wants to be a policeman real bad. Fear's a healthy thing to have on the streets, so long's you use it to sharpen your senses and don't let it get the better of you."

Pasco leaned on the counter, flicked away a crumb with his finger. "Straightening out a kid's never as easy as it looks, Sean. You sure you're not taking on too much? Maybe you should let the force handle it."

Sean silently considered the advice. "It couldn't be that hard. Solid guidance, a firm hand."

"Solid guidance, firm hand, eh? Nice theory. But there's no guarantees, and you haven't even had any experience."

"Neither did my dad." Sean's eyes focused absently on the coffee in his cup. "Besides, you're not quite right."

"What d'you mean?"

"I used to have a son."

"Is that right? Where is he?"

"Dead."

"I'm sorry, I didn't—"

"'Sall right, Pasco. I just like to put it like that, bluntly, to see how people react." He clinked the cup back down onto its saucer. "Everybody's always sorry."

Pasco clasped his hands, looked away to the window. The cardboard pressed in, bellied back out: the wind was picking up.

"It happened a long time ago. A good ten, twelve years. He was eight. Dived headlong into a pool and didn't come back up." He fell silent, then cleared his tension with a light cough. "Anyways, the upshot of that was the end of my marriage. Broke under the strain. My wife always felt I was blaming her and I always felt she was blaming me. Too much finger-pointing, Pasco, too much blame being tossed around when there wasn't any blame, it was just a stupid accident. You can't go nowhere like that. So she took off." He drained the coffee.

"Is that why you're not reporting Kurt? Your son?"

He shook his head. "No. Oh, don't get me wrong, I had my little fantasy of David growing up to be a cop just like me, but he was more like his mother, that was clear from early on. If he'd lived, he'd probably have been a—I dunno—something artistic. A painter or a poet or something like that, dirt poor and sharing a room on Queen Street. No, Pasco, Kurt isn't a substitute. But his dad and his grandad, them I understand. They're probably proud as all hell the kid's on the force. And that's why I want to help Kurt make it."

"All right," Pasco said, his voice tentative. "But if the kid really screws up one day, it's your ass."

"I'll just make sure he doesn't, that's all." Sean stood up, reached for his hat.

"You can't be sure." Pasco followed him to the door.

"You said it yourself, Pasco. There's no guarantee."

Pasco stood in the doorway and watched Sean drive off in his cruiser. The wind was sharp, the sky dark and heavy. In the park, brown leaves rose and fell, and pigeons swerved among the trees struggling against the gusts.

It was a quiet afternoon. Apart from a few street girls warming up for the after-work shift, only two clients came in. The restaurant was empty when the men from the glass company arrived. Pasco decided to close while they worked. Although, as the work began, the point seemed self-evident, he still turned the sign on the door to CLOSED.

The removal of the cardboard once more opened the restaurant up to the world. The sounds of passing traffic drifted in unhindered on the wind, the park came closer, the tables and chairs and Christmas decorations seemed to blend with the street. Every time a streetcar rumbled by Pasco had the impression he was about to be run over. He put on his coat and sat in a booth watching the men work.

Fong, his sweater clutched around him, popped in with the day's newspapers. His face a mask of innocence, he suggested that this would be a good time for Pasco to start a drive-through service. Pasco, equally straight-faced, thanked him for the idea and invited him to join in the venture. He could lay his hands on some good bricks, he said, perfect for throwing at Fong's nice big picture window. Fong declined—"Thank you million, Pasco, thank you million"—but the offer was too kind, he couldn't take advantage of a friend's good fortune.

Pasco, with nothing better to do, flipped through the newspapers.

The workmen donned thick gloves, set about inserting a new sheet of glass into the window frame. Outside, the late afternoon darkness was settling in. Pasco decided that when they were done he would close for the day and head down to the Gate. Not many clients were likely to come by, and a day that had begun with a smashed window deserved to end with an extra beer.

He was rolling the newspapers up for the garbage can when a sharp rapping at the front door startled him.

Sklewy, standing in the doorway, raised a hand in greeting. Pasco shook his head, pointed to the CLOSED sign.

Sklewy rapped again, this time holding up a dollar coin between thumb and forefinger.

Pasco went over to the door, opened it an inch. "Sorry, friend, I'm closed for the day. Come back tomorrow."

Sklewy's face remained blank as always, but he held the dollar coin up to Pasco's face.

"I see you've got money, but it's freezing in here, I—"

Sklewy lowered the coin, following it with his eyes. His face seemed to go slack.

Pasco noticed he wasn't wearing a coat. His suit was growing more threadbare by the day. He opened the door wider. "Okay, okay, come on in."

Sklewy made for the same table at which he'd sat the time before. He sat straight-backed in the chair, bag on his lap, forearms on the table.

"Burger, fries and a coffee okay?" Pasco said.

He nodded once, his right hand reaching into his jacket pocket and groping around for something he couldn't find. Then, with both hands, he pulled the pocket open and peered in. At last, he seemed satisfied.

Pasco bustled at the work station preparing Sklewy's meal. As the basket of frozen fries sizzled into hot oil, the repairers announced they were finished. They declined his offer of something to drink. He wrote out a cheque while one of them laboured over his receipt. They left with dour nods of their heads, and Pasco wondered whether they had expected a tip.

He brought the food over to Sklewy. "Would you mind making

it snappy?" he said. "I'd like to get going soon."

Sklewy gave no sign of having heard him. When he began eating, it immediately became clear that he was in no hurry. He consumed the fries one by one, placing each into his mouth with great deliberation and chewing it well and slowly.

Pasco, irritated, walked over to the new window. The men had done a neat job, had even cleaned up after themselves. He reached his fingers out to the glass. It was freezing. He leaned close, frosted it with his breath. With the edge of a fingernail, he wrote his name. Then, under it, he wrote Edna's.

You see, Edna....

But he got no further. The front door flew open and he had only enough time to say, "I'm clo—" before Emile was standing before him, a cigarette hanging from his smiling lips.

Pasco said, "Can't you read? The sign says—"

"Nice window, man. Looks brand-new." Emile reached out a hand and caressed the glass. "Crash," he said quietly.

"You son of a bitch."

"You know my mother?"

"Look, Emile, I've had enough—"

Emile looked over at Sklewy biting unperturbed into his hamburger. "Business not so hot, eh? You even serve the low-life now." He strode slowly into the restaurant. "How about some fries? Yeah, I could go for that." He snapped his fingers at Pasco. "Yo, cookie, one order of fries."

Pasco wondered where the rest of his gang was. He glanced quickly through the window. They weren't outside. "The kitchen's closed," he said firmly.

"So open it up, you're the boss." Emile perched on a table, one boot on a chair. "And I think I'll have a Coke with that."

"Kitchen's closed," Pasco repeated. "I think you should leave now."

"You haven't served me yet, man. What kind o' rest-o-rant is this anyways?" He flicked his ashes to the floor, took a last hard pull at the cigarette and sent the butt spinning towards Pasco. It fell short. "Get a move on, cookie."

"I don't want to have to call the cops, Emile."

Behind him, Sklewy put his bag on the table and patted at his lips with a paper napkin.

"Cops," Emile said, "should learn to mind their own business. Just like you, cookie. Keep your nose out of other people's shit. You know what happens if you don't?" He reached down and picked up the sugar container from the table, turned it upside down. Sugar streamed onto the table, quickly forming a growing pile. "You get your face rubbed in it till your brains fall out." He shook out the last of the sugar; then, with a quick flick of his wrist, smashed the container onto the floor. "Crash," he said quietly.

Sklewy got to his feet, his hand skittish in his jacket pocket.

Pasco wondered what to do next. The threat to call the police had been an idle one. Emile stood between him and the telephone.

"Now how about those fries, cookie?"

Pasco toyed with the idea of letting him have his fries, was weighing the chances of buying him off when he saw Sklewy take two swift steps towards Emile. Watched, startled, as Sklewy locked his left arm around Emile's neck at the same time that his right hand emerged from the jacket pocket and pressed the point of an open jackknife to the bridge of Emile's nose. Emile squawked, his face reddening, eyes crossing as his pupils zeroed in on the shiny blade. Sklewy yanked him off the table and, using his body as leverage, frogmarched him towards the still-open door and out to the sidewalk.

Pasco watched through the window as Sklewy hugged Emile tightly to him and thumbed the knife shut. Then, as Emile struggled ineffectually against his grip, Sklewy planted a lengthy kiss on the crown of his shorn head and shoved him away. Emile stumbled, doubled over, his hands reaching up to massage at his neck.

Sklewy casually returned the knife to his pocket. Pasco shook his head in disbelief: so the pocket hadn't been empty after all. Stepping back into the restaurant, Sklewy carefully closed the door and, paying no attention to Pasco, returned to his table and resumed his meal.

Pasco knew he should sweep up the sugar, pick up the pieces of broken glass. But he could not, at least not for a while. All he could do was sit on a stool, hands clasped on his lap, mind blank, watching Sklewy methodically make his way through the fries.

Pasco didn't ask Lanny how he'd got the black eye—he already knew that—but he did ask how he was doing. And when Lanny, in a rare foul mood, growled back that he was fine Pasco quickly strode over to the table beneath the saddle. The others were all already there.

Pasco saw immediately that Montgomery was not in good shape. His eyes were bleary, and he seemed withdrawn. He acknowledged Pasco with the briefest of glances, as he might have given to a stranger.

Marcus, bright in a red shirt and green sweater, was sitting on the other side of the table. He looked unhappy. Pushpull, sitting beside him and loudly humming "Deck the Halls", winked at Pasco in such a way that he knew that Pushpull was the cause of Marcus's misery.

He removed his coat and as he sat down Pushpull said, "Hey there, Pasco. So what d'you think? Ain't Markie here real pretty all buffaloed up in his new clothes?"

Cruise said, "Pushpull's driving him crazy, he's—"

"Cut the crap, man," Marcus said.

Pasco glanced at Montgomery but Montgomery, absorbed,

chewing on a toothpick, paid him no attention. On the table sat the remains of his orange: the curled rind, each half of the fruit sucked dry so that it resembled a little white cap.

Lanny brought a beer for Pasco, and another for Montgomery.

Pasco, settling in, told them about the broken window and the visit from Emile, about Sklewy and the lost object that turned out to be a knife. He couldn't get over the fact that Sklewy had once more insisted on paying for his meal—but had pointedly held back the tip.

Pushpull said, "Hope you still have a window tomorrow morning."

"I called my friend Sean. The cops'll keep an eye out."

"You'll need more than one," Cruise said.

Suddenly Marcus said, "Creeps. Bums. Shitheads. Fuckin' ass-holes."

"What was that string of French all about?" Cruise asked.

Marcus sniffed, moistened his lips. "It's this guy at work, another cabbie. Little Jewish guy. Wears that cap, y'know? The guys call him Rabbi."

"A Jewish cabbie?" Cruise said. "Now there's a new one. Those Jew-boys usually own the whole joint."

Suddenly Montgomery stirred, stuck a finger at Cruise. "Watch yourself, man, I ain't like where your words headin'."

"What?" Cruise, stung, threw his arms open in protest.

"Jus' watch what you sayin', Cruise." The toothpick danced from one side of his mouth to the other.

"What are you sayin'? You're sayin' I'm racist? That's it, eh?" Cruise leaned forward in challenge. "If I'm racist, what am I doin' sitting here having a beer with you? No offence, Montgomery, but you're not exactly fleecy white, eh?"

"Offence?" Montgomery chuckled heavily. "But is a compli-ment, man!"

"Anyways," Marcus continued. "Rabbi caught it real bad last

night. Couple o' guys refused to pay their fare."

"Yeah," Pushpull said. "Heard about that on the news this morning. You know the guy?"

Marcus nodded. "Next thing you know, they're both having a go at him. Cops found him unconscious in the front seat."

"He hurt bad?" Pushpull's concern was not idle: he sympathized most with victims when he knew the details of their distress.

"I stopped by the hospital to see him this afternoon. He's banged up pretty bad and he ain't gonna win no beauty contests for a while, but he'll be all right. But you know what he told me? As they were layin' into him he kept wondering why they were doing this? It was only a seven-dollar fare, for God's sake. Seven dollars, and they beat the shit out of him." His voice quivered with muted outrage. "And the thing is, he's just a little guy, y'know?"

Pasco said, "Take it easy, Marcus. You said he's going to be fine, right?"

"Sure, *he* is. But I'll tell you, I'm gettin' a tire iron for under my seat. I'm not takin' no chances. It's gettin' ugly out there, Pasco."

Pasco nodded: where had he heard that, or words to that effect, before?

"And cabbies like me"—his thumb stabbed at his chest—"we're the ones in the front lines. We get all the shit and none of the payoff. We work our butts off—"

"You mean you sit your butts off," Cruise said, but he was the only one to laugh.

"—and what rights do we got? Some guy comes in here or goes into a doughnut shop and starts makin' trouble, you can toss him out. I can't do that in my own fuckin' cab! The Commission says I've got to take everybody, mom, pop, junior and every druggie, pimp and whore that flags me down. Treat everybody equal, they say. Well what about me? I'm a businessman, same like Mr.

Simpson or Mr. Eaton, but anybody can come into my cab and hand me a load o' shit and I gotta sit there and take it."

"So kick 'em out," Pushpull said.

"I kick 'em out, they complain to the Commission and my licence goes out the window."

"Don't knock it, Marcus," Montgomery drawled.

"Don't knock what?"

"This thing, you know, you havin' to pick up everybody even if you ain't like how they lookin'. If they ain't have that rule, a whole lot o' black people goin' to be standin' beside the road catchin' their arse to get a taxi."

"That's bull. Most of the drivers I know don't give a shit what colour you are. Besides, half the cabbies in this city are black anyways."

Montgomery pouted in thought, nodded slowly. "Well, then," he said, "it would be a whole lot o' white people standin' beside the road catchin' their arse to get a taxi." He slapped the table drunkenly and laughed out loud, a harsh and unnatural cackle that brought Lanny's eyes swivelling unhappily in their direction.

When Montgomery called in a slurred voice for another beer, Lanny, for the first time ever, refused. He was discreet about it. Drying his hands on his ever-present towel, he came over to the table and quietly suggested that maybe, at six, Montgomery had had enough.

"Six?" Pasco said. "He's had six beers?" Montgomery usually had two, three on an exceptional evening.

"An' he goin' to have a sevent'," Montgomery insisted.

"Take it easy, Montgomery," Pasco said. "I'm kind o' with Lanny on this one."

"Is my money, is my belly. Bring on number seven, Lanny."

"Sorry, Montgomery. Can't do it."

"What the fock you mean you can't do it? It easy, man. You pick up the mug, you pull the handle...."

Montgomery's aggressiveness alarmed Pasco. He reached a hand of caution across the table. Montgomery brushed it away.

"Lanny, man, I awright I tell you. Jus' one more."

Lanny shook his head. "I think you'd better head on home." He turned and walked away, his body tensed.

Montgomery scraped his chair back. "I ain't ready to go back to Paradise, man," he mumbled, getting unsteadily to his feet. "Laaa-ny!" he shouted.

Lanny stopped, turned slowly around. He was already balling the towel around his right fist.

"Laaa-ny...!" Montgomery cleared his throat, seemed to waver. Then his knees buckled. Pasco and Cruise, already on their feet, caught him.

"Get 'im out of here," Lanny said.

Pasco put Montgomery's arm around his shoulder, circled his waist. Pushpull planted his cap on his head, then held the doors open while Marcus hailed a cab.

As Pasco, staggering, urged Montgomery towards the door, Montgomery sang out, "Laaaaa-nyyyy!"

And the sound reverberated in Pasco's head like a long and clamorous lament.

In the taxi, Montgomery mumbled his address and fell into a fitful doze on Pasco's shoulder.

Pasco had known that he lived in the St. Clair and Bathurst area, but only on hearing the house number on Vaughan Road was he struck by how curious it was that men who spent so much time talking together still knew so little about each other. They'd never been to one another's homes, had only the vaguest idea where and how each other lived.

The driver said, "He ain't gonna barf, is 'e?"

"Depends on how long it takes to get him home," Pasco said.

The car immediately sped up, the driver muttering that he would rather pay a speeding ticket than clean up puke.

Montgomery shifted away from Pasco, pressed his cheek to the cool leatherette.

The taxi hurtled up Mount Pleasant, the driver changing lanes with a split-second timing that jangled Pasco's nerves. The tires squealed when he turned left onto St. Clair just barely ahead of oncoming traffic.

At first Pasco thought that St. Clair, unlike Eglinton, hadn't changed much through the years. The short span before the bridge that crossed the valley was still wide, bordered by residential streets somnolent in the evening darkness. The intersection at Yonge was busier than he'd remembered, the taxi caught in heavy traffic crawling past crowds of people hurrying by or waiting in line for the streetcar. And it was brighter too, the evening brisk with streetlamps, traffic signals, streetcar signals, digital clocks and the lights of office buildings.

Pasco found himself glad to be inside the taxi with the windows up. Outside looked to be alien territory. Danny's territory.

Montgomery, rocked to sleep by the movement of the car, snored intermittently, a jagged, desperate sound that seemed often on the verge of catching in his throat.

Only when they'd left all the lights behind and were on a quieter stretch of St. Clair—the edges of lower Forest Hill on the right, Winston Churchill Park with the towers of Casa Loma lit up in the distance on the left—was Pasco once more able to breathe easily. He saw the traffic lights at Bathurst and realized that here, too, much had been dramatically altered, not prettified but industrialized by an immense supermarket and a mouth that yawned in the middle of the street to swallow packed streetcars into the subway station.

Suddenly he felt Montgomery's eyes on him. "How're you doing there?" he asked.

"Awright." But he was swallowing hard.

"Hey man," the driver called. "You not plannin' on pukin' in my cab, eh?"

Pasco said, "It's Charlene, right?"

He nodded. "The girl take off, man. Help herself to the food money and gone."

"When?"

"Three days ago."

"You reported her missing?"

Montgomery opened his mouth but no words came out, only hacking, strangled sounds. Pasco leaned across him and swiftly turned down his window. Cold air rushed in. As the taxi squealed into Vaughan Road, Montgomery stuck his head out the window and retched.

The driver glanced around. "Oh maaan,..." he moaned in pointless complaint.

Montgomery lived in a lowrise of brown brick and aluminum-frame windows. There was no elevator. By the time they reached the fourth floor, Pasco was sweating and gasping for breath.

"Down there," Montgomery said, nodding his head towards the end of the long, narrow corridor. The walls of Paradise were green, the carpet threadbare.

They stopped before a door decorated with a Christmas wreath. Pasco knocked. The peephole darkened for a moment before the door opened. "Mrs. Bird?" Pasco said. She was a tall, hefty woman, attractive despite her red and swollen eyes.

She immediately reached out for Montgomery, practically lifting him off Pasco's shoulder.

"Can I help?" Pasco remained standing on the threshold.

"No, no, is awright, I can manage." She spoke quickly, a frown on her face. "T'anks for bringin' him home. Good-night." She closed the door in his face.

Pasco remained there for a moment, hurt that his concern for Montgomery had been summarily dismissed. Then Mrs. Bird's face came back to him: distress, yes, but strength too, and pride. He realized that the woman he'd just seen could, as she'd said, manage. It was Montgomery he wasn't sure about.

Chapter Fourteen

Mr. SIMMONS found superintendents to his satisfaction in less than a week.

Danny was thrilled, but he was careful not to let it show.

They said they had to give two weeks' notice at their present job. Mr. Simmons naturally agreed. Then they said they wanted to take a two-week vacation before assuming their duties. Mr. Simmons bargained them down to one.

Danny, with growing dismay, wanted to object. Three weeks: Viv and Deanna would be gone well before then. But before he could find the words, Mr. Simmons introduced him to the burly man and his pallid wife: "This is Dano," he said. "The acting superintendent." Danny felt himself burn, and he could see they didn't know what to make of him when, shaking their hands, he pointed out that he was actually Mr. Simmons's assistant and that his office—he jabbed his thumb over his shoulder—was back there.

In the end, though, he told himself it could have been worse. It could have been months, had the boss so wished. He knew he could survive it, as he could survive the smirk that Sal, bent over his books, made no effort to hide.

He drew the line, though, at using the empty apartment: why make what was already nightmarish even more so?

But Mr. Simmons, following an agenda of his own, personally taped a sheet of paper with Danny's private telephone number to the office door.

The first night brought a midnight phonecall to his apartment when all three elevators stopped working; and the second a two A.M. call after someone had set off the fire alarm for no apparent reason. When the third night brought a three-thirty A.M. call from an inebriated tenant who'd lost her keys, he surrendered and moved in with a camp cot, a radio alarm-clock and his coffee machine.

Danny's approach to the work was, at best, casual. He dealt with the only snowfall of significance not by shovelling, as would have been the best recourse, but by simply broadcasting generous handfuls of salt and watching with satisfaction as the snow melted patchily away.

The most difficult part of the job for him was dealing with the garbage. Once the large metal trolley at the foot of the chute in the basement was full—and it filled quickly in a building of this size—it had to be replaced by an empty one and then trundled from the underground garage to the parking lot at the back. From there, twice a week, a city garbage truck would lift it with metal arms and dump its contents into the whirring maw of its compactor. It was demanding, smelly work, made more unpleasant by Danny's view of the garbage chute as the digestive tract of the building, bags of garbage fed into a mouth on each floor, the bags falling swiftly through the metal intestine and out through the rectum in the basement. The sickly sweet stench of rotting garbage permeated his clothes, clung to his skin, and he would literally run to the shower when he was done.

Yet he was lucky. Handling the garbage was only one small part of the physical demands of the building. As promised, Sita was brought in to help him, and she took charge of the rest. She vacuumed the corridors and swept the stairwells; she neatened and mopped the laundry room; she gathered up the bottles and newspapers from the garbage-chute rooms on every floor. When a vacated apartment needed cleaning, it was Sita who spent the day scrubbing and scraping.

At the beginning of Danny's second week on the job, the building produced more than its usual share of garbage from the many Christmas parties that had been held over the weekend. The trolley filled quickly, bags jammed the chute—but not before several had spilled over the edge of the trolley and split open on the concrete floor. The smell that greeted Danny early that Monday morning was a potent mixture of overripe fruit and suppurating meat. He retreated quickly.

Sal, taking pity on him, sprinkled a liberal dose of the cologne he kept in his desk onto a handkerchief. Danny tied the handkerchief around his face and got to work with a shovel. His eyes watered, his stomach rose again and again, a surging bubble of sourness that threatened to erupt. He fought back with determination, meeting with shaky success until the moment he hefted a large bone, once probably a mouth-watering roast, and saw that it was alive with maggots. They were fat and white and wiggling. And the last straw. Sita had to finish cleaning up for him.

But these were only moments, isolated if onerous. The new duties added no more than an hour or two to his regular workday. An uninterrupted night of sleep was rare though, usually thanks to complaints about noise in neighbouring apartments. Once, three police officers buzzed him awake at one in the morning. They'd got a tip that two teenaged runaways were being hidden in the building and they were there to check it out, apartment by apartment. Danny didn't accompany them, but he couldn't get back to sleep either.

As he found himself growing unusually tired during the day— by mid-afternoon his energy would be depleted—Danny wondered whether this was the reason so many building superintendents drank too much. It wasn't the work itself, he didn't think, especially not when there were two of you. It was more the irregularity of the life—trying to fall asleep at three or four in the morning after dealing with one emergency or another—and the periods of boredom between bouts of hard physical labour.

One night someone regurgitated with gusto in one of the elevators. The discharge, of a peculiar yellowish green, slicked the lower half of one wall and much of the floor. Danny, holding his breath against the odour, took the elevator out of service and left it for Sita to clean up the following morning.

Sita, he was aware, had quickly become the Deanna to his Viv. He was grateful she was there. When Sal asked who she was, as he did more than once, Danny said, "Charity case." When Sal asked why she wasn't on the payroll like everyone else, Danny replied that her working there was just a temporary arrangement and the boss, doing her a favour, didn't want to be bothered with the paperwork.

"But what about her salary? I don't know her full name, I don't have her social insurance number. How can I issue a cheque?"

"Don't worry, Sal, it's being taken care of."

"I'll bet she's Mr. Simmons's secret squeeze," Sal said conspiratorially.

"His *squeeze*?" Sal was a fan of old black-and-white gangster movies. "Maybe you should take it up with the boss, G-Man."

"Or maybe she's yours. A little coffee in your cream, Daniel?"

"Well at least she's safe from you, eh, G-Man? Or should that be G-string?"

Sal turned red. "I just don't like irregularities, that's all."

"Fibre and prune juice," Danny grinned. "Works like a charm."

Only later, as he lay on the camp cot in the dark apartment trying in vain to get to sleep, did it occur to Danny that he had become part of a little conspiracy. Sita's secret, shared with Mr.

Simmons, had become his secret too, as had the responsibility for preserving it. In evading Sal's questions, he had moved from passive observer to active participant—and it still had nothing to do with him. The realization kept him awake for several hours, his mind alert but unfocused.

Once in a while a car, usually a taxi, would pull into the driveway, its headlights shining through the cream-coloured drapes. A door would slam, voices call good-night.

He glanced fretfully at the clock: three A.M.

As the minutes, the hours, flicked by, Danny began feeling himself a trespasser in the apartment, as if it were simply a kind of hole in which he was hiding out for a while. Not a place for living in, then, for that implied a certain emotional possession, but merely a place of temporary refuge. He thought he could never grow accustomed to living like this; it would be too easy to lose himself, too easy to forget that he was a whole person with the needs and drives and desires of normal people. And he wondered, without really wanting to, how Sita managed in the tiny room in the big house in the city that was all danger to her.

One day, as his stint as superintendent was drawing to a close, Danny ran into Sita on the street. He was on his way to the doughnut shop on Bloor Street and she was on her way back from it. They rarely spoke to each other during the day, partly because Sita was usually hard at work somewhere in the building and partly because Danny thought it best to conceal his familiarity with her—from both Sal and Mr. Simmons.

He found her wary of him. They had never seen each other outdoors and here, nibbling on a chocolate doughnut, she looked even smaller, as if dwarfed by the buildings and the trees and the sky itself. In the thin daylight, her face revealed a strain that aged her. He supposed that their meeting like this on the street must have struck her as somehow exposed, dangerous even, so he put the question that had been nagging at him directly to her: How much was Mr. Simmons paying her for the two weeks?

"I jus' helpin' him out, Mr. Daniel."

"But what's he paying you? He must be paying you something."

"Mr. Leon say fait'fulness is its own reward, sir. He does give me lunch money."

Fait'fulness. So was that what it was all about? Danny wondered. Were faithfulness and notions of it at the centre of the game Mr. Simmons was playing with Sita, and with Danny himself?

This is Dano, the acting superintendent. And the burly man had thrust out his bruised and meaty hand as to an equal.

But what about the trust Mr. Simmons had shown in him? Was the boss deliberately testing it? Was he weighing trust against humiliation to see what it would yield? Protest or compliance, indolence or zeal?

As the thoughts shaped themselves in Danny's mind, he realized that the result would reveal something essential about the strength of his loyalties as against the strength of his ambitions. And he felt, even as he appreciated Mr. Simmons's motivation, that the test itself was a betrayal. He had given his all and still the boss, brutish and clever, was probing at him, searching out weak spots. How much of a puppet did a man have to be? The question made him lightheaded.

Sita said, "I have to go, Mr. Daniel. I have wo'k to do."

"Yes, yes," he mumbled. "You go ahead."

At the doughnut shop, Danny surprised the waitress by opting to have his coffee and doughnut there. She had already opened a bag for his order, was already reaching for the maple-sugar and peanut doughnut he always asked for. By the time he found a vacant seat at the window, he was no longer hungry. He pushed aside the doughnut and spent a long time sipping the coffee, watching young men begging outside, listening to old men arguing inside.

On Sita's last day, Danny slipped her an envelope with five twenty-dollar bills in it. He knew it wasn't nearly enough for all the work she had put in, but he didn't mean it as a salary, just as a tip for her having helped him when he'd needed it. Then, in a whisper, he cautioned her not to mention the money to Mr. Simmons. He knew it was important advice but he didn't quite know why, nor did he know whether it was important for her or for him. He just knew it had something to do with the question of loyalty and ambition—and of which was the stronger.

Chapter Fifteen

A FTER WORK on Christmas Eve Pasco crossed the street and followed the sidewalk towards the stone church tucked into the north-west corner of the park. The evening was cold, the air moist but with no hint of snow. The stores on Yonge Street, a comfortable ten-minute walk away, would have just closed their doors, and the road was busy with cars streaming away from the city centre.

Fong, conscientious and quietly driven, was still open. Like Lanny, he made no concession to holidays, although he had stopped by earlier in the day to wish Pasco a Merry Christmas and to present him with a potted poinsettia. Fong's neighbour on the other side—a dry cleaning establishment run by a young Korean couple—had already closed. The interior was dimly lit and an illuminated sign in the window declared:

WE SPECIALIZING IN !
DRAPES

Aldo the cardiologist had stopped by earlier in the day to say goodbye. He would be heading home on Christmas Day. His English had improved somewhat, but his puzzlement over much of what he'd seen had gone undiminished. "I don' un'erstan', Pasco," he'd said. "You Canahdians, you are a strange people." He'd brought up the topic of the health warnings printed on cigarette packages. "This is silly," he'd said, his elegant hands circling his coffee cup. "Smoking is no good for you, everybody's knows that. But how many smokers read their cigarette packs? *SMOKING IS A MAJOR CAUSE OF HEART DISEASE. AVOID SMOKING.* They have nothing else to read? And what comes next? War-nings on beer or wine bottles? How about *CARS ARE A MAJOR CAUSE OF AC-CIDENTS. AVOID DRIVING*? From my experience back home, Pas-co, better they put warnings on ballot slips. *POLITI-CIANS ARE A MAJOR CAUSE OF HEARTBURN. AVOID VOT-ING.*" He shook his head in amusement. "Life is-a full of risk, Pas-co. You Canahdians, you think you should live forever. But what's the point if you get rid of all pleasure? I am a doctor, Pas-co, but life is worth living only if you enjoy it. And like it or not, vice in moderation is part of the enjoyment."

Pasco was amused. He tried to explain to Aldo that most Cana-dians found themselves caught between two types of people: those drawn to hairshirts and those longing to sell them the hairshirts.

Aldo smiled, but his face remained sad. "I am from the old world, Pas-co, a complex place. But after my visit here I think the new world is a very strange place. I prefer Europe. We don't take life so seriously. What is the expression? Live and-a let live?"

If only, Pasco had thought as they shook hands. If only.

He stopped at the empty lot between the abandoned apart-ment building and the church. A Christmas tree stand had been set up there a couple of weeks before but now the lot was deserted, the Boy Scouts who ran it probably all already at home eyeing the gifts piled up under their own trees. The string of light-bulbs that had created an evening air of festivity beside the austere hulk of the church hung unlit between tree trunks. The ground was hard, the grass trampled. Bits and pieces of trees lay around, dry needles crunched under his shoes. A discarded wreath leaned disconsolate against the church wall.

He rooted through the discards and eventually found what he was looking for, a lopped-off branch that had retained enough shape that it could pass for a miniature Christmas tree. He had no interest in the wreath although it was whole; wreaths, even the festive kind, reminded him too vividly of funerals and of the memorial ceremonies to war dead held every year at the modest cenotaph in front of Old City Hall. Had Lorraine not tied balloons to the plastic one at the restaurant, he would not have allowed it.

He took his time walking home. There was no hurry, no one was expecting him. He held the branch loosely in his hand, his glove sticky with the sap, and couldn't help thinking of the many times when Danny was young and Edna alive that he had toted home full-sized trees, their sharp aromas of pine and earth and moist woodland surging with every step.

At home he put the branch into a plastic bucket, secured its base with bricks and placed it beside the fireplace in the living room. He hung on a few frosted balls, the branch drooping under their weight; draped on a string of coloured lights and plugged it in. Several of the bulbs were broken. He replaced them with new ones but even then, he had to admit, the blues, reds and yellows made for a rather cheerless sight. Yet it was better than nothing. If only in memory of times past, if only because his furniture looked so shabby in the living room bright and barren and still smelling of sawdust and fresh paint, the gesture mattered.

The phone rang not long afterwards. Cruise, his voice betraying the merriment of a liquid Christmas Eve, wished him the best. He'd closed the Booksore early—few people gave used books as gifts—and was spending the evening with his sister and her family out in Willowdale. Suburbia was colder than downtown, Cruise said, but folks out here took their fantasies seriously. Trees, lights, turkeys, the whole works. Hell, there was even a smattering of snow on the ground. Behind his voice, Pasco could hear the excited chatter of several young children.

He returned to the living room, a beer in hand, just as an envelope swished through the mail-slot in the front door. He bent down to pick it up. It was plain and white, carefully sealed with tape and addressed to *Pasko*. He quickly opened the door. A fine rain was coming down. A man in a parka, the hood pulled up over his head, stood hunched on the sidewalk out front. It was in his heavy-set frame that Pasco thought he recognized Montgomery. He stepped onto the porch, the dampness seeping through his clothes, and called out to him.

Montgomery, hands tucked into his pockets, glanced over his shoulder. Then he turned and walked with reluctance back to the porch. His hands remained buried in the pockets of the rain-darkened parka. "The wife send me," he mumbled, his eyes avoiding Pasco's. "Is the taxi money for when you take me home from the Gate."

Pasco ripped the envelope open: a twenty-dollar bill. "It's too much."

"Keep it. For the trouble."

"It wasn't any trouble."

"Keep it anyway."

Pasco could see that he was embarrassed.

Montgomery hadn't been to the Gate recently. Pasco, worried, had toyed with the idea of phoning—but he hadn't, for fear of seeming to intrude. He stood aside, showed him the open door. "It's cold out here," he said.

Montgomery left his boots on the porch. Pasco draped his parka over the living-room radiator so that it would dry out quickly and went to the kitchen to fetch another beer.

When he came back, Montgomery was standing uneasily in the middle of the living room. Out of uniform, he looked older, heavier—or had he in fact grown older and heavier in so short a time? His eyes were red, the skin under them matte black. "Any word?" Pasco said.

Montgomery shrugged, took the beer. His face was heavy, unreadable. "I been wonderin'," he said as they clinked bottles, "how the hell to explain chil'ren."

"Lord knows." Pasco indicated a chair but Montgomery ignored it. "And that's the optimist's answer."

"The thing is, Pasco, sometimes you t'ink you doin' good"— his eyes gazed sightless around the room—"but all you really doin' is makin' things worse."

Pasco sat down, ran his finger around the rim of his bottle. "It's all one big guessing game, isn't it. Behind Door Number One, behind Door Number Two—"

"Where I come from, Pasco, it ain't hard to know what a man is. A man is this—" He patted the bulge of his wallet in his back pocket. "A man is food and a house. And a man"—he grasped his crotch in an uncharacteristically indecent gesture—"is chil'ren. Chil'ren"—his voice took on a hard edge—"who know their place."

Children who knew their place? And where in hell is that? Pasco wondered.

"I believe in good ol'-fashion discipline, Pasco. Beat the shit out o' them if you have to. The boy learn his lesson back home from his granny when he was small-small. One step out o' line and bam! Bottom burnin' like pepper. But the girl— Man, lay a hand on that one and she screamin' 'bout rights. What rights a harden sixteen-year-ol' girl have, eh, Pasco? You could tell me? You should hear her. Is the law, is the law!"

Pasco raised his eyebrows. What could he say?

"Fock, man, Pasco. The law? Sometimes I does t'ink this country crazy, you hearin' me? I make the girl, my wife bring her into this world, and now we ain't have the right to straighten her out the way we want? The law should learn to keep its nose out o'

people business." He tilted his head backwards and drained half
the beer.

He began pacing around the room in his thick woollen socks.
"My parents beat me," he said. "And their parents beat them.
Nobody ever run away, everybody understan' is just part o' life."
There was genuine puzzlement in his voice. "You never beat your
boy, Pasco?"

"When he deserved it. And when his mother would let me."

Montgomery stared at a freshly painted wall, his mind scribbling frustrations on it. "Is part of a parent's job, not so? To keep
the kids on the straight an' narrow? But you should hear Miss
Charlene fancy ideas. Suddenly she too good, she too grown up to
listen. *Repression*! Another one of her fancy words. We say school,
not job? We repressin' her. We say homework, not TV? We
repressin' her. We say no party on school nights? We repressin'
her. Accordin' to the young lady, discipline is jus' another word for
repression, we tryin' to prevent her from bein' true to herself—
whatever the fock that mean." He paused to take a breath. "Well, if
you ask me, a little repression never hurt nobody. Hell, man, it
probably even good for the soul." He glanced over at Pasco.

"I don't know anything about the soul," Pasco said.

Montgomery drained his beer. Then he walked over to the fireplace and, with great deliberation, put the bottle down on the
mantelpiece. As he did so, Pasco noticed that his hand shook.
Montgomery flicked a finger at the empty bottle. "You have
another one o' these?"

"You up to it?"

"Is Christmas, Pasco. Time to make merry."

"And your wife? Isn't she—"

"She keepin' herself busy. We not exactly dancin' at home these
days, y'know."

Everyone dealt with his problems in his own way, Pasco
thought, everyone did what he had to in order to keep going.

Montgomery turned to beer, Lorraine to work—and he himself chatted with his dead wife.

He went into the kitchen for another beer. He couldn't refuse a friend.

He thought: You see, Edna....

———————

Later in the evening, after Montgomery had left with a grim nod at Pasco's offering of best wishes, Lorraine knocked at the back door. A coat was thrown over her shoulders, an umbrella held in one hand, a plastic shopping bag in the other.

"Am I interrupting anything?" she asked teasingly.

"Well, there's a wild party going on in the living room—"

"So that's where all the noise is coming from, eh?"

He cupped a palm to his ear. "Pardon?"

"Yeah, right." She folded the umbrella, stepped directly from her work boots into the kitchen. From the bag she took a boxed cake—"Store-bought this year, I'm afraid. Things have been pretty hectic around the centre"—and asked whether he'd put up his branch yet. He said he had, and she took a package from the bag. It was wrapped in silver paper with a green bow on top. "Just a little something to put under it," she said. Then she invited him to a get-together at her house with the people who worked at the centre, "if you can tear yourself away from your little orgy". They had food, drink, music, not to mention a tree in the true sense of the word.

Pasco declined. Across their backyards he could see people standing in her kitchen with drinks in their hands. He imagined their talk to be full of victimization, a venting of pain, but he couldn't tell Lorraine that. Instead he pleaded fatigue, said he would probably make an early night of it after Danny had stopped by, as he usually did on Christmas Eve with a store-wrapped gift.

Lorraine pulled the coat more closely around her. "Well, why don't you both come by," she said. "Magda'll be there later. She and Danny haven't seen each other in years and they used to be such good friends."

Pasco couldn't help wondering why Danny and Magda would want to see each other. Young, they had been the centre of idle dreams. As adults, though, both had brought unexpected conflict to their houses—and apart from this what could they possibly have in common today? Precious little, he suspected.

Lorraine patted him on the arm. "I'd better get back to my guests before they tear the place apart."

"Before you go, Lorraine," Pasco said, "can I ask you something? I need some advice, for a friend."

"That's what they all say. So what's the matter, Pasco? Somebody knock you up?"

"It's a friend from the Gate," he said. "Montgomery. His daughter's run away from home."

"How old is she?"

"Sixteen."

She folded her arms. Two vertical lines furrowed her brow. "Tell me about it."

When he was done, she said, "I'll level with you, Pasco. Your friend's in a tough situation here. His kid's offered herself a Roads Scholarship—"

"A Rhodes Scholarship?"

"She dipped her hand into the cookie jar and took off. That's what we call a R-O-A-D-S scholarship down at the centre. Bad joke, I know, but hell, humour's the only way we can get by sometimes, y'know?" She took a deep suck at an imaginary cigarette. "For now there really isn't much your friend can do. Hope she comes back of her own free will, and the odds are against that. Hope she keeps out of trouble, and the odds are against that too. Hope the cops spot her before some shark does, and I don't have to tell you what the odds are on that one."

"I guess I was kind of hoping she might have turned up at the centre."

"Who knows? Anything's possible." But she didn't sound hopeful. "Get me a picture of her if you can. I can't do anything officially, of course, but I can let you know if she turns up. If she does, maybe I could talk to her. But I'm not going to force her to do anything she doesn't want to do, you understand."

"I know that. But, for Montgomery, just knowing she's all right...."

"Don't hold your breath, Pasco. She could be around the corner or she could be a thousand miles away. Either way—"

"Montgomery's not handling it well, Lorraine."

"If he's the religious type, tell him to pray. If he's not, tell him to hope."

"Doesn't seem like much."

"It isn't. But that's all there is, I'm afraid." She squeezed his arm, stepped into her boots, snapped open the umbrella and went out into the rain.

Pasco watched her hurry through their backyards back to her house. She left the gate in the low wooden fence open. And he wished, in a surge of feeling, that he'd thought of getting her a gift too.

The cake, even though store-bought, was nothing like the industrial desserts he purchased for the restaurant. It was round, smothered in a thick coat of creamy chocolate icing studded with blanched almonds. His mouth watered in anticipation as he cut himself a slice, the knife sinking effortlessly through what he soon discovered to be two layers separated by half an inch of dark, nut-filled fudge. He took it into the living room and, sitting in front of his Christmas branch, ate it slowly, washing it down with the last of his warm beer.

He was licking the icing from his fingers when a key turned in the front door and Danny let himself in.

"Hi, Dad. Getting pretty cold out there." He kicked off his boots but kept his coat on.

"Winter," Pasco said. "Does it every time."

Danny stood before him, held out a package, a shirt-sized box professionally wrapped. "Merry Christmas."

Pasco took the gift. "Thanks." He got to his feet. "I got you something too." He went over to his coat and reached into a pocket for the small package.

"Thanks, Dad." Danny hardly glanced at it before slipping it into a coat pocket.

"You got time for a drink?"

"Thanks, but I'm having dinner with friends."

"Friends? I didn't know you had any."

"Remember Andreas? He's having a few people over."

"Ahh, networking, eh?"

"There'll be some interesting people. You never know. Opportunity lurks behind every drink."

Pasco nodded dismissively. He wasn't in the mood to face Danny's voraciousness. He said, "You look tired."

"Work. Personnel changes. We've sort of had to cover for each other." He glanced at his watch. "Gotta get going, Dad. I'm late as it is."

"Well don't let me keep you."

"Just one more thing, Dad." Danny slipped his hands into his coat pockets, and the gesture told Pasco what was coming. "About upstairs—"

"I haven't had the time to think about it, Danny."

"Dad…." He breathed the word in exasperation. "You must be the world's busiest man. Ever since I was a kid, *I haven't got the time, Danny.* Christ! Some things never change, eh?"

"Take a look in a mirror, Danny. It must be genetic."

Danny, suddenly furious, flung an arm around the room. "Have you looked around, Dad? Open your eyes. Look at what we've done. It's clean, it's bright, it's like brand-new. You can't tell me that—"

"It looks great, Danny," Pasco said quietly. "It just doesn't feel like home."

"You just don't like change, that's your problem."

"As if you'd know what I like or don't like. I've said it before: nothing's wrong with change, if it's necessary."

"There you go again. If-if-if! You if everything to death."

Pasco grunted. "If" had come to represent so much in his life. It was a word resonant with lost possibilities: if his father hadn't been killed; if he had gone to university; if he hadn't bought Pascal's; if he had spent more time with Danny; if Edna hadn't died: all the ifs that continued to haunt him. And he wondered whether, in a sense, Danny wasn't right: was he so enmeshed in what might have been that he failed to consider what still might be? So restrained by the disappointments of the past that he feared the possibilities of the future?

"Dad?"

If: such a small word, with the ability to affect so much. Change *if* necessary: he had never before realized what a curiously hopeful thought that was. Pasco found himself smiling.

"There's nothing funny about this, Dad." Danny eyed him as he would a man descending into craziness.

Pasco was silent for a moment. Then he said, "Of course not, Danny. Nothing funny in the least."

"So…."

"I'll call you."

"*If* you manage to find the time?"

"Merry Christmas, Danny." Pasco spoke gently, but his tone was dismissive.

Danny's lips parted but no response came to him. He felt further words to be pointless, they would just ricochet off his father.

Pasco walked him to the door, waited until he'd driven off before opening the gift: a sweater. Canary yellow—not his favourite colour. And the name of the designer was emblazoned in green across the chest and back. Pasco, recalling a time when businesses gave free T-shirts as publicity gimmicks, didn't believe in paying for the privilege of becoming a walking signboard. Oh well, he thought with a touch of regret as he folded the sweater back into its box, he'd had no idea what to get Danny either, no inkling of what his son might want or need. So he'd bought him a gold-plated pen-and-pencil set, as generic an offering as the sweater.

He went to the kitchen to fetch himself a last beer and stood for a moment at the door looking out through the darkness. Lorraine's kitchen was bright, crowded. The people, lively with the gestures of talk and laughter, were all strangers to him. All except Magda, whom he could see leaning against the counter, a drink in hand.

She had grown from a rather nondescript girl to a woman attractive with the Queen Street look: the hair short, the jewellery silver, the clothes black. Lorraine had mentioned, with some surprise, that she was doing all right for herself as co-owner with her companion, Linda, of a small store selling Latin American artifacts. Lorraine had even been to dinner at their flat above the store. A civilized evening, she had said. Promising.

Beside Magda, shoulder pressed familiarly against hers, stood another young woman, taller, similarly dressed, her hair crewcut and dyed golden. Linda, Pasco assumed. Lorraine squeezed by them, topping up their glasses from a wine bottle in her hand. Magda said something to Lorraine, Lorraine said something to Linda. All three laughed.

Pasco felt a pang of envy.

He returned to the living room and settled back in his chair. Under the Christmas branch, Lorraine's gift glowed festive in the reflected lights. The branch no longer looked quite so dismal. He decided he would leave the package where it was for now. He was in no hurry to open it. Its contents, he realized, mattered less to him than its gleaming presence in his living room.

Chapter Sixteen

I T WAS AFTER seven when the painter put away his tools and, mopping at his brow, took his leave. He was an old Hungarian man with silver hair and eyes squinting through thick-lensed glasses. He had brushed aside Pasco's remark on the lateness of his arrival—outside, the fragile January light was already fading, rush-hour traffic quickening the street—and spread a dirty canvas sheet on the floor beneath the new windowpane.

The work of tracing the lettering on the glass took him a long time. In the man's controlled intensity, Pasco recognized the care he himself practised on abused furniture. It took a special kind of pride, he thought, to bring such purpose to so simple a job.

Once the man had outlined the words in white, he announced he would return the following morning to fill them in with the red Pasco had requested. Pasco locked the door behind him, turned the sign to CLOSED and quickly neatened up the place before heading out.

A fine and lengthy afternoon drizzle had left the street damp. Fong's was still open—it would be until late—but Fong himself was not behind the counter. He usually headed upstairs around seven, leaving the store to his wife, a woman whose command of English extended only to simple mathematics and cigarette brands. For emergencies—and they could be as extravagant as fire

or as simple as a customer asking where he could find dish deter-
gent—his eldest son spent the evening in the storeroom at the
back studying until closing time. Pasco, hugging himself in his
coat, thought that despite the long hours and the early days of
struggle Fong was a lucky man.

He watched a streetcar trundle by. He liked streetcars, especially on rainy evenings. Moving determinedly along on their
tracks, they seemed such assured beasts, their interiors bright and
warm and dry. He would have liked to climb into one now, taking
a seat beside a window and riding through the wet night.

But no streetcar went the way of the Starting Gate. He crossed
the street and headed down the paved path through the park. It
was lit all the way to the other end, the lamps powerful enough to
light the way but too feeble to reach more than a few feet around
their cast-iron standards.

Lorraine had issued an open invitation to dinner, but he
wasn't in the mood. He was tired, would have liked nothing more
than to go home, open up a beer and spend a few quiet hours
sanding and polishing. Home, though, was out of the question
just now. He was expected at the Gate. Montgomery, pleased at
the offer, had promised to bring Charlene's photograph for Lorraine, and Pasco didn't want to disappoint him by not turning up
to receive it.

He was almost through the park when the drizzle began again,
fine and misty in the lamplight. He picked up his pace.

Suddenly a voice came at him from the darkness: "Well, well,
look who's here."

Pasco looked around.

"Behind you, old man."

He turned. Emile was leaning against a lamp post puffing on a
cigarette held in his cupped palm. His right eye was shut, the skin
around it blackened. His lower lip was swollen an angry red. Pasco
glanced nervously around—Emile was, apparently, alone—while,

in his pocket, his hand turned his keys into a weapon.

Emile blew a smoke ring, then an arrow of smoke through it. Pasco began backing away.

"What's your hurry, old man? Scared of a little rain?"

"Don't touch me, Emile."

"Why would I want to touch you? I go for pussy myself." He grinned, his face grotesque in the light. "Like my new look? Had a little plastic surgery done courtesy of your cop friends."

"I had nothing to do with that."

"Who said you did?" Another smoke ring, another arrow—and then Emile was stalking towards him, his hands folding into fists.

Pasco spun around, broke into a run.

"Run, old man, run!" Emile screamed after him. "You ain't worth it, you hear me? You ain't worth spit!"

Pasco barely glanced at the traffic before dashing across the street. Unnerved, he ran on, shoes thumping on the sidewalk, shins aching. Ran on past parked cars and lighted houses, breath wheezing from his lungs. Ran doggedly on until a searing stitch in his side forced him to stop.

"You okay, mister?" a female voice said. "You ain't having a heart attack, are you?"

He panted, doubled over, air pressing in at the walls of his contracted lungs. His heart was pounding, his throat parched.

"Gotta watch out in the park," another female voice said. "Gets kind o' dangerous there sometimes."

"You okay, mister?" the first voice repeated.

"Sure he's okay. Just not up for the Olympics yet, that's all."

The pain in his side gradually subsided. He straightened up, glanced back along the street: Emile was nowhere to be seen. Found himself facing two young girls, one white, one black, who could pass for women only through make-up and the night. It was clear they were working the street together. They must have been new, he'd never seen them before; they lacked the coarseness of face and manner that came with time and experience. Why weren't they in school, he wondered, or working in a bank or an office some place?

"Feelin' better, pops?" the white one said.

He nodded. "Fine," he said, adding "Thanks" as an afterthought.

"Well in that case, would you be lookin' for some company?" She opened the top of her coat to a compressed cleavage. "I'm Sugar."

"And I'm Spice," chimed in the black one. "Two for one. Rainy day special."

Pasco shook his head. "You girls shouldn't be out in this weather."

"Gotta earn a living, pops."

"Sugar and Spice—" said Spice.

"—and everything nice," said Sugar. "So how about it?"

"No, thanks. And do up your coat, you'll catch cold like that."

They laughed, moved aside to let him by. "You don't know what you're missing, pops."

He hadn't taken ten steps before he heard a car pull up behind him, heard the murmur of urgent negotiations. Then two doors slammed. The car squealed away from the sidewalk, flashed past him, its rear lights swiftly bearing Sugar and Spice off into the night.

Pasco kept on walking. The street, suddenly empty, felt a sad and lonely place.

Montgomery, curiously out of uniform, was sitting at the table with the others. He was, under Pushpull's watchful gaze, carefully peeling an orange.

Pasco took his seat, looked straight at Montgomery and told him the truth: "You look terrible."

Montgomery took him in through bleary eyes. "As my granny use to say," he mumbled, "what we have here is the pot callin' the kettle black."

Pasco smoothed his hair. "Do I look that bad?"

"No worse than usual," Cruise teased. "From where I sit, the pot and the kettle're equally ugly."

Marcus said, "We're all treatin' Montgomery here to a round tonight, Pasco, a round each, I mean."

"What's up, Montgomery? Is it your birthday or something?"

"Montgomery's goin' through a bad spell," Pushpull said.

"Yeah," Cruise cut in. "It's called unemployment."

"You quit your job?" Pasco was incredulous.

"What quit?" Pushpull said. "They tossed 'im out."

"That's not possible, he works for the government." Pasco looked over at Montgomery. "You guys are untouchable."

"Not when you're drunk on the job," Marcus said.

"And especially not when you belt the union rep one," Cruise added.

Montgomery put down the orange and the knife, glowered at the centre of the table. "Get it straight once and for all," he hissed. "I wasn' drunk and the fella ask for it, okay?"

"Hey, man," Cruise said. "We know that and you know that, but we know and you know that big unions are no different from big employers. They invent any truth they want, and only their truth exists. If they say you were drunk, you were drunk, period. Don't matter a damn if the only thing in your system was water. Union says H_2O makes you drunk, then H_2O makes you drunk, simple as that."

Trade unions were one of Cruise's obsessions. He claimed to be writing a book about them prompted by the oft-repeated story of his father, a typesetter who, when Cruise was still young, had disobeyed union orders during a strike to smash the windshield of a company executive's car. He had found himself blacklisted, future assured by the union, but not quite in the way promised.

"Look here, fellas," Montgomery said, slicing the orange in half. "That fella was always after me for one thing or another. All I had was a couple o' beers with lunch. He smell it on my breat' and boom! trouble. He accuse me loud-loud of drinkin'on the job. I tell him leave me alone and he lay a hand on me. Well, I don't take that from nobody. I let him have one straight on the nose. Whap!"

Pasco said, "Bad move."

Pushpull said, "You don't know the half of it."

"Nex' thing I know, I sittin' at home quiet-quiet las' night watchin' 'Wheel o' Fortune' and suddenly it have two cops knockin' at the door. Well, I figure it have something to do with Charlene, right? So you could imagine how I was surprise when they grab me and put the cuffs on. Nex' thing I know, I sittin' in the back o' the cruiser charge with assault."

"But the guy provoked you, eh?" Pasco asked. "You have witnesses?"

"Some o' the fellas was around, but—"

"But they have to watch out for their own butts," Cruise said. "It's called solidarity."

Montgomery shrugged. "They have families too."

"Yeah, there's always something, eh? One excuse or another, anything'll do."

"But what about—what do they call it?" Marcus said. "Extenuating circumstances? You know, trouble at home?"

"Sounds more like exterminating circumstances to me," Cruise said. "All they'll say is that he took his personal frustrations out on this guy, that's all. Case closed. Guilty as charged."

"You a lawyer or something?"

"I like facing facts, man, that's all."

"What d'you think, Pasco?"

"I think Montgomery shouldn't have hit the guy."

"So what I was suppose to do, eh? Tell me. I ain't no Jesus Chris', man, Pasco. I have a temper like everybody else, I does get hot up sometimes."

"I hope you broke his nose at least," Cruise said.

Montgomery laughed, bit into one of the orange halves.

But it was a laugh that Pasco hadn't heard from him before. Its tone made him uneasy, for there was an edge to it that told him Montgomery's temper was still far too close to the surface for comfort—his, or anyone else's.

———————

It was almost midnight by the time Pasco got home. His belly was heavy with beer, his eyes red and strained, but the walk through the deserted streets had refreshed him. The drizzle had stopped, the air softened until it held only a hint of wintry bite, teasing with a reminder of the spring still months off. After the tensions of the Starting Gate, he had enjoyed the fantasy of the air turning warmer, the world greener, buds appearing from one day to the next, frail, with a waxy sheen to them. He would sneeze for a few days as he usually did, especially in the mornings and just after it had rained. But his misery would be made bearable by the explosion of leaves and flowers, the buds spreading and fattening overnight. Edna had always been happiest in spring, her joy unconcealed, as if she hadn't believed that the world could escape the tight grip of winter and was delighted to find that it had. Her happiness had never failed to infect him.

He removed his coat and, yawning, ripped open the sealed envelope Montgomery had slipped to him as they were leaving the Gate.

A Polaroid photograph: Charlene.

His heart skipped a beat. He held the picture up to the light, squinted hard at it.

He thought: *Nutmeg.* And his hand shook.

He thought: *Spice.* And the beer rose sour to his mouth.

———————

He was up all night torn by uncertainty. Several times he'd picked up the telephone, several times he'd begun dialling Montgomery's number. And each time he'd hung up before entering the last digit.

Sugar

And Spice

And everything nice

He spent the night in his workroom, fussing distractedly over his furniture, stripping one piece, sanding another, oiling a third. He was unable to concentrate on any of the tasks: they all dissatisfied him.

The last time he picked up the phone, he'd succeeded in entering the complete number—but then he'd hung up before Montgomery's phone could ring.

Finally the dawn came: an overcast day, the sky spitting flurries. The branches of the young tree across the street hung disconsolate in the heavy air.

He dialled Lorraine's number. She answered immediately, her voice thick with sleep.

Two for one. Rainy day special.

She was silent when he told her what he'd learnt, confining herself to confirming what he already knew: if Montgomery was his friend, what choice was there?

His mind was a blank when he once more dialled Montgomery's number. Remained blank as he entered the final digit, as he listened to the buzz urgent in the early morning.

When he heard Montgomery's anxious voice, the words came of themselves, stilted and without premeditation: "I saw Charlene last night. I didn't know it was her till I got home. Then I saw the photo. I…. She was with another girl, she looked all right."

"Where?"

"Pembroke Street."

"What she was doin' there?"

"Working."

"Workin'?"

"The street."

Silence.

In the distant background, the voice of his wife: Who it is, Monty? Who it is? Is Charlene?

"Pasco, you fockin' son of a bitch. You son of a bitch! Fock-youfockyoufockyou—"

A harsh clatter.

Dial tone.

Pasco hung up. He felt empty.

The kitchen door banged. Lorraine called, "Pasco?"

His body went limp when she pressed herself to his back and wrapped him in her arms.

Chapter Seventeen

Danny sat in the darkness and listened to the silence. He had spent months stalking the house, peering into its corners, examining its angles, measuring and sketching, projecting and imagining. And he had managed with great effort to come up with preliminary plans, something to show the boss. But he wasn't pleased with the work—it felt unformed, still not quite within his grasp—and the boss's muted reaction told him he wasn't pleased either. The house was still resisting him, defeating his efforts to draw it fully into his imagination, the vision he had pieced together sitting incoherent in his mind, like pieces of different jigsaw puzzles forced together.

He still had some time—Mr. Simmons wanted to begin work by late spring, once two other projects had been completed—and he took every opportunity to visit the house. He often came, as he had this evening, directly from work simply to sit and listen and feel, hoping that the pieces would sort themselves out, assume a pattern and suggest a natural direction.

The work shouldn't have been so demanding. All the elements had been handed to him. He had only to arrange them in the desired order to achieve the desired effect. But something mischievous—he couldn't tell what—was playing with him, displacing one piece when he was occupied with another.

He had arrived some time earlier, shutting the door behind him—quietly, for the house immediately imposed its silence. And it was as if, in doing so, he had shut out the evening. That was, he suspected, the main problem: the house, its very hulk, seemed connected to nothing. First a family home redolent with gentility, then a rooming house rent by resentments, the structure had lost some essential ingredient of itself, as if the manipulation of its space, the wilful reshaping of its soul, had wrenched away any defining personality it might once have had, leaving it divorced from the neighbourhood. Inside or outside, the house had no context of its own.

How to redefine the house, then? How to recapture—and to renew without trivializing—what it once had been? He had suggested to Mr. Simmons that they ask Andreas to take a look, but the boss had rejected the idea out of hand. He feared that Andreas would turn the house into a carnival version of the past, much flash and little content. "He's good at what he does," the boss had said. "But he's pretty superficial for a man who takes himself so seriously. That's why he's good at lobbies."

Listening for Sita, hearing nothing, he assumed she was out or asleep. He breathed more easily. Then, driven by instinct, undefined and therefore not something he could grapple with, he went directly up to the second floor. He stood at the window through which Mr. Simmons's mother, her sewing or knitting in her hand, would have gazed out at the side street forlorn in the lamplight, the windows of the house across the street egg-yellow on the first floor, dark on the second.

The silence hardened around him.

He drew his fingertips along the windowsill. The paint was dry, peeling in spots. Thin slabs of it flaked off easily under the pressure of a fingernail.

The silence: this was what he had to shatter—and then, somehow, with an effort of imagination, to remake, reordering its pieces into a complete yet totally different whole.

There were no problems, only opportunities. Who knew what rewards pleasing the boss on this project would bring. But resistance had to be met with confidence, a refusal to admit even the possibility of defeat. It was the core ideal of his training.

And yet: idealism divorced from reality was useless.

And the reality of searching for the feel of this house, the sheer effort of it, was not unlike trying to commune with the dead.

The sound, faint and undefinable, was yet definite enough to send a shimmer down his spine.

A shuffle? A sniffle? A knock? The fall of a shoe....

A surreptitious noise. A noise that had sought to muffle itself.

He hadn't been listening for it—not for something concrete— and had heard it almost in split-second retrospect. It might have come from outside: the final echo of a child's shout, perhaps, or the wayward cough of a car engine. But he sensed that it hadn't. His eyes blinked into the darkness behind him, half-expecting to find Sita standing in the doorway, but he saw only the shadowed outlines of the corridor.

Then, again: a soft rustling that seemed to come from every-where, a sound adrift in the air.

He thought of Mr. Simmons's mother: half a startled face in a mirror in a photograph. But he didn't believe in ghosts, not even those of the mind.

He took small, careful steps out into the hallway, peered down the stairs. The light in the corridor was still on, its glow fading out at the fourth or fifth step. He slowly made his way down, sliding one hand along the railing.

The front door was shut, the corridor inanimate in the thick yellow light. But the air was not as it should have been, was alive with dust fibres recently disturbed. He supposed that Sita had come, shut herself up in her room. He was wondering whether he should let her know he was there when another sound gave him pause: a brief and indistinct mumbling from Sita's room.

Curious, breath shortened by a sense of illegality, he crept into the cell next to hers and perched uneasily on the edge of the bed frame.

He listened.

Nothing. Not so much as a whisper.

Then: a creaking of wood and the swift and urgent drawing of breath.

The silence grew brittle.

A sudden moan punched a hole in the silence, startled him.

He wondered whether he should check on her, maybe she wasn't well. Or maybe he shouldn't disturb her at all: curious how a moan could indicate either pain or pleasure, and how indistinguishable one could be from the other. He was considering his choices when he heard once more the low murmur of a male voice.

So that was it.

Wood creaked once more, someone stirring on the bed, or moving about on the floor, he couldn't tell which.

Danny found himself smiling: well, well....

Then the male voice, half-commanding, half-pleading, said, *Be good, be good*

Danny's smile melted away: the few words were all he needed to recognize Mr. Simmons.

Open your mouth

The tone that of a gentle dentist coaxing an unwilling patient.

Wider

A rhythmic thumping shook the wall like light blows from a fist.

A tremor fluttered through Danny's body. He couldn't push away the image the sounds insisted on: Sita—crouched, sitting, on the bed? Yes, her back pressed to the wall. And clothed, surely, he couldn't picture her otherwise. But barefooted.

Yes, yes, that's it

With the boss, Mr. Simmons, standing—yes, it was the only way—pressed close to her. Both feet on the bed, or maybe one on the floor and one on the bed, his middle pressed in close to Sita's face. Supporting himself with his hands on the wall. His face a violent pink, his eyes shut tight. Wearing still his jacket and tie, but with his legs gruesomely bare.

Good girl...

The thumping continued on the wall, the slow and measured beat of a dull drum.

Very good girl...

Beside Sita on the bed, Mr. Simmons's trousers neatly folded, his socks laid out beside them for some reason, his shoes neatly together on the floor. Premeditation was at the heart of Mr. Simmons: there would be with him no crumpling of clothes in the haste of passion.

Like that, just like that...

And despite his dismay, despite the rapping thunder of Sita's head on the wall, Danny felt the tingle of arousal.

Then—the thumping stopped.

What's the matter? The voice was hoarse. *But I'm not—* The tone struggling to be reasonable. *I haven't—*

Coughing, sharp and painful. Whispers: Sita.

Danny pressed an ear to the wall, to no avail.

Is that right? But you don't breathe through your mouth, do you?

More coughing, sniffling.

Fine, then. Stretch out. No, not like that. Face down.

Wood creaked.

Face down, I said.

Wood creaked again: old, dry planks.

Good girl. Very good girl. A heavy sigh, movement on the bed.

"Mr. Leon, no!"

Suddenly, a meaty slap.

Sita cried out.

You don't want to get pregnant, do you? Another slap, sharper this time.

Danny's mouth went dry.

Relax....

"No, Mr. Leon—"

I said, relax.

"Mr. Leon, please—"

Another slap.

"No, Mr. Leon, not there, not—" She choked, her voice cracking, protest dissolving into a gurgle.

The wood creaked, crackled.

Sita moaned long and low to minute splinterings.

The sounds of agony were new to Danny, were like nothing he had ever heard before. His legs went weak, his lungs refused air: it was as if the house itself were smothering him. He hung his head in his hands, felt his insides churn.

Overheard sobs, whimpers of private distress: only the moans of Mr. Simmons's releasing tensions disturbed the memory.

With his father's voice—why was that?—Danny thought: Ignorance is bliss.

When the tears tickled hot and wet down his cheeks, he imagined they were blood.

———

Danny remained sitting in the darkness until he heard Mr. Simmons leave Sita's room. Froze as the boss, still doing up his belt, walked by and trudged up the stairs.

Waited until there were no more sounds, no more stirrings, before quietly letting himself out of the house. He felt emptied, brittle, as if drained of his insides and left only with a shell.

He stood on the sidewalk for several long minutes, looking back at the house, feeling mocked by it. A dull light shone in Mr. Simmons's third-floor flat, but all Danny could see was Simba frozen in silhouette.

———————

Sal called twice the following morning and each time Danny let the machine take the message.

After the second call, Estelle, dusting the furniture, said with concern, "Hibernating, are we?" She was short and plump, her silver hair twisted into a bun at the back of her head.

Danny, lounging on the sofa, simply shrugged. He wouldn't have known what name to give to his mood.

When the phone rang a third time and Sal moaned unhappily into the machine, Danny decided he had to see what he wanted.

"Where have you been, Daniel? This isn't like you."

"In bed."

"Alone?"

"Fuck you, Sal."

"Look, don't you give me a hard time, I've got a situation here."

"Could we make this fast? I'm not up to—"

"Must be something going around. I don't feel too hot either and there's no sign of the boss yet."

"Yeah, right. Now what can't wait?"

A kitchen pipe had burst in 1507, flooding not only that apartment but 1407 and 1207 as well. The tenants were howling and Sal was going crazy.

Had he called the plumber?

That wasn't his job. And, besides, the boss wasn't around to approve the expense.

"Call her anyway."

Sal refused. He'd be damned if he was going to—

"You're pissing me off, Sal."

"Well isn't that too bad."

Danny took the plumber's number and called her himself. She wasn't in, and he left a message with her answering service. "Yes, it's an emergency, dammit."

"We Irish have been everywhere, don't you know," Estelle said when he hung up. "Hell, we've even been to the stars."

"You mean up in space, Estelle?" He stepped into the kitchen for a fresh cup of coffee. He hadn't slept well, and had awoken only when Estelle let herself in.

"Right-o!"

The demons of Mr. Simmons's house had declared themselves, and they were more virulent than he'd expected.

"You probably think I'm farting from the wrong side, don't you?"

"You, Estelle?"

Everything's a product, Dad. Everything can be bought or sold. Even people. The words materialized by themselves in Danny's mind, rising without warning.

"Ignorance'll get you nowhere, young man."

If they're not useful in some way then what's their value? Zero, Pops, a big fat zero: What had that argument been about? Welfare? Unemployment insurance? Handouts?

"All you have to do is look up at the night sky and you'll see him. The hunter, with his bow and arrow at the ready."

Some people starving in Africa. That's what it had been about. His father had donated one day's proceeds from the restaurant. A pointless gesture. They were going to die anyway, why prolong the agony?

"And he's Irish, the hunter?" Danny couldn't fathom why the argument should resurface at this moment, and with an insistence beyond his control.

"But of course he is. Don't you know anything?"

Let them die? Selfishness, his father had said. Tight-fisted, that's what you are. You, you and you, that's all that matters, eh? Why get involved if there isn't a profit to be made? All this crap about sparing them the agony, that's just camouflage and you know it.

"And what makes you say that, Estelle?"

"Why, his name, of course. It's a dead giveaway."

But it wasn't camouflage. Danny didn't believe in a world of misery, but as a pragmatic man, as a man who, unlike his father, viewed the world without sentimentality, he saw no choice but to apply what he thought a natural logic. Money, as the cliché said, made the world go round, and without it a man was nothing. Withered economies and their dormant consumers had no place in it. Why save people who might one day be able to scratch out a living, at the very best? Why help condemn them to an existence without a future?

"I see." Danny couldn't help smiling. "But Estelle, you know it's spelt O-R-I-O-N."

And what about you, Dad? Don't you just give your money so your bleeding heart will let you sleep at night? Your charity has nothing to do with those people. They're just a convenient hook for your conscience.

"That's how *some* people spell it."

Maybe so, Danny, but at least my weakness doesn't result in pain for other people.

Estelle, straight-faced, eyed him for a reaction. Danny couldn't tell whether or not she was joking. He bought himself time by taking a long sip of his coffee. He liked Estelle: if the misconception kept her happy, who was he to disabuse her? What would be the point? He well knew that illusion too had its place. That was what Simmons Construction sold, after all: the illusion of luxury, the belief that a certain way of life could be bought ready-made.

Doing good, as Mr. Simmons would say, was just doing yourself a favour.

Suddenly Estelle broke into a wide grin. "Fell f'rit, didn't you."

Pain for other people.

"I fall for a lot of things," Danny said, rewarding her with a thin smile. "You should be in sales, Estelle. You'd clean up."

"And don't I know it!" She switched on the vacuum cleaner.

In its whine and its moan, Danny thought he could hear Sita's agony.

———————

Estelle left just after midday, the apartment sparkling, the air heavy with the smells of cleaners and disinfectants.

Danny turned to the business pages of the newspaper. It was here among the well-ordered columns of stock-market reports that he often sought comfort and amusement. They were, except in times of market uncertainty, his comics page and his bible. They told tales, offered parables, amazed, delighted and admonished. They provided inspiration and caution, told of wealth already made and of wealth yet to be made. They were damnation and they were hope. They were the past, present and future neatly laid out for all to see, terms precise and mathematical, indisputable, judgements objective and uncompromising.

But not today.

Today their very harmony defeated him, their truths insufficient.

Restless, he went into the kitchen. The counters were spotless, the sink shone. He sat at the breakfast counter and gazed out at the lake: cloud and sun, the island ferry. The world carrying on.

After a while it came to him why that old argument with his father had replayed itself in his mind, as fresh and as spiky as the day they had had it. Sita, with her needs and her hunger and her inability to create answers for herself, was that argument made flesh. The realization shook him.

Behind him the fridge hummed and gurgled, defrosting itself. Danny listened intently to the sounds of ice becoming water.

Chapter Eighteen

FOR PASCO, every new year began slowly. In January, business slowed down as the city sank into a post-Christmas despondency. February, numerically the shortest month, stretched into an agony of rain and snow and dampness under blanketing cloud, inspiring a kind of meteorological depression. The warmth of summer seemed impossibly distant. Pasco's knees and ankles felt continually ravaged.

The biggest blizzard of the season began early one afternoon with the deception of light flakes tossing about on a breeze. They thickened quickly, building into an avalanche of snow that blurred the park. The street turned white, traction treacherous. Traffic slowed down. Pedestrians walking by bent unsteadily into the wind, hats and coats whitening as they struggled forward on unsure footing.

Pasco headed home early. He made himself a coffee, tied on an old apron and spent a few hours working at a coffee table, strengthening the legs and stripping away several layers of paint to the fresh pine underneath. The work—making the old new again—was satisfying, the isolation of the workroom, his picking and rapping and scraping locking out the shudder and hiss of the wind.

Lorraine called just before seven that evening. She had seen the light in his workroom and figured that, since he'd been working at his furniture for all that time, he probably hadn't made himself dinner. She had enough for two: "So d'you feel like joining me or d'you have a hot date lined up with some blonde?"

Pasco snorted. He was grateful for the invitation. His arms were growing tired, the slowed rhythm of the work weakening his defences: he could hear the wind sniffing around the house, sucking through cracks, seeking entry. "She's a redhead," he said. "Only she cancelled on me. The weather, you know…."

It was Lorraine's turn to snort. "Yeah, right."

He showered quickly before hurrying through their backyards already buried under a thick layer of snow.

Lorraine, sipping at a glass of wine, met him at the kitchen door. She handed him a beer and watched in mock admiration— "Wow! One hand!"—as he twisted off the cap. She then motioned him towards the living room. "You know where the coat-tree is, I'll just be a minute. And keep an eye on the fire for me, will you?"

Pasco hung up his coat and stood at the front window looking out. Thick flakes were whipping down through the glow of the trembling streetlight, the street itself defined only by the white humps of parked cars hugging both sidewalks like huddled sheep. It was not a night to be out, not a night to be far from home.

He didn't remain long at the window, soon stepping away from it, and away from the sounds of the wind that were beginning to worm themselves into his head. Stepped closer to the fireplace and the warmth of its crackling flame.

On the mantelpiece was a large photograph of Rick, a posed black-and-white portrait, his large eyes staring frankly into the lens. It was something Rick had rarely done in life; his gaze, even when directed straight at you, had appeared averted, his dark grey pupils viewing the world with a certain wariness. He'd had a fleshy face with full, rounded features, his silver hair plastered back until it erupted in tight curls at the nape of his neck. Pasco wouldn't have described Rick as a happy man; there seemed to be a part of him that was permanently unsettled.

Propped beside the photograph in a little glass case was an Iron Cross military decoration.

"How come you've never asked about the cross?" Lorraine came into the living room with a wine bottle in one hand and her glass in the other.

Pasco shrugged: did he dare say that he'd never dared?

"Everybody's afraid to ask about it," she said, tipping her glass to it. "They all imagine Rick did something unspeakable to earn it. Whenever Magda comes over I have to chuck it behind the photo. She calls it Nazi junk, only it's not Nazi at all, just German. Rick treasured it."

"I didn't know Rick was in the war."

"In a manner of speaking. He was only sixteen but he was already a seasoned soldier, at least as seasoned as you can be at that age. He was a member of the Hitler Youth, they all had to be. The Russians were closing in on Berlin, hell, they were there in the city. And there was only a bunch of kids, Rick included, between them and the big guy. Then one day out of the blue the big guy himself turns up. Only he turns out to be a little guy with sickly skin and trembling hands—at least, that was Rick's impression. He wanted to thank the boys personally. He shook their hands and gave each of them an Iron Cross. Then he went back to his bunker and put a gun to his head. Left the kids to deal with whatever came next. Your typical father, eh?"

"Can't say I blame Magda, Lorraine. I mean, Rick got this thing for defending Hitler."

"Not as far as he was concerned. He was just defending himself. And that's what the medal's for. For surviving. For making it to the American sector then making it here." She stepped to the middle of the living room, gestured with her glass at all four walls as if saluting them. "And it's for all this, for me, for Magda. Everything that came after." A drop of wine flew from her glass and spattered magenta on her white blouse. Her fingers flicked unconcerned at it. "He was a sentimental man, you know, sentimental and angry. Whenever he'd had a drop too much, he'd pick up the cross and glare at it and mutter away to himself. *Der Fucker gave this to me. With his own two hands. Der Fucker himself.*"

Pasco smiled, but Lorraine's seriousness immediately made him feel like apologizing.

"He wasn't an easy man to live with, you know."

Pasco leaned an elbow on the mantelpiece. "Rick always struck me as pretty easygoing."

"Easygoing to you was silence to me." She let herself down into an armchair. "Tell me something, Pasco. Did you ever have a real conversation with Rick?"

"Lots."

"And what did you talk about? Kids? Marriage?"

"Men don't talk about things like that, Lorraine." But that wasn't quite true: he thought of Montgomery.

"So what do men talk about? Cars? Sex? War? *Man stuff*? Like you and your drinking buddies? What? Did Rick tell you how often he screwed me—"

"Lorraine—"

"—or how many Russians he blew away?"

"Not a word, on either count."

"So what are all these things you talked about then?"

"Just things. Hunting, fishing, politics."

"And he never told you about the two biggest things in his life, the war and his marriage." She shook her head vigorously. "You men, you're all the same. You make your lives secret, then you create more secrets to satisfy your need for secrecy."

"What secrets? I don't have any secrets."

"Bullshit. Did you ever tell Rick about your affair? Edna told me."

"Oh she did, did she." His affair: it was not a memory Pasco cherished. His affair—although that was too strong a word for what it had been—with the woman who, for a short time, he'd employed as a waitress.

"She wanted to kill you."

"I know."

"I told her she should."

"Thanks. Really appreciate that."

"You know, Edna never understood why you did it."

He rolled his eyes in irritation. "That was a long time ago, Lorraine. Besides, it was hardly an affair. I only slept with her once."

"That's once too often."

"I was young."

"Your *son* was young."

"Business wasn't good, things were tense between Edna and me—"

"And you really liked the way she poured coffee, eh? Fuck, Pasco, this is bullshit and you know it."

"Why am I doing this?" Pasco said in exasperation. He stalked in a circle around the living room. "I don't have to explain myself to you, Lorraine."

"Of course not. The strong silent man with the big hard dick. Christ!"

"What are you suddenly? Edna's advocate?"

"God knows she needed one. But she wouldn't let me get involved except as the ear that you weren't."

With great deliberation—meant as a demonstration of dignified anger—he put his beer down on the mantelpiece. "Goodnight, Lorraine," he said. "Thanks for the drink."

"Sure. Go on, run." She didn't move from the chair, didn't look at him. "Funny how you have little speeches about everything except yourself. But, oh! I forgot. You haven't got any secrets." She gulped at her wine. "You know where the door is."

But he didn't really want to go. Wanted instead—and without knowing why—to convince Lorraine of…. Of what? He didn't even know that. "All right," he said after a minute. "You want the truth?"

"Only if you feel like sharing." She spoke with exaggerated coyness. "Lecture number sixty-nine, I take it?"

He breathed hard: yet another demonstration of dignified anger. "Look, are you really interested or—"

"I'm listening."

"This isn't easy, Lorraine." He picked up the beer, drank just enough to wet his dry throat. Time had dulled the pain, but the memory could still unnerve him. "She wasn't terribly attractive, you know."

"My-my, defensive, aren't we."

"Just stating the facts."

"And they are?"

"Curiosity, that's all. She offered, I accepted. Nobody was supposed to know, nobody was supposed to get hurt."

"Yeah, nobody's ever supposed to get hurt."

"I wasn't in love with her or anything like that, you know. But there she was, I'd never been with a blonde before."

"C'mon, Pasco. What's the big deal about blondes anyway? They're just albino brunettes."

Pasco couldn't suppress a smile, for he'd quickly discovered in her flat above the restaurant that his blonde dyed her hair. "Anyway," he said, "it was all over pretty fast." An uninspired coupling, his excitement coming from the knowledge of sexual adventure rather than from the sexual adventure itself. "She wanted to kiss me. I refused."

"Whoopee for you."

"I got out of there as fast as I could." How was he to know that she would yap about it afterwards? Of course, the talk had eventually worked its way back to Edna. The worst part of it was that, when she confronted him, he could give no coherent reason for what he'd done.

"Oh, I'll bet *that* would have made Edna feel a whole lot better."

"It's not easy being a saint, Lorraine, you said so yourself. Curiosity got the better of me." He spoke sadly, aware of the inadequacy of the excuse. Years had passed before an unhesitant intimacy returned to Edna and him. "Didn't you ever do something without thinking first, Lorraine?"

"I see too much down at the centre to act without thinking hard first, Pasco."

Pasco turned, looked directly at her. "Edna forgave me, Lorraine."

She nodded slowly.

"But you—"

"I'm the one who told her to kill you, remember?" But there was no anger or bitterness in her voice. She might have been teasing him.

"Can I ask you something?"

"Fire away, I have no secrets."

"How come you never remarried?"

The question amused her. "Been saving myself for the right man. Only trouble is, he hasn't come along yet." She held her empty glass out towards him.

He walked over, picked up the bottle from the floor beside her, filled the glass.

"At least," she continued, "not that I've been made aware of yet anyway."

———

He knew when it happened. He had, over her protests, helped her with the dishes and had just descended the stepladder after replacing the serving dish on the uppermost shelf.

But he couldn't say precisely how it was that he came to be exploring the soft wetness of her mouth. He had seen her eyes flutter, become hooded, as their mouths neared. But who had moved first to bring their lips together? Whose arms had first reached around the other's waist?

His tongue brushed the sharpness of her teeth as her body pressed hard against his. Her breath fell warm and moist on his cheek.

Their lips parted, her hand feeling for his, raising his index finger to her mouth.

His body shuddered with a long-unfamiliar thrill. He said, "Lorraine,…"

And at the sound of her name she bit down on his finger, unsparingly.

He felt her teeth pressing against the bone: a peculiar ache. Promising, demanding: unsubtle in its messages.

She let his finger out of her mouth slowly, pushing at it with the tip of her tongue.

Then she took his hand, led him from the kitchen.

The corridor was a blur, but the darkness of the bedroom—a faint odour of powder, perfumes, a sweet femininity—restored a febrile equilibrium to him.

They reached once more for each other: a tentative embrace. Again their lips met. Hands squeezed, caressed.

And soon they moved to search out clasps and buttons, buckles and zippers.

Pasco's fingers lost their agility, felt thick and heavy as they trembled at their enigmatic tasks. A searing light shone in his mind: these sensations, these actions. They all felt new again.

And a question presented itself to that part of himself that remained distant, coolly observant: was it possible to be chaste once more? Could the years of abstinence have washed away knowledge and made him raw again?

The bed rocked under them as they sank back onto the mattress, Lorraine cradling him in her thighs. The softness, the warmth, the elemental yearning of another body: he could have stayed like this forever, his body electrified, his senses on fire.

They kissed gently. Then, quickly, with ferocity.

When he entered her, it was like a sensation never known yet always known. Time glided away in a spiralling of intensity. He rode deep into her, her legs clasping his, her hands resting lightly on his shoulders, their energies fused in membranes of complicity.

Pasco sensed a tightening of his body, a surge of strength in his hips. Age eased as he followed the dictates of instinct.

Her fingers stroked his back. Growing passion gritted itself on her face, announced itself in her breathing, until her hands stopped their wandering and clasped the small of his back to urge him deeper.

Then, without warning: nothing.

A sudden cessation.

A deadening.

His outstretched arms trembled. He grew soft, felt himself slip from her.

Lorraine smiled at his dismay, her hands moving to soothe. She pressed his head to her breasts, caressed his back.

He relaxed, sensitive to her every sound. And soon, reassured, he took her nipple into his mouth, felt a tingling low in his belly as it hardened against his tongue. A desperation grew in him. He wanted more, faster. The sounds of his hunger rose artless around them.

Lorraine sat up, easing him off her.

His mouth left her breast with reluctance. He lay back, obeyed her whisper to close his eyes. Concentrated, at first a little too hard. But soon found himself drifting, disarmed by her fingers and her lips. She was relaxed, unhurried.

And eventually a knot undid itself deep inside of him.

When she took him into her mouth, he sighed, a lengthy exhalation of surprise and pleasure.

His vigour renewed itself and soon he was reaching for her, her thighs parting at his touch. His heart pounded when his fingers discovered her wetness. He began to sit up but she gently pushed him back down. "Don't move," she whispered, squatting over him, palms on his chest, fingers pinching at his nipples. He closed his eyes as she guided him into her.

The bed shuddered and squeaked under them, Lorraine pressing hard against him, her flesh slapping wetly on his. A dissonance of bedsprings filled the darkness. Her breathing grew heavy, each breath flowing into a husky moan.

Pasco opened his eyes: her body a shadow, her presence clothed in darkness. But he could feel her, wet and alive, eager for more and more of him. His hips rose to meet hers.

Her orgasm shook her violently.

Pasco's eyes welded shut as his body stiffened and the darkness splintered around him.

Maybe, Pasco thought, it was not impossible to be reborn.

"I'll tell you one of my secrets, Pasco." Lorraine's head was on his shoulder, his arm resting lightly on her back.

"I thought women didn't have any secrets."

She clicked her tongue. "That's what I like about men. They're so naïve, they'll believe anything. Each one's the longest, the thickest, the most virile—"

"You mean I'm not?" Pasco said with comic distress.

"But of course you are." She patted his chest. "There, there...."

Pasco said, "So what's this grand secret?"

She pressed her body closer to his. "I once—" She paused, her hand running down through the grey curls on his chest and belly. "I once came real close to killing Rick."

"Oh yeah?"

"I'm not kidding."

"You expect me to believe that?"

"You don't have to. But it's why I believe you about your affair with the blonde bombshell."

"It wasn't an affair—"

"Whatever." Her finger probed into his navel. "It's all about a moment, isn't it? Not great passion or anything like that, just—"

"It's an opportunity that presents itself."

"—and just at that moment you have the ability to change your life completely, if you follow through on it." Her body shuddered against his.

"My moment wasn't that grand."

"It could have been. You could have decided to run off with your sexy waitress."

"Fat chance."

"She might have turned out to be everything you ever dreamed of in a woman."

"But she didn't."

"But she might have, that's the point. What *could* have happened."

"So what could have happened then? With you and Rick, I mean."

"I could've pushed him into a lake and watched him drown."

"Nice. Remind me never to take a bath with you."

Absorbed by the images in her mind, she ignored his attempt at humour. "It was the only time I ever went fishing with him. He'd been asking me forever to come but, let's face it, there's more to life than sitting around waiting for greedy fish to swallow a hook. But this one time I gave in. Had this little dream that maybe out on the lake he'd relax and open up a little. Stupid, huh? You can't talk when you're fishing, scare the fish away. He clammed up, worse than ever. I got so mad—" Her voice shook. "I'm not even crazy about the taste of fish. All he'd say was, 'So we can be together.' God knows, I hated every minute of it. We sat in that dinghy out in the middle of the lake like two statues in a park, each holding a fishing pole. And in the silence, I got this idea: it'd be so easy to push him in, just…" Her palm rose from his chest, punched stiffly at the air. "…push. Rick didn't know how to swim, he refused to wear a life-jacket. He'd have sunk like a stone. And my entire life would've been changed in seconds, with no legal consequences. Accidents happen, after all, and as far as everyone was concerned, things were great between Rick and me. Your normal, everyday couple."

"Didn't you love him any more?"

"Don't be ridiculous. I never stopped loving Rick. But that had nothing to do with it. Opportunities like that don't come along every day, Pasco, and I can't tell you how powerful it was. That possibility of change, something totally different: God, it was tempting. I mean, I could actually feel my muscles tense up, getting ready. I could actually picture myself doing it. No, more than that: I did it without actually doing it, I was so close. And you know, as I pictured him going under, bubbles and all, I felt deeply sorry for him. I mean, he'd be so scared and so puzzled, probably. Just for a few seconds, I know, but still…. And that hurt me, it pierced my heart more than anything else. Because it had nothing to do with him, it all had to do with me and the moment—and the opportunity that presented itself, as you put it."

"I wonder," Pasco said, "if Rick ever fantasized about killing you?"

"Probably. If he was sane."

"Do you still talk to him?"

"All the time."

"Do you—" His breath caught slightly as her hand moved

lower. "Do you find yourself talking to him more now than when he was alive?"

She nodded, her tongue flicking at his nipple. "I'll tell you something else, though—"

"What's that?'

"He's no more talkative now than he used to be."

Pasco was silent for a long time, thinking about that moment which either slipped into oblivion or realigned your life: that moment which, if seized, could remake everything. He said, after a while, "You're a dangerous woman, Lorraine."

"You better believe it." Her mouth closed hard on his nipple.

And when, a few minutes later, she pulled him on top of her he was ready.

———

Lorraine left the bedoom door open when she went to the kitchen to fetch the rest of the wine.

Pasco, for the first time, looked around the room. He could see little in the dim light from the corridor: an open closet with clothes hanging on the door, chests of drawers, a dresser with an oval mirror. He couldn't make out the wallpaper design or the faces in the framed photographs covering much of one wall, but he sensed a personality here; there was a soothing quality to the room, an ordered shelter. And he thought it curious that he felt more comfortable in Lorraine's room, in her bed, than in his own.

She returned with the wine, a fresh beer, a box of crackers and a bunch of grapes. It seemed a grand spread.

After they had eaten and drunk—Pasco, despite himself, silently comparing: Edna would never have permitted this, she abhorred crumbs in the bed—Lorraine ran her hands up and down her thighs, fingers pinching at the loose flesh. "Cellulite," she said. "No matter what you do, cellulite." She raised her right foot into the light, wiggled her toes. "Look," she said.

He looked: large feet, plump toes bunched and squeezed together, the nails ridged and bulbous and the colour of old ivory.

"See what vanity did to me?" she said. "When I was growing up all women had small feet. Or at least small shoes. I never bought my size, always one smaller. And we're amazed at the Chinese! Almost destroyed my feet." She chuckled, turning her foot this way and that. "That was the greatest benefit to me from the women's movement. I threw away the bra and, well, you can see the effect that had. But my feet will be eternally grateful."

Pasco said, "Edna never threw *her* bra away."

"And she never got rid of those stupid high heels either."

"Lorraine, do you think—" He hesitated, unsure of whether to ask the question.

"Yes?"

"Do you think,..." He ran the tip of his tongue around the rim of the bottle, buying time. "Was Edna happy?"

"I think she was fulfilled."

"But happy?"

"That's a kind of happiness. Not rah-rah happiness but,..."

"You make her sound like a nun."

"Well, she kind of fell for it all, eh? The grand myth. Beauty, motherhood and all that. I have the feeling that if she were still around today she'd be the best-dressed midwife in the city, pushing breastfeeding and natural childbirth—as if childbirth can ever be unnatural. Danny was the most important thing in the world to her, more important than you. Even if she didn't understand him."

"She was his mother. You must understand that, you're a mother."

"Sure I do. I'm as maternal as the next woman. Hell, you can't go through pregnancy and childbirth without feeling *something*. Not when just turning in bed becomes a major engineering feat.

Not when just hearing the baby cry makes your milk flow. But you've got to keep things in perspective. You listen to some women and you get the impression having kids is all that matters. Well, it's wonderful and all that but—call me cynical—but, you know, cows do it, horses do it. I don't see why motherhood should be *the* most important thing a woman ever does."

"Somehow I didn't think you were like that, Lorraine."

"Like what?"

"Without a single romantic bone in your body."

"So what has this evening been? Slam-bam-thank-you-Sam?"

"I didn't mean—"

"The thing is that sometimes romance is just a nice way to hide myth. Prince Charming's just the flip side of the helpless female, after all. That's women's biggest problem, if you ask me. All the damned myths we fall for, from feet to maternity."

"Not only women, Lorraine."

"I know. *Blondes have more fun*, right?"

"Christ, you still on that? All I want to say is that what you call myth some people call truth."

"Right, you take a little truth, you embellish it into a stereo-type, add a dash of romance and abracadabra! you've got a strait-jacket."

So Edna had lived in a strait-jacket. The thought would never have occurred to him.

As if guessing his thoughts, Lorraine reached over and laid a comforting hand on his chest. "It's nothing to worry about, you know," she said. "As I said, Edna was fulfilled."

"And you?"

"Me? I'm content."

"Is that good or bad?"

"It's the next step after fulfilment."

"And happiness?"

"It's the worst of all. Because you can never be always happy the way you can always be content. You have to feed happiness constantly, and that implies a deeper dissatisfaction."

Pasco sighed. "I guess I'm content, then."

"Good," she said. "Because it's a gift, especially at our age. The thing to remember is, what you know doesn't matter all that much next to what you understand. Know what I mean?"

"Know what you mean."

———————

Lorraine switched on the bedside lamp, took a slender book from the drawer in the night table. "My diary," she said, flicking through the pages.

"Adding a new conquest?"

"Do you mind? You get a silver star."

"Who gets gold?"

"None of your business." She gave a throaty laugh.

Pasco said, "I tried keeping a diary once. Several times, in fact. It never worked, there wasn't much to write."

"That's hard to believe." She lay back holding the open book up to the light.

Pasco watched her heavy breasts flatten against her ribcage. "I wasn't interested enough in myself," he said. "For breakfast I had toast and coffee. For lunch I had a burger and a coffee. For dinner I had—" He reached up with a finger and traced invisible arrowheads on her yielding flesh. "Who cares? As my friend Cruise would say, not exactly immortal prose."

"I don't write about myself much, at least not stuff like that," she said, slowly turning and scanning the pages. "Listen to this, for example. 'To me,'" she read, moistening her lips with her tongue, "'the greatest terror would be to look back with regret on the life I have lived. Memories should not be shadows stalking the edges of consciousness. They should not haunt every thought and limit every action. They should not be allowed to sculpt the present into a grotesque caricature of the past. Memories should be nothing more than mental notes, keepsakes that we drag out from time to time the way we do with photos in an album: to help keep the present in context. That is why I keep the photo of Rick on the mantelpiece: not forgotten but most definitely gone.'"

Pasco let his hand rest on her breast. "That's not about you, eh?"

"Want to hear the last line in the entry?"

He shrugged.

"I wonder," she read carefully, "what Pasco has done with all the pictures of Edna." She closed the diary, put it back into the drawer. "It's not just about me," she said.

After a minute, Pasco said, "Am I the first since—"

"No."

"You're my first since—"

"I know."

A moment later her fingers reached down and wiped away the tear that had formed in the corner of his eye.

————————

They stood together on the threshold of the kitchen door looking out at their gardens snowbound in the pale morning light.

Pasco said, "Edna always got depressed around this time. Remember that? The long winter got her down, as if she was afraid the snow would never end."

Lorraine, clutching her robe shut at her neck, nodded. "All depends on how you look at it, I guess. I don't think it's sad or depressing at all. It's more like the womb between pregnancies, kind of settling down and resting up before incubating new life again. That's why I like gardening, you know. It's all part of a larger continuous cycle. Knowing that calms me down, somehow.

And that's why I like working at the centre too. Every abused kid or battered woman that comes in is an interruption to that cycle, and I like helping them find their places in it again." She paused in embarrassment. "Christ, listen to me. I must sound like some kind of born-again gardener. Come one, come all, plant a tulip and save your soul!"

Pasco slowly buttoned up his coat. "How come you and Rick never had any more kids?"

"But we did. Two years after Magda. A boy. There were complications, he only lived a few hours. And after that, well, it just wasn't possible any more. Physically, I mean."

"I didn't know. Rick never said anything."

"Well, it wasn't man-talk, eh?"

"Did Edna know?"

"She knew."

"She never said a word to me."

"There's a lot you don't know about me, Pasco."

"So you have secrets too, eh?"

She smiled, and gently pushed him out the door. "Keep warm," she said.

He waded through the snow back to his house. They had managed to get only a few hours' sleep and he felt the effects of it in a tightness around his eyes, in a heaviness in his legs.

Only when he'd let himself in and was trudging through the silence up to the bedroom did he realize with a twinge of surprise that the night had come and gone and with it had retreated, unnoticed, all hint of the hectoring wind.

Chapter Nineteen

"Y OU FEELING OKAY, Danny? I've never seen you looking so tired."

"I'm fine. Work. You know."

"The usual?"

"More or less."

"You got the time for something to drink?"

"Sure, Dad, why not?"

"What'll you have? Scotch, beer, wine?"

"Since when do you buy wine?"

Lorraine had slept over the night before and, in the passion of the evening, had managed to finish only half her bottle. "A friend brought it," he said. "There's still some left."

"I didn't know you had any friends who drank wine," Danny said suspiciously. "Is it any good?"

"I wouldn't know. It's got a French name."

"Sure, I'll give it a shot."

When Pasco returned with a full glass, Danny had removed his coat and was lounging on the sofa beneath the window, a distracted look on his face, eyes staring vacantly into the cold fireplace.

Pasco sat in his armchair, twisted the top off his beer bottle. "Cheers," he said.

Danny raised his glass at him, sipped, grimaced.

"No good?" Pasco said.

"It'll do." He put the glass on the floor beside him and continued staring into the fireplace.

After several minutes of silence, Pasco said, "So what do I owe this visit to?"

"It's time to get moving, Dad. On the house, I mean. I'd like to get it done as soon as possible."

"What's the hurry?"

"Oh—" Danny linked his fingers on his stomach. "I guess I'm getting kind of restless at Simmons Construction. It's time I made a move."

"And I'm your way out?"

"Gotta start someplace."

"Well, Danny,"—Pasco was surprised that the words were coming easily even though he hadn't thought it through, at least not consciously—"it's my house."

"I never said otherwise."

"And I know you've been counting on inheriting it. But I have to die first. And, Danny, I'm not dead."

"Dad—"

"Didn't Simmons ever teach you not to count your chickens before they hatch?"

"What d'you take me for?"

"A businessman, first and foremost."

"There's nothing wrong with wanting to be rich, Dad."

How many times had Danny said that to him? But now he spoke without the challenge in his voice. "I never said there was. But what's important is how you get there."

"Don't you think I know that?"

"Do you? I wonder sometimes."

Danny took a sip of his wine. "Everybody's got his own way. And some of us have to make do with what we've got."

Pasco thought about that for a minute. Then he said, "What would you say if I told you I was thinking of selling the house?"

A stillness descended on Danny. "I'd say you're crazy."

"But you've always thought that."

"No, foolish maybe, stubborn definitely. But not crazy. This is new."

"But don't I have the right to—"

Danny suddenly sat up. "Have you thought this through? So let's say you sell. Where are you going to live, tell me that."

"I"ll find a place."

"Where?"

"At Lorraine Neumann's, for example."

"What? She going to rent you a room or something?"

"Oh, I don't think Lorraine would charge me rent, Danny. Of course I'd pay my share."

Silence. Then, disagreeably: "I see."

"I told you, I'm not dead yet."

"You and the widow Neumann—"

"It hasn't been easy without your mother, you know."

"And have you talked to her about this?"

"No, not yet. It's just an idea." An idea that had only just come to him, triggered, he suspected, by Danny's hunger. "I thought I should talk to you first."

"Oh yeah? Well, thanks a lot, Dad."

Silence. Then, with a trace of a smile: "You're welcome."

Danny's head shook in agitation. "And what if she isn't interested? What then?"

"I don't need a lot of space. Maybe you could help me rent a room from Simmons. A hot plate, a fridge—"

"I've got a crazy man for a father."

"No, Danny, not crazy. It's just hard sometimes knowing how much I should do for you and how much I should do for me."

"You've had years to figure that one out."

"And what about you? How much should you do for you and how much should you do for me? Have you asked yourself that?"

"You're the family philosopher, Dad."

"The world's full of questions, Danny. You should try one on once in a while."

"I live in the real world. I haven't got the time."

"But you've got the time to plan and scheme, don't you?"

"All right, you want questions? Here's one for you. Why the widow Neumann, Dad? Her belly's bigger than her breasts."

"There's no need to be disgusting, Danny."

"Just stating a fact."

"It's not true and you know it. And even if it were, what does that have to do with anything?"

"It's just that I never figured—"

"Well you better start figuring."

"Why her?"

"Why not? You got something against Lorraine?"

———————

Danny remembered Rick Neumann as a large man. Tall, rotund, with a broad fleshy face and thick cigars for fingers. His nails like eyelids of hard, white plastic, always a little long and sharp-looking. Not the hands, Danny had always thought, of an appliance repairman.

His workshop had been in the basement of their house and he could often be seen carting radios or toasters or televisions from his old Rambler up the stairs. He invariably wore baggy work pants, a white undershirt and, even on the hottest summer days, a faded blue work coat that hung halfway down his thighs, its pockets heavy with screwdrivers and pliers and swirls of copper wire. On his feet were battered work boots which he never laced up—the same boots which, so many years later, the widow Neumann still wore in the garden.

Not an unfriendly man, but not a talkative one either: his English wasn't quite up to it. Danny had often wondered how he and Mrs. Neumann—who, as far as he knew, spoke no German—managed to converse with one another.

It was in the basement workshop that Mrs. Neumann found her husband one hot summer afternoon when Danny was twelve. He was slumped unmoving on the littered work table—details of horror, whispered and overheard, were never forgotten—a screwdriver clutched so tightly in his hand they had had to pry his fingers open.

Danny recalled being shushed and shuffled to his room while his father hurried over to the Neumanns' in response to an urgent phonecall. From his dusty bedroom window he watched his mother trot through the two backyards to the Neumann house.

A siren wailed in the distance and presently an ambulance, light flashing, hurtled by on the street. It fell silent in front of the Neumanns' house, stopping out of Danny's sight but leaving a chilled wake in its path.

His room felt airless, the high afternoon sun burning the day into an unnatural stillness. He pulled the window open. A greater heat billowed in and he shut it again.

The day remained shredded by the scream of the siren: the sound, always exciting, suddenly become fearful.

After what seemed an eternity, the ambulance pulled slowly away, its light flashing. Although he listened very hard, Danny never heard the siren. He concluded that, for whatever reason, there was no longer an emergency.

He stood at the window waiting for his parents to return. They didn't come. He grew drowsy in the stuffy heat and curled up on his bed.

He dreamt that the lake was boiling, steam wafting through

the city, transparent bubbles drifting lazily among tendrils of wispy smoke.

When he awoke he found he'd pulled the blanket over himself. His clothes were drenched in perspiration, the room dark, the day almost gone. Lights were blazing in the Neumann house, and he could see people congregated in the kitchen. Someone was moving around downstairs.

His mother was in the kitchen looking drawn and tired. Her eyes were red. A ham was baking in the oven. The smell of its honey-and-clove glaze clung to his skin, his hair, coated him in its sweet thickness.

Preoccupied, she told him he would be spending the night at a friend's place. She had already made the arrangements.

He asked if Magda's mother or father was sick.

Mr. Neumann had had a heart attack, she said.

Was he going to be all right? He couldn't bring himself to use the word *dead*, although the silence of the ambulance as it drove away had told him everything.

His mother hesitated briefly, and her hesitation confirmed his suspicions. Mr. Neumann, she said, hadn't survived. Did he want to pay a visit to Mrs. Neumann? Or Magda? They would appreciate seeing him. He didn't have to say anything, just be there.

But without a word he ran back up the stairs to his room, climbed into bed and pulled the blanket up to his neck. How could he face them, Mrs. Neumann and Magda? Maybe he could say hi to them—but then what? All the usual words seemed hollow, all the usual games seemed to have lost their meaning.

His heart thumped hard in his chest, and he wondered what it was like to have it stop. What it was like to feel the darkness come over you.

He remained there, trembling in the heat, until his father came to take him to his friend's place.

He stayed with his friend for several days—his parents didn't insist when he refused to attend the funeral—and when he returned home he found himself going out of his way to avoid both Mrs. Neumann and Magda. He felt assaulted by their sullenness, by the air of depletion that hung around them.

Some weeks later, his mother asked him to take a freshly baked nut-loaf over to Mrs. Neumann. Cooking seemed to be his mother's way of dealing with the tragedy. The ham had just been the beginning of an edible assembly line. Over the next weeks she plied the Neumanns with food, more, Danny thought, than the two of them could possibly eat, even with their constant visitors. Cakes, pies, breads, muffins, stews, roasts—as if they could somehow overwhelm their sorrow with food.

Danny wondered whether this was what his mother herself was doing: overwhelming her own sorrow and fear. He understood the need to keep busy. It was the only way to draw back from the anxiety that had taken hold of him, the awareness of sudden extinction, for himself as well as for his parents. That was the summer he damaged himself playing baseball: running too fast, trying too hard. Chasing a goal—he wanted to be his team's top scorer—that had nothing to do with home, its stresses and demands.

He reluctantly took the nut-loaf, warm and fragrant and wrapped in a kitchen towel, over to the Neumanns. At least he wouldn't have to deal with Magda; she was spending some time with Mrs. Neumann's sister and her family at their cottage on Georgian Bay. There was no answer when he knocked at the kitchen door so he let himself in. He called out, but softly, for the form of it, and was glad when there was no reply. He put the loaf on the kitchen counter and was hurrying to leave when he was stopped by a choking sob from farther in the house.

Go, said a voice in his head, don't hang around.

But another sob came and he found himself creeping along the shadowed corridor that led away from the kitchen towards Mrs. Neumann's bedroom. The door was half-open and when he peeked in he saw Mrs. Neumann lying on the bed, her feet facing him. She was wearing a bathrobe, her head, wrapped in a towel as if she'd just come from the shower, propped up on a pillow. Her eyes were closed, cheeks wet. She was sobbing quietly.

Mrs. Neumann moaned, shifted her weight in the bed. Only then did Danny notice that her right hand was inserted between the folds of the bathrobe. She was rubbing herself between the legs, sobbing and choking and whispering her husband's name.

He knew what she was doing. The winter before, he and Magda had been playing in the basement of his parents' house and there, behind a stack of boxes, she had shown him what she did when she was alone. He had offered to reveal his own secret already obvious through his shorts but she had fled, promising to kill him if he told.

When Mrs. Neumann's breathing deepened, when her body went stiff and her toes curled back hard, Danny ran from the house. He had understood Magda's pleasure, but Mrs. Neumann's frightened him. This was a passion, it seemed to him, that should not be: Mrs. Neumann was making love with a dead man.

"When a woman wants a man," Pasco said, "it doesn't matter what she looks like. She becomes beautiful to him. And vice versa."

"I just don't understand why you're involved with *her*, Dad."

"You make it sound like we're doing something dirty."

"Dad, this probably isn't any of my business, but did you ever—I mean, before—you know, with the widow Neumann?"

"Say what you mean."

"All right, fine. Did you have an affair with her?"

"*Affair* isn't what I'm hearing in your voice, Danny. What you really want to ask is, did I screw Lorraine when your mother was alive, right?"

"Put it any way you like, I don't care."

"Don't you? This isn't really about me, is it. It's about your mother. So if it'll make you feel any better, no, there was nothing between Lorraine and me."

"So between you and who, then?"

"That's none of your business."

"So there was—"

"Nothing that's any concern of yours."

"Was that the time Mom was so upset?"

"Danny,..." Pasco closed his eyes, managed to keep his tone calm. "Don't try to claim every part of my life."

Danny grunted, his tongue probing around his mouth. Even a partial answer was better than no answer at all; at least it cushioned the pit the question had dug for itself. "You aren't planning to marry her, are you, Dad?"

"It never crossed my mind."

"If it ever does—"

"You'll be the third to know."

"I thought you were, you know, more or less happy." He had had no reason to think otherwise. His father's undemanding way of life, its very predictability, had offered no hint of dissatisfactions.

"I was. Am. In most ways." But there was more too. "It's just that— Danny, don't you think I've mourned long enough for your mother?"

Danny glanced at him, then looked away: it was a question without an answer.

Pasco's eyes searched the window above his son. "You forced me to learn self-sufficiency, you know, Danny." It was so new, so large, yet gave access to so little: the house glittering across the street, the tree enfeebled against the porch light. "I suppose I should thank you for that."

"How so?"

"I needed support and you weren't there, that's how."

"That's not fair, Dad."

"Maybe not but—"

"I'm sorry I disappointed you." The words were offered not as apology but as rebuff.

"D'you know what it was like, Danny? She lived—kind of—for days. Oh, there were people around. Lorraine. My friends Push-pull, Cruise. And I kept waiting for you, I kept thinking, my son won't let me down, Danny'll be there for me. But you never came."

"I came, Dad."

"You didn't stay, did you."

"What'd you expect, Dad?" But the challenge emerged blunt, his conviction weakened.

"Maybe for a while. A day or two."

"Work…." His voice failed him. Work had long served as his escape from the suffocations of the moment: a world more predictable, its complications intellectual. Until now.

"Work? So maybe you lose a few dollars. But not everything, Danny." One hand tightened around his beer, the other massaged nervously at a bicep. "Not the way I did. I never thought—" Then, without warning, the words were gone. "I mean—" The lecture, frequently rehearsed in feverish insomnia, retreated into reticence.

Danny said nothing, kept his eyes locked unseeing on the darkened fireplace.

Pasco took a long swallow of his beer. "And afterwards, the house, it suddenly became bigger, emptier. Quieter. Everything was sucked out of here the way…the way life was sucked out of her." He snapped his fingers: "Like that. Gone. A balloon bursting." He settled a challenging gaze on his son.

"I called as often as I could."

"I know. Like you used to do before she died. You can't really touch someone over the phone, you know, that's just another lie. Advertising. I thought you of all people would know that. We needed to *see* you, Danny. Just as I needed to *see* you. Afterwards."

"Why didn't you say so?" But he had known.

"What difference would it have made?"

"I've got a brain, Dad." He had known, and the knowledge of his father's needs had frightened him.

"I know that. It's the heart I'm not too sure about."

"The heart's fine, thank you."

"Yeah, but are the two connected?"

The words hung pulsing in the silence that opened up between them.

After a moment, Danny said, "Fine, Dad." His voice had hardened. "You want to play hardball? Let's go back a few more years. Remember the first night I ever spent away from home?"

Pasco turned away. He knew where Danny was heading. He said, "This is absurd."

"You don't remember, do you."

"Of course I do." There was no escaping it. "You must have been ten, eleven—"

"Nine. And I called home and I said, Hi, Dad, guess who this is."

Pasco's face began to burn.

"And you couldn't. I mean, Christ!, how many people in the world called you Dad? You had no idea who I was."

"Just for a second, Danny. I had a lot on my mind, I—"

"You always did."

"There were bills to pay. The restaurant wasn't exactly— You're a businessman, you know what it's like."

"That's why I expect you to understand, too, Dad. How busy you can get sometimes, I mean."

"I always thought I could make it up to you. Always intended to, your mother and me."

"I didn't have the time to wait around for you to do that, Dad. I wanted more. I wanted Mom to know that her son had made a success of his life."

"What I don't understand, Danny, is if you were so anxious to impress your mother, how come you never came over, eh?"

Danny closed his eyes, ran his hand tiredly through his hair. "Too busy," he said. "Too busy trying to do it all. Dreams, Dad, big dreams. Me, Danny Taggart, the son of a short-order cook—" Danny paused, jolted by his own frankness. "Dad, I didn't mean—"

Pasco sighed his hurt away. Was it natural that sons aspired to being better men than their fathers? And was a certain contempt a necessary part of that urge? "That's okay, Danny. I know what you mean. I hoped I would live a better life than my dad too."

"So what's the point, Dad? That we're both guilty?"

"It's not a matter of innocence or guilt."

"So what's the point?"

"To tell you the truth, I'm not sure." Pasco raised his hands one by one to the light, examined them: the wrinkles of age, a smattering of liver spots. "Maybe it's just that I'm really not such a bad person, Danny."

"I never said you were."

"Not in so many words."

"It's just that sometimes you seem, well, kind of naïve."

Pasco chuckled. "Do you think I'm growing innocent in my old age, Danny? Naïve isn't a word I'd use for someone who calls Simmons a son of a bitch."

"Let's leave Simmons out of this, okay?"

"Fine." Pasco, without quite knowing why, was amused. It had, he thought, something to do with this unexpected reluctance to discuss Simmons. And it occurred to him that maybe he and Danny were more alike than they cared to admit. If he himself had sought a certain self-protection by pulling back from the anxieties of the world, hadn't Danny simply taken it one step further by denying the world and recognizing only his own urges? Pasco drained his beer, rubbed his hands together in satisfaction.

Danny yawned, hand cupping his mouth. "So, Dad. The renovations?"

Pasco studied Danny: in this light he could see Edna in his son. And he said simply, "So when d'you want to start on the bedrooms?"

Danny looked over at him, his eyes narrowed into a frown.

"I'm not doing this for you, Danny. I'm doing it for your mother, remember that." Not the whole truth but, for the time being, a comfortable one, for them both.

Danny got to his feet. "I'll call you in a couple of days." He reached for his coat, slipped it on. "Sounds like the wind's kicking up," he said.

"The wind?" Pasco cocked an ear. "That's not wind, that's rain."

"That's the sound of wind, Dad." He smiled. "Getting deaf in your old age?"

Pasco shrugged, showed Danny to the door.

When he stepped from the porch into a light rain, Danny looked back and laughed.

Pasco stood in the doorway and watched him walk to his car. The night was utterly still. The only movement was in the silvery curtain of raindrops descending through the streetlight.

He thought: You see, Edna....

Chapter Twenty

I T WAS a Sunday morning, the air crisp and bright in the spring sunshine. The sidewalks at Yonge and St. Clair were busy with couples young and middle-aged strolling around window-shopping or manoeuvring baby carriages into restaurants.

Lorraine nudged Pasco in the ribs, directed his gaze to a bookstore window and its display of the Doctor's latest bestseller. "Want a copy?" she said.

"Don't they kill trees to make books?" he replied without breaking stride.

They had been exploring for a while, east to the bridge across the valley, a wrinkle of greenery that roughly separated the commercial from the residential; south to the park that hid the midtown water reservoir, clumps and ribbons of iced snow slowly melting into the grass; west to Avenue Road past imposing condominium and commercial buildings and sedate apartment blocks in one of which, Lorraine said, the pianist Glenn Gould had once lived. At tiny Amsterdam Park they admired the tulip display before making their way back to Yonge Street.

They stopped in at a restaurant and from the display case crowded with baked goods Pasco chose a raisin bun. Lorraine, pronouncing him boring, picked a large cookie studded with multicoloured candies. The price, with two coffees, surprised Pasco but he was too embarrassed to protest.

They stopped not far up the street, at a little park beside a large church of honey-coloured stone. Lorraine led the way across the springy lawn, past an old woman puffing at a cigarette and contemplating the sky, to a bench sufficiently distant from the traffic to afford an illusion of privacy. Across the street, renovated houses sat pretty in the sunshine.

Lorraine broke her cookie into discreet pieces and ate them one by one, as if consuming peanuts. Pasco bit into the raisin bun, sweet and sticky and fragrant with cinnamon. A silence settled on them: the little park in the midst of the vibrant city, steps from a busy street, might have been under glass. The blended scents of thawing earth and fresh greenery rose around them and for several long minutes there came to Pasco a sense of lightening, a sense of the world claiming him from himself. In the gentle warmth, it was a pleasing retreat.

Lorraine said, "Magda and Linda came by yesterday."

"So that's what's been on your mind, eh?" He had noticed her silence but had remained respectful of it.

"Kind of." She fed him a piece of her cookie. "Actually I've been on my mind."

He waited for her to go on.

"There's this woman I work with down at the centre. Janine. We were shooting the breeze the other day and she said something funny. She said that her parents were really open and liberal, they let her have as many of her black and Chinese friends over as she wanted, they just made it clear she wasn't to marry any of them. And I kind o' got a glimpse of myself in Janine's parents. You know—lesbians are fine, except when it comes to my daughter."

"Nasty fight yesterday?" Pasco guessed.

"Actually, no. But I'm getting to know Linda a bit, and you know what, Pasco?"

"And you're all going to live happily ever after?" Pasco winced at the echoes of Danny in his own voice. Or was it, he quickly wondered, the other way around?

"You know better than that. But Linda and I both like French red wine and fat Russian novels, and we're both ex-smokers struggling to keep the ex alive. We didn't fall into each other's arms or anything, but…" She looked away, her gaze following a squirrel that had darted from behind their bench and settled onto its haunches three feet in front of them. "I still can't wrap my mind around her making love to my daughter, but I guess we're learning to get along." She tossed a piece of cookie to the grass, watched the squirrel lunge for it then skip away. "Differences are easy to find. It's the similarities you really have to dig for."

After a moment, Pasco said, "Sometimes the differences overwhelm the similarities."

"But only if you let them," Lorraine replied.

———————

They walked south on Yonge looking at the changes time and money had brought to the street. The slightly seedy two-storey buildings—cheap flats above convenience stores, greasy spoons worthy of the name, barber-shops and other establishments too nondescript to be memorable—had given way to office buildings, antique stores, clothing and jewellery boutiques, expensive restaurants and specialty-food shops. Renovated, rebuilt, scrubbed; glass, chrome, brass: all of it glittery, all of it attractive. And yet Pasco began to find the evidence of wealth depressing in its sameness.

He was pleased that the railway line still crossed Yonge at the dip in the land below Summerhill, the concrete and steel of the underpass as dank and grimy and pigeon-plagued as ever. He was strangely reassured by its stench, felt better about the changes he'd

seen. Lorraine, doing an impossible dance around the bird droppings, noticed a small smile on his lips. She pronounced him per-
verse.

They paused for a rest at Ramsden Park, across from the
Rosedale subway station. The cries of playing children attracted
Pasco's gaze to boys hectic with hockey sticks dashing about a
rink. The ice had melted and they were chasing after a tennis ball.
Farther in the park, on a rise in the land, a chainlink fence surrounded tennis courts, while, closer in, partly hidden in a depression, rose the batting cage of a baseball diamond.

The shouts of the young voices, the sight of the batting cage:
Pasco was reminded of Danny sliding hard into base, felt afresh
his pain at the sight of the blood and gnarled flesh and Danny's
gritted teeth.

Lorraine said, "You all right, Pasco? Not too tired?"

"No, I'm fine. Just thinking." A train rumbled and hissed into
the subway station. He said, "Lorraine, can I ask you a question?"

"You don't usually ask permission. Must be serious."

"I'm wondering what you'd say if I were to sell the house and
the restaurant, invest the money somewhere safe and live off the
interest." The idea, invented to unsettle Danny, had remained
with him. He was intrigued less by the possibility of carrying it
through than by the idea itself. There seemed a certain liberation
in lightening the load, in leading a simplified life.

"Retire?"

"More or less. Maybe I could turn the furniture refinishing
into a kind of sideline. Nothing grand, just something to occupy
my time."

"If you can afford it, why not? But if you sold the house, where
would you live?"

"Maybe Danny could help me rent a room from Simmons."

"You can't go from a house to a room, Pasco. What's the point
of that? Rooms are for transients. Besides, you'd need more space

if you're going to work at your furniture."

"Danny wasn't thrilled with the idea either. And to tell you the truth, me neither for that matter."

"So what's this all about then?"

"I'm not sure. But—"

"Yes?"

"Well, the other idea I had—"

"Do I have to drag it out of you?" She reached up and gave his ear a friendly tug.

"Well, I was thinking you might have some extra space in your house...." His voice fell off, letting her infer the rest of the sentence.

After a few seconds Lorraine put her hand to his cheek and nudged his face towards hers. "Pasco," she said quietly, "don't go making plans for us, okay? I like things the way they are."

He laid his palm on her thigh. "I know that."

"I hope you're not too disappointed."

He examined himself. "No," he said, and he knew it was the truth. "It was just something I had to clear up. With you and Danny. And with myself. I guess I kind of like the way things are too."

They sat in silence for a few minutes, listening to the muted sounds of the world. When they resumed their walk, Lorraine pressed close to him and linked her arm with his. A wave of warmth surged down Pasco's chest and back.

Lorraine said, "Maybe one day, Pasco. You never know."

"Good enough," he replied, but despite himself he thought: You see, Edna....

At Bloor Street, Lorraine left him for the subway. She had to attend a strategy meeting at the centre: "Funding, what else? Our budget isn't even shoestring."

The intersection, said to be the busiest in the country, was deserted. Pasco remembered Cruise once saying that you could spend a weekday at Yonge and Bloor and never see the same face twice. But this was not a weekday, the stores and offices were closed. People had no reason to come here. Pasco was a minute or two before understanding why the desertion struck him as strangely familiar: this was how, years before, he had visualized the city on the eve of nuclear attack.

A billboard high above the intersection caught his eye. It showed, in shades of black and white, a toxic bog with rotting cartons and rusted cans bobbing among unhealthy shrubs. The stripped hulk of a car lay half-submerged in the water, the grey background a burnt-out field gouged and pitted and dotted with dead trees. Beside the superimposed title of his new book, the Doctor squinted in colour, smiling doom down at the empty streets.

He knew something was wrong when, on approaching his house, he caught sight of Pushpull sitting on the porch. He was leaning against the front door, legs drawn up, elbows on his knees, cheeks in his hands. He was staring at the wooden floor between his salt-stained boots.

"Pushpull?"

He looked up, his face drawn.

"Everything okay, Pushpull? Old lady thrown you out again?"

"You haven't heard?" The adam's apple bobbed tightly in his neck.

"Heard what?" Pasco mounted the stairs, stood looking down at Pushpull with his hand on the railing.

"About Montgomery."

Pasco's heart skipped a beat. "What about Montgomery?"

"He's dead."

Pasco froze. A chill ran through his body.

"Cops shot him."

His insides hollowed, legs went weak: he pictured himself falling among skittish legs. His fingers grasped at the railing in an effort to steady himself.

"Sorry, Pasco, I thought you knew. It's all over the news." Push-pull reached into his shirt pocket for a cigarette, lit it up.

"I left early. Went for a walk. With Lorraine." His own voice sounded distant, thinned, strangely inconsequential.

"Cops shot him."

"You said— You said that already." He could barely get the words out; his lungs were as if collapsed.

"Did I?"

Pasco gulped at the air, with incomplete satisfaction. He fished his keys from his pocket. "Come inside, I—"

Pushpull shook his head. "I'm not goin' inside."

"I need to sit down." He became aware of a pressure building inside his head.

"I said I ain't goin' inside! Can't breathe inside." Pushpull, snif-fling, speaking through his teeth, leaned his head back against the door, stared glassy-eyed past Pasco to the street. "They shot 'im inside."

Pasco hesitated, then carefully lowered himself to the porch floor. He noticed as if for the first time the cracks in the wood, the chips in the grey paint, and he wondered that it all seemed foreign, alien, disconnected from himself.

"I keep seein' it, Pasco. Like a fuckin' dream that won't stop."

"But you weren't there." A man walked by with a dog on a leash. Walking a dog. Poop-and-Scoop: why did the normal sud-denly seem so obscene?

"I listened to every news report. Just had to, couldn't help it. Every fuckin' little detail."

"You sure it was him?"

"Christ, Pasco! How many Montgomery Birds do you figure

there are in this world? Who used to work for the post office yet?"

"Tell me."

"What?"

"What happened." And he heard in his voice a control that disguised the trauma within: *Aneurysm? What's an aneurysm, Doctor?*

"What are they saying?"

"Who? Everybody's got something to say."

"The cops."

"They say he came at them with a knife in the corridor outside his apartment. So they pumped two bullets into him. Self-defence."

"What the fuck were they doing there?" He looked out at the world: the street, the houses, the sunlight suddenly dense. None of it was quite as it should have been. It was all tilted, all askew.

"They say he threatened a neighbour. You believe that?"

"He hasn't been himself lately...." But even as he said them, he knew the words to be unfaithful. He thought: a time and a place.

"Hey, man, don't I know that? But I know Montgomery too. You should hear what they're sayin' about him. You'd think he was some kind of violent criminal. They're bringin' up the tussle with the guy at work, the charge against him, you name it. A real fuckin' snow-job." Pushpull stubbed out the cigarette, lit another. "And then there's this guy. Some lawyer. He's already mouthin' off. He's claimin' the only reason they shot Montgomery is 'cause he's black. He's sayin' Montgomery wasn't right in the head, he had mental problems, problems at home and at work and the cops had been harassin' him. You know anything 'bout that?"

Pasco shook his head. Montgomery hadn't visited the Starting Gate much recently and, when he had, his silence had been unsettling. Pasco suspected that Montgomery hadn't forgiven him for the news about Charlene. "They say anything about the cop who shot him?"

"Not much. Some young guy. Hasn't been on the force long. Kurt something-or-other."

Pasco shut his eyes, his strength leaving him with a low moan.

Pushpull blinked at him. "You goin' to the funeral?"

"Can't say." His voice was almost inaudible, even to himself.

"Man, I just can't get it through my head. Dead and funeral and Montgomery all together. It don't seem real, y'know?"

Pasco said nothing. Kurt, Sean, Montgomery: the images seething through his mind left no room for thought.

"Hey, Pasco, you know what else?"

Pasco waited. A jet screamed by overhead.

"I don't think I can go back to the Gate, man. Not ever." And his voice broke.

———————

Pasco sat in the kitchen and watched the sunlight harden on Lorraine's garden.

Watched it fade over the bristling lawn, darken the upturned earth of the flowerbeds.

Counted the birds that pecked at the feeder.

Sat in the darkness, waiting.

When the lights at last went on in her kitchen, he stirred his stiffened muscles and made his way through the night to her.

———————

Montgomery's funeral was held a few days later. Pasco chose not to attend, and he chose not to go to work either. It was the first time since Edna's death that Pascal's remained closed on a legal working day.

Lorraine didn't agree with his decision to avoid the funeral.

She tried to convince him that he should go, that his mere presence would be important to the family, and to himself. She insisted that funerals offered what she called catharsis, their ceremony a way of soothing the ragged edges of the wound. Bidding farewell to the body, she said, was the first step in bidding farewell to the grief. Remember Rick's funeral, she said, remember Edna's.

But Pasco refused to be convinced. He was not, he said, sentimental about funerals. When he attended one, it was to be with those left behind—if he knew them, if he cared about them. The deceased, after all, was well beyond taking offence, or even notice. And he didn't accept that showing up at a funeral was a sign of affection or respect, either. Those were emotions valuable only when revealed in life; their public display after death was meaningless. "You know, Lorraine," he said, "the body doesn't matter." The conviction in his voice quieted her.

She offered to remain at home with him—she could get someone to fill in for her at the centre—but he preferred to be alone. She brought him a shepherd's pie, instructed him in how to heat it up and warned that she would be calling to make sure he'd eaten. When she opened the fridge to put it in, the smell of a goat cheese she had brought over the week before—Pasco had left it unwrapped—wafted out like a gas attack. "Your fridge," she said wrinkling her nose, "has bad breath." But she couldn't even raise a smile from him.

He spent the morning carefully stripping an old rocking chair. Its arms were ornate, its back intricately carved, but the task, minute and painstaking, was well suited to his mood. As he worked, he let his mind drift easily over his memories of Montgomery, attempting to recall as much about his friend as he could: to preserve, to honour.

He remembered that, after having been bitten once and attacked twice, Montgomery had taken to carrying a little store of pebbles in his pant pocket for dealing with troublesome dogs on his route.

Remembered his tales, only half-believed, of hunting birds and iguana "back home" with a slingshot: "For the stew, man, for the stew!"

Remembered a story he'd told of having been tossed out of history class one day for talking. The teacher, furious, had told him he'd be staying out "till Columbus come back". Montgomery's gleeful cry, a few minutes later, of "Ship ahoy!" had led to an encounter with the teacher's leather strap.

Remembered Montgomery's voice, his gravelly laugh. Knew—and was saddened—that, in years to come and despite all his efforts, the sharpness of his memory would be dulled and his friend would fade in his mind the way Edna had: the tones flattened, the colours paled.

———————

Pushpull called around eleven. He and Marcus would be attending the funeral. Did Pasco want to join them?

He declined with intentional gruffness—he'd had enough prodding from Lorraine—and he could tell that Pushpull was disappointed.

Had he heard from Cruise? Pushpull asked. He seemed to be making himself scarce. Not even Lanny, who had sent a wreath to the funeral home in the name of the Starting Gate, had seen him.

Maybe he was keeping himself busy, Pasco suggested, longing to return to the rocking chair. "Everybody mourns in his own way," he said.

Hanging up, he thought back over their evenings at the Gate, the arguments and the laughter, the pain of dealing with Charlene and Montgomery's quick slide into despair. He saw a toothpick bobbing between Montgomery's lips, saw his deft fingers slicing the peel off an orange. Saw the little pocketknife, thought: Surely to God not....

Lorraine called at one-thirty to find out whether he'd eaten. He said he had no appetite. She said she wouldn't hang up until he'd put the pie into the oven. He did so, noisily. "Happy?" he said into the phone.

"You can still make the funeral, Pasco. There's time." When he remained silent, she sighed in resignation. "Gotta go," she said. "We've got a little bit of a crisis on our hands."

"That's why you're a crisis centre," he said without humour.

He plunged back into his memories, his hands busy on the ill-treated wood.

How are things, Montgomery?

T'ings easy, mahn.

Minutes before the funeral was scheduled to begin, he put down his tools, washed his hands and sat quietly in the armchair in the living room. After a few minutes, as the weight of the moment pressed down on him, he smelled smoke. He hastened into the kitchen. Smoke was curling from the oven—billowed out in a cloud of intense heat when he pulled the door open. He removed the shepherd's pie, tossed it into the sink.

His face felt hot. And then his sight blurred. He couldn't fathom why it was the food charred and steaming in the sink that finally brought the tears.

———

Lorraine got in late. She didn't say a word when she saw the burnt pie, simply gathered it up and threw it out. She'd brought with her a copy of the *Sun*, the front page taken up with a colour portrait of Kurt on the left, a black-and-white one of Montgomery on the right. Pasco glanced briefly at it, rolled it up and put it next to the ruined pie in the garbage can.

She made them cheese sandwiches, poured him a beer, herself a glass of wine. They ate in silence and watched the late news together on television.

Montgomery's funeral was the third item, a position of distinction that signalled the importance of the controversy that had flared up around his death.

There was a picture of him, the same as in the newspaper. A brief shot of the apartment building where he had lived, police cruisers parked outside, his bagged body being wheeled away.

Paradise

Then, cut to: the church, the choir, the energetic singing. The pastor preaching forgiveness in a voice of fire and brimstone, urging the bereaved to find solace in "warship".

Cut to Montgomery's coffin—white, elaborate, grander than the man had been—being carried down the steps of the church to a waiting hearse, behind it his wife, Mrs. Bird, walking with difficulty, assisted by her son on one side and her errant daughter on the other.

Charlene Nutmeg Spice

Pasco found himself shaking his head sadly. Lorraine squeezed his hand.

Cut to a group of solemn young people, many blacks with a few whites sprinkled among them, holding up signs: END RACISM NOW! CHARGE HIM WITH MURDER! KURB KOP KILLINGS!

Cut to a man familiar from the news, the lawyer Pushpull had mentioned, a grave and elegant man: "Today is a day of sadness and anger for us...."

Cut to another man, yet another face grown familiar in recent days, identified as a black activist, less polished than the lawyer but a dapper dresser still: "We will not take this lying down. I put this racist society on notice...."

Cut to a police spokesman announcing that the constable

involved—cut to a photograph of Kurt—had been suspended with pay pending the outcome of an internal investigation.

Cut to Montgomery's coffin being slid into the hearse, the door closing, the hearse driving away.

The reporter signed off unseen.

Lorraine switched off the television.

Pasco sat for a long time staring at the screen, at the point of light in the centre of it that took forever to fade. He was troubled. The report had had little to do with Montgomery. The man himself was being lost, simplified into one thing or another. Claimed for a cause by the agendas of others. Where was the Montgomery he had known? Montgomery had not had a racial vision of life. He had not seen the world through the colour of his skin. And yet his life, and his death, were being given a racial tint. Pasco felt the stirrings of anger at this betrayal of his friend. Barely in the grave, Montgomery was already being made into an object.

Lorraine said, "Have you heard from Danny?"

"No, not a word."

"Did he ever meet your friend?"

"Once."

"He probably didn't remember him."

"Probably not." He couldn't bring himself to believe it, but he took comfort in Lorraine's faith anyway.

Chapter Twenty-one

S AL SAID, "What's up, Daniel? We hardly ever see you much around here any more."

"Busy."

Danny had taken to coming to the office early, arriving before everyone else, arranging his day and then heading out to evaluate the requisitions and visit work sites. He would take long lunches, sometimes meeting with bank loan-officers in search of capital for the renovation of his father's house, sometimes going to Mr. Simmons's house to work on the plans—but only after ensuring no one else was there—or, a couple of times, even heading home for an afternoon nap to try to make up for restless nights. He would return to the office late in the afternoon to write up his reports.

"Busy with what?" Sal asked.

"What are you? The boss's spy?"

"Do you need to be spied on?"

"Fuck off, Sal."

"You got something to hide, Daniel?"

Danny grabbed a handful of the pink slips, scattered them on his desk like large confetti. "Half the damned rooming houses are falling apart, the High Park town houses need major electrical repairs. One fucking thing after another. Spit and string."

"You know the boss. Keep 'em going as long as—"

"Aren't you getting sick of this, Sal?"

"I just do my job, don't ask questions. Besides, Daniel, how many tenants do you see moving out? They're not exactly leaving in hordes, are they."

"No, but the places are falling apart around their ears, and I've got to run around like a fool sticking the pieces back in."

"But you've always done that. What's the big deal?"

"Time for a change," Danny said glumly.

"Must be spring fever. Or something. You should take some time off, Daniel, go to some resort down south and add a few notches to your bedpost. I know a resort in Mexico where you can get anything you like, whatever turns you on."

Danny swung his chair around in irritation. The window behind him was filled with the soft light of a late spring afternoon.

"Oh, I almost forgot." Sal reached into his desk drawer, took out an envelope. "This is for you."

"What now?"

"It's from Mr. Simmons. He's been looking for you. He had to leave. I don't think he's too happy with you, Daniel."

He'd been spending as little time as possible with the boss, meeting with him only when it was unavoidable—and then hurrying things along by explaining that he was putting the finishing touches to the plans and wanted to spend as much time as possible at it. The truth, which he kept to himself, was that he'd been able to add little to his original concepts: the vision remained as soulless and as static as before.

The last time they had met, Simmons, pleased with his eagerness, had been accommodating, quickly rejecting more than the usual number of repair requests. At one point, though, he had peered closely—suspiciously, Danny had thought—at Danny's face. After a few seconds, he simply warned him not to get too tired, he didn't want him getting sick now that they were on the verge of starting the actual restoration work.

Danny, gathering up the papers, had assured him that he wouldn't.

"Good," Simmons had said.

Be good, Danny had heard. *Be good.* He'd felt the blood drain from his face.

"What's the matter, Dano?"

Open your mouth

"Mr. Simmons?"

Wider

"You're not yourself these days."

Face down I said

Danny had shrugged.

"Have you seen Sita recently, Dano?"

Relax...

"No, she hasn't been around. Why?"

Good girl

"No reason. Just wondering."

Very good girl...

When he'd opened the office door to leave, Danny had heard wood splintering wood in the creaking of its hinges.

He ripped the envelope open. Mr. Simmons's note said: "Meet me at the house. Six o'clock. Bring the plans."

"A little billet-doux?" Sal said coyly.

"Something like that. Jealous?"

Sal made a face, shook his head. "He's not my type, you know that."

———————

The flashing lights—red, white, blue—formed a well of pulsing brilliance in the evening darkness. They caught Danny's eye from a long way off. He pulled up some distance from the house—the road up ahead was blocked off by the emergency vehicles—and walked the rest of the way, the air cool, odorous with exhaust fumes.

An ambulance was parked in front of the house, several patrol cars scattered around it blocking off the street.

A crowd had gathered, mostly Chinese but with smatterings of immigrant colour. They were quiet, watchful. Neighbours peered through windows and from porches. Policemen milled about on the sidewalk and the roadway, relaxed, arms folded, chatting quietly with one another. The school was brightly lit, its playground deserted.

Danny eased his way through to the front of the crowd just as the ambulance crew began making its way out of the house with a stretcher. As they wheeled it into the ambulance, he caught sight of the boss, his head heavily bandaged, an oxygen mask plastered to his face.

Mr. Simmons—

Danny felt nothing. *What you think of Mr. Leon? You like him?* He searched himself: absolutely nothing. Even as the ambulance doors were closed and the vehicle moved off with controlled urgency. Nothing, save the vaguest awareness of relief that it hadn't been Sita lying on the stretcher.

He stood at the edge of the crowd unsure of what to do. He watched the comings and goings of policemen uniformed and plain-clothes, listened for clues in the undecipherable murmurings of those closest to him. All these people standing around: what were they waiting for? What were they hoping to see, expecting to learn?

An irritable mother pulled her young son away, the boy stumbling along behind her, his legs barely able to support her pace.

Danny made up his mind. He signalled to a constable. "I'm

Simmons's executive assistant," he said.

"So? Who's Simmons?" He was a middle-aged man with a sad, tired face.

"The guy they just took away in the ambulance." Danny held out his driver's licence as identification.

The policeman glanced at the licence. Then he looked up. "Hey, you Pasco's kid by any chance?"

"You know my father?"

"Yeah, makes the worst coffee in town. So that's *the* Leon Simmons, eh?"

"Can you tell me what happened?"

"That's what we're tryin' to figure out. Who called you?"

"I was supposed to meet the boss here to go over some plans. We're working on this house."

"Come with me."

The policeman led him to a man who, in his three-piece suit, resembled more a business executive—upper management and rising, Danny estimated—than a police officer. He was standing the way Mr. Simmons had when he first showed Danny the house, with one foot on the lowest step, and taking notes from a driver's licence. His father's friend spoke quietly to the man, winked at Danny and headed back to the crowd.

Danny asked about the boss's condition.

"He's been bludgeoned about the head. I'm no doctor, of course, but between you and me ten to one his brain's messed up, if he makes it."

"Any idea what happened?" Danny realized he wasn't so much looking for answers as for—fearfully—confirmation of a dawning suspicion.

"Looks like your boss walked in on a break-in. Looks like. The third floor's a mess. He doesn't live here, does he? The address—" He held up Simmons's driver's licence.

"No, it's kind of a den, a study. He goes there to think."

"Would you be able to tell if anything's missing?"

"I've been there a couple of times."

The policeman led the way into the house. All the doors in the corridor were open, two uniformed policemen puzzling over the graffiti. "There's more of that on the second floor," Danny said. "But it's months old, years maybe." The policemen nodded non-committally at him, and Danny took the opportunity to glance into Sita's room. It was bare, the mattress gone, even the light socket empty.

Danny followed the policeman up the stairs, noticing in passing the changed air of the house. It was fresher, less musty, the collected dust unsettled and flushed by the bustle of many bodies through the open front door.

The door to the den was open, the lock and the wood around it shattered. The furniture was all in its place but every drawer hung open, contents spilled. The photographs Danny had so carefully examined littered the floor. A dark stain darkened the centre of the carpet.

"Look around," the policeman said. "Take your time but don't touch anything." He remained at the door.

Two other policemen were in the room, one stalking around taking photographs, the other patiently brushing a fine powder onto the shaft of a hammer in search of fingerprints.

The glass of the bookcase had been smashed, the ceramic lions scattered in pieces on the floor among the shards. The box that had held the pictures of the bedrooms lay empty on its side. A glance through the scattered papers and photographs told Danny that the green hardcovered booklet wasn't there.

"Anybody else live in the house?"

"There haven't been any roomers for months. Mr. Simmons grew up here. He wanted—wants—to restore it." He looked into the bedroom. It was overturned. "How'd you find him anyways?"

"Someone called nine-one-one. A woman, or a girl. Accent of

some kind. She just gave the address. We sent a car to check it out. Would you have any idea who that might have been?"

Danny turned the question over in his mind. Finally, he shrugged.

"Is your boss married, got someone in his life, anything like that?"

"Not that I know of. He never said much about his private life."

"Did he, as far as you know, pay for company?"

"I wouldn't know anything about that," Danny said sharply.

"Look." The policeman, hands in his coat pockets, stepped closer to him. "This'll probably come out eventually. Your Mr. Simmons was picked up about eighteen months ago in a street-sweep downtown. Communicating for the purpose. You know. Except she was a bombshell with a badge. He sent in some high-price lawyer and everything was taken care of hush-hush. I'm just wonderin' if maybe this was a trick that went sour."

"You'd know more about that than me," Danny said, careful to leave open the possibility.

"There's one thing I don't understand," the policeman said. He led Danny to the corner by the window. "Take a look."

Danny followed his gaze to the floor. Simba lay at the base of his pedestal, his body beaten out of shape, his head smashed almost flat.

Simba—

"Now what do you figure that's all about?" the policeman said with a look of distaste.

"I guess whoever did this wasn't a cat-lover." Danny had to struggle against the smile that rose through his gravity. It wasn't just what had been done to Simba. It was, too, the sudden realization that the house had, for the first time, failed to impose its silence.

The policeman escorted him back outside. He seemed disappointed that Danny hadn't been able to help and asked him to call if he thought of anything that might be of use in the investigation.

Some of the patrol cars had left but the crowd had grown, their talk more animated now that there was little to see. He supposed they were exchanging information, speculating on the continuing spectacle of emergency vehicles. A television crew was filming the house, the camera light bright and piercing. His father's friend, chatting with another policeman, waved to him.

The crowd, eyeing Danny with the curiosity they reserved for anyone who emerged from the house, parted to let him through. He had barely stepped out of the circle of light, walking in the direction of his car, when he saw her. She was wearing her heavy coat against the light coolness of the evening, her suitcase on the ground beside her. Absorbed in trying to peer at the house over the heads of the crowd, she hadn't seen him.

He walked slowly up to her. "Sita?"

———————

For a long time, neither of them spoke.

She sat in silence beside him in the car as he drove through the city streets, aimless, going nowhere in particular. Her coat remained tightly wrapped around her, her suitcase sat flat on the back seat.

Finally, Danny said, "You're the one who called the police."

Sita, biting at her lower lip, stared straight ahead, her gaze hard and uncompromising.

"Right? It was you?"

She turned her gaze on him, defiant. "Where we goin', Mr. Daniel?"

"You tell me." He spoke harshly, recognizing his cruelty only when it was too late. Then, more quietly, he said, "This area is called the Beaches."

She turned away, looked out the window at the passing lights: clothes boutiques, small restaurants, video stores, a cinema. People were out strolling on the sidewalks, mostly young couples, many with babies strapped to them or in strollers.

"So why'd you call them?"

"I jus' wanted my passport, not'ing else."

"And?"

"Mr. Leon try to stop me."

Danny braked at a red light. "How many times did you hit him?"

"Only two or three." She said it easily, in a voice of simple speculation, as if he had asked how many coffees she drank per day.

"And the mattress?"

"I put it down in the basement, with the others."

"You thought of everything, didn't you? Even the lightbulb."

"What you tryin' to say, Mr. Daniel?"

"Well, you got hold of a hammer, you knew where to hide the mattress—" Danny deliberately avoided a tone of conclusion, hung the words between them in the car. He let her contemplate them for a long minute. Then: "You know the word 'premeditated', Sita?"

But she was ready for him. "You sayin' I plan it, Mr. Daniel? You sayin' I want to hurt Mr. Leon?"

"You tell me." He spoke harshly once more, this time the cruelty intended. "You had reason, didn't you."

"I jus' wanted my passport," she said, losing the fire in her voice.

Danny drove on: what was he doing here with this girl? Mr. Simmons's problem, now more than ever. Shouldn't he be going straight to the police, turning her over, telling them all he knew? It had nothing to do with him, after all. Did it?

Sita glanced uneasily at him. "Mr. Daniel?"

"What?"

"I ain't hurt Mr. Leon too bad, eh?"

"Sita, you hit him with a hammer. Two or three times. What do you think?"

"He not goin' to die, eh?"

Danny concentrated on the road, swung around a stalled car.

"It wasn't to hurt him, Mr. Daniel. I jus' wanted my passport. Is why I call the police. He help me so much, I ain't want Mr. Leon to die—"

"No? Look, Sita, I was in the house the night he—" How to put this? What were the delicate words for an indelicate act? "You know—when he was in your room." He forced himself to glance over at her. "I heard everything."

Her eyes remained fixed on the rear lights of the car ahead. She offered no hint of a reaction.

"He hurt you." Not a question, not a statement, but somehow both.

Her hands fastened together on her lap, wrung at one another.

"Did he hurt you like that often?"

She shook her head slightly in an intangible no. "That was the firs' time."

"He never touched you before?"

"Usually he did jus' want—" Her voice wavered. "—my han' or my mout'."

My han' or my mout': only her accent added a plaintive edge to the words. "I see," Danny said drily. Simmons: it hardly seemed possible. "Why'd you put up with it?"

"But how else I was goin' to pay him back?"

"Pay him back for what?"

She looked over at Danny again, her face set in furious defeat. "How you goin' to understan', Mr. Daniel?"

Danny turned into a quiet street—parked cars sentient in the webby streetlight, houses with windows frilled and laced filtering the light of normal lives—swung into a quick U-turn, and headed back the way they'd come.

Sita began to cry quietly.

Sounds that haunted: Danny's fingers tightened around the steering wheel. She was right, of course. How could he understand? There were no neat columns here, no tabulated figures, no expert opinions logically expressed. Make a list, advantages to the left, disadvantages to the right, check out the bottom line.

But, he thought with a shiver, there is no bottom line.

Yet the problem remained: what was he to do with Sita? He could drive all night, cover every inch of the city and never find the answer.

Soon they entered the downtown core, the sidewalks deserted, the traffic sparse.

All he could offer her, he decided, was flight. He turned onto Bay Street, pulled up in front of the bus terminal. "Here," he said, handing her all the money he had in his wallet, about two hundred dollars. "Take this. It isn't much, it can't make up for anything, but—" But what? "Just get on a bus and go."

"Go? Go where?"

"Anywhere. Far from here. The police don't know about you except for your phonecall. You'll be all right." Even as he reassured her, he knew he was lying.

"But go where, Mr. Daniel?" she repeated, the money resting on her open palm, unclaimed, unaccepted.

"I don't know, Sita." His fear, for himself, for her, was making him irritable. "Pick a town, there are lots of them. It's a big country."

A look of genuine puzzlement came across her face. "It strange, eh? Mr. Leon din't want me to go and you pushin' me to go. And both ways I ain't gettin' nowhere."

"So what do *you* want to do?"

"What you care?" Her fingers crunched the bills. "I guess it ain't really your problem, eh?"

"No."

She struggled to undo her seatbelt.

"But—" No, she wasn't his problem. But his or not, there she was. And he knew at that moment that he couldn't very well just toss her out. The streets would chew her up. "What did you want with your passport?" he said.

"What you t'ink? I want to go home." Her voice cracked over the word *home*.

Danny put the car into gear and pulled out into the traffic.

———

As he gently pushed a reluctant Sita into Pascal's, his father looked up from behind the counter.

"Danny?" Pasco said, his eyes curious on Sita.

"Dad." Motioning to his father to wait, he settled Sita at a booth, giving in to her insistence on sitting in the farthest corner facing the street. She didn't respond when he asked whether she was hungry. He saw in the light that she had grown even thinner than she had been when they first met. Her cheekbones and her jaw were tensed flush against the skin.

He went over to the counter. "Could she have something to eat, Dad? Maybe some fries."

There was only one customer in the restaurant, a middle-aged man in a ragged suit with a bulky supermarket bag on his lap. He paid no attention to them, concentrated on his plate as if seeing images in his hamburger and fries.

Pasco, restraining curiosity, turned on the fryer, tossed a handful of frozen fries into the basket. "I heard about Simmons on the radio," he said. "Can't say I'm sorry."

"What'd they say?"

"They say he got beat up by a thief. Is that what happened?"

"Did they mention his condition?"

"Touch and go. He's in a coma. Intensive care." Pasco lowered the basket into the oil. "You didn't answer my question."

"A thief. That's what the cops told me."

Pasco recognized an evasion when he heard one. He said nothing, but he locked his eyes onto Danny's with a look that said he was not so big a fool as all that.

And Danny wavered.

Pasco said, "You in trouble, Danny?"

"No," Danny said quickly. "Yes. I—" He glanced across the restaurant at Sita. She was sitting limply in the booth, staring at the tabletop. "I don't know."

"It wasn't you, was it?"

"No, of course not."

"What's going on, Danny."

"I just need some time to think, Dad."

"Why don't you tell me, maybe I can help."

"Dad, you don't want to get involved."

"If you're in trouble, yes I do."

Danny sat on a stool, propped his elbows on the counter. No columns, no bottom line: nothing had prepared him for this, a problem that was not an opportunity—not that he could see anyway.

Pasco agitated the fries, got out a plate and a bottle of ketchup. Went over to the front door and turned the sign to CLOSED.

Folded his arms, waiting.

Finally Danny said, "Okay, Dad, here goes." And in whispers, his father leaning in close, he told all that had happened.

Pasco listened without interruption but he couldn't help wincing several times. A hammer, two or three blows: even Simmons....

Several times, too, Danny had to pause to take a deep breath, as if to fight back the tension that kept building in his chest.

"Christ," Pasco said when Danny was done.

"One more thing, Dad."

"What?"

"You've got a friend who's a cop?"

"Yeah. Sean. Hasn't been around in a long time, though."
Hadn't been around, in fact, since Montgomery's shooting.

"Well, he was at the house. Don't mention this to him."

"What d'you take me for?"

Danny shrugged. "Just thought I'd mention it."

Pasco shook the fries free of the oil, emptied them onto the
plate.

Danny took them over to Sita, sat quietly talking to her, urging
her to eat. She seemed uninterested.

Pasco kept a discreet eye on them, watched a new side of his
son emerge: Danny picked up a french fry, chewed at it the way he
might in trying to tempt a reluctant child.

Sklewy pushed his chair back, nodded at Pasco and made his way
out to the street. Ever since the incident with Emile, Pasco had
refused to take his money and Sklewy, dignity intact, hadn't insisted.

When Danny returned to the counter, Pasco said, "So what
now?"

"Haven't figured that out yet."

"I have an idea for you."

"I'm listening."

"Why don't we take her over to Lorraine. She'll know what to
do. I'll call and let her know we're on the way."

"The widow Neumann? What can she do?"

"She's a crisis centre counsellor. And Danny, this is a crisis,
isn't it."

"I don't know, Dad."

"You have a better idea?"

Danny let his silence give his answer.

A little while later, as they all left the restaurant together, Sita whispered to Danny that the ragged man they had seen was Mr. Bell.

"Mr. Bell?" Danny said.

"The fella from the upstairs room," she whispered. "The fella who put the writin' on the wall."

———————

Lorraine said, "Danny, you know the police'll be around. They're probably speaking to the neighbours right now. And they'll be interviewing the tenants in the building where she worked."

"I know all that."

"They're not stupid, they'll find out."

"Nothing. Tenants probably hardly noticed her, they saw her around, that's about it. As for the accountant, Sal, he had nothing to do with her. She was there for a few weeks then she wasn't. She's just a face and a first name." He glanced over at Sita sitting swallowed in an armchair. "Right, Sita?"

"Yes, Mr. Daniel."

"You didn't talk to anybody else?" Pasco said.

"Nobody, sir."

"Neighbours?" Lorraine said.

"No, m'am."

"Any of the tenants?"

"Never."

"You know you could just go to the police," Lorraine said quietly. "With your story…."

Sita's eyes shifted away to the floor.

"It's all right, dear, don't worry." Lorraine patted Sita's knee. "That's not really an option, is it." She turned to Danny. "She can use Magda's room."

Danny nodded.

"But Danny"—her hand traced the path of a plane taking off
—"the sooner the better. And pay cash."

He nodded again: he'd already decided that the ticket would be
bought for her by Nathaniel Price. "But won't they stop her at the
airport when they check her passport?"

"There's no passport control on the way out. She'll be all
right."

While Lorraine coaxed Sita into taking off her coat, Danny
fetched her suitcase from the car. When he came back in, Mrs.
Neumann had already shown her to the bedroom.

Pasco took the suitcase from him. "I can't believe you're doing
this," he said. "You, of all people."

"What would you have done?"

"Nothing different, I don't think."

Danny, expressionless, considered his father. "I was afraid
you'd say that."

Lorraine came back down the stairs. "You both realize we're
breaking the law," she said.

"Is there a choice?" Danny looked frankly at her.

"It's just that I wouldn't have expected that of you. Either of
you."

"Me neither," Danny said.

She reached up, squeezed his arm. The gesture, brief, earnest,
her fingers clasping at his arm for no more than a few seconds,
meant more to him than he would have guessed. As he turned
away to the night, he saw her slip her arm around his father's
waist, saw his father's arm encircle hers.

And he thought that it would not be easy, after all the years, to
stop calling her the Widow Noymann. As he unlocked the car
door, he looked up and saw them—his father, Mrs. Neumann—
silhouetted in the window. His father raised a hand at him. Danny
returned the greeting, knowing as he did so that despite the difficulties he would manage.

Chapter Twenty-two

CRUISE said, "Everything's changed. The Gate's not the same. Not without you and Montgomery. Feels like I'm going through some kind o' fuckin' change of life. Once again."

Sunlight was pouring in through the window, reflecting off the table where they were sitting beneath PASCAL'S in mirror image. Deep in the park, the pigeon lady sat on a bench tossing crumbs at the birds.

Cruise sipped his coffee, grimaced. "It's weird drinking coffee with you, man, my tongue's expecting beer." He cocked an eyebrow. "And you look so fuckin' cute in your little apron, too."

"Do you see ever Pushpull or Marcus at the Gate?" Pasco was tired. He'd been up late waiting for Danny's call from the airport. It was well after one in the morning when the phone rang and Danny confirmed that the plane taking Sita home had finally departed. Just before going through security she had asked him what she should tell her family. He hadn't known what to say, so he'd suggested the truth—a novel concept, Pasco said—and the last Danny had seen of her was her head shaking no at him.

"Marcus usually, Pushpull sometimes. How come you don't...?"

Pasco shrugged. He didn't feel like explaining anything, didn't know whether he could find the words to describe the fissures in him: the one that Montgomery's death had opened up, the one that Lorraine's affection had filled in. The Gate and their regular table in the corner beneath the saddle were now simply out of the question.

"Never mind," Cruise said. "I think I got it. It's kind o' like the day that chick jumped from the top of Rochdale." He clinked a fingernail furiously against the cup. "Decades seem to crash around my ears."

"What have you been up to?" Pasco asked, trying to change the subject.

"Writing."

"Oh yeah?"

"No shit. Writing."

"Your great Canadian novel?"

"Well, it's a novel, it's Canadian and it's mine. As for great, we'll see. Doesn't really matter, though."

"What brought this on?"

"Montgomery. At least, the day they shot him. I don't know. I'm still figuring it out."

"Is it about him?"

"I don't know yet. I don't think so. At least not— Like, it's not him, not really. Look, don't get excited, eh? It's nothing grand. Just a simple story. I'll tell you one thing, though. When it's done, if it's ever published, I'm going to dedicate it to him, *Muntgumery Bird de t'ird.*" They both smiled.

The door opened and a young man came in. Pasco knew at a glance who he was. He'd seen him only once before, and only for a second or two on television, but he would have recognized Montgomery's son anywhere. He stood awkwardly at the door, tall like his mother, solidly built like his father. An old army satchel weighted down with books hung on his shoulder. His eyes darted uneasily from Pasco to Cruise and back again. "Mr. Pascal?" he said.

Pasco stood up. "Just Pasco will do."

"I'm—"

"I know." He offered his hand, and the young man took it shyly. "This is Cruise," Pasco said, indicating him with a nod of his head. "He was your father's friend too."

They shook hands, and in the seconds that they murmured hello to each other Pasco knew that he was looking at Montgomery young, Montgomery as he had been years before they met: the Montgomery who had hunted birds and iguanas with a slingshot. The resemblance was unsettling, and when the young man turned back to him there were several seconds of uneasy silence before Pasco could say, "So...."

"I have something for you." He unslung the satchel from his shoulder, busied nervous fingers at the buckle. He handed Pasco a white envelope. "My mammy thought you might want this."

"What is it?"

"Have a look."

The envelope contained a photograph of Montgomery taken several years before. He was grinning mischievously at the camera, his hair chaotic with that atrocious haircut. Cruise looked over his shoulder and together they stared at the picture.

How are things, Montgomery?

T'ings easy, mahn

Oh God, Pasco thought, Oh God.

The young man buckled up his satchel, slung it back on his shoulder.

Pasco said, "How come..."

"My pappy talked about you all the time." He had his father's voice, but the accent, pure Toronto, was all his own. "It was always Pasco this and Pasco that."

"But wouldn't your mother rather—"

"We have enough pictures. Besides, she hated that haircut."

"She wasn't the only one."

A thin smile: Montgomery again. He turned to leave.

"Hold on," Pasco said. "So how—" His voice softened. "So how are things going?"

"All right. Easy does it."

"Your mother?"

"Holding up."

"And Charlene?"

He was silent, his face tightening and turning to the window. "I don't want to talk about her."

"Is she okay?"

"I suppose."

"Is she back home for good?"

"She was never home for *good.*"

"She's your sister, man," Cruise said.

"Look, this is one case where water's thicker than blood." He shook his head. "But if you really want to know, yeah, she's home. How long for is anybody's guess."

"You should try to convince her to stay," Pasco said.

"Stay or go, it's her decision."

"Your father—"

"My father should have listened to me." He glared for a moment at Pasco. Then his eyes watered. "Anyways," he said more quietly, "she's found herself people to listen to now."

"What d'you mean?"

"They keep shoving cameras and microphones in front of her."

Pasco didn't have to ask who "they" were. The controversy continued with demonstrations and press conferences, accusations flying back and forth.

"Even Mammy's getting caught up in it. She's planning on joining a demonstration at Queen's Park tomorrow."

"And you?"

"I've told 'em to fuck off, I don't plan to be anybody's victim. My sister, she likes that, eh? She likes being told she's a victim. I dunno, Mr. Pascal, it's all turning real weird. These people, they won't leave us alone. They see a racist under every bed. One of 'em even told my sister that having white skin automatically means you're racist. Guilty until proven innocent. Well, just saying that is racist, if you ask me. They say they're on our side, but there's only one side as far as I can see, and that's *their* side. If they didn't have us, I don't know what they'd do. They'd be nobodies. Well, I want no part of it. I have a life to live."

Pasco looked at the picture again. Montgomery had had the kind of determination he was hearing in his son's voice, the steady strength it took to insist on leading his life as he saw fit. He said, "I think you're going to be all right."

"I can manage." He hefted the satchel more comfortably onto his shoulder, opened the door.

"Listen," Pasco said. "If you ever feel like just dropping by…."

The young man paused, nodded.

Pasco held up the picture. "Thank your mother for me."

"See you." He closed the door behind him.

"By the way," Cruise said as they watched him run for an approaching streetcar. "What's his name?"

Only then did Pasco realize he didn't know. "I'll ask him the next time," he said.

———————

Pasco went home early that evening. The sky was grey except for one spot directly overhead, an opening like a tunnel through fragile white clouds to the pale blue of sky. Across the opening and lower down, trails of thin grey cloud scudded by like the plumes of a distant fire thinned and pushed along by wind.

By the time he got home, much of the grey had shredded, the blue darkened, and a spring chill had set in.

He headed down into the basement, rummaged through

several boxes before finding the framed photographs, each care-fully wrapped in newspaper, that he'd packed away so many years before.

The first he unwrapped was of his and Edna's wedding: among the faces of Edna's friends hardly recalled now even in name was Pushpull, slimmer, younger, like Pasco and Edna themselves, Pasco with one arm around his new wife, the other around his mother. They had just emerged from City Hall and had arranged themselves on the steps for the photographer, a friend of Push-pull's, when surging clouds cast a shadow and a strong wind gusted up Bay Street. The photographer managed to squeeze off three frames before squinting eyes, fluttering hair and hands grasping at hats and wayward hems caused him to give up. Two of the pictures had captured faces frozen in half-dismay. Only one, the one they had framed, had shown them, in Edna's words, "looking human".

Pasco unwrapped several more pictures before finding the one he was looking for, a black-and-white portrait of Edna Danny had taken. It wasn't from a particularly happy time in their life together, but Danny had managed to capture something essential about her. She hadn't really posed, hadn't prepared herself, and a contentment deeper than the hurt somehow managed to shine through.

He removed another of Danny's pictures from its frame—a view of the house from the street—and, along with the other two photographs, took the empty frame upstairs. It was cheaply made, a piece of glass held to a cardboard backing by four pieces of soft wood, but it would do. He cleaned the glass carefully and, when it showed spotless against the light, put Montgomery's picture into it. Then he dusted off the mantelpiece and arranged the pho-tographs on it: Edna to the left, Montgomery to the right, the wedding in the middle.

Pleased, he dialled Lorraine's number. There was no answer,

and he remembered she'd said she would be working late at the centre tonight.

The heat was off in the house, and the air was growing chilly.

He returned to the basement, retrieved from behind the boxes some kindling and two pieces of firewood.

It didn't take him long to get a fire going. Danny had had the chimney cleaned, the wood—stacked in the basement for years—was dry. It burnt well.

He pulled the metal curtain across the face of the fireplace. Felt the warmth from the flames as he settled back into his armchair.

He thought: You see, Edna....

But he had nothing to say to her.